THE SCORPION SCAR: THE COMPLETE

TALES OF KOROPOK, VOLUME 2

THE SCORPION SCAR:
THE COMPLETE TALES OF
KOROPOK
VOLUME 2

SIDNEY
HERSCHEL
SMALL

ILLUSTRATIONS BY
FRANK KRAMER

ALTUS PRESS • 2015

TABLE OF CONTENTS

THE BLEEDING SUN

A ONE-LEGGED JAPANESE guard poised his long club before rattling it again along the square wooden bars of the cages of the one unburned Tokyo detention prison. He was listening for the wild wail of sirens which would mean the approach of *Amerika-jin* bombers before he continued his pre-dawn duty of awakening the inmates. Behind him, in the narrow corridor open to a sky so obscured and black with smoke that no morning light had been able to end the night, the prisoners were creeping out, to wait on all fours for a bowl of fish-offal soup and a two-inch chunk of a brownish substance which had no name. Ahead of the nervously listening guard, unaroused men slept body to body on the dirt floor.

After being fed, the inmates would be herded off to some war plant which was still smouldering and gutted from the jellied gasoline dropped by the bombers, to salvage what little was possible. Among the prisoners were a few shriveled old Japanese, petty thieves and a few boys in dirty wadded school kimonos who were accused of having failed to complete their daily war work tasks; and the boys looked almost as pinched and thin as the old men. But most of the men listed as being held for questioning were pariahs, the despised Ainu outcasts who had once populated Japan. Stocky, dark, bearded men, long ago beaten into abject submission, they were jailed merely because their conquerors feared to allow even half-starved and unarmed slaves to live in their former pariah settlements outside of the cities.

The guard looked up, eyes caught by the sudden skyrocketing of color into the blackness overhead; an instant later and the belated explosion somewhere in the Tokyo area rattled through the prison.

"*Wazawai wa shimo kara,*" the guard muttered. "Calamities surely come from the heavens. What will be the end to all this?"

Because such a thought was unpatriotic, he stumped around and, with the point of his wooden leg, jabbed at the neck of the nearest kneeling Japanese, so that the face of the old man in brown prison uniform was shoved into the dirt.

"I am punishing you for thinking evil thoughts about the war," yelled the guard, in true Japanese fashion attributing to the other what had been in his own mind. "I curse you, end your father and your sons. I hope that you die like a flea crunched between the teeth of Inu-gami, the dog god."

"*Hito wo noroebo ana jutatsu,*" the prostrate old Japanese

whispered instinctively as he put a wrinkled hand to his torn
and bloody neck. "Curse a man, and there will be two graves."

"What?" squealed the guard.

Never before had an inmate of the detention prison dared
to speak to a guard, much less chide him. The guard's eyes narrowed to slits as ugly purple blotches appeared on his puffy
cheeks. He was working himself into a rage. He felt that he
had been reprimanded by the old man's use of a proverb, the
meaning of which was that a curse struck not only him against
whom it was pronounced, but also him who pronounced it. He
had been insulted. He, a guard, an official, a former Imperial
Marine, had lost face not only before useless old thieves and

*One grim yank pitched
the Japanese face
forward and sent the
wooden leg flying
down the corridor.*

sniveling boys and worn out geisha, but before pariahs. Ainu dogs had witnessed his disgrace!

The entire corridor, as if aware of what was taking place within the guard's head, cowered in silence. It was so still that the moans of a Korean who was hanging suspended by his ankles could be clearly heard; and the moans were scarcely more than a shiver in the prison's stinking air, because the Korean was almost dead. In the silence no man dared raise his head, although some of the boys smiled secretly, in anticipation of what they hopefully expected to see.

Just to one side of the old man who had provoked the guard's anger knelt an inmate who was as ragged and gaunt and bearded as any of his fellow pariahs, but who was no Ainu at all, although he was accepted by Japanese and pariahs as Koropok the Ainu. Stocky, bearded, speaking the clipped Ainu dialect he had learned as a boy while living with his doctor father in northern Japan, Llewelyn Davies, lieutenant, Army Air Forces, had re-

Old Sujino Atuji moved his wrinkled
head to stare at Koropok.

turned to Japan disguised as a pariah before Manila was attacked. From that time on he had carried out his orders to cause
trouble for the Japanese. Again and again he had managed to
escape detection, which would have meant unbelievable torture;
now, with Japan more fearful than ever of the people whom
they had beaten down—Koreans, Ainu, Chinese—he knew
that he must be doubly careful.

Davies had seen a wildly jubilant Japan four years before,
when America, at Pearl Harbor, had been caught unawares. He
had next seen a Japan content with great loot, satiated with
conquest, and feeling completely safe behind the barriers of
distance and the fortifications of Guadalcanal, Guam, Saipan,
Manila, Iwo Jima, Okinawa. And then he had seen a glimmer
of doubt appear as the belt of American steel began to tighten
around Japan's gorged and distended belly. Imperial Marines
killed to the last man by American Marines? Oh, not possible!
Lies! The Imperial Navy, *Dai Nippon Teikoku Kaizan*, while
waiting in a safe place to attack and destroy the American fleet,
itself attacked by carrier aircraft? Impossible! And next, as time
passed, he had seen fear. Stark and naked fear as death and
destruction and defeat came out of the skies.

He recognized fear now, in the guard, although Koropok the
pariah was kneeling with his eyes on the dirt floor. Fear drove
the guard to accuse the old fellow of the same thing; fear of
lost face was whipping the one-legged Japanese into a frenzy.

He'll beat the old boy to death, thought Lew, *and give me a
couple of wallops because I'm next to the old Jap*. Although he had
no feeling one way or the other about the prostrate old man, a
coldness grew in Davies, intensified by the snicker of some
grinning boy. It came to the American, suddenly, that the old
man was no temple-sweeper, no ordinary thief; the voice had
been modulated, the accent without the slightest *nigori* impu-
rity. The proverb which had been uttered was not one common
to the streets. Added to this was the fact that the old Japanese
had spoken at all, an amazing thing for a prisoner to have done.
All of which, Davies told himself, *is no skin off your ear*. However,

if the guard's rage did not expend itself and burn out during the process of clubbing to death, Davies himself, as the nearest Ainu, might receive the same fate.

All that Davies wanted was to remain alive, now that the day of an American landing must be approaching. He hoped to find some way of reaching the landing party and giving them information regarding Japanese defenses which they could receive from no one else. He had no idea how this could be managed. He did not know where the Americans would land, or when, although Japanese divisions were constantly being shunted to one point or another along the coasts, depending upon where bombers had struck last. Davies did know that from now on it would be foolish to do anything at which the Japanese might catch him, even if it were something which would hurt their war effort. The time for that was over. The important thing was to remain alive, so that when the attack on Japan itself started, he might contact the invaders.

SINCE WAR had roared in the Pacific, Davies had been in Japan, an outcast, a pariah; he had been beaten, he had been hungry, he had been completely alone. He had not permitted himself to think of home—his people, friends—but he found himself thinking of these things now as he watched the guard working himself up to near insanity. The one-legged Japanese' face was the color of pickled eggplant, and his eyes were glazed.

In a moment, Davies knew, the guard would begin what was similar to a *banzai* charge, and there was no way of telling when the Jap would stop swinging his club, particularly if the first blow crushed the old man's skull. For Davies, there was no way out. *What a hell of a way to have things end,* he thought bitterly. *I get knocked on the head like a steer when the finish is in sight, and what can I do about it?* There was no sense in telling himself that the guard had no reason to club anyone except the old man; Davies was sure that a single killing would not satisfy the ex-soldier guard. *Only I don't get slaughtered, on my knees, like an ox,* Davies decided, cold as ice. *I've got the right to go fighting.*

It would feel good to get the guard around the knees, slam him down and, with the guard's own club, fight until fighting became impossible.

Davies had no time to think more. "*Jibun ga war'i!*" the guard shrieked. "Heads up! You must all watch! Heads, up, dogs!"

When Davies, along with the others, lifted his head obediently, he saw what he had not seen before, since his sidewise glance had been fixed on the guard's face. The infuriated Japanese had backed himself against the bars of an unopened cell-cage, and had unbuckled his wooden leg. The old Japanese, face hidden, was in easy striking range, as was the younger man known as Koropok; but a sudden hope surged in the latter, although nothing of it showed in his face.

The guard had dropped his club in favor of the heavier, uglier weapon, and why he had done so soon became clear.

"You have called attention to my honorable infirmity," he howled, although the bowed old man had done no such thing, and the statement was all a part of what the guard had worked up to produce his rage. "You have cursed me because I did not die on the field of battle! In cursing me you have cursed his Imperial Majesty... *aaaaaa!* the *Tenno!*... and, before you die for that, announce your name! Come! I cannot permit you to breathe the same air as loyal men! Your name!"

The old Japanese' mouth said, "Sujino Atuji."

Davies recognized the name instantly. There had been gossip in Tokyo about Sujino Atuji, an official who had risen to great power, but who had gradually slipped from favor in spite of his cleverness... until he had ended here, in a detention prison. Neither wealth nor shrewdness could prevent disgrace if the Japanese' advice in council was bad, or if a scapegoat happened to be needed by a superior.

Sujino Atuji's reputation, when he had been in power, had been that of a cruel and unscrupulous person. Once a great land owner in the tea district, he had never been above selling *bancha*, old tough leaves, as *gyokuro*, jeweled dewdrops. How he had fallen so low as to be here, "*held for questioning*," with the scum of the city, Davies had no way of knowing; but, *I'll bet the prison authorities didn't expect he would do anything which would cause him to be killed by a crazed guard*, Lew guessed. Then, as he remembered that the old man had formerly been a confidant of the Imperial Minister for Defense, and not so very long ago, the disguised army lieutenant wished that he himself knew what Sujino Atuji must know about Japanese defense plans.

The one-legged Japanese spat down on Sujino Atuji's head. Either the name meant nothing to him, or he was too frenzied to recognize it. Thick spittle dribbled from the guard's mouth, turning into froth and bubbles as he jerked out a stream of ugly curses. At the end of each he would pause, tighten his grip on the heavy weapon, and damn the old man with, "*Inu! Inu!* Dog! Dog!"

Beating a prisoner to death was nothing to interest other guards, nor would it bring any prison official running to the scene. On the other hand, as Llewelyn Davies knew, a Japanese of Sujino Atuji's class had the right to demand that he be permitted to kill himself honorably by performing *seppuku*.

Why the old man was not insisting on this right seemed strange. *If I could manage to keep him alive long enough so he can rip his own belly open*, Davies thought, *maybe I'd have a chance to ask him what would sound like a fool Ainu question... and maybe he'd be grateful enough to answer it*.

Davies had already figured out, when he had first seen the manner in which the guard intended to beat the old man, how Koropok the Ainu had a chance of avoiding the same treatment. The problem, now, was altered. How could he keep Sujino Atuji alive until a prison official could get to the corridor?

Into Davies' head, as the guard's howling turned the word dog, *inu*, into what was truly the mad howl of a beast, came an idea which would bring the other guards and whichever official was on duty all running. It would work. It was certain to work. But it was dangerous, damnably dangerous.

There was no time to weigh the plan, because the guard's horrible weapon swung up like a decapitating sword in the hands of a *kaishaku*. The whistle of its upward swing was repeated in the delighted indrawn breaths of the Japanese boys, all excited at the wonderful spectacle they were about to witness. One whispered to another that it was almost as good as watching the beheading of an *Amerika-jin* pilot, with the exception that the *Amerika-no* would be pleading for mercy.

Up. As the bludgeon reached the top of its arc, with Sujino Atuji finally beginning to mumble that he should be permitted to perform *seppuku*, anyone who looked at Koropok would have seen that the stocky outcast, on hands and knees, had moved swiftly and noiselessly nearer the guard, while his right arm snaked out toward the one-legged executioner. Then Koropok had the guard's ankle gripped. One grim yank pitched the Japanese face forward and sent the wooden leg flying down the corridor.

The guard fell across both Koropok and Sujino Atuji. One short, fierce blow drove the one-legged Japanese' dripping venom back down into the poison-sacs of his own throat.

AT THE same instant, everyone in the corridor, everyone in the detention prison, heard, "*Gassh'koku!* United States spy!"

The words, so dreaded by the Japanese, echoed down the corridor once, and then the pounding feet of running guards obliterated the sound. The on-duty official was shouting orders as he raced after his men. Questions were shrieked at the one-legged guard even before hands pulled him to his one foot and held him upright; but he was unable to reply at all.

Out cold, thought Davies; but he, too, was cold. He had taken a terrible chance. What would be the result?

Rough hands jerked him erect and away from the prostrate old Japanese. It seemed to Lew, as he came up limp and with pariah-like drooping head, that Sujino Atuji moved his own wrinkled head enough to stare at him, and that the old man's eyes, no longer dull, glittered with excitement. As before, Davies

had no time to do any figuring, because Koropok had to meet
the questioning of the assistant warden, whose medals, awarded
him for his ability to force confessions, hopped up and down
on his scrawny uniformed chest and jingled when he took a
deep breath.

"You lie!" the official screamed, before asking Koropok a
single question. A furious slap rocked Koropok's head. "Who
shouted '*Gassh'koku*'?" Another slap, harder than the first
"Answer!"

Koropok muttered, "I listened and obeyed the orders of the
honorable lord who is the guard. Surely only he could have
spoken, great lord."

Since this was what the assistant warden himself believed,
and since the guard was still unconscious and not able to speak,
Koropok was slapped again. "Why did you place your filthy,
hairy body where the guard would stumble over it?" demanded
the prison official, indicating to Davies how the assistant warden
had figured out what had taken place. "If it were not for you,
Kichibei would have seized a spy! It is your fault! You will be
tried as an enemy!"

While guards were doing their best to shake Kichibei, the
one-legged Japanese, back to his senses, the assistant warden
suddenly bowed deeply, seeing that Omashu, the warden
himself, had appeared. The latter cut through his assistant's
explanations with, "Any inmate who knows what took place,
and who informs me truthfully, will receive a fine reward."

All of the pariahs remained silent, as always, Koropok along
with them. What the assistant warden had said regarding punishment for the pariah Koropok would never materialize, Davies
was reasonably certain, because workers in Japan were becoming scarce. The assistant warden had merely been sounding off.
But when a Japanese boy, after fidgeting with the ragged edge
of his kimono until bits of sweat-packed wadding came off in
his fingers, bobbed his shorn head and pleaded for permission
to speak, Davies' heart began to turn over.

What had the damned kid seen? Too much?

"*Mappira go men nasai,*" the boy said, humbly enough, snuffling a little at his temerity. "Please be so good as to excuse me. I saw."

As Davies glanced about involuntarily, in a place where no escape was possible, he could see how more guards had taken the places of those who had rushed to the corridor. The word "spy" had raced through the prison; and if anyone could be apprehended, guilty or innocent, he would never get away.

"Stop wiping your nose and tell us what you saw," commanded the warden, "or I myself will beat you."

"The dirty old thief attacked the honorable guard Kichibei, with the assistance of the dirty Ainu," the boy said. "I saw this. I swear to it. Firstly," the boy went on, beginning to giggle with nervous exhilaration as he found himself assuming what seemed to him a position of importance, "the Ainu dog spoke secretly to the thief, and then the old thief replied, and then—"

"Kick the old one over so I can observe his treacherous face as he listens to this damaging testimony," the warden ordered, and a guard flopped the old Japanese around on his back. Whatever the official was about to say, he changed it to an uneasy, "Oh! Sujino Atuji *sama!* You were to be confined privately. We are so overcrowded in these days, so busy!" The warden bowed and showed all of his teeth, including the gold one which had once been in the mouth of a soldier at Singapore. "A mistake has unhappily happened," he continued, bowing again and sucking in his breath. "Omashu! Assist Sujino Atuji *sama* instantly to his feet."

The old Japanese permitted himself to be helped up by the perspiring assistant warden, Davies saw that a great change had come over the old man. No longer did he appear hopeless and dejected. Instead, his beady eyes, as at the moment when he had turned his head while on the floor to stare at Koropok, were as shining as polished *tsuguri* steel, and his mouth was thin and firm.

Being recognized and treated as a person of samurai class wasn't sufficient to bring about this swift alteration, Davies thought Sujino Atuji had something working in his shrewd head. What? Had Koropok some part in this? Did the old fellow, alone, understand what had happened and who had shouted?

If he did, nothing of it was indicated in what he said, and Davies breathed a little easier. "I have the right," said the man who had once been in highest favor, "to summon men of my own class as my assistants in the sacred and honorable rite of disemboweling myself... if I must do this, as I must if the intention of a guard to kill me is found a just and proper punishment—"

The warden hastily assured him that such punishment was unthinkable. Oh, how the warden—also impressed with the old man's sternly confident attitude—regretted this horrible mistake.

"As much a mistake," said Sujino Atuji, "as the nonsensical and idiotic shout of the guard concerning the presence of an American here. There is as much sense to that," smiled the old Japanese, "as the ridiculous statement of the dreaming child who swears that I attacked the guard."

Does he mean that? wondered Davies. *Or is he playing a game? If so, what game could it be? I don't like all this,* Lew told himself.

KICHIBEI, THE one-legged guard, suddenly squirmed back to semi-consciousness. He stared around wildly, seeing bearded Ainu faces, and then wailed, because of the beards, "American Marines! They attack again, with flame and fire! I feel my body burning! *Banzai! Banzai!*"

"That one," grunted the warden, "is crazed. Yes, it must have been he, out of his head, who shouted '*Gassh'koku.*' He thinks he is still on the battlefield, still fighting against the cowardly American Marines as they run panic-stricken from our victorious troops. Take him to the hospital." He bowed to Sujino

Atuji. "What took place is plain," he said. "Please, great apologies to you."

Sujino Atuji bowed in return, and smiled again. "Imagine," he said softly, in a light voice like the hissing of silk on silk, "imagine an American, and not known for what he was, in one of our detention prisons. What secrets can be discovered in a prison? Why, not even an American would be so stupid as to come voluntarily to a prison... and certainly *our* officials, men of keenness and intelligence, would be aware of such a thing if it were ever to happen."

The warden was delighted to see Sujino Atuji not angry or vengeful; for while the old man had been ordered to the detention prison camp yesterday, tomorrow Sujino Atuji might be in a high place again. One never knew, in these days, who was "in," or who "out." Next, the warden remembered to give an order which would assign

The Hellcat roared earthward at a nasty angle, guns streaking fire.

the boy, who had imaginatively spoken, to a long and unpleasant duty. Lastly, not being a man to forget, he turned on Koropok.

"As for you, Ainu," he snarled, "see to it that you are never again in front of a brave ex-soldier who has given his leg and his senses to... *aaaa!* the *Tenno!*... so that he can fall over your filthy body. Even if he desires to beat you, do not dare move so that he might lose his balance!"

"*Sonna mon' desu,*" commended Sujino Atuji.

"Nicely stated. And yet," chuckled the Japanese, "if the guard had not stumbled, his club might have given me a headache. So possibly I owe something to an... Ainu."

Davies caught the little pause.

Does that mean what it could mean? the American worried. *Can the damn Jap have guessed that I'm no Ainu? Because if he could prove who I really am to some other topside ring-tail, he'd probably be rewarded with the order of the Golden Kite. Is that why he's all pepped up?*

The warden did not approve of a Japanese owing anything to an Ainu pariah, but preferred to smile widely rather than indicate disapproval of what a man of the samurai had remarked. A quick word to the assistant warden was relayed to the guards, who kicked the inmates off the floor... and as Koropok shuffled off with the others, there was time for him to recall what was not reassuring.

It seemed to Davies that Sujino Atuji had gone into the act about performing *seppuku* in order to be able to talk with a man of importance and inform him about the pariah Koropok.

All I can hope, thought Lew grimly, as he swallowed the nauseous prison fish-soup and snatched the brown square of food which must last until night, *is that he isn't absolutely sure and doesn't intend to make an accusation which mightn't stand up under investigation.* But this hope was slim. Davies couldn't forget how Sujino Atuji's eyes had glittered, how his attitude had changed. *Neither he, nor anyone in Japan, can prove that I'm not an Ainu,* Davies tried to tell himself, *but they can torture me to death while trying to prove it....*

With sudden bitterness, Davies remembered that all of this would take place close to the time when Americans might land on Japan.

"Hell!" he muttered, and then he bit his lip. Fortunately only gobbling inmates were near enough to have heard the ejaculated word. But Sujino Atuji, now gone with the warden, would have needed little more to be able to present satisfactory proof that the supposed Ainu was actually what Japan feared most.... and then, soberly, Davies realized that the old Japanese could, and would, swear to anything in order to present evidence that Koropok was an American.

CHAPTER II

AINU DECOY

OUTSIDE, IN the early morning, black and white smoke curled up from the burned-out buildings; destruction was everywhere as the thieves, pariahs, and boys followed a guard along the twisting, ruined Kojimachi Street. Down near the river-bank, flame had broken out again as fire had eaten down to some basement; beyond, a column of blacker smoke marked where oil tanks were burning.

Past the walls of the Imperial Palace, untouched by bombs, the work gang walked. Davies noticed a few old women walking along the broad street called the Road of Triumph, but no men, walking there to pray for the Emperor. He wondered if the Emperor himself was bowing and explaining to his ancestors how it was that Japan, beyond any doubt, was about to be invaded. The Emperor would be in a "hall constructed of cream-white knotless timbers, polished smooth as mirrors," those mirrors which were the symbols of the sun-goddess.

There were no protective planes overhead, but only geese, which, rising from the palace moats, flew with heavy wings across the palace grounds. No planes. None. When Davies, disguised as Koropok the pariah, had first come to Tokyo, there had been many, winging triumphantly over the city; now, those which did not rise high to meet aircraft, the like of which Davies had never seen when he had piloted a P-40, were destroyed on the ground.

Japan was being prepared for invasion. But Llewelyn Davies, in his ragged Ainu jacket, was too sure that not only would he never be able to be of assistance to the landing forces, but he wouldn't be living. Sujino Atuji had been seized by an idea, at which Davies could only guess; but what the American knew was this: the wily old Japanese intended to make good use of it.

When Koropok was set to work, razing a brick wall where an aircraft retracting mechanism plant had been gutted, he had come to the decision that he might as well, despite the obvious nearness of invasion, attempt to do any one of the things which he had previously discarded as not being now worthwhile. It would be better to hurt the Japs again, if he could, and if there were sufficient time before Sujino Atuji set the wheels in motion.

Around Koropok there were old men, women, and boys, all breaking up brick but not chipping them for future use in building. It was rumored that the bricks were to be used, in some way, for new coastal defense installations, and from the manner in which the guards drove the prisoners, there could be truth in the whispered word. Therefore it was instinctive for Davies to work slowly at something which would aid the enemy, and he had to force himself to do the opposite. He worked so well that he earned what was almost the admiration of the guards.

He had his reason for this. Getting away would be possible only if the guards' vigilance were relaxed.

By the noon five-minutes-for-rest period, Davies had decided that Sujino Atuji must be preparing to do one of two things.

Either the shrewd old man intended to make the Ainu known as Koropok *appear to* be an American who insisted on sticking to his disguise in spite of all proof, and possibly even after torture... or Sujino Atuji was really of the belief that the stocky, bearded prisoner *was* actually an American. If the former were the case, Davies didn't see how he had a chance. Had he any if it were the latter?

There's this much, thought Lew, obeying the order to labor again. *The old Nip is going to work on me soon. He won't just have me turned over for questioning, where somebody else gets the credit, but will be in on it himself, if he can find a way to wangle it, because success will raise him to a spot of importance again. With rewards and medals.*

It was ironic, Davies felt, to be caught so close to the time Japan's end was in sight. Tokyo was smashed, Nagoya was smashed, Osaka was burning again. Yokohama's docks and warehouses and shipyards were a memory, power plants had become wreckage. Transportation was being systematically knocked out. Equally important, there was violent dissension between the Army and the Navy, and between branches of both services. There was even greater and more vitriolic dissension between *samurai* militarists clinging to control and the *nankin* industrialists who had found this war increasingly unprofitable. Most hopeful sign of all—as even a pariah in a detention prison could both see and hear—there was trouble between the dominant and arrogant Shinto priests and the jealous Buddhists, who had been early shorn of all influence, until they had not the right to carry their begging-bowls through the streets as they prayed for food.

And at a time like this, thought Lew, not stopping his work when sirens howled anew, *I'm going to get the business, all because I was too damned cowardly to take a few cracks over the head from a one-legged guard.*

But he was unable to convince himself of this, even now. If he hadn't acted as he had, his brains, as well as those of the old Jap's, would have been splattered all over the floor. However, that might have been better than what he was sure he would be called upon to face soon.

To keep his eyes on his work was not easy as American aircraft, whistling like steam from the locomotives they must be attacking along Tokyo's all-important Belt Line, flew low over the city. The Central Station was a mass of twisted steel, and was beyond repair. Uyeno Station had also been abandoned, and Osaki Station, Megura, Ebisu, Shibuya, Harajuki, had been destroyed one after another. Just how Japan was going to manage to move up reinforcements to defend an initial attack on a vulnerable coast line was something in which Davies had been long interested, after it became apparent that America was closing in for the kill. Such a plan for general defense, when the strange vessels about which all Japan whispered were beached to disembark troops and tanks, must have been made almost useless by American blasting of communications, of railways and bridges.

When Koropok had been a despised *hakoya* at Number Nineteen, in the Yoshiwara, he had overheard what drunken officers had boasted would happen to American units if Japan should be so fortunate as to coax the United States forces into attempting a landing on Nippon's sacred soil… and Davies knew that once the Japanese got an idea, such as a basic defense plan, into their heads, they seldom changed what was decided upon. He had hoped, for weeks, to get what information he had picked up, and his deductions from it, to the landing Americans—and he had started to hope also, that with his real usefulness over, he could get away.

Now, the word "home" choked him as he sweated away, a chunky, tattered, gaunt-faced pariah, on the streets of ruined Tokyo.

A SINGLE-ENGINED Hellcat fighter shot out of the smoke and swooped insultingly low over the Imperial Palace. *So near and yet so far,* thought Davies, as he flattened to the ground at the guards' cries. So near and yet so far—the

Arms tied to his sides and a rope around his neck,
Koropok was led along the wrecked streets.

closeness of the American aircraft to where its pilot must believe Hirohito lived, and the plane's nearness to an Air Forces officer who wished desperately he could be at the controls... and the nearness of an American victory without that same officer, Llewelyn Davies, being alive to see it. Davies thought of those things one after the other—all in the same fragment of time in which the pilot must have seen the prone figures around the previously blasted war plant, and must have decided the prison uniforms meant Nip soldiers....

The Hellcat roared down at a nasty angle, guns streaking fire; and then the firing stopped just when it would have been most murderous.

I'll bet he suddenly saw Ainu beards, Davies supposed. *When he gets back, he'll turn in a report about how he attacked American prisoners. I wish,* thought Lew, as he had more than once before, *that we'd bomb the Imperial Palace. Maybe Hirohito's inside, but, from some of the signs, maybe he isn't.*

Davies' guess was that the palace was being used as military headquarters, and was the nerve center of Japan's crumbling defense.

Guards from the prison, headed by the gesticulating assistant warden, came racing along the street almost before the inmates had been ordered to resume work or the wounded pulled out of the workers' way. The minor Japanese official was waving his arms as he rushed up; his face was purple.

For a moment he was too breathless to speak. Then he gasped, "*Ki 'i to i' ni!* Who has been killed? *Hayaku!* Who?"

"No harm has come to any of us," the guard in charge of the working party simpered. "Not a scratch to us. Only a few prisoners were—"

"You?" cried the assistant warden. "You, cow-face? Who cares about you? Oh, I wish you were fighting against flame-throwing American Marines! I wish.... Where is the pariah Koropok? If he has been killed, you will be punished for having permitted such a thing to happen! Where is he? Bring him to me! Do not stand there as if your toes were roots! Where is Koropok?"

A guard bawled, "Koropok! Ainu dog!"

As Davies shambled up, he thought, *I was right. Sujino Atuji is going to get out of his mess, and rise to a position of influence, on the shoulders of Koropok. Or—on Koropok's body. The old devil has convinced somebody that I'm not a pariah. And so now, I face the toughest one of all... with my life at stake... just when Japan, torn by dissension, truly faces defeat.*

Koropok, as if too dumb to bow to the official responsible for having him summoned, lowered his head meekly before one of the inferior guards.

"Yes, lord," mumbled Koropok.

The assistant warden's face purpled again, this time with anger. He raged, "I am the lord to whom you should bow, fool!" and his hands obviously itched to knock the pariah down. His control of them was proof to Davies that, as Koropok, he had become valuable, although he was certain that no minor official had any idea what his value was to Sujino Atuji. "Bind him," the Japanese commanded.

The American wondered if it might not be better to put up a fight here, hoping that he would be killed... but the Japs wouldn't kill him. Lack of slaps from the assistant warden meant that Koropok was to be handled carefully. With this in mind, Davies stood with hanging head while his arms were lashed to his sides. A chance in a million was the best he could expect. To take advantage of it, he knew that he must be unbattered and alert when the time came.

When the official was satisfied with the way the pariah's arms were bound, another rope was looped tightly around Koropok's neck, and then tied about a guard's middle. "March!" ordered the assistant warden. No pariah was escorted as was Koropok the Ainu. Guards were ahead of him, to each side, and behind, all armed. The official had his own gun out.

Here and there, on the wrecked streets, old women shuffled

homeward with their daily handful of millet or scrap of dried fish. "Stand back!" the guards screamed at them. "Back! Out of the way!"

The pariah must have done some terrible thing, the old women knew. Oh, it was sensible to kill him, and all pariahs, because the nasty *Amerika-jin* intended to return all lands to their original owners, and a person could guess what the Ainu would then do to the Japanese! Yes, the safe thing to do was to kill all outcasts, Chinese, Koreans, Formosans.

If Davies could have overheard this, it would have been additional proof of the change which had come over Japan. The assurance of victory was gone. And the doubt which followed had been replaced by certainty again. Defeat.

A limousine, with two soldiers sitting stiffly in the driver's compartment, was parked in front of the prison. Whoever had been driven in it must be an important personage, because Japan's supply of gasoline was virtually exhausted and no tankers could get through the cordon to bring more, while the synthetic plants had been bombed out of existence. So Davies was prepared to find someone high in authority waiting to have a look at him, as he was half-shoved, half-pulled inside. Then he was pushed into the warden's office, where he stood, cringing and stupid, with his eyes fastened unseeing on the red carpet underfoot.

A crisp voice said in Japanese, "Unbind him," and there was a pause while the assistant warden had the order obeyed. He bowed low when informed that he might leave the office. Then the same crisp voice, now directed at Davies, said quietly, in excellent English, "Won't you sit down?"

Koropok did not so much as blink.

"The jig, as you Americans are saying, is up," Davies heard Sujino Atuji say lightly, but with an urgent undertone. The old Japanese also spoke in English. He continued, "You see, I have been, as Americans also are saying, around places. Yes. And when I are in Wales, I remark that some of the inhabitants is much similar in looks to the Ainu. It are causing lots of joking when I am there. I suppose you have a father from Wales?"

THIS TIME, in the brief pause, Koropok scratched in his black beard for what his intent watchers would believe was a flea. He did not raise his head, although he wondered if he would recognize the second person in the room, whose English was far superior to the old man's, but whose voice was also Japanese.

"Possibly you are being in Japan so long that Japanese language are easier understood than are English," Sujino Atuji suggested. "Very well. *Anata mazu do iu go ryoken…* it was in the prison corridor that I became aware of your identity. Would you care to know what convinced me? Well, I, like all Japanese, am interested in courage, in fighting, in personal combat. Naturally, when I was in the United States, I went to see your contests-with-fists. The blow which you struck the one-legged guard," the old Japanese went on smoothly, "was truly a beautiful uppercut. Right on the button-hole! No Ainu, nor any Asiatic, could have delivered such an expert blow. But what I am curious to learn," the old man concluded, with no alteration in his tone, "is why you attacked the guard?"

Slick, thought Lew, realizing the cleverness of the questioning, done by men far more intelligent than blundering gendarmes with their kicks and slaps. *Slick as hell. I've got to really watch my step.*

Koropok said nothing.

"You did attack the guard, you know," the first speaker remarked.

Koropok, as if finally understanding that this was why he had been brought to the warden's office, mumbled, "Oh, great lord, I am only an Ainu. I was down on my knees. I attacked nobody. Do not beat me, lord."

The first speaker began to laugh. He said in English, "You do it magnificently. I see you are not to be trapped. We should have known this, or you would have been caught before." His voice became precise, chill. "Since you have doubtless been in Japan for years, and therefore are aware as to how we can make a man talk when he is stubborn, let us waste no time. I have not the slightest desire to have your flesh sliced like pieces of cold-water fish in order to make you talk—as you will, at the end. So let us be civilized about this."

Koropok kept his eyes on the carpet. He knew what the speaker was seeing—a tattered, stupid, ignorant pariah who might be a masquerader and, if so, a great catch. And he knew also what the man who spoke good English must be wondering, as proved by Sujino Atuji's own question—why had Koropok, if he were actually an American, attacked the guard?

The longer the pause between questions, Davies felt, the better his chances, if he had any at all.

Suddenly Sujino Atuji exploded, "Kakebachi"—and now Lew knew that the other Japanese was an Imperial Minister of the Household—"a little twist of an arm, of a leg, and we will have the truth out of him. Like that!"

If that's what is going to happen, thought Davies, *I've got to remember to cry out like a Japanese, 'yaiiiii!' instead of like a white man.* He wondered whether, in agony, he could remember this. *I've got to remember,* he told himself. *I've got to!* Was there any way out? He could think of none.

"If he is an American," said Kakebachi, discussing the situation placidly but, as Davies knew, undoubtedly studying the tattered figure intently, "I would like to know it. Yes. So would you, because his apprehension will be to your credit. As your friend, I wish this for you, of course." The minister paused; Davies could feel the cold eyes fastened speculatively on him. "If we kill him during an inquisition," went on Kakebachi, "and he is only a pariah, it will be no loss to anyone except himself. However, I do not intend to have envious officials whom we could both name laugh at me for mistaking an Ainu for an American. That would be very bad for you—and for me. If the American were cooperative," the minister ended, "I think something might be worked out for him. I can promise that his life would be saved; and possibly in one way or another, due to my official capacity, I could get him back to his own people."

What damned nonsense, thought Davies. And then, that moment, a notion came to him—came to him firstly because he was fighting for his life, and secondly because, no matter what happened, he would never again be allowed to prowl about in Japan. Was there any way in which it could be managed, or was it too impossible even to consider?

Then, when Kakebachi said mildly, "It is unfortunate that one who has the appearance of this pariah has no intelligence, or he could serve His Imperial Majesty, the Emperor," Lew's heart began to pound. Hard. Fast.

Don't bite at that, he warned himself. *Wait!*

Kakebachi lit a cigarette, and blew smoke to tantalize Davies. "Have one?" the minister invited. When Koropok gave no indication that he had heard the question, the minister sighed. "Old friend," he said to Sujino Atuji, "that American uppercut must have been imagined, or else this fellow is smarter than I am, which I doubt. And if he is smart enough to fool me, he would never, for no purpose, have attacked a guard."

Sujino Atuji muttered, "Then my hopes are gone—"

"Not yet," the minister said. "Of course I am willing to say that this pariah is an American, and that he died while being questioned. Thus you will receive credit for having discovered him. Am I not your friend? But another thought occurs to me—if only the fellow were not such a fool! Surely he is the most stupid Ainu dog I have ever seen."

HERE goes, thought Davies. He lowered his head until his beard was on the tatters of his jacket, and when he spoke the two Japanese had to lean forward to hear what he was saying. "*Maido g'yakka' sam' d'su,*" he began, in clipped Ainu dialect. "I am only an Ainu, and I dare not mention the Great Name, but I, too, would fight against the dirty *Amerika-jin.*..."

Will that give him an idea? hoped Davies. *He's got one already. Will this push it along? Will it?*

The minister was laughing. "Even an Ainu bundle of filth calls the Americans dirty." Then he said, like ice, "What good are you, dog?" but, swiftly, he began to whisper to Sujino Atuji. Now and again the older Japanese broke in with an amused "*ma!*" of satisfaction, or a quick question or suggestion which Davies could not hear....

Sweat began to trickle down Davies' arms. It would be ironic if, when the Japs were satisfied that Koropok was truly an Ainu, perspiration, the difference in the odors of Occidental and Oriental sweat, gave him away, he who had not bathed since being in prison. But both Japanese were smoking, and both were deep in whatever was under discussion.

Kakebachi said, "If only the pariah were not such a fool!" which, to Lew, meant clearly that if such were the case the Ainu could be put to good use.

Now the minister said, "I am going to shave off your beard, Koropok."

"Lord!" whimpered Davies. "No, lord! An Ainu will die without his beard!" Then Koropok played what he hoped would remove the last shadow of doubt, "But if—if my beard... torn from me... will show my—my obedient reverence to... the Great One, then—my beard...."

"I think your father must have been part Japanese," said Kakebachi. "Well, we are not going to cut off your beard, Koropok, although"—last vestige of doubt—"I wonder how you would look without it. No, you may retain the beard which is a part of your bear-dog religion. You are going to take a little journey with Sujino Atuji *sama*. How will you like that?"

Koropok said, "I cannot go with a lord. I as a pariah. I—"

"If the lord can stand it," said the minister, "I think you had better make no objections. Do you know," Kakebachi added, to his crony, "if I were not an intelligent person, I would swear that the pariah's idea and mine occurred at the same time." He began to laugh at himself. "Now I am as stupid as he." The minister chuckled. "This will be in your hands, old friend," he said, sobering. "I will arrange everything. But remember this— if it goes well, I share the credit. If it goes badly, it was your idea, and your execution of the idea."

The word "execution" must have come unpleasantly and with finality to Sujino Atuji's ears, because he shivered. Davies guessed that the old Japanese was remembering the horrors of the detention prison and how near he had come to being killed there, as well as the fact that if he did not go along with what Kakebachi offered, he might remain in jail for years.

"Naturally," said the minister, shrugging when Sujino Atuji failed to reply, "if you do not care to go through with it, I can only believe and report that you have not had the good of the Empire at heart."

Right between the eyes, thought Lew. What a difference there was between Japanese and American friendships! *His pal!*

Sujino Atuji said, "I will need a special pass for him," and then everything was jovial again between the two men.

Each of them, Davies knew, was playing his own game and for his own purposes. Each would betray the other, if any profit were to be had by betrayal. They would work together only so long as each believed it would benefit himself.

Davies' own game, as an American and a man, was hazy and unclear as yet, but it had possibilities. At least he was out of a tight spot for the time being. Perhaps what he was getting into would be equally tough, and he would be less fortunate in escaping from it. What he hoped was that his estimation of Japanese logic, which he knew so well, had been correct. The basis for his hopes was Kakebachi's belief, as expressed during the inquisition, that Koropok the pariah could be put to some good use because the Ainu could be mistaken, by Americans, for a white man of Welsh descent. Logically, this must mean that the minister intended to place the pariah where the Americans could find him.

The two Japanese, heads together again, were studying him. *And what they're cooking up,* Lew believed, *won't be dumb. Not as they see it.*

Davies made no effort to try and figure out what the Japanese intended; knowing only what he did, it would be pure guess-work. Even so, he couldn't help wondering whether the Japs might use him as a decoy in an attempt to get across to the Americans certain authentic-seeming but incorrect informa-tion. Something about the Japanese' inexhaustible supplies. Something about the undefended point or points where land-ings might be made, but where the landing forces would be wiped out?

"He is such a fool," Davies heard Sujino Atuji say, "that nothing will come out of him except what we put in." The old man's voice lowered so that Davies had difficulty hearing what followed. "And when we achieve success," said Sujino Atuji, "there are a few people here and there to whom I owe something for having degraded me! They no longer fear me because I have fallen so low. *Hotake no kao mo, sano-ddo,*" whispered the old man, voicing the Buddhist proverb that even a Buddha's face could be tickled only three times, the Oriental equivalent of "the crushed worm will finally turn."

Kakebachi snapped, "Careful! Japan is now Shinto. It was your championing of Buddhist priests which started your down-fall, my friend. Do not make the same mistake again! Keep away from priests! All priests!"

"I will not forget," promised Sujino Atuji solemnly.

Davies thought, *Neither will I,* but what the American meant was that here was something which he might put to use.

After that, the formalities were quickly arranged with the warden. Koropok the Ainu, the minister explained, had not confessed; there was actually doubt as to the pariah's guilt. And Sujino Atuji was important as a witness. "After all," Kakebachi told the warden, "this must all be done secretly… and I know that you would not like questions asked as to why only a single one-legged guard was in the corridor. Oh, I understand. You are short-handed. But the Minister of Justice might not understand—unless I explained it to him."

After the warden had bowed his gratitude, he himself brought the street kimono and straw hat for Koropok to wear while in the limousine... and then, Llewelyn Davies, for the first time in years, was in a car again. When he closed his eyes, it was easy to imagine that he was in the States, and home. The sensation of riding, of motion, of familiarity, was enough to tighten his throat.

Home!

In order to get there, thought Davies, *I've got to be more careful than I've ever been before.*

CHAPTER III

LESSONS IN MADNESS

KOROPOK WAS seated between the old Japanese and Kakebachi, with one of the two soldiers crouched at his feet. The ride was rough; the streets over which the car traveled was ripped and torn. Once the minister cursed the pariah fluently for having bumped against him, and after that Koropok did his best not to permit his dog's-body to touch that of the noble lord again.

The drive was only as far as Kakebachi's town residence. The minister and Atuji said whatever remained to be said in private, undoubtedly arranging all details. Koropok stood in a room with the soldier; it, too, was strange after the detention prison's noise and filth. The matting was thick, soft and white, the stands lustrous contrasting ebony. The scroll on the wall bore a pair of secretary birds, another of copper pheasants, and a third pair of ducks, all symbolic of domestic fidelity. But the minister, as Davies knew, had been one of the most constant visitors at Number Nineteen in the Yoshiwara.

In ten minutes, the journey which had begun at the prison

was resumed, this time without Kakebachi but with his personal aide, a supercilious captain with a fringe of mustache on his upper lip and without campaign ribbons on his spotlessly correct tunic.

His first words to Koropok were, "How dare you wear a hat?" and when Sujino Atuji intervened, the captain snarled, "With his dirty beard, and a hat on his head, he looks like a cowardly *Amerika-jin*."

Sujino Atuji, whose spirits seemed to have mounted after his discussion with the minister, and possibly also because he was no longer in prison, and out from under Kakebachi's thumb as well, smiled. He said softly, "I am unfamiliar with your combat record, Captain Toshi. Please relate it to me."

Captain Toshi lit a cigarette instead of replying, using a sulphur match from Singapore. He did not blow out the flame. Instead, he wiped the fire to a smudge against the back of the pariah's hand.

"With his dirty beard and a hat on his head, he looks like a cowardly Amerika-jin,*" said Captain Toshi.*

"You will not do that again, Captain," said Sujino Atuji. "Nor anything like it. Kindly bear that in mind."

The captain's face was black. Koropok's face had twisted with pain, but became smooth again under Davies' control. Sujino Atuji's was a puzzle, not to be guessed at; but the American believed that the old Japanese' eyes had flicked curiously at the gaunt face of one who was believed to be an Ainu. Curiously? Or with a grim, unaltered understanding? There was no way of knowing.

But the pain disappeared, as the limousine rolled and bumped along, and was replaced by a deep fear. Sujino Atuji, man of the world, shrewd, calculating, was a man to be feared, because he would stop at nothing in order to profit himself. Acquiescent patriotism was not so important to the former government favorite and landowner as his own position and skin.

And he's sure of himself, decided Davies, *or he wouldn't have needled the officer.* Just why Sujino Atuji had been so willing to cause the captain loss of face by chiding him in front of a pariah was something else to worry over. *I've got to watch out,* Lew told himself again.

Through Tokyo the car was driven, and into the outskirts. Once Lew saw the foul huts of the Ainu settlement where he had once been kenneled, and once had a glimpse of the Yoshiwara roofs, from which all but a few girls had been taken, in order that soldiers in the field might be comforted. Then the car turned from destruction to a quiet highway, narrow, field-bordered.

A full hour passed, without another word being spoken, when suddenly the captain's bottled fury exploded.

He snarled, "*Tomeru!* Stop!"

"Drive on," Sujino Atuji objected, without opening his eyes. "We cannot drive at night, and I want no delays. I—"

"You are a disloyal man," fumed Captain Toshi.

The old man opened his eyes; and Davies saw what Sujino Atuji had not noticed at first. The old Japanese said, "I was asleep. I did not see." He said it placidly, and not as an apology. "No person questions my loyalty," he added, preparing to rise and leave the automobile. "No one."

The captain did not apologize either, but stepped ungraciously out to the road and toward the object which had brought on the words.

A beautifully kept Shinto shrine had been erected beside the road. Grass grew before it, except where feet had trod along one path. The shrine was roofed with dulled tile, lest the shine from it attract *Amerika-jin* airmen who, the villagers were untruthfully informed, delighted in obliterating sacred places. Inside the unwalled shrine were the objects to be worshiped, the visible evidence of Japanese Shinto gods and goddesses. The *shintai*, the god-bodies, were many here, and there were the mirror and the sword, of course.

BEHIND THE shrine was a recently built house, an expensive one, of translucent paper and polished wood, and as the old Japanese and the captain approached the Shinto god-bodies, a Shinto priest stepped from the building. Brilliant mid-morning sun illuminated his dazzling white surplice. His feet were shod in black lacquered wooden shoes, his head was covered by a black lacquered cap. His face shone with good living. He did not speak until the two travelers, after bowing deeply, placed currency in the wooden bowls which were between the *shintai* on the altar. These offerings must have been satisfactory, because the priest's face, itself as smooth as a lacquered surface, broke into a satisfied smile.

He said, "Give me your names. I will include them in my prayers." When he became aware of the identity of the old man, however, his smile vanished. "You are the person who has failed in worshiping the god-bodies and, therefore, the Emperor," the Shinto priest condemned him. "Have you reformed?"

Something tells me, thought Davies, as Sujino Atuji bowed more deeply and more humbly than before, *that the old boy is far from a reformed character. Except for his own benefit.*

"I have regretted any improper thoughts of mine," Sujino Atuji said. "Please offer prayers for me."

"I will," snapped the Shinto priest. "'For any who should deny our sacred faith, Heaven will send a curse and Earth a plague. Demons will slay them. Men will smite them. They will die in agony, and their souls will be tortured for ten times ten thousand years.' That is the prayer."

"Possibly Sujino Atuji desires to perform purification," suggested Captain Toshi, so pleased with himself that he giggled.

"Excellent," the priest purred. Without asking the old man's consent, the Shintoist said, "Repeat after me:

" 'To the end that my impure thoughts may be annihilated,
These hempen leaves, cutting with many a cut,
Purify me.'"

While the priest directed the old Japanese in the prayer, which Sujino Atuji had no choice but to repeat, Davies was realizing anew the inner conflict in Japan between rival religions. When the prayer was ended, the Shinto priest selected one of the knives on the altar, one whose hilt was formed by intertwined hemp leaves of brass, with silver leaf-veinings, and handed it to Sujino Atuji. A tremor seemed to shake the old Japanese. The cut, the sign of purification, which he gashed on his bared forearm, was far from straight.

"I am old," he said, while the priest frowned at the uneven and bloody mark. "Forgive the unsteadiness of my hand, honorable priest."

"*Ono ha soto*," the priest said shortly, ending the ceremony. "You are a pure man. The devils have escaped through the cut."

When they were in the limousine again, moving along the quiet road, Sujino Atuji seemed to be trying to compose himself. But Captain Toshi kept chuckling, as if greatly amused, until the old man grated, "There are those who have fought only on Tokyo—at desks. Possibly some day such men will perform *seppuku*, and their devil, Cowardice, will escape through the slice in their bellies...."

*The cut, the sign of
purification, which
Sujino Atuji gashed
on his bared forearm,
was far from straight.*

After that, the captain did not chuckle. Koropok, the Ainu,
could become the object to be minister had assigned his aide,
a fanatical Shintoist, to accompany and watch over Sujino Atuji,
who was not a believer in Shinto at all. The situation, to Davies,
would have been amusing, if it had not been for the importance
of it. It was entirely possible that he, as Koropok the Ainu could

become the object to be ground between the antagonism of the two Japanese.

At last the old man dozed, and then slept.

It was late afternoon before Sujino Atuji's tea plantation was reached. It, like many others, spread up a terraced hillside to the plateau above. When Davies stepped stiffly out of the limousine, which had stopped at the end of a long and winding narrow road, he saw the rows of neatly pruned tea bushes, with some, not cut back, looking like gigantic green toadstools.

He saw something else, too, before being prodded into the low house; men were about, as if returning from the day's labors. But the picking of tea and most of the work on a tea plantation should have been done by women. The pickers, as the disguised American knew, were often the daughters of neighboring farmers, and were called "pick-up wives" as well as pickers, because young men, their own long day's work ended, hung about the plantation to select girls who worked so sturdily that they would make good wives. Nor were these men stupid peasants, although they were dressed in tattered cotton jackets and trousers.

Koropok was hurried into the house, and had no chance to look around carefully, so as not to be caught at it. Instead of being taken to some dim one-mat corner, he found that he was actually being poked by the soldier-guard in the same direction taken by Sujino Atuji; and when a panel was pushed back, in a chamber where a maid bowed to the lord, the old man ordered the guard to go where he would be fed, and then to return to Tokyo. Captain Toshi, who had come along behind the pariah, was examining the maid.

Sujino Atuji said shortly, "She is the wife of one of my managers, and serves in the house only because we have sent most of the women to work in factories. I ask that you remember that, Captain."

Captain Toshi said, "You are insulting!"

"I am sure you will forgive me," Sujino Atuji retorted. "I

mentioned it merely because her husband is a very jealous man, and one who might forget that you wear His Imperial Majesty's uniform."

Is he deliberately needling Toshi? wondered Davies. *Or is he giving him an idea, which will later pay dividends?*

Captain Toshi was standing stiff as a ramrod. "I was told to carry out your orders," he stated. "That does not include being insulted. I—"

"My first order," said the old man, "is that you go to the room assigned to you, that you bathe, attire yourself in a cool *yukata*, enjoy a smoke, and then dine on what country fare we can offer you. I also wish you," said Sujino Atuji, "a restful sleep." He paused. "Alone," he ended.

WHATEVER THE officer was about to say he stifled. He bowed. Sujino Atuji bowed. The maid bowed. Only Koropok remained erect. When the shuff-shuff of Captain Toshi's footsteps could no longer be heard, the old man said, "*Biiru ip-pon motte kite o kure.* Bring me a bottle of beer. Then dinner. Also bring food for the pariah. Do not talk about it. *So shicha ikenai.*"

The maid, staring at the tattered and bearded Ainu, allowed herself one startled indrawn breath, and then hurried out. After she had gone, Sujino Atuji said in English, "Must we continue this foolishness? I have never changed my mind, you know."

Davies waited for whatever would be said in Japanese.

"If I needed further convincing," Sujino Atuji went on, "I received it in the machine. You braced yourself automatically for the curves. A very, very small thing, but I observed it. No Ainu would have done that. I admit," said the Japanese, "that it was an excusable error, but it was revealing."

He could be right, thought Lew, *but he also could be giving me a chance to spill. So I continue being a dumb Ainu.*

"As a matter of plain fact," the old man remarked, "proof is terribly simple. I am glad that the minister did not think of it. You see," he said, settling back comfortably on a cushion on the matting, "you are going to be given a part to perform, for Japan.

You look like a Welshman, and we are going to turn you into one, but one who has been so tortured by the enemy that he has lost his wits. In order to do this, my friend, you must be taught a few words of English with which, of course, you are quite familiar. And there," said Sujino Atuji laughing, "is the crux of the entire matter. The proof. And absurdly simple, really."

Koropok waited, his face unmoving, nerves tense.

The old man was still laughing. He shifted to Japanese. "*Mo yaku ni...* I wish you to repeat exactly what I say. You understand, Koropok? I had better call you that, no matter what your name really is. Koropok. Now, repeat a word after me, exactly as I say it. Now say, 'man'. Come! Let us get on with it, although I feel rather stupid conducting such a performance. Say, 'man'."

Koropok ignored everything except the order. His bearded lips moved once, then again, as if trying to utter the strange-sounding word. Then he said, "man," in a muffled voice and with a short *a*, Japanese-fashion.

"Excellent! Next, if you please, 'devil'."

When the pariah finally managed to repeat the word, but with the sound of the *l* turned to *r*, a pucker appeared between the Japanese' eyes.

Got out of that one, thought Lew. No Japanese, except one with the education and long foreign experience of Sujino Atuji, could pronounce the letter *l*.

Davies almost was tripped by "question," Japanese having no *q*; he made the sound of *k*, stuttering a little to show the difficulty in trying to repeat so unfamiliar a sound.

"Either you are very smart," said Sujino Atuji in English, "or" he continued in Japanese, "very stupid, and an Ainu. What are you?"

Koropok said, "Lord, I am the son of my father."

"Of that I have been sure," the Japanese agreed, "but who was your father? Do not answer that question. Go away. Get out of my sight. I am sick to death of you. I will become more worn out with you as the days pass. I—" he stopped. The maid had returned, followed by another, and both carried trays. "The pariah is to be fed in the next room," Sujino Atuji said. He looked once more at Koropok, and added sadly in English. "I had hoped for a little intelligent companionship. I—"

He stopped a second time, as a plantation worker shuffled into the room; and the fact that the laborer had not asked permission to enter was enough to cause Davies to wonder. Sujino Atuji said, sharply enough, to the newcomer, "You bring the report concerning the new manure pots?" but, even so, the American sensed that the tone of the old man's voice was different from what it would have been had the Japanese who had entered been merely a peasant. The maids, too, had lowered their eyes as soon as the man had come into the master's room.

However, what the newcomer said sounded like farm-talk. "*Sum tenki wa ki no iranai,* Sujino Atuji *sama,* I came to say that I fear this weather."

"You need not be afraid of it," said Sujino Atuji. "No."

Double-talk, thought Lew. *Could be.*

He was ordered into the next room. A maid followed him, and placed a tray of food on the floor, not bothering to put it on a stand. Koropok, immediately, began to gobble, and continued to eat like a pariah even after the maid left, lest hidden eyes were observing his actions. He would have liked moving closer to the paper panels separating the two rooms, but, for the same reason, did not dare. He heard the murmur of voices. Perhaps the laborer was reporting to the master what was going on at the plantation—and perhaps he was not.

Food, quiet, cleanliness about him, and the steady murmur of voices were all sleep-provoking. Davies must have dozed, until words, formerly whispered and soft, and now still whispered, but with a fanatical sharpness and tingling timber which buzzed into his head, told him what was taking place.

" 'As void one should look upon the world,
Ever being mindful
To destroy the theory of self,

Then he will overcome Death.'"

A Buddhist prayer was being intoned by a Buddhist priest, now in hiding on the plantation. When the prayer ended, and the priest must have slipped away, Davies realized anew one of the forces which was ripping Japan apart from the inside. Yes, there were worms gnawing at the Japanese nut.

For a long time Davies played with the notion of admitting to Sujino Atuji his identity. What would happen? What had the shrewd old boy in mind? Davies was almost sure that the former favorite, who had stuck to Buddhism almost to the point of death, would propose something whereby, in return for cutting down the life-cost of the invasion, the Buddhist priests might return to power.

What was to be gained by admitting his identity? Didn't the Japanese intend to turn a dumb Ainu into what would seem a half-insane and tortured white man? Wouldn't this get him, Davies, back to the American forces? Whether Sujino Atuji really had something in mind such as Lew guessed at, or was merely making sure that the bearded pariah was a pariah indeed... what difference did it make?

D A V I E S A W O K E at the time the prison inmates were usually kicked out of their cells; and it was a strange thing to hear the birds' sun-song. How well the American had slept was proven to him by the rubbed-out cigarette in the empty *hibachi;* Sujino Atuji must have come in to take a look at him. Nor had Davies heard anything about the house talk that someone un-identified had tried to slip into the maid's room during the night....

The old boy is building up his story in case he finds the captain a nuisance, Lew decided.

At the master's orders, the pariah was stripped of his rags, scrubbed by one of the maid-servants, and then told to put on peasant trousers and jacket. Then the lessons in English began again.

During these, Sujino Atuji tried trap after trap, stubbornly,

"We are not stupid people like the Germans," boasted Captain Toshi. "Oh, how we will slaughter the landing forces!"

to catch Koropok. None worked; but more than once Davies shivered as the steel almost closed on him. Captain Toshi dropped in more than a few times to listen, to squat on the matting and smoke cigarettes and pour himself thimblefuls of electric brandy, purple and hot. And it was Captain Toshi, elegant and bored, both guard for the pariah and spy on the landowner, who let something drop which stirred Davies deeply—and made him more anxious than ever to get away....

What the supercilious Captain Toshi had said after plenty

of brandy was, "*Doann yosu ka to omette*. I have been wondering what we have up our sleeves, and now I am satisfied. What a surprise awaits the overconfident *Amerika-jin!* Truly, their arrogant plans to invade Japan will receive such a terrific blow that they will be ready and very eager for peace. How clever we are!"

"We are preparing a reception," agreed Sujino Atuji.

Then the captain, refilling his tiny bowl, had said what Davies believed was an exposure of the Japanese strategy. Captain Toshi could not help talking about it; Davies was not surprised that he did, because such boasting was typically Japanese, as he had learned at Number Nineteen.

"What the Americans have been attempting," said Captain Toshi, "is apparent to a military man. They repeat their successes in Germany, but we are not stupid Germans. The Americans wreck our factories. They explode our ammunition dumps. For a long time they have been burning our oil. They pound away at our transportation. Soon they will be convinced that we have no aircraft with which to oppose a landing... and then we have them!"

Koropok, squatted with downcast head, gave no sign that he was listening. What pleased him was that Sujino Atuji no longer made the slightest pretense of watching him, as if the old Japanese was by now entirely convinced that Koropok was Koropok the Ainu, and nothing else.

"We are not stupid people like the Germans," boasted Toshi, "but we learned to do the sort of thing about which they talked and did nothing. What I have seen here has brought me pleasure. Oh, how we will slaughter their landing forces! What a pretty sight it will be! And it will be justice, too, Sujino Atuji *sama*. We have been burned out of our caves at Okinawa and Saipan—and out of our caves vengeance will come! How glad I am that I was assigned here, although at the beginning I thought it a degrading post for an officer."

Davies was not surprised that the officer became silent. Here, again, was something typically Japanese: having started to boast, a Jap would stop, as if cunningly, craftily, before announcing a conclusion. But, also as in the past, Lew could do his own summing up, and he did so now while playing parrot for his teacher.

What Captain Toshi said he had seen, and which delighted him, had been here in the tea country. It had to do with the destruction of American landing forces; it came out of caves. Well, there were no caves in the tea country, so far as Davies knew, but there were long series of terraces on which the shrubs grew. A perfect set-up for concealing aircraft. Hundreds of them. Thousands. And, guessed Davies, fighter-bombers. All gassed and ready. And undoubtedly what had been done here had been done on other tea plantations....

Proof, Davies knew, would be in finding a take-off strip. And yet this could easily be made invisible. Davies had no intention of slipping away from the half-hearted guarding of the captain; he was satisfied, now that he had the clue, that a word here, or something happening there, would be sufficient proof.

What had him puzzled was this: on the one hand, the minister undoubtedly intended the pariah to be used in some way which would expose the landing Americans to an overwhelming defeat... but was that what Sujino Atuji intended? What did the old Japanese intend? Whatever it was, Davies had reason to believe, an American could have been put to good use. Sujino Atuji had been disappointed that the bearded, stocky man had turned out to be an Ainu.

As the days passed, Koropok's lessons began to change. Words were drilled into the obedient pariah, words in English, but there was no coherence about them. Words. Simply words. There was a single clue to the purpose of the instruction: when the old Japanese said, for example, in either Japanese or English, "What is your name?" the pariah was taught that this phrase, and a few others, were not to be repeated as were the individual English words. Instead, when Sujino Atuji demanded, "What is your name?" Koropok learned to reply, "Name? Name?

My name?" and then, after a long pause, to say, "Ar... ar... arthur... I... do not... re-mem-ber."

It took time before Koropok could learn this.

The basic notion was clever, diabolical. An Ainu, turned into a tortured white man, and used as a means—how, Davies did not know as yet—to assist the Japs. But he did begin to realize the thoroughness with which it was being done. Sujino Atuji, now advised by Captain Toshi, began to work on Koropok's appearance. It began when the pariah had the phrase learned pat. After that, Davies realized that he was being slowly and expertly starved. Nor was he allowed to sleep at night except for a brief half-hour intervals. Once he was supposed to be terrified out of what few wits an Ainu possessed by a sword-tirade by the officer....

Day by day, night by night, the ugly training and treatment continued, until Koropok's eyes, now sunk in his head, sometimes glittered with what approached lack of reason. There was deadly danger in all of this, to Davies, and he knew it. How far would the Nips go? So far that he might forget his disguise? Mightn't it be better to reveal his identity to Sujino Atuji? Because, earlier, the old Japanese had hoped to use the pariah for what he had believed him to be, an American....

Davies thought about this as, with lights glaring in his room in the plantation house, he tried to sleep. What was the old man's original intention? Surely it was anti-Shinto, in one way or another.

Suppose I were to say to Sujino Atuji, in English, "Look! I've had enough! I'm what you first thought I was." What would happen?

It was days later, with Davies husbanding every remaining portion of his dwindling strength, that he found out. He knew that the final action could not be very far away, for even here, in the country, clouds of smoke rose, as American bombers sought out every small city in the systematic destruction of Japan's ability *to* resist... and when he learned, he knew that his growing weakness, the sapping of mental as well as physical powers, must have prevented him from learning earlier what should have been obvious from the start.

He knew that the time was nearing. More and more men were appearing at the tea plantation, until Captain Toshi was moved to the servants' quarters, proof that he must be out-ranked. These men were never in uniform but they were not laborers, nor did they labor. They were bombardiers. Pilots. And many men about whom the maids spoke breathlessly as those who would perform honorable *seppuku* in a new and patriotic manner, taking Americans with them when they died. Suicide pilots. Called, by the maids who offered themselves to them, also patriotically, those-who-died-for-Japan.

Sometimes Lew's hands shook, uncontrollably. Sometimes he would sit and pick at nothing on the floor. But always he fought, *Hang on, boy. Hang on.* But a fellow could only hang on for so long....

CHAPTER IV

THE HAIR OF THE PARIAH DOG

O N T H E last afternoon Sujino Atuji come to Koropok's room. The peasant who, as Davies had learned, was actu-ally a Buddhist priest, accompanied the master of the tea plan-tation; and he, like Sujino Atuji, examined the bearded figure bowed down before them both. He put a bony hand under Koropok's chin, and raised it. Shrugging, he said, "He cannot stand much more."

"It has been a lengthy and complicated business," said Sujino Atuji, "The other way"—did the sly old man stare just once more at Koropok?—"would have been so much simpler. He could have managed it since, if he had been an American, he would still have been fooling everyone except me. And, of course, you. Yet there might have been complications. Perhaps this way is better. Shall I... is it time? We want no one to ques-tion him."

"It is time," the Buddhist priest said. "I go here and there, as a worker. From what I have heard—so carefully kept from you, because when this is over no person knows whether you will be restored to favor or not—the generals have finally decided that no more delay can be risked. They take him tonight."

Into Davies' head flashed, *Take me!* and then he thought, *Home!*

Sujino Atuji sighed. "Koropok," he said, "you are going on a strange journey. When it is over, you will go to live with your people, free, in the mountains in the north. You will have a wife. Children. You will be a chief. Soon...." The old man stopped, glanced at the priest, and then said, to the Buddhist, "It is so complicated, and so dangerous, and—"

"Continue," the priest said coldly. "Are you a Shintoist?"

The old man bowed. "No," he said. "I have attempted," he went on, still to the Buddhist, "to secure the attire in which they will dress him, but that has not been possible. I have tried—"

The priest said again, like ice, "Continue. In no other way can we oust those essences of untruths, the Shinto priests. Continue."

I was right, thought Lew, none too clearly. *Back of it all is the division between two sets of fanatics.* Half-dizzy as he was, he still realized that whatever the Buddhist and Sujino Atuji wanted accomplished, it would not be the surrender of Japan, nor assistance to the invaders, the Americans. *It's past me.* Davies was suddenly afraid. Then—

"Koropok," the old Japanese said, bending over, "I place something in your beard. It is a charm. An Ainu bear-charm. It is very great, and very old. Remember this: *your life depends upon it!* Do not touch it! Remember!"

The Japanese' thin fingers worked in Koropok's beard, fastening something small to Davies' chin, and under the hairs.

Sujino Atuji came erect; there were sounds outside. "Remember," he repeated, in a voice as thin and cold as his fingers, "if you speak of it to any man, or if it is taken from you, you are certain to die, and your soul will turn into nothing. I say again, you will die."

Just before the panels were roughly pushed aside, the old Japanese said wearily, "And we will die also."

"Death," the Buddhist said, "is only an illusion. But the actions of the Shinto priests are reality, and not to be suffered any longer."

"Our fate," whispered Sujino Atuji, turning to meet the men who were about to enter through the opened panels, "is in the hands—or in the beard—of a pariah dog, in whose stupidity we must trust"

Davies' hand, when both Japanese' backs were to him, went experimentally to his beard. In it, covered with black hair like his own, was a small cylinder, in which, Davies could readily guess, was a message.

Slick, he thought, his hands at repose again. *After I've gone into the act for which I have been so beautifully trained, and will appear to be a starved white man, tortured out of his senses, I'll be hospitalized. And shaved. Then the message will be found.* He could see why Sujino Atuji would say nothing relating to the discovery of this message by the Americans; there was no reason why this should be told to the Ainu. Nor did the old Japanese care how much of a fight Koropok might put up, so long as the message got to its destination.

Into the room came a number of Japanese staff officers, headed by a general. Sujino Atuji bowed deeply, and the Buddhist priest hastened away as if in his present disguise as a peasant, such glory was not for him to see. Behind the general, immaculate in a pressed uniform, was Captain Toshi; and Davies saw the antagonism flare in his eyes the moment he observed the old Japanese.

The general wasted no time. "*Ni shutatsu guru yoni chanto shitaku...* everything is ready. Is *he,* Sujino Atuji?"

The old Japanese bowed. "He is ready."

"Very well." The bald-headed general blinked and then smiled sourly. "What a stupid-looking one! Yes, in appearance he is like *Ingurisu* soldiers I have seen. I myself have slapped many of those English officers, and some of their women also." The general picked at his upper lip, and then pushed it forward with his tongue. "Is it your opinion," he rasped at the old Japanese, "that the pariah will not be able to answer, sensibly, questions about Japan which might be asked of him? Some of those American Intelligence officers are not fools."

Sujino Atuji answered question with question. "What can such a one know?" and the general was satisfied.

But Captain Toshi suggested, "Why not cut out his tongue? Then we are certain he can say nothing, nor write anything, since pariahs cannot write. If—"

"You are so great a fool that at times I feel sorry for you," the general said. "The entire plan hinges on what the Ainu says, which will convince the Americans that he is of their own despicable race."

Captain Toshi bowed, but shot a look of hatred at the old Japanese, as if Sujino Atuji, and his plan, were responsible for the rebuke.

"Get him dressed properly," the general ordered. "You, Toshi," continued the staff officer, "may remain and assist in the attiring. Perhaps then you will not be so quick with ridiculous plans. Although," ended the general, "the one thing I do not like is that the Ainu might say something—how, I do not know—of a damaging nature."

He turned on his heel and left. A junior lieutenant, before following him and the rest, dropped clothes on the floor.

IT TOOK only a short time to dress Koropok in the sweat-stained and tattered uniform once worn by a soldier in the Welsh Grenadiers.

Sujino Atuji, staring at him, said uneasily, "What have I created?" and then, once again, asked, "What is your name?" in English.

By now Koropok had the answer perfectly. He said, with the clipped Ainu manner of speech adding to the illusion, "Name? Name? Name?" and then, after the proper long pause, "Ar… ar… arthur… I… do not… re-mem-ber."

"Perfect," said the old Japanese. "Perfect."

Captain Toshi must have thought the same thing. "And because of such a performance," he said, "an ignorant old person

*"Why did you
do that?" the old
Japanese demanded
of Koropok. "Why?"*

who is not faithful to Shinto will become important. I do not trust you, Sujino Atuji *sama*."

"No?" said the old man, grinning.

"No!"

Sujino Atuji, Japanese to the core, laughed. "Have you a better plan? As I recall, the general did not care for your suggestion."

The room became electric with conflict. *The old boy can think rings around a desk-hugging officer,* thought Lew, *and he certainly enjoys twisting the knife in Captain Toshi.*

Davies' head was beginning to spin from weakness and nervous strain.

"I do not see," shrilled Toshi, "why the pariah must be received alive. It is too great a chance for us to take. Why could he not be found washed up on the rocks of Okinawa, with the message on him? Answer that!"

Sujino Atuji explained contentedly, "That is simple. After the pariah has given proof of what the Americans will suppose him to be, he will be asked, 'What was your outfit?' or 'Try to remember your name,' or 'Where were you taken prisoner?' or someone may say, 'Those damned Japs!' No matter what, as you should know, his answer, as I have taught him will be the same. He will say, 'In my uniform. Uniform. Uniform.' And in it will be found what we want found."

"Suppose," said Captain Toshi, with growing excitement, "that instead of being questioned by a stinking white officer, he is questioned by a brown dog of a Japanese-American? Such foul persons are fighting with the American Army. What then, I want to know. Suppose a damned Japanese-American soldier is ordered to speak to the pariah? Suppose the traitor to *aaaaaaaa!* the *Tenno!* addressed the pariah in Ainu? *Ho! What then, old man?*"

As a frown puckered between Sujino Atuji's glittering eyes, Davies knew what was racing through the Japanese' head: if Koropok were dead, the message concealed in the Ainu beard would never be discovered. For an instant Davies, weak and unalert, was amused. Then he realized that it was he himself, as Koropok, who would be dead, and that there was sense in the objection raised by the supercilious captain, whose turn it was to grin.

He'll speak of it to the general, thought Davies, *because it might restore him to favor as well as save the face he just lost by being reprimanded. And it will be a slap at Sujino Atuji, a slap at a non-Shintoist.*

Davies did his best to rouse himself, nerveless as he was. The old Japanese' face told Lew that the old man was really worried.

With hands hanging at his sides, where he stood after being dressed as a prisoner of war, Koropok took one shuffling step forward. Captain Toshi's grin by now was a broad smile. Koropok took another step. *Can I do it?* Lew asked himself. He had no choice. None. This was it!

The panels were still open. Outside, he saw, without really seeing anything, a bright blue sky, and the blue hilltops up to which the terraced fields spread their dark tea shrubs. There were no parties of chattering tea pickers now, no women with baskets on their backs, no barrows being hauled, no smoke rising where the tea was being manufactured. None of these things. Here, instead, waiting to attack and destroy some great landing force, were many of Japan's dive-bombers—here, and at other tea plantations, all magnificently concealed in the terraces. And the general's haste meant that invasion must be coming soon. As Davies, head whirling, took that one automatic look outside, he could see, coming from the far south, what could have been a rain cloud, black and with a silver edge, but which was smoke—smoke, where Japan burned and burned.

Can I do it? wondered Davies. *But I've got to!*

His shuffling footsteps did not rouse the wily old Japanese, who was obviously trying, and uselessly from his dejected expression, to find an answer to Toshi's question; nor did they attract the captain himself, who was feasting on the look on Sujino Atuji's face.

Captain Toshi's sword hung to his belt. Against the sword, and in a scabbard of bronze, was the captain's *wakizashi,* the short dirk with which *seppuku* was performed. Davies slipped it out of its thin scabbard. The razor-keen blade flashed up, and down. Once. Deep. Sujino Atuji's eyes saw what had happened at the moment that Toshi's mouth writhed open. The old Japanese stepped aside to allow the captain to pitch to the floor.

"Why did you do that?" the Japanese whispered. "Why?"

Davies strove to gather his wits. The sky, as seen through the open panel, was getting blacker and blacker; and that must be the smoke. But everything was getting black. The effort had cost the weakened, starved American the last of his strength and senses. He did not sway. He fell, as the captain had fallen, as if he, also, had been knifed to the heart.

Nor did he hear the old man mutter, "I will never know if he did it because he is what I first thought he was." And then, "Toshi's fooling with the married maids must be the reason he was killed, by a maid or by a husband. I can have an excellent explanation which the general, disliking Toshi, will gladly believe. Yes. I am going to say that Koropok and I waited while the captain went on an errand, in the house, and then staggered back… to die. Everyone will be questioned… nothing will come of it. Nor will I have the answer to Koropok either." Although his lips moved again, it was in Buddhist prayer.

Nor did Davies know that Koropok, head lolling, was carried to what he would have recognized as an old Fourteen, still in Japanese service. Not until the transport plane was in the air, flying nervously low, did the drone of the motors penetrate into his consciousness at all, and then only as sound, as noise, as dizziness. Lew Davies had truly reached his limit.

He did not see Tokyo from the sky, scorched and blackened, nor Yokohama and the vanished installations and docks, nor Nagoya blazing again, nor Osaka with Kobe to the east, both devastated and crawling with rats… nor Kagoshima, where Japan's fleet had tried to hide.

AT TUKONOSHIMA, north of Okinawa in the Ryukyus, the Fourteen was set down on an airfield almost one-hundred-per-cent useless; all that Koropok saw of the island and city, previously by-passed by Americans who had already landed nearer Japan, were the ruins of a castle on a hill—once massive, but still not so obliterated by centuries as a single American bombing would have been accomplished....

Then he was in a native boat, small, seaworthy, manned by Japanese seamen in the nudity of natives; and torrential rain was beating down on the thatched forward cabin. He was content to lie there. Just to lie. He was, he knew, only about half alive. Spells of dizziness shook him; what thoughts he had were incoherent. He was never sure whether the rolling of thunder, overhead, was thunder or the roar of motors, nor if the hissing of water against the sides of the craft was water or the politely venomous sound which accompanies Japanese speech.

He did know this: *I must not speak. Not anything. Not here. I haven't got the sense to open my mouth. I don't know what I'd say.*

Am I going home? he thought, in the darkness. And what would home be? Darkness? Death? Or... *home!*

The rain hammered down. Thunder crashed. None of the seamen, including the *taii* lieutenant in charge, paid any more attention to the pariah Koropok than to drop wet cloths on his face from which, if he wished, and were able, he could suck water. They had been ordered to set him ashore, alive. No one was to speak with him, because, which they were not told, the first words Koropok the pariah was supposed to hear were intended to be, "What is your name?"

Once he got to his knees, only to fall flat to his face again.

The slim native craft, in rain and night, slipped close ashore.

That's how I landed in Japan, Davies remembered hazily; and he was not positive that this was not what was taking place now. Maybe he was just setting out on his mission. Maybe Pearl had been bombed. Maybe the Nips hadn't yet ripped Manila's airfields apart.

There was the black curtain over him again. But this time, when he stirred, he was no longer on the boat. He was on shore.

He tried to get off his back. No sweat came from him. He had been drained dry. It was minutes before, in the dark, he managed to roll on his side, then to his belly. Somehow, he began to crawl. Once he got to his knees, only to fall flat to his face again. Coral cut his mouth, his cheekbones.

A red sunrise found him on his face... and when a posted guard suddenly shouted, a twitch passed through the American on the coral of Okinawa. A twitch. That was all.

What desperate measures were taken to bring him to consciousness he did not know; but whatever shocked him to life was accompanied by, "Your name! What's your name? How'd you get here? What—"

Automatically, in the tone of Koropok the Ainu, the man now on a hospital bed mumbled, "Name? Name? Name? Ar... ar... arthur... I do... not... re-mem-ber...."

"British," an Intelligence officer whispered. "Poor devil! The Nips've tortured him to death."

"It's not exposure," agreed a doctor grimly. "No real signs of that."

The bearded figure tried to speak. A little something was trying to light the darkness in the gaunt man's head. But when he spoke it was what had been drilled into that head. "Uniform," said Koropok. "Uniform. In my uniform."

It was beside the bed, on a stool. The Intelligence officer's swift hands were at it. "He's been in Japan," the G-2 officer said slowly. "Somehow he's managed to draw up a sketch of their major coastal defenses! There's no time to lose on this! We're about set, but this'll change matters. I'll—"

Lew Davies' mouth said, "No."

That was all. No.

Medical and Intelligence officers stared at him.

"No," said Davies again, and shivered.

"Out of his head," a doctor remarked. "Poor devil."

Davies said once more, painfully, "No."

Things were clearing for him. Slowly. Too slowly. The Intelligence officers didn't believe him; he knew that somehow.

One hand crept slowly, as slowly as he had crawled before, up toward his thick, matted beard. At first his fingers refused to do his bidding.

"He wants a shave," said a doctor quietly. "They all do. First thing. Even if they can't live."

Davies' fingers closed on his beard. He opened them. Where was it? Where was the thing which was fastened, concealed, there? Ah! He had it! And he could see a little better now! If only his jaws would unlock, and say what he wanted to say. He was still so horribly mixed up....

KEEN EYES at last saw what he was doing. The cylinder was detached, and opened. Reading, the ranking G-2 officer's eyes widened even more than before. "A list of men to whom post-war Japan can be safely trusted," his lips formed. "Men who want peace. Good Lord! Here's a real name in Japan—and here's another, one of the abbots and a Buddhist... and another...."

"Where'd you get this?" insisted the G-2 officer. "Get him to talk! He's got to talk. What a story he must have! Who can he be?"

A doctor said, "Better send his description to London, Captain, and, although he's no American, to Washington. From his appearance, and his uniform, he's as British as a cup of tea—"

"Tea," said Davies. "Tea!"

The word seemed to loosen his tongue, and the driving urgency of what, half subconsciously, he knew he must say seemed to pound at the barriers against speech, and at length break through.

He began to talk then, monotonously and without accent, as he had not spoken since he had been in Japan. It was as if he spoke without volition—of tea plantations and terraces and dive bombers. Not until he had finished did any of the men move so much as a hand for a cigarette. When his eyes closed after the semi-conscious effort, every man in the room who was on his feet turned instinctively toward where the strange landing craft about which Koropok had heard were waiting—waiting, with fighter planes protectively high above, for the beginning of the Japanese invasion....

Then the G-2 officer said what was in every mind. "In a day or two, there'll not be a tea plantation remaining in Japan!"

But Davies did not hear this. He slept.

Not until the sun had slid down to China, leaving a sky which was clean and blank after rain, did the bearded hospital patient waken. He dared not open his eyes, lest the bed under him turn out to be a kennel in Japan, such as were permitted to the pariahs who had once inhabited Japan. Then, beyond any doubt,

he knew that what had been so illusive, so fragmentary, was real.

Home!

He opened his eyes, blinked, and opened them wider.

A nurse was beside his bed; a girl—an American girl. Davies saw the soft hair under her cap, and her eyes, and her mouth—and—and now she was smiling. An American smile. Home!

"Good evening, Major Davies," the nurse said.

Davies wanted to say, "You're real!" but the best he could manage was, "Lieutenant." He saw the silver bar on her cap. He wanted her to talk to him, to keep on talking, so he could listen. "You outrank me," he said.

"There have been communications and orders, Major," she told him. "We know who you are." She added hastily, "I must report that you are awake, sir. But, oh, what you've done—everything you've done...."

"They know they're licked," said Lew.

He didn't want to talk about it, here; there would be enough of that soon. For this moment, he was home. "Home," he said slowly, "I'm home," and saw that the nurse was smiling again; and then he saw that her eyes were wet.

Home!

THE SWORD OF SHINTO

I T W A S so still and cold that the water in the bronze font which had stood for centuries in the paved, empty courtyard of the Shinto shrine had become a block of ice long before midnight. The night was one of enormous white stars and almost no shadow. There was no moon.

The ice, even with Tokyo's winter starlight glistening on its surface, had no real color of ice at all. It was brown, like the color of long dead *mitsu-aoi* leaves, those leaves of the wild ginger which, when pointed inward, were used by a fierce samurai family as a crest.

No paunched and black-robed Shinto priest shuffled out from the sleeping quarter to chip away the ice block and refill the container with the water which should be used by devout or boastful or fearful Japanese in the age-old ceremony of purifying their bodies in the sight of their ancestors and the gods. No worshipers were expected. There had been no lack of them before, not since the day when a short dagger was first thrust into the ground and, along with the hand which wielded it, buried where the shrine was to be built.

The dagger and hand thus became the first offering made to the god of war; a good many offerings had been made since that time.

Perhaps the lack of worshipers was why the fat and warm Shinto priests remained comfortably in their quilts. On this night there was no chance of their being awakened by the sound of shrill bells carried by the worshipers who raced through the streets to receive purification at the shrine. Once these *hada-kamairi* had run naked, in order that weaker persons could admire their physical strength. As years passed, and the new century began, they covered themselves with thin white kimonos, to satisfy the stupid authorities, but neglected to belt the light fabric about their middles. The *hadakamairi* continued to carry bells, but these were intended to warn those weaklings who could not look upon strength, and admire it, to turn their heads away.

Now, the streets of their own city, the capital of Japan, were forbidden to all Japanese after dark. Men could not be purified, at a time when purification was needed. In addition, the war god went unworshiped during the hours of night when prayers could arise where the sword-edge of the moon cut a hole in the skies. No soldiers could come to the shrine, nor sailors, nor merchants who had prayed for a continuation of the profits coming from conquered lands, nor women praying for strength for their husbands and sons in combat, so that their men would find the enemy weak.

Never had purification been so desperately needed. Japan had been disgraced, humbled, and defeated completely for the first time in all Nipponese history... and by the despised *Ameri-ka-jin*, the weak ones, the cowards.

What must the gods be thinking? What must the god of this temple, the angry-faced god of war, be thinking?

And why had not the sacred *shintai*, the object for veneration of the god, not already leaped from the earth, in the hand of the hero who had sacrificed hand and dagger, and driven the accursed Americans from Japan? Where were the *Ika-dzuchi*, the dread ghostly warriors who had been generated from the putrefying corpse of the husband of the sun-goddess herself?

Perhaps this was what the priests were discussing in the sleeping quarters. A dagger was mentioned in what they whis-

pered together while they stuffed their bellies with midnight rice and pickled egg-plant; a dagger, but not a hand.

Any of them would gladly have thrust one of the shrine's many knife-*shintai* into the backs of the two American infantrymen on guard in the courtyard. *Ai-ya!* Oh, no more fat and beautiful days for the Shinto priests, warm here in winter, and cool, at some seaside shrine, in summer.

No more succulent little lobsters whose scarlet claws could be sucked on while reciting prayers. No more delicately flavored raw fish so thinly cut that the light could be seen through the pale slices when held up before a lamp. No more slender young maids sent from Siam and Indo-China to serve in the shrine after they had already properly served the glorious heroes of the army, the true worshipers of the war god. And no more opportunities to observe what prison camp commanders did, so delightfully, to captured *Amerika-jin* soldiers who arrogantly refused to bow and to answer questions.

Instead, as if the Americans who had tricked Japan into

*The two infantrymen
stared at the sprawled
body on the matting.
"Gutted himself," one
soldier said to the other.*

defeat by something which the priests did not understand, were
not in themselves evil enough, the Americans were permitting
a plague of ascetic Buddhists to leave the prisons, fools who
had been jailed for not praising the glories of war. The Shinto
priests hated these men as venomously as they hated the Americans, as greatly as they hated Japanese who had accepted a
cowardly religion which worshiped a carpenter-god and peace,
and almost as greatly as they hated defeat.

Shinto was hate.

But the priests intended to do more than hate, and were
whispering about this in the sleeping quarter. *Jigoku no sata mo,*

kana shidai: even hell's judgments could be swayed by money, and the shrine was a wealthy one. Money bought what men desired. It could buy swords and daggers. It had bought one of the latter, a thin *wakizashi*, because if one of the shrine's dagger-*shintai* were employed in killing, the blade might be traced back to the shrine.

A dagger was being discussed, in the warmth of the sleeping quarter, while the two infantrymen walked their cold, lonely posts along the edge of the courtyard. A dagger. And a head which had been hacked from a neck.

The head was in the block of ice.

" *HOTOKE no k'o mo san-do,*" announced the head priest, a man as ponderous as a Japanese wrestler, and with a face just as gross. "We will not be crushed. We are supposed to be worms, but we have became snakes. Our efforts," he said solemnly, puffing out his thick lips, "are blessed in the sight of the gods. It is a great and noble service."

A younger priest said, "Nor will the stupid *Amerika-jin* realize what we are doing. If they come... here we are. At prayers."

"How long will it be before Kokochuji is missed?" asked another subordinate, reaching for a fat Egyptian cigarette which had come from Singapore. His fingers shook slightly as he picked up a coal from the brazier and lit the cigarette. "It is certain," he continued, "that the *Amerika-jin* will come here, when Kokochuji's head is discovered, and then we will be questioned."

Tadami-uchi, the head priest, took the cigarette from the other, and drew in a great breath of smoke before replying.

"You have not studied carefully," he chided, chuckling. "Do you not remember your lessons? '*Todai* moto *kurashi.*' Below the candlestick is the darkest place in the world. The head is here, in our font of purification. Would *we,* if we had done the deed which separated it from the neck, have placed it here? No! The Americans will reason so."

"We will be questioned," the younger priest muttered.

"Assuredly. We know nothing. We have faithfully, according to orders, remained within the sleeping quarter. The soldiers—out in the cold!—will truthfully state that they have not seen us in the courtyard."

"But we will be questioned."

"Yes. With words. The *Amerika-jin* do not torture to discover truth. We can lie safely, laughing to ourselves as we do so, because there will be no filling-belly-with-water, or"—he put the glowing end of the cigarette near his flaring nostrils—"other little pleasantries which we invented. And the Americans say we can invent nothing! *Mah!* Who invented the Divine-Wind airplanes? Who invented the defenses-of-caves? Who invented the glories of war?"

The youngest of the priests asked respectfully, "Oh, lord, how could the devils we hate have found a way to open the heavens so that the thunder and lightning could come down, destroying two entire cities? How—"

"That was not done by the *Amerika-jin*." growled the head priest. "It was caused by lack of prayers to the war god, who in his anger wiped out the cities. That is the truth. I learned it while I was at prayer."

"But—"

The head priest snarled, "Doubts? You will not sleep tonight. You will pray. For doubting. Be glad," he roared, "that I do not slice away the tip of your disloyal tongue. You are as big a fool as any Ainu pariah."

The youngest priest lowered his head.

His superior, finishing the cigarette, seemed to be studying the young priest. "Go to your prayers," he ordered suddenly.

When the young priest rose, bowed, and shuffled out of the warm central chamber, Tadami-uchi said, as if nothing had happened, "It will not be long before the *Amerika-jin* will become tired of a dead man here and a dead man there, right under their big white noses, and when that time comes, brothers, we will act. And what has been planned will be successful. The Americans intend to bring about order and peace. If the Buddhists fail, if the members of the old Peace Party fail, we will have our chance." He rubbed his hands together softly. "As for young Wazashimo"—the departed priest—"I am a little worried."

The other priests looked from one to the other, nodding slowly.

Tadami-uchi sighed, and placed his hands, clasped, over his capacious middle. "It is not good for a priest to have doubts," he said.

*"A good blade," he said. "Strike well
and deeply, Brother Sumebosu."*

There was a long silence, in which the footsteps of the sentries could be dimly heard.

"Well, brothers?" asked the head priest, sighing again.

Someone said, "He is weak."

" *'Ushi wa ushi-zure, uma wa uma-zure,'* " quoted the priest who had been chided for lack of remembrance. " 'Cows consort with cows, and horses with horses.' If he is weak, who can tell with whom Wazashimo will consort one day?"

"I think we agree," said Tadami-uchi.

The quoting priest lit a second cigarette for himself, again not offering it to his superior. A pucker of thought came between Tadami-uchi's thick eyebrows as he marked the lack of courtesy.

"Sumebosu," the head priest said suddenly, "yours is the honor."

The lesser priest jumped to his feet.

Face suffused, he said hoarsely, "Which blade shall I use? This will be an act of devotion to the war god."

Tadami-uchi slipped a nine-inch dirklike weapon from one of his sleeves, and tested the blade by touching the edge of his own robe with it.

"A good blade." He smiled. "Strike well and deeply, Brother Sumebosu. Remember to clap a hand over his mouth," the head priest continued, in the gentle voice of a father, "in order that the sentries hear no outcry."

Sumebosu promised, "You can rely on me!" He rose, took one quick stride, and then, before he was out of the room, moved in quick cat-steps.

He opened a panel, closed it, and was gone. Tadami-uchi said, very low, "Brothers, how long will it be before the head of our enemy, the head of Kokochuji, is discovered? We should not be wasting time in our efforts for vengeance and power. Is this not a good time for discovery?"

"It is not easy to sit, waiting," a wizened priest said, "when the spark which we will set off, the lesson which all dutiful men must learn from us, is being delayed. But we dare not go outside ourselves and discover the head. It may be a day or two before it is seen by chance—"

"And until it is discovered," agreed the head priest, in a voice as hard and as cold as Kokochuji's severed head in the bronze receptacle, "nothing will happen. I believe," he went on, after pausing to listen, "that Sumebosu is a man determined to play a great part in that which we intend."

The priests nodded. Like their superior, they, too, were listening. Their lips, as they squatted on their cushions, were tight; one, automatically, was reciting a prayer for the dead, and trying to recall whether the youngest priests's shadow, as cast when he had walked from the room, had truly become thinner, which was what always happened to a man about to die.

SUMEBOSU'S FOOTSTEPS could not be heard on the matting, although every priest, so enormous was the stillness, heard the boots of the American soldiers on the icy stones beyond the font of purification.

"He is a clever one, Sumebosu," muttered one of the priests. "He does not hurry. The youngest brother will never know that he approaches."

The head priest's frown due to this praise of Sumebosu was infinitesimal. He whispered softly, to the cadence of the soldier's boots, "Surely Sumebosu will therefore approve of playing a greater part than even he imagines will be his."

Tadami-uchi drew one leg more comfortably under the other, and with one hand smoothed a wrinkle in the cushion's silk.

The silence brought sweat to the faces of the priests... and then there was a short, savage grunt to be heard in the shrine. Sumebosu, having crept up behind his praying brother, had driven the knife deeply.

A priest said, "*Aaaaaa!*"

Tadami-uchi gave a final delicate smoothing to the vermilion and gold brocade of the cushion over which his huge bulk overflowed. Then, without the slightest preliminary lifting of his head, he screamed, twice, with all the force of his lungs. If the first scream was one of fear, the second had in it the simulated agony of death.

In the tiny fragment of time afterward, during which the head priest sat immobile, and the lesser priests all turned toward him, their eyes wide, the sound of the American soldiers' footsteps stopped—for one brief moment. An instant later there was the clatter of boots on the courtyard's paving stones as the infantrymen rushed toward the great door of the priests' quarters. As an undertone to the pounding feet was the softer sound within the shrine made by the stockinged feet of Sumebosu, hurrying back to rejoin his fellow priests.

The bloody knife was still in his hand as he ran in. He asked, "What has happened?" because, so far as he could see, nothing had happened at all to have caused the screams. Everything seemed as it had been when he had left.

"Come here, Brother Sumebosu," the head priest said swiftly.

Sumebosu obeyed.

"Kneel," said Tadami-uchi. "Kneel before me. Good. You have performed a noble and valiant deed. I wish to express my gratitude."

The younger priest, confounded and amazed, and yet smiling with satisfaction and pleasure, did as he was told. He half turned his head as he knelt squarely before his superior, so that the two Japanese were belly to belly; the movement of his head was instinctive, because of the banging on the massive door as riflebutts were hammered on it.

Sweat greased Tadami-uchi's face. A muscle jumped in his neck. As delicately as he had stroked the silk of the cushion, he had slipped a second knife from his sleeve... and he now brought the blade up so that it ripped the belly of the younger priest clear to the breastbone.

Tadami-uchi's free hand closed over Sumebosu's mouth like an iron claw until the stabbed Japanese' flesh was crushed against his teeth, and his shrieks modulated to an agonized and

*He even accompanied
the soldiers outside
and part way through
the courtyard.*

muffled *ugh–ugh–ugh*. At the same time, the head priests's powerful wrist twisted around, the knife with it, and brought the
blade back along the same cut. Halfway. There, the head priest
made a swift crosswise cut. Without pause, he pulled the
weapon free, and, with one more terrible and blood-spattering
blow, drove it to the hilt under his victim's left arm.

The banging on the door was more furious.

Tadami-uchi dropped the dying priest to the matting, and let the knife fall beside him. The matting soaked up blood until the fiber became the identical color of the cushion on which the head priest squatted.

"Permit the ignorant *Amerika-jin* to enter," said Tadami-uchi harshly. "*Seppuku* is what they think they will see," he told his stunned subordinates. "The recovery-of-honor by suicide. Sumebosu," the head priest continued, as if in explanation to the shocked Shintoists, "performed *seppuku* because he violated the shrine of the great war god by shedding blood, here in the shrine, which was not warrior's blood. Remember that, brothers; Now, unbar the door."

While one of the priests rose to obey, another whispered, "But, lord, Sumebosu was carrying out your august orders—"

"He was," the head priest agreed. "Orders more clever than he himself was able to imagine. The head of that peace-lover, Kokochuji, is certain to be found now, I believe. Therefore Sumebosu, in dying, performed a noble act. His memory will be worshiped. Thousands will soon bow before his grave. He will become as famous as the Ronin, the greatest of all heroes." Tadami-uchi went on solemnly, "Brothers, repeat the vow of the Ronin so that it will give us, and other loyal men, needed courage in these days of disgrace to do what duty demands we do."

The priests began to chant fanatically: "We cannot live under the same heaven as the enemies of our lord." None intoned the vow, known to every Japanese, more fervently than Tadami-uchi, the head priest.

It was this sound of chanting, of prayer, in a strange and foreign lamp-lit chamber, which brought the two infantrymen up short when they entered. It was some time before they marked the sprawled body on the matting, the body of the man who, when dying, certainly must have done the awful screaming.

"Gutted himself," one soldier said to the other.

There was another dead Nip in the shrine, also. The big head priest, not such a bad guy, and very helpful, took the infantrymen to where, before the gleaming sword-*shintai* of the war god, the youngest of the priests lay, face forward. The head priest was polite and courteous, although he was unable to reply to questions in English, which neither soldier expected him to understand. Neither soldier caught the tightening of the head priest's mouth when one of them remarked that it was a relief to be around a Nip so freshly killed that he didn't stink, which was compensation for the reports which would have to be made....

Yes, the big guy was pretty decent. He even accompanied the soldiers outside and part way through the courtyard, until they remembered their orders to keep all the priests inside. It was a good thing the head priest had come outside, however, because when he stumbled and bumped against one of the soldiers, just when passing the funny sort-of-a-fountain, the soldier saw what was in the bronze bowl there.

The severed head was frozen as solid as a Gulf oyster being shipped to Ohio; but a fellow didn't see things like that, Stateside.

CHAPTER 11

RETURN TO THE YOSHIWARA

EVERY AMERICAN officer sitting around the table was worried, but none of them was more worried than the G-2 colonel at whom the others were snapping. Damn it, they insisted, this was his job, and he was fumbling the ball. This had to stop. The absolute limit had been reached. Washington was screaming and, unfortunately, had plenty to scream about.

Colonel Humphreys tried to put up a defense. "It's that damned own-the-earth militaristic Black Dragon Society," he protested. "The boys who started the war. But we've got most of the ringleaders rounded up now, and—"

"And the killings go right on," a division commander accused. "Bad as ever. Or worse. What gets me down," he growled, "is that the Nips always pick a spot where my boys are on guard duty, and kill whoever we are supposed to be protecting. I'm sick of it. Makes us look foolish."

"That could be a part of the killers' plan," the C.O. said soberly. "We must find some way to end this killing of those Japanese who were held in prison previous to the occupation. They, the men who objected to Pearl Harbor and war, are the core of a future Japanese government."

"Yesterday," said the division commander, "another was killed. His head came rolling down the street, where my men were, like a football."

Humphreys said, "Nichimura's head. The Minister of Education, who had ordered a change in children's text-books."

"What is the opinion of the liberal Japanese?" asked the C.O.

"Obvious," the G-2 officer said. "Someone is seeing to it that no Japs cooperate with us. But is that all? We don't know. The Japanese," Humphreys added, "have gone in for this sort of assassination for generations. They even worship the memory of a gang of thugs Ronin, Wave-Men, who avenged an insult to the honor of their lord. There were forty-seven of them. The Forty-seven Ronin. Every person in Japan knows the story. But," grunted Humphreys, "those thugs are dead."

The C.O. relit his pipe.

"A successful occupation means there must be a change in Japanese thought. This can only come about through the Japanese themselves. If this doesn't happen, we will be forced to occupy Japan for years, or face another war. And what is going on," the C.O. said, "must be stopped."

"What I'll not do," said Humphreys bitterly, "is send any more of our Nisei, American soldiers of Japanese descent, out to try and find out what's what. When those boys are detected, we find an arm on one street and a leg on another. And yet the fellows continue to volunteer for that duty."

"From killing cooperative Japanese to killing us will be just a short step," said the C.O. "This conference," he admitted, "is exactly where it began, gentlemen. Has no one a suggestion?"

"One of my officers," said the Air Forces general, "who has been hospitalized in Okinawa was flown here last night. I asked him to report. I did this, frankly, to ask him what he thought of all this."

"And?"

The general shrugged. He smiled slightly, and then said, "He has an idea that we are nowhere near a solution."

"Hell!" barked the G-2 officer. "We all know that. I suppose," went on Colonel Humphreys, "that your pilot wants to be transferred to Intelligence and solve the mysteries of the universe?"

"He doesn't want to solve anything," General Griffith said. "He wants to return to the States. But he came over here with me, and I thought you gentlemen might wish to question him. He knows Tokyo. And Japs."

The C.O. said, "Bring him in."

A moment later a stocky officer entered the room. He was closely shaved, but even so there was a hint of darkness on his cheeks, proof of the heaviness of his beard, and that it must be the same black color as his close-cropped hair. He was broad-shouldered and swarthy, although hospitalization had faded the tan of his face. On his jacket were medal ribbons, but no theater-of-war ribbons at all.

His superior said, "Major Davies, gentlemen."

The G-2 officer jumped up. "The hell you say!" he said excitedly, shaking Davies' hand while the others rose.

"Any man," said the C.O., "who could remain undetected in Japan, all through the war, has a chance to get to the bottom of this."

Colonel Humphreys' excitement bubbled over. "We'll turn

you into an Ainu pariah again, Major," he said. "Your final operation. It won't be anything compared to what you've already done, but we need what you can learn damned badly. You won't have any difficulty in roaming around and finding out what's behind all these murders. It'll be like shooting fish in a barrel for you."

Davies remained silent.

The C.O. said grimly, "You know what has been going on?"

"Yes, sir," said Lew.

"We are not only losing those Japanese who want to govern Japan decently," the C.O. told Davies, "but we are losing face because we can't stop the killings. It is safe to assume that the seeds of real future trouble are already sprouting. I do not intend," the occupation commander said gravely, "to *order* you to see what can be found out, Major Davies, because you have already served your country far beyond the call of duty. But—"

The room became silent.

Davies said, "Sir, as Koropok the Ainu I had shaggy hair and a beard. I was able to fool the Japanese." Lew ran a hand over his chin. "I'm afraid, now, that I'd be licked before anything could be accomplished. The first Jap," said Lew, who knew only too well, "who sees me where there is no occupation soldier around on duty, and supposes me to be an Ainu pariah, will grab me by the beard before slapping me to my knees. And—well, the false beard will come off."

"The Japs' days of slapping others around are over," someone remarked.

Humphreys disagreed. "A good slap, given a pariah who won't report it, restores a little of the Nips' lost face and makes 'em feel superior again," he said. "I can see why my suggestion won't work. Oh, well, it was an idea." He sighed. "Anyhow, Davies can have a look at the records."

"Thank you, sir," said Lew.

BECAUSE EVERYONE seemed to be waiting for him to say something, the man who, as Koropok the Ainu, knew exactly what had gone on in Japan during the war, said, "If those Japanese who desire the establishment of a decent government are unable to explain who is responsible for the murders, I don't see how any of us, who think like Americans, will get very far."

"They know *what* is responsible, and so do we, and so do you, Major," the G-2 officer said. "They don't know *who*. If we could get at that... if only we could find out who is the head of the damned gang."

Davies said, thinking aloud, "That's not easy. It could be any one of a dozen groups. It could even be men who seemingly are cooperating with you, sir." The man who had masqueraded as Koropok asked suddenly, "Who was killed first?"

"Uriju Kokochuji. We had him slated for an important job. His body," Humphreys stated, "was found in his home. His head was frozen in the receptacle outside the big Shinto shrine. A couple of our men found it," went on the G-2 officer, "when they went to investigate a yell they heard in the temple—the shrine, I mean. One priest killed another priest, and then killed himself. Blood and guts all over the place. We wasted a lot of time," said Humphreys wryly, "trying to connect Kokochuji's death, and subsequent murders, with the priests."

Nodding, Davies said, "Nobody hates us more than the Shintoists. Next to the militarists, they've lost the most by defeat. Those priests had fat years. "Not," said Lew, "that the skunks who were given the opium concessions in China are very happy now. They've taken it on their financial chins. As have a lot of Japanese who ran the licensed quarters. So there are plenty of Japs who'd like to push us out of Japan." Davies broke down his own conclusion by remarking, "But a continuation of outrages will keep us here just that much longer."

"Right," agreed the C.O.

"Perhaps," Davies said quietly, his thick black eyebrows—his one resemblance to Koropok the Ainu—drawn close together, "perhaps whoever is planning these murders prefers us to having Japanese run Japan. That's a possibility."

"Rather have the Four Freedoms than the way it was?"

Lew said, "Perhaps."

"Why?"

Davies said, "If I could tell you that, maybe we'd have the answer, sir."

"At least it's the injection of a different idea," said the C.O. "We have worked on the opposite theory, Davies."

"Yes, sir," said Lew.

As the C.O. rose, dismissing the conference, Colonel Humphreys promised Davies that the reports would be made available for him, and that he should question any of the men mentioned in the reports, as well as those who had done the investigating for G-2. All of the officers were standing, and the Air Forces chief was speaking to his major about lunch later, when a technical sergeant entered the room. Without delay, he placed another report before Humphreys, who read it quickly. As the Intelligence officer read, a grim look appeared on his face.

"This time," said Humphreys, "it is Matsu Shikibu, a member of the Imperial Household. Found, decapitated, within the grounds of the Imperial Palace. His head has not yet been found."

Unnecessarily, another officer explained, "He was one of the Moderates. Not a bad old boy, for a Jap. But it isn't possible that he was killed within the palace grounds. We've got them carefully guarded—"

"By *my* outfit," mourned the division commander. "It was done from the inside," he snapped. "Somebody in the palace did it. My boys have the grounds so well watched not even an ant could crawl in. I—"

The C.O. interrupted wearily, "And what Washington will say to this, you can all guess."

Davies had been rubbing his chin. "Colonel Humphreys," said Lew suddenly, "I wonder how much of a jerk a false beard could stand. We could try it out." A wry grin twisted his mouth as he put a hand to his head. "The Nips never grabbed me by the hair, top-side," he said. "Maybe that isn't *bushido*." He glanced down at his crisp uniform. "From riches to rags," grinned Llewelyn Davies. "And here I was all set to give the gala a chance, Stateside. Oh, well."

The C.O. said, as lightly as Davies, "No girl at home, Major?"

"No, sir," admitted Lew. "I was thinking of playing the field. Or perhaps I've been waiting for a little blonde to grow up. I've always been partial to blondes, sir. Now there is one I remember—"

"You needn't try to fool me," said the C.O. gently. "I know what chances you are taking, Major." The C.O.'s hand shot out and gripped Lew's. "Good luck. We'll see to it that we keep an eye on you."

Davies said sharply, "If the beard business will stand up, you are to forget that there will be a pariah known as Koropok in Tokyo. If any attempt is made to watch or protect me, I won't make the try. Is that plain?"

Not until later did Davies realize the manner in which he had addressed the commander of the occupation forces; but when he did recall it, he also remembered the way in which the C.O. had smiled.

I F N O worshipers could run to the shrine of the war god, naked, when the late afternoon winter sun slanted down, white and cold, and if few came there to worship at all, hardly more Japanese walked toward Tokyo's licensed quarter, although far better entertainment could be expected within the district. Those who did come, at an afternoon hour when Japanese were permitted on the streets, bowed deeply before the M.P.s posted at the entrance, stationed there as visible evidence to all GI's that the famous district was out of bounds.

The M.P.s stood under the bare branches of a tree which drooped over the gate; a twisted and gnarled ancient trunk rose inside the gate. The look-back willow. Lang ago, in feudal days, it was the custom of Yoshiwara maids to accompany the guests of the night as far as the gate, since no girl, once entering the quarter, after being sold into it by her parents, was allowed to leave. But when the nightly guest passed through the gate, he would turn back for another glance at the maid. Thus the tree got its name.

The pariah who shuffled along the street toward the licensed quarter did not lift his eyes to see the willow. He was not looking back; he had everything ahead of him. As he approached the licensed quarter, he was dirtier and more ragged than the sorriest beggar who held out a mendicant's bowl for a handful of millet. He was filthier than the small boys who screamed at the Japanese who walked toward the Yoshiwara.

The pariah's beard was thick, black, and matted. His shaggy hair was a little less black; dirt had made it look gray. The Ainu jacket which he wore was tattered; one sleeve was entirely gone, as if ripped away.

Once, as he shuffled ahead, he gripped one wrist with the other hand. Koropok the Ainu.

He was thinking, *The coldest day of the year! Why couldn't I keep my damned mouth shut!* But, in spite of Major Davies' thoughts, the eyes which were supposed to mirror thought were as dull, opaque, and as truly like the eyes of a pariah as only Lew's years in Japan, in disguise, could make them.

The Japanese boys were screaming their curious wares, pieces of printed paper made to resemble a treasure-boat, in which the seven gods of luck appeared, together with pictured gold coins, coral, and other indications of wealth. On the sheets was a Japanese poem,

> *Na ka ki yo no,*
> *To o no ne fu ri no,*
> *Mi na me sa me,*
> *Na mi no ri fu ne no,*
> *O to no yo ki ka na,*

and no matter which way the poem was read, whether from

start or finish, it read the same way and produced the same meaning.

Davies, deep in his own job, gave no thought to these *otakari-uri* sellers as they vended wares which had been sold for generations.

The boys each had a portion of their faces covered with a handkerchief, also according to custom, and all of them hurried

As he shuffled ahead, Davies was thinking, The coldest day of the year. Why couldn't I keep my damn mouth shut?

toward the licensed quarter, because it was well known that the
maids within were generous when purchasing the Sheets of
Luck… although, on this afternoon, the men who were walking
to the district were not the excellent purchasers they had been
in the past.

Each man bowed to the M.P.s, just as they had always bowed
to their own soldiers, but Davies wondered how many of the
men in civilian attire might have been soldiers a short time ago.
When he reached the gate, he bowed also, more deeply than
any of the Japanese.

One of the M.P.s said, "You goin' in there, Gran'pa?"

Koropok bowed again.

"He don't look like no Jap," said the other. "He looks suspicious. Maybe he's tryin' to look disguised as a Russky? Look at them whiskers! Maybe we better hold him for the sarge. The looie says to grab everybody suspicious and then let somebody figure it out later. So maybe—"

"Wait a sec'," broke in the first M.P. "The sarge gets sore as hell when we yell for him and it ain't nothin'." He demanded, as he had been taught, "*Oh nam yee wa nan to ooo?*" asking, in something like Japanese, for the man's name.

The army major masquerading as a pariah stared at the soldier as if he did not understand, and then bowed again.

"*Oh nam yee wa nan to ooo,* damn it!" The M.P. yelled, in English, "Don't you understand your own monkey talk?"

When the M.P. yelled, Koropok dropped to the ground.

A pudgy Japanese, bowing himself, said in excellent English, "Can I be of any assistance?"

"Ask him his name."

"*O namaye w' nan to iu?*" snarled the Japanese. "And speak rapidly, dog, or the *Amerika-jin* devil will cut off your tongue!"

Davies whimpered, "Koropok, lord."

The Japanese spelled it for the soldiers. "He is an outcast," said Nishu Benji. "A pariah. A person who performs menial tasks. He—"

"Who asked you what he does, Harvard Charley?" harked one of the M.P.s. "Get along inside, both of you."

The pudgy Japanese dodged around a couple of urchins, with their Sheets of Luck, in hurrying off. The ragged pariah rose slowly, looked fearfully at the two M.P.s, and then stepped behind them. In English, swiftly but clearly, Davies remarked, "You two act like a pair of dumb cops."

He regretted the impulse instantly as the M.P.s whirled; but both shouted a warning after the hastily departing Nishu Benji, thinking that he must have done the jeering in English.

Davies, on the principal street of the licensed quarter, warned himself, *Go ahead acting smart. Do it again, and you'll probably mess everything up and get a knife in your neck as a dividend.*

M A I D S   F R O M the houses were running out to purchase the Sheets of Luck, which they would place under their pillows and hope for the happy dream which would mean happiness and good fortune during the coming year.

One girl, standing before the particular house, Number Nineteen, where Koropok had been the lowest of servants before being seized and sent to Formosa to labor in the camphor jungles along with hundreds of other pariahs, stood on the step under the carved eaves and read from the sheet, in a high-pitched nasal monotone:

> "*Na ma ki yo no,*
> *To o no ne fu ri no,*
> *Mi na me sa me,*
> *Na mi no ri fu ne no,*
> *O to no yo—*

and then she stopped abruptly.

Instead of reading the final words of the ancient poem, she shrilled, "*Hayaku! Hayaku!* Come quickly, everyone! See who is arriving! Oh, what a very strange happening! *Hayaku!*"

Unengaged maids ran to look; the fat manager of Number Nineteen, Suriga himself, pushed through the girls to see what was exciting them, hoping that it would be many customers, although the cry of the maid was not the polite manner in which guests should be greeted. An oily grin parted his thick lips, and he laughed at what he saw as he begged ironically, "*O toshi mose!* Show the honorable person in! We must not keep such an important guest waiting!"

When Koropok was inside, Suriga said sharply, "So you have returned!"

"Yes, lord. I—I am hungry."

The pudgy Japanese, Nishu Benji, apparently dissatisfied with arrangements at a different house, had entered the hallway of Nineteen. Unnoticed, he watched and listened, his hands folded across his stomach.

"You are hungry!" snarled Suriga. "Who is not hungry? Everyone is hungry! Why should I feed a pariah dog? You would not earn your food here. Few guests arrive in these evil days. Go away!"

The manager grabbed the pariah's
beard and flung him to the floor.

Koropok cowered down, but Davies was thinking, *When he's finished he'll allow me to stay here, and work like hell, for no money and little food. This is all an act. But I take whatever he gives, because a house in this district is the best spot to find out what goes on in Tokyo… and Nineteen always received Number-One guests.*

Japanese curiosity made Suriga ask, just when Koropok began to turn as if to leave, "Where have you been?"

Koropok mumbled, in clipped Ainu dialect, *"Ich' ne' tat'nu 'chi 'i.* In a land where we died." The masquerader, heart beating fast, held out his wrists, and an involuntary grunt issued from Suriga's mouth, while the staring girls instinctively put their own hands over their own wrists. "We were bound at night," explained the man disguised as a despised pariah, "so we could not run away, lord."

Suriga examined what appeared to be the marks left by thongs.

Those G-2 boys really know their stuff, thought Lew. Even to Davies, the condition of his wrists looked real. *Now if Suriga yanks me around by the beard, and it doesn't come off, I'll feel safer.*

The manager did exactly that, to cover up what might have looked like sympathy. He grabbed the pariah's beard and, as Davies carefully gave to the jerk, not too obviously, flung the man in rags to the matting of the floor.

"How dare you criticize the actions of our soldiers," squealed the manager of Nineteen, "Oh, how I intend to beat you! Go instantly to your kennel beside the kitchen, and when I am ready I will give you such a beating that—"

"If you beat him so greatly," said Nishu Benji, who was so pudgy and short that he had remained unseen behind the girls, "he will not be worth anything to you." He stepped through the lane which the girls, hastily moving aside, made for him. "How did you get back to Japan, dog?" he asked Koropok.

Koropok did not lift his head from the matting. He said, "We were brought here by the *Amerika-jin,* lord." But silently Davies was asking himself, *What's this Jap's interest in how a*

*pariah was returned? Does he actually give a damn, or is it the usual
Japanese curiosity?*

"Lord," continued Koropok, intending to find out, "we—we
were told by the *Amerika-jin*... oh, I cannot say it!"

"You had better say it," suggested Nishu Benji, "or the beating
which the manager promised you will be like the tickle of a fly
compared to what I will give you. Come! What were you told?"

Koropok whispered hoarsely, *"Dat'kushi no yo' bim'nin.* If I
say, you will kill me, lord."

"If you do not say, I am certain to kill you!"

"We... the pariahs... are to be as—as other men," whispered
Koropok, covering his head as if to ward off a kick. "The *Amerika-jin* told us that we will be permitted to—to go where we
wish, to do what we wish...."

Nishu Benji shrugged.

He said, "That is as was expected." He was about to give the
pariah a casual shove with his foot when, half under his breath,

*Koropok saw their faces. Round.
White with powder. Stupid.*

he repeated what the groveling masquerader had said. " 'To go where we wish!' Honorable brothel-keeper," the pudgy Nishu Benji said softly, "beat him very little. Very little. Or not at all. And do not allow him to run away. Remember that!"

Suriga bowed. "But how can I keep him, in these unfortunate days, against his stupid and unintelligent desires?"

"I will supply a bit of help there," promised Nishu Benji. "However, until the help arrives, bind him well. If he gets away," smiled the pudgy Japanese, "I fear that your own head may be the price of negligence."

"I will tie him until he is a cocoon!"

No flicker of interest betrayed Davies. Actually, Nishu Benji might be merely inferring that Suriga would be punished severely should he allow the bearded pariah to get away. On the other hand, there might be more behind what the pudgy English-speaking Nip had threatened.

DAVIES WAS not at all surprised at what was taking place. A Japanese brothel like Number Nineteen was the best place in Japan to find out what went on. During the war, here, admirals, in their cups, had first boasted as to the date they would sail into San Francisco, and later whined at the lack of army cooperation. And generals had explained to other generals why the navy was responsible for the failures to hold important island positions. And the new-rich *narikin* had blamed both army and navy... while the military men had been caustic concerning the desires of the merchants and manufacturers. All of the talk had been of no concern to the maids of Nineteen, who, doll-like, performed their duties and repeated nothing.

Koropok, on the floor, saw their faces now. Round. White with powder. Stupid. He had seen them in the past, without komonos. Brown bags.

He saw, too, the faces of the two men. Suriga's was questioning; Nishu Benji's seemed elated and excited.

"As for you, dog," the latter said to the man on the floor,

"believe only what we, your lords, tell you. Obey us. And do not listen to American lies."

"No, lord."

Nishu Benji opened and closed a hand, as if a sword were in it. "He is better than nothing," said the Japanese. "Or—is he?"

A true Nip, thought Lew. *First he makes up his mind to do something, and gets all worked up over it, and then he becomes doubtful. That's why the devils didn't land on Hawaii after Pearl Harbor, and just keep on going. So now I've got to give Harvard Charley a push, and it had better be good.*

He sat in the reception room of Number Nineteen, watching maids of the house serving the Japanese guests.

"Lord," he whined, "must I become a dog for the *Amerika-jin?* Oh, great one, I do not wish for such a terrible thing to happen."

"Why not?"

"Because they killed my brothers," said Koropok. "They killed my brothers with a death coming down from the sky, lord."

The pudgy Japanese smiled slowly. He licked his lips as if he had been eating succulent fat eels simmered in their own juices. He actually reached down and patted the shaggy head of the supposed Ainu, which made Davies' heart almost stop because of the anchored wig. But while Nishu Benji was clearing his throat with the customary hiss before speaking, three more men, well protected against the cold, entered Number Nineteen.

The oldest of them jibed, to Nishu Benji, "Ho! Is this where you select your maids for the night?" and continued, sternly, to the manager, "What has Number Nineteen become? A place of fourth-class entertainment? Where the maids appear to the guests in a showroom? This is disgraceful. Defeat or no defeat, do you think we will tolerate such indecency?"

Nishu Benji cut through Suriga's attempted apologetic explanation. The English-speaking, pudgy Japanese said, "One day, Number Nineteen may become a shrine equal to"—he bowed—"Sengakuji, most sacred of all shrines, because here—"

"You have been drinking! The next thing we know," the old Japanese said bitterly, "you will tell us that future generations of Japanese, instead of bowing as is proper before the statues of the most courageous and loyal of all men at Sengakuji, will bow before the bearded statue of a filthy pariah!"

Nishu Benji bowed to the older Japanese. "Perhaps I will," he said. Through a chorus of protests at such sacrilege, the pudgy Japanese whom the M.P.s had called Harvard Charley added, "He is more than a pariah."

With this Davies could agree.

Nishu Benji whispered something to the oldest of the Japanese, who, after listening carefully, nodded in agreement.

"I have decided not to have you bind the pariah," Nishu Benji informed Suriga. "He comes with me. Now take us to the reception room."

Davies, shuffling down the corridor with the guests, was disgusted and uneasy. This was not what he had wanted, not at all. He had expected to be able to get around; this would be impossible now. The "help" which Nishu Benji had mentioned earlier, in regard to holding the pariah secure, would certainly be secretly armed Japanese. The best Davies could hope for would be that later he might elude them, if he found out anything… but his opportunities for making any discoveries would be limited.

He did not forget that Nishu Benji's first interest in him, however, had only become apparent when the Japanese realized that an Ainu could go where he wished, without being checked on. Would the places he went, and the messages he might carry, give Lew what G-2 wanted—the person responsible for the killings, for the trouble the occupation commanders feared would follow?

At about the time the gang must be gathering for a drink before dinner, Major Davies was sitting in the reception room of Number Nineteen watching maids of the house serving the Japanese guests with tea and brittle cookies. He knew that there would be liquor, but that would come later.

CHAPTER III

THE DEADLY RONIN

HE HAD plenty at which to guess, did Llewelyn Davies, as he squatted in a corner of the room. Japan was, and always had been, a land of plotting. Army against navy. Moderate against conservative. Religion against religion. Military violently opposed to manufacturers. And there were plenty of cliques within cliques. G-2 was convinced, with logic behind the conviction, that the murders were intended to end Japanese cooperation with the occupation authorities. Davies had no fault to find with G-2's conclusion; but did it go far enough?

If I could do something which would cause the Nips to be doubtful about their original plans, they'd get all excited, Jap-fashion, decided Davies, while the two singing-maids droned away to the accompaniment of a samisen. *Then perhaps I'd get something positive to go on.*

Nishu Benji and the three other Japanese were up to something. Were other Japs meeting in other houses? There was no way in which Davies could find that out at present.

The pudgy Nip had threatened Suriga with the loss of the manager's head; that, however, might have been said merely because what was taking place all over Tokyo was common knowledge. However, Nishu Benji intended using a pariah in something which had to do with a Japanese-style deed of loyalty and courage, akin to what had been accomplished by the celebrated and deadly Ronin....

Davies' figuring continued until squat black bottles of saki appeared on red-lacquer trays, along with taller bottles of Scotch from Singapore. Nishu Benji and the others paid their *najimi-kin,* intimacy money, so that they could be served by personal and individual maids.

Saki and Scotch were indiscriminately imbibed; the faces of the guests, in the tightly closed reception room, became sweaty and red. Suddenly Nishu Benji shouted, "Sing the song of the Sheets of Luck!" and a singing-maid began it.

> *"Na ka ki yo no,*
> *To o no ne fu ri no,*
> *Mi na me sa me,*
> *Na mi no ri fu ne no,*
> *O to no yo ki ka na!"*

At the final line, all of the liquor-excited Japanese first raised their bullet heads, and then, to Davies' amazement, lowered them reverently. The mouths of all the guests were moving, but silently. Here and there Davies caught a monotonous and un-

The pudgy Japanese added, "He is more than a pariah."

accented syllable, enough for him to guess at the familiar remainder; and what the four Japanese were mouthing was: "We
cannot live under the same heaven as the enemies of our lord!"

So that's it, Davies realized. *Modern Ronin! Modern murderers, vengeance-killers.* The word "Ronin", the American knew,
meant, literally, a wave-man, one who was tossed about as a
wave of the sea. It designated men of samurai blood who were
entitled to bear arms, and who were prevented, by their own
acts, or dismissal, or fate, or defeat, from continuing to serve a
master.

Davies knew also why the song was connected with the
Ronin and the vow. Translated, it meant, "We wake from sleep
after a long night, and we listen to sounds of the sea and of the
waves."

He had no opportunity to start piecing together what he
now realized, even if this had been possible. Nishu Benji had
leaped to his feet.

The pudgy Japanese' entertainment kimono was open to the
waist. Liquor, fury because of defeat, and the vow itself had
readied him for a banzai-charge; it took the form of words
instead.

"*Tepyo motaba uchi-korosu no desu,*" he howled, glaring at the
squatted pariah. "I would kill him if we did not need him! Oh,
I have killed more than one shaggy-haired person, even if I was
not in the army! Oh, it was my duty to question the American
prisoners, whose hair had grown long like this dog's! Let me
tell you I was not easy on them!"

"There was usefulness in that," simpered another of the
Japanese. "*Ai!* We had practice in the severing of heads! How
that has helped us now! And how successful we are in—
aaaaaaaaa!—serving our lord!"

Davies was all ears. He listened to the repeating of the vow,
"We cannot live under the same heaven as the enemies of our
lord!" and his thoughts were racing now. It was apparent to him
that the Emperor *should* be the lord of his subjects, but unless

what Davies had read in the G-2 reports was badly bungled, the decapitated Japanese were men who had been loyal to the Tenno. The sole argument on the other side was that the assassins, the Ronin, considered the advice given by the moderates to the Tenno to be bad and disloyal advice, which warranted death. Davies rejected the latter argument.

If the Tenno were not the lord whose honor must be avenged, who *was* the lord? Davies had not the slightest idea. He maintained his physical masquerade perfectly as he squatted in the room, with the singing and noise and sound of drinking around him; he looked a pariah, a dog, an outcast.

Thought did not pucker his eyebrows. Then, as a notion came to him, his mouth puckered involuntarily... and he whistled. Once.

THE GUESTS' noise stopped abruptly. Nishu Benji, who had been standing with a bowl slopping over with whiskey in his hand, let the blue and white porcelain drop to the matting, where the fragile object shattered.

"Who whistled?" he whispered. "It is not yet time! We will not act until there is a word from Tada—"

The oldest and least drunken of the Japanese had risen. He clapped a skinny hand over the pudgy Japanese' mouth.

"Silence!" he ordered. "*Baka!* Fool!" The old Japanese snarled at the pariah, "Did you learn to make that sound from the *Amerika-jin* dog?"

Koropok said, "Sound, lord?"

"Yes! The sound of a whistle!"

"I have no whistle, lord,"

Nishu Benji said, "I heard it."

The Japanese stared from one to the other. Finally the old Japanese said, after drawing a relieved breath, "It must have been the disorderly conduct of the American military police who stand at the gate. They do not behave as is expected of civilized soldiers. I have heard them make the impolite whistle-noise when some maid passes. This sound must have carried to us."

Davies, also, was relieved. *That's twice I've slipped,* he told himself in disgust. *Three times is apt to be out.*

But the excitement of the Japanese caused by his brief involuntary whistling, and what they had said, gave him some-

The maid's footsteps sounded ta-da ta-da ta-da, *like the portion of the name Lew wanted.*

thing more on which to figure. The sound of a whistle was involved in the Nips' plotting. The whistle was to be a signal. Davies believed he knew why and how it was to be used.

His reasoning was simple. The Japs, as shown during the war by the manner in which they first attacked, then later defended their stolen gains, invariably followed an established pattern. They intended to follow custom again, in a plot where the signal would be a whistle.

This sound of a whistle, long ago, had been the signal for the assassination of a samurai called Kotsuke no Suke, who had insulted the lord of a defeated band of retainers known as Ronin. Wave-Men. This Kotsuke no Suke had taken the other lord's wealth, power, and importance from him. All modern Japan worshiped the memories of these murderers, whose tombs were at Sengakuji.

What Lew did not know was on whom the vengeance was to fall. "We will not act until there is word from Tada—" Nishu Benji had said, before he could be stopped from speaking. This name, or portion of a name, must be that of the person who was at the head of the plot, and, therefore, apt to be the Jap whom the plotters intended to avenge. Someone who had lost wealth, power, and importance. Who? Lew wished there had been fewer Japanese names in G-2's reports, so that he might have remembered this one.

Getting out of the district to find out, now that Nineteen's manager had him back, was out of the question.

And whatever was going to happen could not be far off in time.

Quietly, Davies made up his mind, there on the floor of the reception room, that what he had planned, which had caused him to whistle, must be carried to completion. If the Nips could be jerked out of secrecy by the unexpected whistle, Lew was positive that what he had considered doing would really set them on their ears. He hoped he could manage it! When the oldest of the Japanese remarked that it was growing late, Davies began to sweat a little, because in a matter of moments he would know whether or not his guess as to how Nishu Benji would act was correct. It was.

Nishu Benji said shortly, "The pariah comes with me," because the pudgy Japanese intended to see to it that all credit for what was to be done, by means of the Ainu, would come to Nishu Benji.

He himself, with his belly stuck out, led the way along the corridor. Behind him trotted the maid for whom he had paid the intimacy money. Koropok shambled along in the rear; and Davies was delighted that he followed unwatched, since it proved that Nishu Benji had no doubts about him.

The maid's footsteps sounded to Lew like *ta-da ta-da ta-da*, like the portion of the name he wanted. Threatening Nishu Benji with death would not get it. But there was a way to get it. If it worked, and Davies did get to the bottom of the plot, he had to get the account of it to men who would go into immediate action. Getting himself killed, after finding out, would serve no purpose.

It'd be a hell of time to be hacked to pieces, thought Davies. *The war's over and I'm all set to go Stateside.*

The chance he was going to take made him cold. But he was able, as he followed the Japanese man and the Japanese maid down the long perfumed corridor, to take a deep breath, unobserved. Then the maid whispered a giggled apology, hurried to slide back a panel for her guest, the honorable Nishu Benji.

The pudgy Japanese swaggered in, stumbling slightly until Number Nineteen's maid assisted him unobtrusively to a cushion on which he squatted. He stared at Koropok the Ainu, and then exploded into laughter,

"Oh, nothing like this has ever happened to me before," he wheezed. "This is a new experience, even for me."

"Yes, honorable guest," agreed the maid, moving a smoking-stand nearer to him, and pouring another cupful of liquor before kneeling beside him.

Nishu Benji pushed the cup aside. "I am not one who speaks only to be answered by silence," he flung at the pariah. "Ho! When the shaggy-headed *Amerika-jin* would not speak to me, I knew what to do about it! You! Dog! Speak!"

"*Dan' sa' yor'shi'rba wa'kush' g'zar'mas',*" mumbled Koropok. "It will be a new experience for you, lord."

NUMBER NINETEEN. In some other room another guest was being entertained more formally than Nishu Benji desired; Davies, as he stood waiting while the Japanese smoked, heard the tapping of a drum, at first slow, and then running into a quick, rousing tempo. There, a dancing-girl was performing the same dance as was always performed, in exactly the same way—just as the Japanese always followed the customs of the past. Her arms would be outstretched, Davies knew, and her sleeves would be swaying, while her fan invited and promised....

Here, the maid busied herself with tending Nishu Benji, until Davies wondered if she would ever rise and go for quilts and mosquito netting. When she did stand, to beg permission to leave for a moment, the pudgy Japanese grabbed at her kimono; the silk of it hissed through his fingers. She smiled down at him, and then pattered from the room.

Davies took two long, swift strides. His fingers were around the throat of the Japanese before Nishu Benji's mouth could open, and almost before the panel had been pushed closed by the departing maid.

"A new experience," whispered Davies, in a voice as hard as steel and in English.

He didn't know whether the popping of the Japanese' eyes was because Harvard Charley understood the language and the words, or whether the pressure of Lew's fingers was forcing the eyeballs out of the ex-torturer's head. He didn't care.

The rest was butcher's work. Davies knew from living at Number Nineteen exactly where, according to custom, a maid would keep her long gift-knives. But it was an ugly, bloody business.

He wiped his hands, at the end, on the Japanese' own kimono. He examined his own rags. Not spattered. He looked again at the outer wall; the window there was shut, but not fastened. He ran to it, and put a blood-smear on the lacquered sill. After that, he searched Nishu Benji swiftly and found a Sheet of Luck. *Maybe they use 'em for communicating,* he thought, but he dared not take the time to examine the sheet carefully, nor did he dare attempt to conceal it.

He paused now and took a deep breath. Would this do it, this headless body? Or would this be the finish of both Koropok and Davies?

There was the rapid beating of the drum, the brittle tinkling of a stringed instrument, and the voice of a maid as she sang an ancient song. Somewhere in Nineteen, coarsely, a man laughed.

Davies put his fingers to his lips. Once, shrilly, he whistled

The laugh and the drum and the music stopped. The softly singing provocative voice fainted away to silence.

Clearly, loudly, in Japanese vastly different from the clipped dialect of the Ainu, Davies chanted, "We cannot live under the same heaven as the enemies of our lord!"

After he had done that, he crouched down in the dimmest corner of the room, as far as possible from the window.

Number Nineteen's panels shook with shouts. Bare feet thudded in the corridor as guests ran to investigate, forgetting all politeness as rooms were unceremoniously entered. The oldest of the Japanese came running out of one of the rooms, sputtering with worry. For a moment he was bumped this way and that, and finally against Nishu Benji's maid. She and her quilts were knocked down; she whimpered as, on her knees, she collected the night-paraphernalia again.

Suriga, the manager, was first in Nishu Benji's room. What he saw there—the decapitated body on the blood-soaked matting, and the grinning head on the little lacquered smoking-stand—turned his face the color of a dirty tomb-cloth. He gagged, covered his mouth with both hands, and stared.

The withered old Japanese, shaken mentally and physically, his face gray also, was the first to speak. What he said proved how thoroughly Davies understood the Nipponese psychology.

"He must have been disloyal," snarled the old man, "and therefore Tadami-uchi ordered his death."

That's that much, thought the man in tatters. *Now let's see if he doesn't become doubtful of his own reasoning, Jap-fashion.*

The old man did. "But why would Nishu Benji's head remain here?" he said, as he thought aloud. "The *Amerika-jin* will never find it here! They are forbidden by their own authorities to enter the district. They—"

"Perhaps it is because Nishu Benji was disloyal, and not like those Japanese who wish to injure our lord," a Japanese of the party suggested. "It may be that all our lord required was his death, not that it be learned about by the Americans. Perhaps that is why Nishu Benji died here."

"But the whistle! The whistle!"

As Davies had figured, the Japanese were terribly confused, just as they were whenever the unexpected took place. He was positive now that he could give G-2 the information needed. Tadami-uchi! The characters forming the name leaped like zigzags before Davies' eyes: Tadami-uchi, the head priest of a powerful Shinto shrine, who was fighting to recover what the Shintoists were losing to both the Americans and the rival sect of Buddhists. The head priest had organized fanatics into a band like the famous Ronin, the Wave-Men, who would willingly die in order to avenge an insult to their leader.

It also occurred to the American, as puckered foreheads told him the sound of the whistle was completely puzzling to the Japanese, that if peaceful Japanese could not maintain order under the occupation forces, Shintoists who would assume a different cloak could again secure control. It was not a simple affair; but neither was anything in the Orient.

Keiri Bassaku, the old Japanese, broke the silence.

"The pariah," he demanded. "Where is he?"

Koropok did not move, not until he was dragged from his corner.

"How many men killed Nishu Benji?" he was asked.

"Only one man, lord," whined Koropok.

"How, fool?"

Davies raised a trembling finger, and pointed toward the window.

"And when Nishu Benji, who must have been part Ainu dog, was dead, what did the other man do?"

"He took a little shining something from his jacket, lord. He put it up to his mouth. He puffed into it and sound came. I—"

Keiri Bassaku said, "The whistle!"

"He has seen and heard too much," someone grated. "We had better kill him at once, here and now."

The old Japanese said sharply, "No. Not yet."

He stepped over to the stand, picked up Nishu Benji's head by the black hair, and looked down at the stand, as if a message might have been placed underneath. A cigarette rolled to the matting, but that was all. Keiri Bassaku dropped the head. It fell with a thud and, like the cigarette, rolled a little.

A QUICK, belated search of the body disclosed nothing. When the Sheet of Luck was found on it, the Japanese crowded around, all reading that which they should have known by heart.

"There is nothing on it but the time and place of our meeting here," the oldest of the Japanese said; and Davies' immediate guess was that the ancient poem, containing almost every Japanese syllable, must be secretly marked in some manner. He didn't especially care now. What he did hope was that the old man, given time, would arrive at what was the one conclusion.

Davies landed
heavily on stones
in the courtyard.

Again the American who had been so long in Japan was not mistaken.

Keiri Bassaku said to Suriga, "Send the maid about her affairs, and you go about your own. I need not tell that your life depends on silence, although you know all of us for what we are—"

"You are men of ancient families," said Suriga quickly, "and your fathers came to Number Nineteen when my father was the manager, and—"

"I am going to borrow your pariah," snapped the old man.

I am the only messenger he can find, thought Lew, which was what he had been thinking before, and the reason the plotters had been originally interested in a liberated Ainu, who could go where he wished. *And he's got to find out what has happened, because of the whistle and the chant.*

There was a discussion when Keiri Bassaku announced that

a carefully worded message of inquiry was to be sent to the Shinto shrine. Could the bearded pariah be trusted with it? Perhaps Keiri Bassaku himself should go. The foolish Americans might permit him to walk to the shrine; the Americans were gentle toward old men. Or perhaps the smallest of the party here could dress himself like an *otakari-uri* selling Sheets of Luck—one of which would be used for the coded message— and be allowed on the streets by the stupidly kind American guards who would think him a young fellow merely out too late? Or perhaps—

"No," said Keiri Bassaku. He pounced on Koropok while Davies was congratulating himself and his perfect luck; he clawed at the pariah like a cat sharpening its nails; thus, in true Japanese style, beating down someone who was to be used. Davies did not dare protect himself, although he tried to roll his head. One of the vicious old man's fingers prodded at a corner of one of Lew's eyes, bringing bright blinding pain. Keiri Bassaku ended the typical threat—a warning as to what additional punishment could be expected should the pariah fail in obedience—by raking all of the fingers from eye up to temple. The black wig, so carefully fastened down, began to give, first just slightly, and then....

Keiri Bassaku was shrieking, "What have we here?" when Koropok the Ainu flung him, with one terrific motion, against two of the other Japanese. The tattered figure of the pariah was out of the window before anyone else could shout or jump forward.

Again, Japanese were trapped by the unexpected.

Davies tried to twist around in mid-air, but landed heavily on the stones of the courtyard. He did not try to yell for the M.P.s at the gate as he jumped. It would have been better if he had, because head and shoulder struck together, and red and black sparks alternated before his dazed eyes. Even so, he managed to get to his knees before the Japanese came tearing out of Nineteen, and he could hear, although hazily, what they intended, which was to cut him off from the Americans at the gate.

Instead, looking more like Koropok the pariah than ever before, his face plastered with dirt, dust, and blood, Davies crawled for shadow, and then, limping as he ran, headed away from the gate toward the nauseous black canal bordering the northern portion of the licensed quarter.

There would be danger wherever sentries were posted. He knew that. And it was the Nips, not Davies, who knew the nearby posts.

These Japanese were desperate, and since they had already discussed ways by which they might be permitted on the streets at night, they would certainly try to do so now. Davies knew another fact: while the Japs would make every effort to get him before he could contact the American occupation authorities, other Wave-Men, without any delay or the wasting of a second of time, would, in desperation, take the word of what had happened to the Shinto shrine and Tadami-uchi.

The head priest, lord and motivating force of the fanatical Wave-Men, would immediately vanish… and continue to direct the assassins.

Davies went waist-deep into the canal. His feet squashed down in ooze. Foul smelling as it was, Davies cupped water in his hands and slapped it against his face until his head had cleared.

It doesn't make much difference if we've got a hundred thousand or a million men in Japan—not to you, boy, Davies told himself grimly. *If the head priest is to be grabbed, it's your party.*

He had been utterly on his own all through the war; he did not mind being so now. The one important thing was to get to the Shinto shrine before Tadami-uchi disappeared… and Koropok the Ainu, better than any Japanese, knew all of the dark alleys which were the short cuts through Tokyo. When he had lived there as a pariah, other streets had been forbidden to him. So, now, the dim, filth-line passageways were familiar.

At this hour the narrow, angled ways along which Davies ran were deserted except for those cats which had escaped the cooking-pots, hordes of big bronze night flies, and an Ainu man and woman asleep against a filth-can.

THE SWORD which was worshiped in the Shinto shrine of which Tadami-uchi was the head priest was a famous one. This sword-*shintai,* according to tradition, had been found by an ancient samurai warrior in the tail of the Great Serpent. It was not a huge sword, and the handle was only of iron orna-mented with inlaid silver threads, but the blade, resting on a piece of silver on the altar-stand, glittered like a slice of the moon. Priests spent whole nights tapping the steel with a tiny bag filled with polishing powder.

The *shintai* gleamed just to the left of Tadami-uchi, who squatted on his cushion in front of a semi-circle of the priests of the shrine.

In spite of earlier regulations, American officers had come to the shrine itself to question the priests. With them, acting as interpreters, were two Japanese-American sergeants. Colonel

*The sword-*shintai *had been snapped
by the shot, but not shattered.*

Humphreys, of G-2, was in charge. Sitting beside him, in silence, was an officer, whose single gold bar seemed to mark him as a second lieutenant, and whose breath came rapidly, as if he had been running.

This officer's uniform was ill-fitting. The sleeves were too long, and the suntan blouse too tight across shoulders and chest.

Davies had seen the cars drive up just as he dashed toward the courtyard. He had been lucky in that the sentries posted under the *torii* of the gateway had snapped to attention as the officers had been driven up, otherwise he might have been shot.

His first question, when answered, told him that G-2, in desperation, had started again at the scene of the first of the murders—the shrine; his second question had resulted in the removal of his wig and beard with the assistance of a belt first aid kit, and the transfer to Davies of the uniform of the second lieutenant who had been with the investigator. The latter, shivering, was driven back to Headquarters, and swiftly.

Before entering the shrine, Davies had told the colonel, "What we've got to watch is the old banzai charge. That's what the spirit of the Wave-Men has turned out to be. It's the idea that death doesn't matter if you achieve your vengeance."

A quick look around had shown Davies how small the group of Intelligence officers really was. Even so, it was pretty fine for the man who had been on his own for so long, to be backed by and be a part of the United States forces. It felt good to be in uniform, even one as badly fitting as the lieutenant's. And there was a splendid feeling in sitting opposite the plotting priests and to know that the plot was going to fail.

Tadami-uchi had greeted the Americans graciously enough. Davies had almost grinned when the head priest, the servant of the war god, had spoken of peace. He did not speak at all, nor did he interrupt obvious lies when Tadami-uchi expressed horror and surprise, even now, when reminded of the head which had been frozen in the font in the courtyard.

What the head priest offered was, thoughtfully, "Possibly

that dead man caused the jealousy of a woman? I have heard stories about his households, something which we, here in the shrine, frown upon."

Davies, briefly, thought of the shrine's dancing-maids.

This fencing had not gone on for more than a few minutes when a Japanese slid softly into the chamber, not by the main door, but, Davies supposed, probably through the priest's passageway itself. It was the thin, boy-sized Japanese who had been a guest at Number Nineteen. He bobbed his head, dropped on all fours, and approached Tadami-uchi. As he sidled over the matting, his eyes fastened with venom *on* the two Nisei sergeants....

He knows they'll understand Japanese, thought Lew, amused, *and he knows he's got to be careful.*

The wiry Japanese finally choked out, "A sacred *shintai,* the goddess-mirror, has fallen, oh, lord. Please come and recite prayers before it, or something terrible will happen."

Not bad, decided Lew, while one of the sergeants softly translated what had just been said. *It would have worked. Tadami-uchi would have gotten away.*

"Inform your masters what I must do," the head priest threw at the sergeants, as he stood up ponderously, his robes hissing around him.

"Tell him to put his fat bottom back on the cushion," growled Colonel Humphreys, and Davies' eyes glistened as the sergeant proceeded to furnish Tadami-uchi with an exact translation.

There was a rustling of robes as the priests moved slightly. Every beady stare was fastened on a separate American; here and there a hand slipped up a sleeve, so that Davies, and most of the G-2 officers, knew that the priests were armed.

The chamber was silent. Behind the priests was the raised sanctuary, now empty of the sword-*shintai* which was beside the big head priest. Offerings stood on the high altar, bronze perfume burners, handfuls of rice in bowls, miniature wooden swords and daggers. A long white scroll hung motionless.

The shrine was so still now that approaching footsteps made a frightful sound. Into the room came old Keiri Bassaku, almost tottering. The wizened Japanese froze stiff as he saw the two semicircles of silent men.

Davies' mouth barely moved as he said, "It's coming. The banzai charge." He, and the Americans who expected it, heard the soft thrumming of cars approaching the shrine. "Maybe I can hold it up a sec'," said Lew.

A second… a minute… enough to change the odds. That might do it. If not—well, it would be bad. Bad because Americans would be killed here, and priests would be killed and a shrine violated. Much could be made of it, at home and in Japan and throughout the Far East.

DAVIES STOOD up slowly, so no knife would be thrown.

"Keiri Bassaku," he said, gravely, in excellent Japanese, "you are tired. It is a considerable distance from Number Nineteen to this shrine. Please sit and enjoy a little rest." One of the old Japanese' hands fluttered, but he gave no other sign of astonishment. He, like all Japanese, was caught by the unexpected. His old eyes saw an *Amerika-jin* officer, short, dark, erect… and, Japanese-fashion again, he was unable to refrain from, "How did you know?"

When Davies remained silent, Keiri Bassaku shot at him, "You have been listening to lies!" which meant that the American had believed what a pariah, or a person disguised as a pariah, might have said.

In clipped Ainu dialect, Davies mumbled, in the voice of Koropok, "*N'ma b'y'o wa o-kiz' n' mot'*. Were the lies your lies?"

The wiry Japanese screamed, "Koropok!"

He was leaping up at Davies while he shouted. Lew's short, savage blow pounded in an uppercut just as the Japanese' knife flashed out.

Tadami-uchi had heard enough to guess the rest. With one hand he produced a tiny shining whistle, which was almost lost in his thick lips as he blew wildly on it; with the other hand he grasped the sword-*shintai*. One huge hand began to swing it in a great arc of light.

Davies saw it coming, but had not guessed that a priest would employ the sacred weapon. He saw the streak of white-and-silver lightning and, in the same split second as death was presenting itself to him, he knew the lengths to which Tadami-uchi and his Wave-Men would go.

But if the sword were the lightning of the war god, a revolver shot became the thunder, to fill the chamber and set the scroll to trembling, so that the characters on it changed form.

The priests were on their feet; knives were out. None darted from brown hands, however, because the great door had been flung open, and the Shintoists became immobile as they saw the soldiers with whom the lieutenant had returned come swarming in.

The sword-*shintai* had been snapped by the shot, but not shattered. Tadami-uchi continued to grip the handle.

Keiri Bassaku shrilled. "Use what blade remains, lord! Perform *seppuku* honorably." A despairing plea of, "Swiftly, lord!" did not cause the head priest to recover the last of his honor by disemboweling himself.

Davies' first thought was, *Let him!* but that would have brought about questions concerning the death of a priest. So, with one fluid motion, he had the bulging sword arm of the ponderous head priest pinioned. It was like squeezing fat. There was no strength in the gigantic arm when death called to Tadami-uchi.

"A coward," Davies said in Japanese. "A leader of Ronin? No!"

That does it, realized Davies. *He's got no face left. No honor. No anything. He's through. So are the Wave-Men, because you can't swear not to live under the same heaven as the enemies of your lord when your lord is a bust.*

Proof of what Lew was reasoning became apparent from the manner in which the old Japanese, and the younger one, and even the priests, hid their shamed faces in their hands. They, too, were dishonored and disgraced by the cowardly action of Tadami-uchi, who should have shown them the way to honor.

Colonel Humphreys said, "Well! You've got to explain most of it to me, Major. I never saw anything like this in my life."

"It took me a good many years in Japan to understand it myself," said Lew. He went on quietly, "This ends my duty here, sir? I'm all finished?"

"You certainly are!"

"May I drive a car when we return, sir?"

"Good Lord, yes. All of 'em! We're damn grateful to you, Major."

"You see, sir," said Lew, giving his shirt a loosening yank, "when I'm back in the States, I hope to go out with a gal, and I haven't driven a car since the first bomb was dropped."

The G-2 officer nodded absently. He said, thinking aloud while the soldiers waited for orders, "No sense in arresting the priests now, is there? They'll behave, even if they're not on our side. We'll not have any more Nips murdered when they try to work with us, will we?"

"No more," agreed Davies.

Colonel Humphreys said, "Take any car you want. Anybody's. Mine." With a hand on Lew's shoulders, he asked, "Is there anything else, Major?"

"Yes." Davies paused and began to smile. "Yes. There's something else. I want to go home."

THE SILKEN SCABBARD

MAJOR LLEWELLYN DAVIES, just re-
turned from Stateside furlough, listened to what was
being said by the Japan Civil Control Authority commissioners at Headquarters, and his earlier amusement began to change
to resentment and rising anger. Sitting far down the conference
table, he was hearing why he had been ordered to remain in
Tokyo instead of receiving flight duty which would have been
such a welcome assignment. And he was understanding what
fellows meant when they talked about a castor oil assignment.

The discussion was going on as if he were not present at all,
as if he were a pawn. What annoyed him was that the JCCA
men who were doing the pushing knew less about the game
than he did. All during the war years he had been on his own
here, disguised as a bearded and miserable Ainu pariah. Now,
he sat listening to theorizing by men who had never been in
Japan before, but who were deciding, right down to the final
details, what he himself was to do. Davies had no intention of
doing it, if there were any possible way out.

"Major Davies," the newly appointed head of the JCCA said,
speaking directly to Lew for the first time since the C.O. had
introduced the men, "I take it that you will begin immediately."

The dark, stocky Davies, who had been known to the Japanese as Koropok, looked down the conference table to the C.O.
But when the general shrugged, and refilled his pipe instead of
speaking, Lew realized that the C.O. was helpless, and that it

was up to Llewellyn Davies to escape from what he believed was a senseless task, and one in which he wanted no part.

Davies did not believe that these JCCA men, who kept talking about the need for wholehearted cooperation, would want to work with a man who wouldn't give it. Lew thought grimly, *And I won't leave any doubt in their minds, either.* He said flatly, "Your plan won't work."

"I should think," snapped Brown, the head of the JCCA, "that you would have considerable sympathy for the Ainus, Major, and a desire to help them. Or have you, through long association with the Japanese, unconsciously donned the kimono? Have you acquired a Japanese viewpoint toward conquered peoples?"

The C.O. took his pipe from between his teeth, and a G-2 officer beside the general opened his mouth in protest, but Davies spoke first.

"When I say that your plan to rehabilitate the pariahs won't

Slowly and humbly, Koropok laid the
dead rats on the earth floor.

work, it's because I know them. You can't change such perse-
cuted and kicked-around people into men who can take care
of themselves. Not over night."

"Let us be the judges of that, please," Brown retorted. "You
underestimate the latent abilities of primitive people after they
become free. I repeat—you, a man who is accepted by the Ainus
as one of their number, are to lead them toward self-respect
and decent work. They will prove themselves capable of taking
an important place in the new order in Japan."

Davies said, "If I could persuade them to take jobs which
were forbidden them in the past, d'you know how I'd do it? By
telling their old men that if they didn't obey they would be
killed by the new lords. Us."

"You will tell them nothing of the sort," snapped the JCCA
head. "We have made a comprehensive study of the psychol-

ogy of the Ainu people, and they will follow a leader. You are to be that leader."

"Not me," said Lew.

"I assure you, Major, that we would prefer to work with someone who has faith in the regeneration of the Ainus, and in democratic principles. I admit I am amazed that you have raised the slightest objection."

This was what Lew had hoped would be said; a little more needling, he believed, and he could slide out. He said, "You want me to go around to the pariah quarters and toot on a horn and have the Ainus follow me in order to get food, clothes, and yen. The Pied Piper of Tokyo. The Japs will laugh when it fails, and the Ainus will be worse off than before. So I'm not going to do it."

HOPEFULLY, DAVIES observed the choleric tightening of the Chief Commissioner's lips, but Brown finally said levelly, "The Japanese will believe that the pariahs are asserting their independence. The plain truth, Major, is that you are actually making mountains out of mole-hills. In Japanese," said the JCCA head, "that would be '*Hari hoda no keta wo ba hoda ni,*' I believe. You see, Major, we have not only carefully studied Asiatic psychologies, but the language as well. Come! Go along with us, Major Davies, and do it… willingly."

The last word, emphasized slightly, was proof to Lew that

he would be ordered to do what the JCCA had decided upon; but the fact that the C.O. was allowing him a chance to get out of it, if he could, made Davies bold. If only he were able to make these theorists believe that he could wreck their high hopes for the pariahs by failing to cooperate, he was sure they would finally leave him out of their plans. And no matter what they eventually did, without him, it would be better for the poor devils whom the Japs had booted around.

Lew said, "I hope your understanding of the Ainus is better than your *seiyo-jin* type of the Japanese language."

"I did not expect that my phraseology would be perfect," said Brown coldly. "I like your attitude even less than you like our plan, Major."

Got him going, thought Davies. He had hit below the belt, he felt, but it had been necessary. *Now I'll rub it in,* Lew decided.

He quoted swiftly and perfectly,

> " '*Kono hana wo*
> *Kataku oru-na!' to*
> *I' tate-fude mo,*
> *Yomenu kaze ni wa*
> *Zehi mo nashi.*"

The Intelligence officer said, "That's too fast for me."

Davies said, "A translation would be that even when a sign is inscribed with the words 'It is strictly prohibited to pluck these blossoms' the warning is useless against the wind, which is unable to read."

The C.O. looked up at the ceiling as Brown demanded, "What do you intend to infer by that, Major? What I think you mean?"

Davies' shrug and silence practically said, "Exactly. You think I mean you are too dumb to heed my warning, and I do." He marked the exasperated manner in which two of the JCCA commissioners, sitting together, were whispering, and when both of them whispered to Brown, Lew was reasonably positive that they were telling their chief they'd had all of Major Davies that they wanted. And so, from the way Chief Commissioner Brown was nodding and biting his lips and tapping on the table, had the head of the Japan Civil Control Authority.

He said, "We will omit you from our plans, Major Davies."

"Thank you, sir," said Lew. Because he was certain that he was right, and also because he felt a little like a heel, he said, "I'm in accord with your basic idea, which is to make men out of the pariahs, but surely there is some other way to do it. I would not have refused if I were not certain. If you will talk with some of the Japanese who are playing ball with us," ended Davies, "I believe you will find that they will corroborate what I have told you, sir."

One of the commissioners said, "Quite the contrary, Major. An important Japanese agreed entirely with us."

"Perhaps he was agreeing out of politeness," said Lew.

"I wouldn't exactly call Mr. Suzuki-mura a polite man," said Brown.

"I wouldn't either," replied Davies, grinning, who had seen Japan's wealthiest and most ruthless silk manufacturer many times at Number Nineteen, where Suzuki-mura had paid the highest of fees to be entertained by fresh young girls of the house. "The old so-and-so," recalled the man who had been Koropok, "gave me the hardest kick anyone ever planted on me when I was a bit clumsy in handling the quilts which his maid was waiting to spread on the matting as soon as the old swine swilled enough Singapore Scotch to put him to sleep. He—"

"His morals are not our concern, Major."

"And how he could curse!" remembered the man who had been Koropok at Nineteen. "He always outdid himself when he mentioned Americans, giving us the business and... Incidentally, how come," Davies wanted to know, sitting straighter in his chair, "you're discussing anything with him?"

"He is a powerful industrialist," explained Brown, "and naturally he is in a position to assist us without long delays."

"What's he getting out of it?"

The Chief Commissioner said, with cause, "I fail to see why you should interest yourself, Major."

"Because Suzuki-mura was in with the sword-rattling boys, and—"

"He had no choice," stated Brown. "Do you believe, Major Davies, that he, as a prominent manufacturer and exporter of great quantities of silk, was made happy by the loss of his business?"

Lew said, "He made a bigger profit out of opium in China. He was in on every racket. Oil. The boosting of the price of rice and millet and from the way he was allowed to act at Number Nineteen, I always thought he got a cut out of the profits there, too. No Jap," Davies said earnestly, "was ever smarter at keeping in with the boys top-side. Suzuki-mura entertained Tojo at Nineteen. When Tojo finished himself by trying to establish a shogunate and was caught at it, Suzuki-mura dropped him so hard that The Razor was knicked all over. I wouldn't trust him with a tub of spoiling saki. He looks like a benevolent god of fortune, but I'd hate to rub his belly the wrong way."

"Major Davies' analysis of Suzuki-mura agrees with our own," the Intelligence officer said. "He is a dangerous man."

"He must behave himself," the JCCA head remarked. "In order to resume manufacturing, he must have our consent. In order to secure our consent, he must engage a percentage of Ainus. He must give them instruction, pay a standard wage, assure a decent work-day in hours, and afford them equal opportunities for advancement. Mr. Suzuki-mura has not only agreed to every one of these JCCA provisions, but with a good spirit. I would say that he has done so enthusiastically."

The other control commissioners nodded.

DAVIES COULD see that Suzuki-mura had probably jumped at the chance to put his long-idle spinning mills and raw silk conditioning establishments back in operation before his competitors could get going, and that the wily old devil was undoubtedly again taking advantage of a change on control. On the other hand, the astute Suzuki-mura must know that few pariahs could perform any of the silk factory tasks, work performed before the war by deft-fingered Japanese girls who had labored from five in the morning to seven at night. And if Suzuki-mura's competition in the making of silk fabrics came from factories employing these girls, experienced and accustomed to be driven at top speed for long hours, his Imperial Nippon and Far Eastern Silk Association would be driven out of business.

Suzuki-mura was too smart for that.

"I don't understand it," Davies said slowly, which was an understatement. "I don't see how the pariahs can be taught to work with machines. A few can, perhaps. The younger ones. But—"

"Mr. Suzuki-mura raised that point also," returned Brown, smiling, "and he had a solution. Those Ainus who are unfitted for factory work will be sent to the country to be engaged in sericulture. Any of them can pick mulberry leaves, or chop the leaves so that they can be fed to the silkworms, or maintain fires in the rearing-chambers. In addition to furnishing the Ainus with healthful and gainful employment forbidden them in the past, it sets them on a plane with the Japanese, and forces them away from the squalid pariah quarters in which they now live."

Davies leaned back in his chair. Looking at the plan coldly, it sounded reasonable. Suzuki-mura was after an edge in silk manufacturing and exporting when silk would bring enormous prices and profits in the States; the Japanese industrialist was delighted to scrape and bow and smile and agree to anything which would enable him to get his mills back into operation. He would become the top dog in Japan. And what a dog! The JCCA would pat him on the head since the commission's chief concern was the rehabilitation of the Ainus; and all Japan would enjoy the shrewdness of Suzuki-mura and how he was fooling the Americans.

Was the outcome, the doubtful regeneration of the pariahs, worth the price, which would be the loss of American face and the elevation of Suzuki-mura to importance and power again? Lew did not think so.

He said earnestly, "I was at Number Nineteen when the news was brought that the first American flyers has been executed. Suzuki-mura grabbed a fan from one of the geisha and hopped up and down like a *taikomochi*, like a wild man. I can't get that out of my mind. I can't forget the things he yelled. I tell you," said Davies, "that I am afraid of the man."

"His actions and words were part of the general war hysteria, Major," Brown said, soberly and kindly. "I have no affection for Suzuki-mura, but we simply must be realists and utilize the tools which we have."

The figure of the wildly exhilarated Suzuki-mura dancing and shouting refused to dim before Llewellyn Davies' eyes. He blurted, "Are you sure that you won't be the tool in Suzuki-

He recognized the silk-hatted Suzuki-mura as the one who bowed most deeply to the commissioners.

mura's hand?" He stopped whatever the Chief Commissioner was going to say in protest by continuing, "There is something behind the old devil's acquiescence. I don't know what. But I think it is more than just getting back into the manufacturing and exporting of silk—and I don't see how he can do even this working under the handicap of Ainu workmen. Sir, drop the plan. Or—"

"Or what?" asked Brown.

Davies reached for a cigarette, lit it slowly, and sighed. Then he grinned as he looked at the paper tube. "During the final year of the war," he said, "there was little tobacco. Old women kept themselves alive by picking up the last sodden quarter inch of soldiers' cigarettes and selling the remaining tobacco for use in pipes. You can guess what chance a pariah named Koropok ever had to smoke. When a big boy like Suzuki-mura came to Number Nineteen, and smoked fat Egyptians right up to the war's end, and blew the smoke in my face, I wanted to send him to join his ancestors. What I was thinking," ended Lew, with everyone staring at him, "is that it shouldn't be so bad now."

"What has tobacco to do with what sounded like a threat if we didn't change our decision to go through with our plans?"

"I was just realizing that I've got to play along with you," Davies said, "and I was telling myself that it shouldn't be too bad now. But there's one thing I've got to know, sir—how many people know of the plan's details? Does Suzuki-mura? I mean as regards my proposed part in it. If—"

"It is too late for you to accept, Major," said Brown, finally managing to break in. "We would be working at cross-purposes."

The C.O. cleared his throat. "My orders," he said placidly, "are that Major Davies is to be assigned to work with the Japan Civil Control Authority for this particular operation. Until such orders are rescinded, gentlemen, it is necessary for the major to work with you. I could not," the general said virtuously, "allow the plan to go into operation unless Major Davies is connected with it. Surely, gentlemen, you see my position."

Leave it to the Old Man, thought Lew. He said quickly, "Mr. Brown, if the Ainus can be helped, I want to do it. I may," went on Davies, in an admission which he did not actually believe, "have raised objections without having given the matter enough thought. I'll work with you, sir. The best I can."

"It would take weeks, and involved explanations to Washington, to bring about a change in orders," Brown admitted to his fellow commissioners. "We have no choice, I regret." He said honestly to Davies, "You believe that Mr. Suzuki-mura's expressed intentions and expectations cloak something which you admit is unclear to you, and we, frankly, do not. On our part, we intend to regenerate the Ainus without a waste of time, with which you are not in sympathy. If, however, you will carry out our plans, which you have already heard and know, toward that latter end, then we must be satisfied, Major Davies, under the circumstances."

The C.O. rose. "Those are his orders," he said.

"Mr. Brown," said Lew hastily, as the meeting broke up, "does Suzuki-mura, or anyone except those of us who are here in this room, know that an American disguised as a pariah is to have a part in your plan?"

"We have told Mr. Suzuki-mura only enough to explain the basic idea. I believe he did raise the question as to difficulties in moving the Ainus from their settlements. If I recall correctly, he suggested that we herd them, with our troops, to wherever they are to be sent to work. Naturally I explained to Mr. Suzuki-mura that we do not operate in such a manner, and that we would see to it that the Ainus went willingly. He did not ask how we would do it."

THAT WAS something, anyhow. Davies' thoughts, as he walked from the room with the G-2 officer, were already busy with the problem of how to begin the assignment; he saw, when he reached the corridor, that several Japanese were waiting there, and he recognized the silk-hatted Suzuki-mura as the one who bowed most deeply to the commissioners. The others, Lew heard the Intelligence officer remark, were officials of the Imperial Nippon and Far Eastern Silk Association. It was perfectly in order for them to be waiting here, to hear the result of the conference, and they would know that whatever was to be done by the JCCA must have the C.O.'s consent.

But Davies, as the G-2 officer slyly suggested one last stiff drink before Davies once more took on the identity of Koropok the Ainu, was aware of the fact that although the group of formally attired Japanese seemed to be listening with complete attention to what Chief Commissioner Brown was telling them, their eyes managed to take in the two younger officers and catalogue them. Undoubtedly they had met the Intelligence officer, or knew who he was from previous visits and interviews. But the dark and stocky major on whose uniform was the Air Forces insignia—what was he, a fighting man, doing where policy and business were being discussed?

Davies could almost hear the Japanese as they silently asked themselves this question. He knew how curious they were, so like the East Island monkeys which the Chinese called them; and he knew also that they would go to any ruthless ends to satisfy their curiosity.

Should he tell Major Blake, the G-2 boy, to explain later to the Japanese that he, Davies, had been called in to the discussion because in civilian life, he had had knowledge of textile manufacture? No. It would be too difficult for G-2 to explain later why he hadn't stayed on the job. The best thing, Davies decided as he walked past the group, was to leave well enough alone.

But I'll bet, he thought, *that in one way or another one of the Nips asks a commissioner who I am. Oh, it'll be done shrewdly and politely, of course. I only hope that whoever answers the Jap doesn't fumble the ball.*

Just as he was about to enter the G-2 office with Blake, before setting out on his assignment, he turned quickly. He was willing to swear that where, before, five Japanese had been listening respectfully to the commissioners, only four now stood gathered around the JCCA men.

Davies said flatly to Blake, "What'll you bet I'm going to be followed after I leave?"

"If they follow you," said Blake, "we'll follow them. We have Japanese-Americans trained and ready for such duty. Good boys. If any Jap follows you, they'll grab him up in short order."

Davies weighed the desirability of this. It would be a fine feeling, even for a short time, to know that he was being protected in case the Japanese attempted to pull a fast one, should they fear that he, someone unknown, might interfere with whatever their plans might be. If they made such an attempt, it would be absolute proof that there was something damned funny about Suzuki-mura suddenly becoming a good and cooperative fellow. But it wouldn't be of much help in revealing what he was really up to.

On the other hand, it was equally necessary to assume the dress and identity of the Ainu, Koropok, without being detected, which could not be done at Headquarters, since all Japanese would stare when a parish shambled out... while Japs who were interested would wonder what had happened to a stocky, dark Air Forces major.

It was necessary to his plan that he become Koropok without being detected, and, as Koropok, get to the pariah settlement.

Davies made his decision. "You'd better not have me followed. It might give the Japs an added chance to keep close check on one Davies. You see," added Lew, grinning, "if I can't give a fat official of the Silk Association the slip in Tokyo, I'd better give up before I start. Just have someone drive me along Atagoma-chi, and I'll hop out when I'm ready. And vanish."

"The C.O. wants us to keep an eye on you," said Blake.

Davies didn't like that. "Is it an order?" he asked.

"What the Old Man said," replied the G-2 officer, chuckling, "was that we wouldn't know where you were until you got back."

It occurred to Davies to ask Blake to find out just what had been said by the Japanese and Suzuki-mura to the commissioners, and what had been said in reply, and why one of the Nips had slipped away, all of which could be important. Then he decided that, no matter what had been said, the important thing was to get out of Headquarters at once, in case the Jap who had left so hastily was really up to something which might cause trouble.

CHAPTER II

SEND AN AINU TO CATCH AN AINU

THE CORRIDOR was empty as he walked along it, although he recognized voices, the commissioners' and Suzuki-mura's, coming from some adjacent office. At the outer doorway, Davies returned the sentry's salute, glanced down the street, already dim in twilight, and wondered how it was that where some buildings had been utterly bomb-razed, another, not far off, stood practically undamaged. He walked down the steps in a leisurely manner, clicking off in his head the arrangements made by G-2 intended to help him in the job ahead.

A jeep, ordered by Blake, was waiting. The soldier behind the wheel was a big, redheaded MP; the corporal beside him was a dark, thin Japanese-American, able to ask directional questions which made driving easier and much faster than a constant consulting of the maps of the Tokyo streets.

"Atagomachi," said Major Davies.

He was stepping into the jeep when the crack of a nearby gun and the *pinnng!* of a bullet rang in his ears. His cap was knocked from his head, and into the sound, before he could move, was blended the quick gasp of a man who had been hit. Lew saw, all in the selfsame moment that the bullet's course whined in his ears, that the corporal had slumped forward in his seat.

"Push him out of the car," Davies snapped, as a second bullet snarled past. "Fast! And get going!"

The sentry at the entrance was firing now, in the dusk, at wherever he believed the shots were coming from. Firing rapidly.

"Sir," pleaded the driver, "George is hit—"

Davies shoved the corporal out of the car with one swift push. "Damn it, drive!" he ordered. "Snap into it!"

The start of the car almost jerked Davies' head from his shoulders. Not until the jeep had swung right at the street's end, with the driver obeying the major's directions by slowing down after making a skidding turn, did Davies say, "It was a rough spot. We had to get away."

"George was a good guy."

And you think I'm a heel for pushing him out and leaving him, realized Davies. *You think the Japs shot him for being a Japanese-American. But it's me they want out of the way. Why? Just because I was in on the discussion and they aren't sure why I was there? Could be. Or because somebody said something?*

"Whoever got George," muttered the driver, "will keep shootin' into him, the way those rice-bags do. George didn't have a chance. Not a chance."

"Turn left," said Davies. He said later, paying no attention to the understandable antagonism of the soldier, "Slow down when you pass over the next bridge. I intend to get out while the car is moving. Don't stop, even if there shouldn't be anyone around to see. When you are off the bridge, turn left again and keep going until you reach the first broad street. It takes you back to Headquarters."

The driver said, "Yeah," and added grudgingly, "sir."

But when he saw the district into which he was now entering, and the black, slimy canal flowing under the bridge, he said, as he slowed the car, "You sure this is where you want to go, sir? George told me, a few days back, that this is a crummy part of town. Maybe you got the wrong address, sir. If—if George were along, he'd give you the dope. Maybe—"

"This is it," said Davies. "Did Major Blake tell you that you are to say nothing to anyone as to where I got out?"

"Yes, sir." The car was approaching the bridge. "Look," the soldier muttered, nodding toward the canal. In the sluggish black water, floating slowly and only partially discernible in the gloom, was a body.

There was movement along the banks of the narrow canal, too, as if the ooze and mud were stirring, and the driver shivered when he was aware that what he saw in the growing darkness were giant rats.

He was also aware, suddenly, that he was alone in the car. The dark and stocky major was no longer in it; and when the soldier glanced instinctively around, and then back, the major had disappeared.

KOROPOK THE Ainu was not taking the usual way which led to the pariah settlement on the far edge of the city. He was taking no chance on being stopped before he could again become as like the other pariahs in appearance as one added grain of sand; he was fully cognizant of the fact that Suzuki-mura knew that a stocky black-haired major had been driven safely away from Headquarters, and that Suzuki-mura would do everything possible to find out where Major Davies had gone, and why, and what he might be up to.

There was an additional danger, which Davies had considered while making use of the room in the deserted portion of bomb-smashed Tokyo which G-2 had prepared for him and this venture; which he had thought over while assuming the matted beard and wig waiting there, and attiring himself again in the foul rags and tatters of an Ainu. It was this: how much, if anything, had the commissioners intimated to Suzuki-mura? If too much had been said, or ferreted out by the shrewd and hidden questions of the Japanese, Suzuki-mura would have a cinch. All the old devil had to do was wait until a leader appeared among the pariahs—one who directed their steps toward the silk mills or the silk-country, or persuaded them to listen to the voices of the *Amerika-jin* who wanted them to do it—and the jig would be up.

What I've got to do, Lew had thought, while putting on a belt of worn leather which had once looked like bear-hide, *is get to the settlement without being seen, establish myself immediately as just one more outcast, but arrange things so that if it becomes necessary I can get the chiefs to listen to me. Above all, I've got to keep my eyes open, and act like an Ainu again.*

Davies had then torn away a length of bamboo, not rotted

He was stepping into the jeep when the crack of a nearby gun rang in his ears.

like the softer wood of the deserted hovel, and swung it around until the feel of the makeshift club, a good three feet long, become easy and familiar.

When he left the room, he was actually beginning to carry out all of those decisions which he had made as he now began the slow, strange journey which would take him to the mud-walled huts in the hollow where the Ainus lived because in the past they had been forbidden to live anywhere else by the Japanese... and because in the present they were too inert and terrified to move away....

He did not climb back from the canal and the place where he had turned himself into Koropok to the black street above. Instead, after making positive that he was unwatched except by the glittering eyes of the rodents along the banks, he started to run to get under the bridge.

A rat, possibly wounded in a fight with another, was slow in getting away. Davies stepped on the big furry body, stumbled, and half fell. Instantly, another rat fastened its teeth on the man's bare leg, and Davies struck him away, his leg bleeding from the rip made by the gnawing, blood-hungry teeth. Had he fallen, the rats would have been upon him.

They backed away as he struck out with the club; backed away, but began to follow him. He moved quickly, but carefully, until he was under the bridge, because he had been visible from the street; when a rat more vicious or more hungry than the rest slipped too near, Davies slashed at him with the club. They were clever, too; one would dash at him, while others would wait until the man struck out and the club was extended, and then try to get a jawful of flesh by attacking from the opposite side. Their teeth were like samurai blades.

They fight like Japs, decided Lew, when he was under the bridge. *How far up the canal will they be, anyhow?*

Instead of continuing at once, and finding out, he waited, He waited, and the rats waited; and when hunger drove them, two or three of the rodents would come ahead on their bellies, and then race forward. Davies' club finished them, although some were able to set their teeth in the American's stocky legs and had to be torn loose and then kicked away.

If they've learned enough from their Nip brothers, thought Lew grimly, *they'll make a* banzai *charge, and that'll get me.*

He kept at the strange business until there were fifteen or more dead rats around him. Whenever he could, after that, and always with his stick swinging furiously, he would stoop, grab up a rat, and thrust the body through his loose belt. He continued to do this until the belt began to sag, tight as it had become, and then started out from under the bridge and up the canal.

If he were seen now, by anyone except some searcher sent out by Suzuki-mura, it would make little difference. True, some Japanese might take the fat bodies of the rats from him, and he would be forced to secure more, but that was not too important. The Japanese would not kill the rats themselves, hungry as they were, because the rat-god was as vindictive as the more familiar fox-diety... but the Nips would eat the rats without religious scruples, as would the Ainu, if someone else did the killing.

Koropok continued walking up the canal's bank, his progress slow at first because of the rats, but soon the number of rodents began to thin out in the upper canal, until finally they were only a nuisance. He was able to move more quickly then, because there was no longer the danger of being attacked in a body by the loathsome creatures if he should fall; he was able, also, to formulate his plans and to prepare and rehearse what was ahead.

When he would arrive at the settlement, the old men, the chiefs, would recall that several years before an Ainu from the north, named Koropok, had stumbled to the hollow. This Koropok, being from the mountains, had been recognized as a hunter and a man of strength, whose vitality had not been drained away by the Japanese; and, as a hunter, bringing food, he would be welcomed on his return to the settlement.

The members of the outcast village would accept what he brought without question, and would be sure that they knew where he had hidden during his absence.

THEY WOULD believe that he had been living with the *Kawaramono,* those other outcasts, but of Japanese descent, whose very name meant that they existed under the bridges and burrowed in the banks of riverbeds and canals and whose bodies, after death, became offerings to the rat-god because of the sins of their ancestors. Some of the original *Kawaramono* had been merely criminals, others were samurai who, disgraced because they were unable to fend off the defeat of a lord to whom they had pledged allegiance, and lacking the courage to cut open their bellies and die honorably by performing sep*puku,* had slunk away to live in misery. Renegades.

Their women were those too old to continue in places like Number Nineteen, and too stupid to be wanted again by the parents who had sold them into the Yoshiwara of which Nineteen was a part.

The *Kawaramono* dared not show themselves; they were more despised by the Japanese than were the Ainus, since the *Kawaramono* had been Japanese themselves. But, because of some amazing Japanese logic, they were allowed to live and to continue breeding, and it was rumored that some of the outcasts had been permitted to go on suicide missions which could wipe out a little of the sins of their ancestors.

When Davies had first lived in the pariah settlement, he had learned that the Ainus actually envied the *Kawaramono* who had some food, but none of the true pariahs had had the courage to challenge the descendants of cowards. But when Koropok returned with the rats around his middle, they would remember that he had been a hunter in the northern mountains, and therefore must be an Ainu who was a fearless man. Or so Davies reasoned.

The Ainus, who never so much as defended themselves, had cause to be afraid of the river-bank folk. Sometimes a *Kawar-*

*Another rat fastened its teeth
on the man's bare leg and
Davies struck him away, his
leg bleeding from the rip.*

amono, needing a woman, snatched one in the settlement. And at intervals one of the bank-dwellers, possibly driven by a hidden force which he himself did not understand, would leave his hole and, with a knife, come out slashing and killing, racing as far into Tokyo as he was able, killing as many as he could, until the police shot him.

But only twice, as Davies walked, did he see any of the outcasts. Once an old woman cursed him for a dog of an Ainu as he passed where she was filling a wooden pail with the black water of the canal. Again, he saw a pygmy of a woman, squatted down with a baby on her back, who might have been waiting for the return of the male with whom she was kenneled. Davies passed her near enough so that, even in the gloom, he could see the leper sores on her upturned wizened face; and he walked the faster after his glimpse at her.

This was the sort of thing hidden behind the silken screen which, in the past, tourists had seen. Davies wondered what was behind the manufacture of silk in which Suzuki-mura was interested, and kept wondering about this while he stuck to the canal as the safest way to reach the Ainu settlement. It was also the shortest, as it cut diagonally across Tokyo.

At last the shambling, bearded figure crawled up out of the canal, where now only a trickle of water ran, and took the narrow path above which led to the mud-walled huts of the men who had once inhabited Japan.

Someone was dying in the village. Davies could hear the moaning voices of the dying person's relatives, who were pleading with the stricken one not to return to haunt them, but to permit his after-life form to be dissolved by the wind. With the frightened prayers in his ears, Davies headed for a hut in the middle of the settlement, where the old men, the chiefs, should be nodding, half asleep with age and half with hunger, as they kept the wick burning which they hoped would carry the dead man's breath up on the smoke.

Unnoticed, he shuffled along between the walls of the huts;

when he pushed aside the dirt-stiffened cloth which covered the low doorway to the chiefs' living-quarters, the five old men in the room cowered down and waited to die. Only devils could be abroad on a night of death; and if devils entered a room, you were dead. Only devils, or the Japanese. And death came with them, too.

Davies stood there silently. Seated on the floor, where the wick flared feebly as it sent smoke up and through a hole in the torn thatch of the roof, were the leaders of these Ainus. White of hair. Tremulous of hand. Ragged. They shook with fright; and Davies knew that every Ainu in the pariah village would have shaken and cowered as did the chiefs, should the curtain across other huts have been opened. They were utterly beaten down.

The hut was the best in the settlement; the walls of it were crumbling. Only a black cooking-pot was in it, a heap of rags for bedding, and a few horrible-smelling clothes. That was all.

And these are to be silk-workers, thought Davies soberly. *Chop-chop. Right away.* He almost said it aloud, thinking of what had been planned for the pariahs' immediate future as well as the odor of unwashed bodies and the smells in the room. *The whole thing stinks.*

H E B E C A M E an Ainu. He mumbled, "*G' b'sat' it'sh'ma'ta,*" to say that he had returned, and then stood with his head down, First one and then another of the old men gathered courage to look up. It was no demon who had entered, but a man. An Ainu.

None of the old men, when they had glanced fearfully up, showed interest in anything except the booty dangling from the newcomer's belt. Hunger caused them to count, "*Ip pi', ni hi', sam bi' shi hi',*" as the pariah called Koropok slowly and humbly laid the dead rats on the earth floor.

Not until all of the rodents lay in a heap did the oldest chief ask tremulously, "Is this the first of the great fine food which we are to receive, Koropok?"

What great fine food? wondered Davies. Probably, he figured, the Ainus already had heard stories of how the Americans intended to help the Ainus. So he said, "Oh, old one, the *Amerika-jin* will not allow us to starve."

"They? No. It is the lords who give food."

The Japanese? Before finding out about whether the Japanese had changed their attitude toward the pariahs, Davies decided to establish his position with the old man. So he said, "I killed this food and brought it to you," and let that sink in before adding, "Why do the lords give food?"

"We are to do a thing for them," said the chief, smiling just

He saw a pygmy of a
woman, squatted down
with a baby on her back.

enough so that Davies saw the thin, dry old lips as they parted. "No longer will we be a hungry people. No. We do a thing for the lords."

"Work?" asked Davies.

The chief smiled again. "Yes. But not the mending of *geta* such as you did, Koropok. Nor the killing of animals. No. We are to do things which the lords do. We will make cloth. Some of us will care for the little bugs which make threads, although we must remember not to eat them. But we will not want to eat bugs," announced the chief, "because the lords will see to it that we have food which is fatter. And," he concluded, licking his lips, "we will be given saki. Yes."

So they've already been told, thought Davies. *Suzuki-mura must be all set. It doesn't make sense.*

The people in Japan, the Japanese, Davies realized, needed

Even in the gloom,
he could see the leper
sores on her upturned
wizened face.

employment, especially in something backed by the JCCA, just as much as did the Ainu, and were better able to perform the work. Had Suzuki-mura agreed to the engaging and training of pariahs only in order to get permission to begin manufacturing silk ahead of everyone else and reap the profits? Did he intend to use the despised, useless pariahs as a blind in order to hire as many experienced Japanese workmen and girls as possible? Or… what?

Davies did know this much: the supposed difficulties in getting the Ainus away from the settlements might have been planted in the commissioners' minds by Suzuki-mura. Now that the pariahs were starving, they would go anywhere if food awaited them at their destination. Not even Davies, who had left the settlement upon becoming attached to Number Nineteen, had fully realized the depths to which the Ainus had dropped. Possibly Suzuki-mura, aware of it, had wanted to make JCCA believe that he could accomplish the transplantation of the pariahs in the face of real difficulty, which would cause the commissioners to feel that the Japanese was exerting great effort in his desire to cooperate.

Even if Suzuki-mura were merely inquisitive, merely curious about where the Air Forces major had gone, Davies had no intention of permitting the manufacturer to add two and two. And the shooting indicated, to Davies, a lot more than common Japanese curiosity.

He said, "If the lords know I am here, perhaps I will be forbidden to secure more food."

The old chief pulled his eyes away from the carcasses on the floor, destined for the cooking-pot. Then, beaten-down leader of a beaten-down people that he was, a glimmer of light came to his eyes.

"Koropok is a brother," he quavered. "We say nothing."

Realization that there was a spark left in the ancient Ainu gave Davies the deepest of warm feeling.

"*M'kot' n' shib'rak'*," he said. "I have been long gone." Then, as if the white-bearded chief were again the respected leader of free mountaineers, and Koropok a returned hunter who, with knife alone, had killed a bear for food and hide, Davies said in the old form, "Have I done well?"

The ancient conventional response did not come; the chief's spark had vanished. He whined, "The next *koy'* is for strangers. Go there. It'kish' sleeps in it. When he wakes, he will hunger. Say nothing of the food."

"Who is he? A visitor?"

"*Wat'kush' n' kwank g' n',*" mumbled the chief. "The son of a woman taken by a lord. It does not matter. I am tired of talking. Go away."

"When did he arrive?" asked Koropok.

"Just before you... go away!"

Koropok shambled out as if it did not matter in the least. One of the old men hurriedly closed the curtain behind Koropok, lest the departing spirit of the dying man crawl into the hut.

Outside, in blackness and with the moans of the dying man's relatives in his ears, Davies hesitated. It was possible that the newcomer, Itikishi, had been sent here by Suzuki-mura, either to be around when the JCCA plan went into operation, or to be able to report whether a stocky American officer, who might speak Japanese, came to the settlement for any purpose at all. On the other hand, Itikishi might be only what he said he was, the son of an Ainu woman and a Japanese, come to the pariah settlement for any one of a dozen reasons.

I've got to watch out, thought Lew. In the past, he could never relax; but in one way this was more dangerous, because Itikishi—if actually on the lookout for a dark, stocky man—might more easily penetrate Davies' disguise. And in the past Koropok's hair and beard had been real.

It occurred to him that the Japanese were the world's cleverest monkey-see monkey-do face, and that if Brown and the commissioners had said anything, or let anything slip, about

Koropok, Suzuki-mura might attempt to do what the Americans had accomplished. Disguise a Japanese as an Ainu.

CHAPTER III

PARIAH RECRUITS

THE GUEST-HOUSE was black as the pit inside; Davies heard snores as he entered. Had they started when he pushed aside the curtain? He was not sure because, as the curtain had crackled, the pariahs' moaning for the dying had suddenly turned into wild screams for the dead.

If Itikishi were a full-blooded Ainu, Davies was thinking, the fellow wouldn't have been sleeping at such a time. Either the man was a half-caste who, having lived with his Japanese father, didn't realize what the departing spirit could do to him, or he was a masquerading Nip badly coached for his job here. The third possibility was that Itikishi had come to the settlement utterly exhausted and, a true Ainu nevertheless, slept because he could not keep awake.

Davies himself became all Ainu. He dropped to his knees, not to fumble in the dark for some filthy pile of wadded cloth on which to sleep, but to whimper in simulated terror, "*Tor' m' k'san' genk'... Ts'a y' 'kur y'r'r....*"

If the so-and-so is a Nip, decided Davies, as he prayed away, *and he has doubts about who I am, it's easy enough for him to find out. All he's got to do it wait until I'm asleep, and then give my beard a work-out.* In the past, many Japanese had given Koropok's beard a jerk, just for the fun of it; but then it had been really his own. *So what I do,* Lew thought, *is find out about him, first.*

He dared not wait to match wits with Itikishi, in case the man were here on Suzuki-mura's business. If he waited, the fellow could yank at the beard with one hand and drive home a knife with the other. Anything else was preferable. No time would be better for the test than right now.

Even so, while determining the other man's exact position on the floor of the hut, Davies paused. Itikishi, if the son of a Japanese man and an Ainu woman, must understand much Japanese and some Ainu. But if Itikishi had been assigned to this pariah settlement as a person clever enough to penetrate another man's disguise, a Japanese trained for such work, it was certain that he would know more than Japanese and Ainu. This might also be true should he have been sent here merely for the purpose of reporting to Suzuki-mura what went on concerning the JCCA plan for the regeneration of the pariahs... but if that were the case, his reactions to what Davies intended to do would be vastly different.

Davies did not seem to move, but, where he had been kneeling, he now crouched, muscles tense, eyes straining in the gloom.

He stopped his wailed prayers. As if speaking to himself, he said, "*S'u tonk' ik' d'su...* a spirit should fly off in smoke."

"Yes," said Itikishi. "What is your name?"

Ten-to-one he's a gendarme, thought Davies instantly. *He can't wait. He's got to ask questions.*

But that was only guesswork. And so Lew proceeded as he had intended. "I hope the evil spirit is gone," he said worriedly. "Oh, I hope so." Then he went on, in the same tone, "How about it, rice-bag?" but in English.

He heard Itikishi's instant and involuntary hiss, like water running up a long beach. *Sssssss...* How many times Koropok had heard the sound, when, in Number Nineteen, a Japanese was surprised. *Sssssss....*

Would that be all?

If it were, nothing had been proven. But it wasn't. Itikishi was moving. His hand. Quickly. For a weapon?

Davies didn't wait to find out. He sprang; and while he was all over Itikishi at once, flattening him as he tried to rise, he managed to roll the hissing man's head into the quilts as he pinioned one of Itikishi's arms with a hand while his own stocky body pressed the hisser's other arm deep down into the wadded cloth, rendering it useless. At first the man who called himself Itikishi jerked furiously to release the arm which Davies had jammed down; then he began to jerk only in an attempt to free himself; and then he began to make hoarse muffled noises which changed to rattling gasps.

Outside, the screaming had diminished. What the pariahs in the settlement did not know was that another man was dying.

Davies stood up at last.

Othello, they call me, he thought grimly. *You,* he told the dead man silently, *got off easy, compared to what I'll bet you've done to others.*

There was no hurry now, but Davies did not waste time. He

He rolled the hissing man's head into the quilts... the hoarse muffled noises soon changed to rattling gasps.

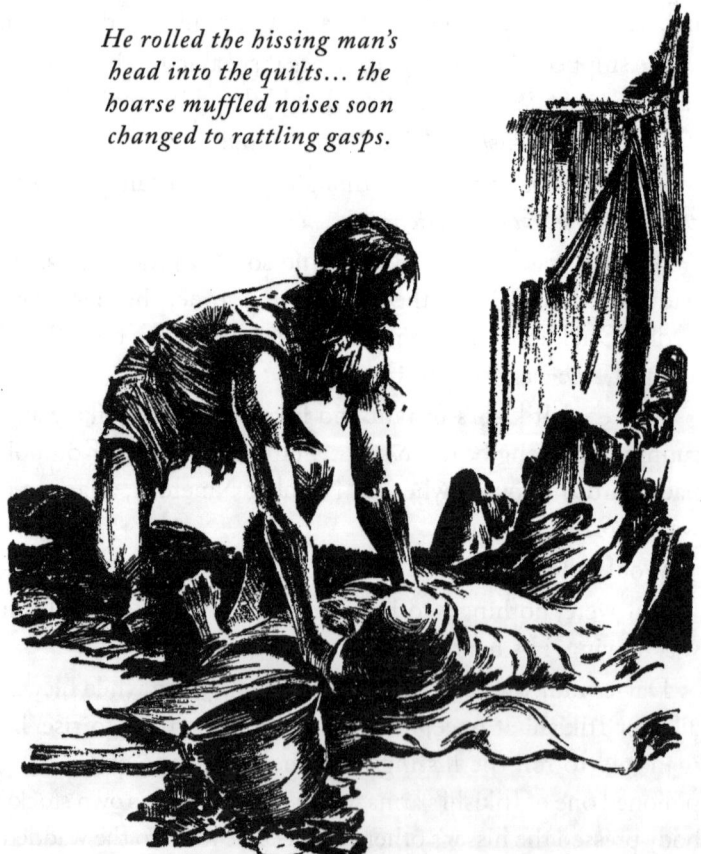

disentangled Itikishi from the quilts, made certain that the man had been smothered and was dead, then picked up the body and carried it as far as the curtain. No Ainu would be out of his hut on a night-of-death; even so, Davies looked about carefully before leaving the guest-hut with his burden.

He carried the body past the chief's hut and deeper into the village until he came to the small clear space where a peeled pole was stuck in the ground, the only symbol of worship of a people who had no priests, and who did not remember why the powerful-bear-post-to-heaven was there at all. Long ago, before subjugation, Ainu hunters had prayed to the bear-god for strength and courage, and Ainu women had prayed for fidelity and devotion to their children; but now it was merely a something to be vaguely feared.

Yet Koropok, as he deposited the body before the post, might have been a hunter when the Ainus had been free, when men slain by bears had been buried at the foot of the sacred post. Koropok, in his rags, looked like a man.

Howls of fear would go up in the morning when the body, showing no marks of violence, was seen. The pariahs would believe that Itikishi had been killed by the departing spirit of the Ainu they had known was dying, and that was how they would explain Itikishi's death to anyone who questioned them.

Davies considered giving them a few fancy touches regarding the death of the late lamented, such as saying that Koropok had seen a hissing serpent crawl into the guest-house and carry Itikishi off, or that Koropok had heard a rushing wind, on which Itikishi had vanished. But if he did either, attention would be directed toward Koropok should someone come to the settlement to get a secret report from Itikishi; and Koropok did not want to be singled out.

TWO JAPANESE did come to the settlement in the morning, a morning on which Davies was the last person to leave his hut, having remained stretched out while the Ainus cowered under the presence of Itikishi's spirit, which they knew must be hovering over the village. The pair of Japanese was in Health Department uniforms, although Davies grinned to himself when he saw them.

Sabers, and not thermometers, were what they should have been carrying. The pair looked like secret police.

The old chief, in response to sharp, brutal questioning, as to whether anyone except the dead Itikishi had arrived, kept shaking his head. No. No one else. No other person. No one.

Those rats must have tasted good to him, thought Davies, *and he isn't taking any chances that there won't be more.*

At the end, the pair of strutting Japanese, after whispering together, informed the chief that the *Amerika-jin,* temporarily in Japan for reasons which no fool of an Ainu would understand, had requested the Health Department to see to it that only strong and healthy pariahs were selected for tasks which would give them food and a place to live, and therefore all Ainus must come to the open space in order to be immediately examined. The chiefs would call out the names of men and women, and the names would be written down.

Davies thought, his skin prickling, *It isn't conceivable that the JCCA would let Suzuki-mura weasel the name of Koropok from them.*

It made no difference to Davies whether the pair of Nips was checking on the death of their probable fellow gendarme, whether they were searching for some dark, stocky American officer, or if they were actually beginning to select Ainus for the regeneration plan; he had to be around to observe and listen. He was not here to take chances, but he wasn't here merely to save his skin.

The examination, conducted squarely before the peeled post, went along just about as Davies expected, with one exception. It looked to him as if the stronger of the men, the most sturdy women, were actually being rejected, and that didn't make sense. He kept wondering why the pariahs were not to be moved away from the settlement in a body; hadn't the JCCA stressed that all of the poor devils were to be regenerated as far as possible? About the only thing he could figure was that perhaps something other than work in the spinning mills or the mulberry country had been arranged for the stronger pariahs, something about which he did not know. Suzuki-mura would not like getting only the weaklings. The best of the Ainus would be none too good....

I don't get it, thought Lew; and then it was his turn to shamble away from the shivering pariahs and go up to the peeled post.

One of the Japanese stared at him, briefly.

"Koropok," quavered the old chief.

"*Hone to kawa to ni,*" stated the Japanese. "He is skin and bone. Let him remain here to die. He is no good."

Koropok was certainly the sturdiest of all the pariahs; and Koropok, unlike any of the other Ainus, had the courage to

The old chief, in response to the sharp, brutal questioning, kept shaking his head. No, no one had arrived.

whimper, looking at his feet, "Great lords, I hunger. Cannot I go where there will be food? I am strong—"

"Strong?" said the Japanese who had been writing down the names of those pariahs being selected. "I wonder how strong, Kano?"

Kano, his companion, giggled. "We will find out shortly." He whipped out at the dejected figure of Koropok, "Since when do dogs ask questions? Do you think that because we have permitted the *Amerika-jin* to come here, in order to make use of their gold, that you are less an animal? Or we less your masters? Stand where you are. At the post. I will soon give you an answer!"

Davies could guess what the answer would be. What he did not know was why the supposed Health Department Nips were rejecting those pariahs who could be expected to produce a halfway decent day's work. To make certain that regeneration of the Ainus wouldn't work? Were certain Japanese working at cross-purposes to Suzuki-mura? Was that it?

Unfortunately, getting a beating from the gendarmes would tell Davies nothing. He did know this much: the pair had come to do the selecting, and not primarily to look for a mysteriously-disappeared American officer. It looked as if they had asked about a stranger, a newcomer, only because of the death of Itikishi. Well, the beating was coming. *I hope I haven't softened up,* thought Lew wryly, *because these two boys would love to hear me yowl.*

THERE WAS one advantage, however; he was standing where he could watch the ridiculous examination. It told him nothing more than he had already observed until a man more ragged than the others, more shaking and fumbling, hobbled before the two Japanese. This man was old, older than any of the pariahs; old, wrinkled, and beardless.

"*Hai-ya!*" ejaculated Kano. "Name!"

The old man covered his face with thin hands.

"Name!"

"*Kaze wo hikimashita*," whispered the old man. "I am sick. I—"

"Name!"

The old man said, "Tetsugaku Shakwai."

Davies instantly recognized the name as that of an official close to the Japanese throne and an Imperial confidant, an official who had disappeared instead of killing himself after Japan's surrender.

Both of the "Health Department" investigators blinked. Kano sucked in a brief, noisy breath before snarling, "Coward!"

The old man bowed his head.

"Your sons have removed your name from the family tablets," squealed Kano. "A house in the Yoshiwara has bought your granddaughters!"

Kano, realized Davies, was working himself up to a fine Japanese fury. *In a minute,* thought Lew, *the old banzai charge. Bingo!*

The pariahs, while Kano's face swiftly became a muddy purple-brown and his eyes began to pop, remained uninterested and abject.

"You," shrilled Kano, shoving aside whatever invective his mate was about to bring up, "you, a Japanese, live with these dogs! Their food went into your foul and cowardly mouth. You begged them for it! Oh, disgraceful!"

Tetsugaku Shakwai pleaded, "I intended to die among the *Kawaramono,* which has been permitted in the past. I went there to die. I am sick. I will die soon. But when I was on the canal… Oh, the rats… the rats…."

"You are the rat!"

"If I had known… the daughters of my sons…."

"A rat!" screamed Kano, His revolver was out as he spoke; words and discharge were one, neither less deadly than the other. Both of the infuriated pair began to kick the former Imperial councillor the instant he fell to the ground; and Davies, his heart beating swiftly, knew that their Japanese blood-lust would not be satisfied with what they had already done to their slain countryman, and that in a moment they would turn on him.

Kano did not wait for so much as a moment; he had already whirled, with his gun rising jerkily toward Koropok's middle.

"No, no," shouted the other Japanese, thereby stopping Davies' fist. "Oh, wait, Kano! Tetsugaku Shakwai was a Japanese. He died from a clean bullet. But this dog is an Ainu. He should not die pleasantly. No! These other dogs must see what we do to a pariah who questions us. If—"

"I will kill him slowly," promised the red-eyed Kano. "He shall be tied to the post. I will cut away one finger. Another finger. And when all of his fingers are gone I will cut away his toes. One after the other. That is what I would do to all Ainus, because they have seen our defeat. What is Suzuki-mura think-ing of," cried the Japanese, by now beside himself with whipped-up anger, "to arrange that pariahs should eat and work? Is that right? No! And—"

Kano stopped. Abruptly.

The redness of his eyes seemed to stain down into his cheeks, leaving the eyes white, frightened, and staring. He first, and then Davies, saw that a number of men were walking, rapidly now, as if they had observed what was taking place, past the last of the huts and toward the central pole.

The second Japanese was saying, "Suzuki-mura knows what he does. He must have a deep and patriotic plan, or he would take the strong ones," when he, too, saw the approaching party. His mouth remained open, but no more words issued from it. He began to puff like a stranded fish.

Davies thought, *Should I sneak into the crowd of Ainus and keep out of sight?* because he saw not only the waddling figure of Suzuki-mura—responsible for the change in Kano's behav-ior—but also the Chief Commissioner of the JCCA and several Americans in uniform, including the G-2 officer and the C.O.'s chief of staff. *If they recognize me, and show it,* Davies knew, *I'm*

through here. If they do not, and I stay with the two ex-gendarmes,
there are going to be more spirits of dead men around. Their's, or
mine.

The thing to do was to wait and see what happened. It was
entirely possible for Davies to go off safely with the Americans,
and he knew it; but he wanted to manage otherwise if he could.

The pair of "Health Department" men was bowing deeply
now to a Japanese in army uniform who first reached the space
about the pole.

The uniformed Japanese demanded sharply, "What has happened? How is it that you what-ever-your-name-is, possess a
gun, a weapon?"

Kano had already slid down from being a lord and a deity
to a person who was as cringing and low as the lowest of pariahs.

"Sir," he whined, "I had no weapon. It was the dead man who
had the weapon. I took it from him when he drew it, and in
the struggle—"

"Why was anyone killed?" asked Brown, the Chief Commissioner. "We do not want force. That is the last thing we want."

Suzuki-mura said, oil dripping from his words, "The dead
man attempted to interfere with the selection of workers, my
dear Mr. Brown, and became violent. The investigator from the
Health Department was forced to wrest the weapon from him.
Is not that what took place, Captain Yamu?"

"It is what was said," said the Japanese captain shortly.

Brown nodded. The account seemed reasonable. Even so, he
hesitated before asking the captain to have the check on the
pariahs resumed; Yamu snapped an order to Kano, disbelief on
his face, and then stepped back.

KOROPOK THE Ainu moved forward just a little, as
if he had been waiting to be examined, or as if the examination,
for him, had not been concluded. Brown and the Americans
looked at the short, stocky figure curiously, taking in the sturdy
mud-caked legs, from Davies' walk up the bed of the canal, the
broad shoulders, and a lean, exposed belly, fouled by dried blood

from the rats which he had brought for the chiefs. And the hanging head, the slack mouth almost hidden by the befouled black beard. An Ainu. A pariah. The dirtiest of thousands.

"*Waki ye yore,*" muttered Kano. "Go away."

Brown's understanding of Japanese, when Koropok began to move off very slowly, was sufficient for him to ask, "Why? He looks husky." Hastily, the Chief Commissioner changed his question into halting Japanese.

Kano mumbled, "He is sick."

Suzuki-mura queried Kano so swiftly and blurringly in Japanese that even the former gendarme had difficulty in following what was being said. When Kano, fearful of disagreeing with an important man, nodded, Suzuki-mura said to the head of the JCCA, "The Ainu is subject to illness. He is sick most of the time, and also suffers from… ah… mental derangements. Yes."

"Did one nod tell you all that?" asked the G-2 officer.

Koropok stopped shambling off.

Suzuki-mura laughed and shrugged his shoulders. "My dear Mr. Commissioner," he said, "if you want this fellow, of course you shall have him. Should he become ill, we are prepared for hospitalization. Of course you shall have him! Put down his name," he commanded the ex-gendarme who kept the list.

"Your name?"

Davies acted as if the question were not being hurled at him; he did not reply until Kano came running to him and pushed him back to the post. Then, when the demand was repeated, he said indistinctly, "Koropok."

The G-2 officer had been taking out a cigarette; Davies couldn't see whether or not Major Blake's fingers halted in what they were doing, or if startled and surprised recognition showed in the Chief Commissioner's face, because, warily, he was watching Suzuki-mura.

The fat Nipponese' mouth was puckered, Japanese-fashion, with thought. It didn't look to Davies as if Suzuki-mura were putting on an act, which wouldn't be worth while trying if the Chief Commissioner had mentioned Koropok's name earlier; that is, unless Brown were unaware of having named Major Davies as Koropok. Suzuki-mura, however, couldn't be positive whether Brown would be unaware, and would not be fool enough to go into an act, which would be bound to jog the Chief Commissioner's memory. Suddenly the paunched Japanese began to laugh until every roll of fat was jellied with his amusement.

"Koropok," he gurgled. "Koropok!"

Davies said, "Yes, lord."

Suzuki-mura turned to Brown. "I recall the name," he chuckled, "although who can tell one Ainu from another? Yes, I remember it now. Koropok! There is an Ainu who needs regeneration! Do you know what he was, Mr. Brown? *Hakoya* to Number Nineteen in the Yoshiwara. Sometimes I entertained there, not because I enjoyed such entertainment myself, but because it was expected of a man in my position. And I assure you that being *hakoya* is very low. Such a one must do the most degraded tasks. If," Suzuki-mura ended solemnly, "we are able to make him into a self-reliant man... oh, what a great accomplishment!"

"It is a challenge," agreed Brown; but, Davies saw, without acknowledgment, that the name Koropok meant nothing to him at all. "A real challenge."

Major Blake said, "Isn't it?" and finally lit his cigarette.

"Koropok," repeated Suzuki-mura. "Oh, I remember how he was called upon to perform menial services. 'Koropok, come and wash my back!' and, 'Koropok, come clean the *benjo!*' and, 'Koropok, a drunken person has soiled the matting!' Oh, if we do make him into a man, and I will do my best, I will be happy."

Koropok had memories of his own concerning Suzuki-mura's behavior at Nineteen, and he knew exactly how much interest the fat Japanese opportunist had in regenerating the Ainus. None. The so-and-so wanted broken-down pariahs as workmen, and not those who could really do a day's work. Why? Perhaps to prove that pariah labor was unsatisfactory, and that experienced Japs must be hired?

That's not enough, decided Davies, waiting beside the post. *It'd take too long to prove. Other manufacturers would get going before Suzuki-mura could convince a theorist like Brown that the plan's unworkable.* Well, what was the Nip up to? Certainly he didn't give a damn about the Ainus. *He's after plenty for himself,* Lew was positive, *but what?*

"How I would appreciate a servant like this Koropok," said Suzuki-mura sadly. "Trained to give any service." The Japanese sighed, and then brightened. "But he would not be entirely satisfactory as a house-servant anyhow," Suzuki-mura consoled himself, "because I seem to recall that he was often sick at Number Nineteen. I hope his health remains excellent when he is my workman. Oh, I hope so."

What does he mean by that? wondered Davies uneasily.

Major Blake said, "I hope so, too."

Davies wished that the veiled threat of the G-2 officer, voiced after what Suzuki-mura might also have said as a threat, had not been uttered... although it could only be considered as a warning if Suzuki-mura knew too much.

CHAPTER IV

SILKEN FABRICATION

THE WAY to the silk country lay through the prefectures of Saitama and Gumma; Koropok, on the train with the party of pariahs, was careful not to show interest in what was to be seen. A few farmers were threshing a scant crop of barley. On dry-land patches, where the grain crop had been harvested, soya bean, sown between the rows of grain long before harvest, was becoming bushier now that it was out of shade. Japan's food for the poor, sweet potatoes, was being set out. Small patches of tea had already been scrupulously picked for the second crop; no longer did red Formosa tea come to Japan. Water, at this time of the year when the rice was small, spread over the paddies, with here and there, on a rock outcrop, a sacred clump of trees in which a Shinto shrine gloomed, and around which, moss-grown and untended, were the headstones of the dead.

When the train climbed out of the plain and the first mulberries began to appear, Davies saw them as shoots from treestumps or as tall standards. Gradually, the mulberries usurped the landscape. It was not long before Davies marked whitewashed low buildings, gray and scaling from lack of attention during the war. The cocoon houses of silk factories. Few of the former tall red, blue, and white iron chimneys remained. Metal had been needed for munitions.

The railway stations, too, showed that it had been years since silk had been manufactured. There were none of the familiar stacks of large flat bean-cakes used for fertilization standing about, nor any sign of activity save for one old Japanese, with his striped flag, at each station. No boys ran along the train offering *bento* boxes containing rice, cold omelette, pickled plums, and fish shreds, or pots of tea. Japan was inert. Stunned.

Not so the half dozen Japanese who had been sent in charge of the Ainus. They, drawing pay from the JCCA, were in excellent spirits; and if they kicked a pariah now and again, it was from sheer exuberance and without real ill feeling. Oh, it was a fact that the Ainus were useful, since without them the half dozen Nipponese would not have been receiving pay, or food, or expecting comfortable quarters in a silk factory. True, the attendants did examine the blankets and supplies which the JCCA had given to the Ainus, and here and there made a little exchange... but the pariahs did not mind. After all, no Ainu had ever seen a toothbrush before, and as for tubes of shaving soap, they were not even good to eat.

Shortly after leaving Tokyo, the Japanese conductor of the group had taken a military jacket from his cloth-wrapped bundle, together with a squat black bottle, and, after donning

the first and draining the second, prepared for sleep. He gave
only one order to his men. "If you cause any of these dogs to
cry out with pain," he warned, "and it awakens me, I will throw
you off the train. I was a soldier. I fought. I did not skulk in
safety, calling myself gendarmes, as you did. So let these dogs
be." Then he slept, and snored.

Only one attendant, Davies observed, showed the least resentment at such talk. This was a stubby, lax-mouthed Japanese,
who frowned. He, of them all, was the only one who kept any
sort of watch over the pariahs… and, if he appeared the most
stupid, and was sometimes the butt of his companions' crude
jokes, Davies did not believe he was stupid at all.

When Lew considered his fellow-pariahs, and saw their
condition, there was no doubt in his mind but that Suzuki-
mura must have some strange use for the Ainus. These pariahs
were the scum of the settlements. The half-blind, the lame, the
old. Women who stared at nothing, and were good for nothing,
and hoped for nothing. Davies continued to be amazed that
the Japan Civil Control Authority had consented to the engaging of such people.

His guess was that the commissioners were anxious to bring
about the regeneration of the most miserable of the Ainus, and
to do so immediately. In this he was not entirely correct. The
question as to the type of Ainus selected for the experiment
had come up, but when Brown had raised it, Suzuki-mura's
statistical assistants were ready with facts and figures to prove
that the old and weak actually did the best delicate work, particularly in certain types of preliminary production. Oh, Suzuki-mura himself had promised, the stronger Ainus would receive
work a little later, work for which they were much better fitted.
Yes. On his word of honor.

There were other things the Japanese and the JCCA had
discussed about which Davies did not know, and which, pleas-
ing as they were to the JCCA commissioners, who did not know
Japan, would have been interesting to the man who was again
Koropok. But these things had been recommended by Suzuki-

mura after the first trainload of pariahs was on its way, and only when the plan was in actual operation. Recommended shrewdly and subtly. And accepted with satisfaction.

The route became mountainous, but terraces of mulberries continued to spread up to the very summits. Here, in the district into which the train was advancing, the finest leaves were plucked, producing the finest of all silkworm food. This was the true silk country... where the train puffed up and up, through tunnels, over chasms and ravines where, in the rainy season, torrents roared down to ruin the land below with rock and debris.

This'd be a hell of a place to leave in a hurry, thought Davies;

If Japanese women couldn't take it in the silk factories for long, what would happen to the weak, sick pariahs?

and he wished that Suzuki-mura had selected a silk district nearer Tokyo in which to begin manufacture. Perhaps this prefecture had been chosen because some of the factories in the interior had not been completely gutted of metal for the war... perhaps Suzuki-mura, briber and politician, had seen to that.

IT WAS night before Kofugano was reached. The pariahs were herded from the train to a wood dormitory in which factory girls had formerly lived, Davies along with the rest. Over the doorway hung a *gohei*, wood and straw, hung there by some Shintoist, a phallic symbol before which the entering girls must have bowed. There was the motto of the establishment itself: "I hear the voice of spring under the shadow of the trees"; that, Davies knew, was true irony. All that the girl workers had ever heard was the clack of machines and the hissing of steam.

If the Nips drove their own girls until the maids dropped on the job, thought Lew, *what's going to happen to these Ainus?*

He knew, from the past, what a silk factory in Japan was like. The steamy and fetid spinning bays became intolerable with silk dust and heat, and the strange technique of spinning as performed in Japan precluded the admission of fresh air. Hellholes. If Japanese women couldn't take it for long, what would happen to the pariahs, of whom Koropok was the one sturdy person?

Did Suzuki-mura expect them to break down? Would he go to the JCCA, after he received reports of the incompetence of the Ainus, and ask for Japanese laborers, girls and men? But how could he justify the type of pariahs whom he had been perfectly willing to have sent to the silk country? Surely Suzuki-mura didn't think that Brown's memory would be that short.

It doesn't make sense, Davies told himself again, as an attendant indicated the spot on the dormitory floor which was to be Koropok's; after the previous night's lost sleep, Koropok slept heavily.

In the morning, after standing in line for his bowl of hot

buckwheat, which he wolfed down along with the others, he went with the others to where a smiling Japanese in his middle forties was waiting. Here, after a word from the laughing manager, the Ainus were separated into gangs, and Davies found himself assigned to sweeping and carrying and general cleaning. He was amused at the reason he'd been given such work. He was strong, he heard some assistant say, and, being of a strong body, would not be here unless he had a simple mind....

And what should I make of that? wondered Lew.

Pariahs, with someone to instruct them, were sent out to pick mulberry leaves. Others were put to work chopping up these leaves to be fed to the silkworms. To the Ainu women went the task at which Japanese girls "never loosed their *obis,* their sashes" because sleep was almost impossible—the twenty-four-hour continuous feeding of the voracious silkworms. They, too, had Japanese male instructors....

Davies, before the first day was over, discovered that Japanese men, and hundreds of Japanese girls, upon coming to the wood-walled location of the factory and asking for the sort of work which they had performed in the past, were refused. Back in the villages, these Japanese would surely feel resentment toward the Ainus and the Americans also, and this antagonism would grow.

Was that what Suzuki-mura desired? Had he been ordered, by someone high in the old Japanese government, to bring about just such a condition? Wouldn't it be the easiest and surest way to unite the Japanese, from the bottom up, now that Shintoism and emperor worship were things of the past?

Against this, Davies weighed what he knew of Suzuki-mura; if all of what Davies first thought were true, it did not balance the scales, because Suzuki-mura was a man who was interested in only one person—Suzuki-mura.

Working against the shrewd Japanese was one man, and this man soon established the reputation of being the dumbest pariah within the factory walls. Why, as Ikanu the manager remarked, if you told this Koropok to sweep a walk, he would sweep and sweep until someone told him to stop, although the first sweeping would have cleared the path. Oh, this Koropok was as intelligent as the very broom which he plied, neither more nor less. And this was a fortunate thing, because a stupid Ainu with a strong body had his uses.

Ikanu, following instructions, kept watch, along with his assistants, over the pariahs, because of the warning from Tokyo that the *Amerika-jin*, priding themselves on their Intelligence, might keep check on the work at the factory. He did this well, once causing a pariah to disappear for no other reason than that the man caught on to his new tasks rapidly... too rapidly, the factory management decided, for an Ainu. Maybe he was a nasty spy.

But Koropok? Koropok was a fool.

It was because of this positive belief that one of the lower assistant managers suggested to Ikanu that possibly Koropok's

The silkworm moths' eggs, **tane,** *were placed on cards which were then kept on trays and slid into bamboo racks.*

outdoor duties might be altered so that the broad-shouldered pariah could do some interior cleaning also....

"You are tiring of being sweeper-coolie?" Ikanu had asked, laughing. "I do not blame you, Kitabara. Yes, it should be perfectly safe to entrust some of your duties to the Ainu. Of course, we must be careful. *Kai-inu ni te wo kamareru.* We do not want to nurse a viper in our bosom. But Koropok... we need not worry about him. Had it not been for his lack of intelligence, he would never have been permitted here. No. So you have my permission to beat his new duties into him."

"Beat?" asked Kitabara. "Is that a new order?"

Ikanu chuckled. "No. It was a slip of the tongue. The Ainus must be treated kindly and gently. We can never tell when there might be inspection by the *Amerika-jin* jackasses. And some idiot of a pariah might pour words of ill-treatment into those long American ears. Be kind with Koropok." The Japanese laughed. "The reward will be worth the price. Cannot you imagine Kitabara again in Tokyo, his pockets heavy with money, being entertained by the prettiest of maids, and right under the noses of the Americans, who will never know how it happened?"

Kitabara could well imagine it... and the beauty of what could be expected later pleased him so that even Koropok wondered at the gentleness with which he was told about another little task which would be his to perform.

He was interested in the possibilities of this task, too... because he had wondered why it was that only the men who were actually fairly important in the factory were allowed to do work which should have been done by girls. He had supposed that some day, after preliminary training, the pariahs would do such work, but as yet this had not happened. Was this to be the start of it? And, if so, why select Koropok, most stupid of the Ainus, to begin? Or did the fact that he was to be permitted to go places forbidden the other pariahs actually mean that Ikanu was testing him out, to see if he were Koropok... or someone else?

There was no way for Davies to know. So far, he had learned exactly nothing. And he was sick of the walled factory, buckwheat mush, brooms, and broad Japanese smiles... sickest of the smiles, because he did not know what was behind them. They were like silken coverings of samurai blades. What did they hide?

THE SINGLE silk-work chamber which was put into operation was kept at fever heat by iron *hibachi* in which charcoal was kept burning. When Koropok stirred the smouldering coals, as he had been taught by Kitabara, the already vitiated air in the badly ventilated chamber made him gasp for breath. Sweat dripped from him, to sizzle into the open burners; what was worse, he feared that his beard and wig, subjected to constant moisture, might loosen.

It was easy to see why Kitabara had wanted to shunt the job off on a pariah, a job which had taken health-toll from many Japanese girls when many chambers had been in operation; the big room was like a deep corner of hell, and the job was practically a continuous one. Kitabara often came to the chamber, but only to examine what Koropok was doing....

"He is the perfect person for such a task," Kitabara told Ikanu, the manager. "He is a hair-coated machine. If we were going to make silk," said Kitabara, "this Koropok would make a good workman! If—"

"Silence," Ikanu said. "Do not speak of that, even to me."

Davies would have liked to have heard more of the short conversation....

So far as he knew, the factory actually intended to manufacture silk. That only a single silkworm hatching chamber was being operated was not anything for him to wonder at: after the years during which the factory had been shut down, it certainly seemed necessary to make a small beginning in order to get going. And so he did his jobs, and continued to curse them, and where he was, and the fact that he was finding out nothing. He had agreed to the assignment solely because he didn't believe Suzuki-mura could intend anything decent. He was disgusted and fed up, and considered himself a bigger fool than even the Japanese thought him.

The silkworm moths' eggs, *tane*, were placed on cards, which were about a foot square; the eggs were arranged in exactly twenty-eight two-inch circles on each of the cards, on which the eggs appeared like the heads of pins. The cards were kept on trays; row on row slid into bamboo racks in the chamber. Around each of the two-inch circles was a bottomless round tin, in which the *tane* had originally been deposited during the early season, several months previous.

On Koropok's fourth day in the chamber the first minute caterpillar appeared, hardly more than a tiny pale thread on the paper, and by the time Kitabara appeared for his hourly check, hundreds of eggs had hatched. Koropok was sent hurrying for Ikanu; and when he returned, shambling behind the scurrying manager, he heard Kitabara say, "At least I was spared four days of this sweat-box...." After that, the managerial staff was kept at work, along with Koropok, who did the dirtiest of it.

The emerging caterpillars had to be fed, and fed all day and all night, with the finely chopped mulberry leaves which the pariahs continued to gather. As the caterpillars grew, the leaves fed them were less finely macerated, until by the tenth day they were given whole leaves, and by the twentieth the shoots and leaves both. There were daily casualties, and Koropok had to examine every tray, in addition to his other tasks, removing the misshapen or dead chrysalises.

The cocoons on the racks were finally covered with thin sheets of paper in which a number of round holes about an inch in diameter had been cut. It was out of these holes, and into the light, that the moths would creep, to reach the upper side of the paper, to mate, and to produce the millions of *tane* which would start the factory into real production.

All through the rearing of the caterpillars and their formation into cocoons Davies had been inwardly alert; yet he had learned nothing except facts concerning sericulture, the producing of silk. However, he had seen winks, and heard pleased giggles, sure indication that the Japanese staff, instead of being resentful at performing hot, endless, menial work, was actually delighted. Why? Japanese girls had easily raised the moths in the past. Were the Nips tickled that a pariah was being fooled about something? Impossible. They didn't give a damn.

Well, what was it? *They're too pleased with themselves,* thought Davies, who knew the Japanese. Was it because the Imperial Nippon and Far Eastern Silk Association, by getting the edge on all other manufacturers because of the JCCA assistance, would reward them well? Was that enough?

It looked as if it was, because on the twenty-ninth day Davies heard the talkative Kitabara remark gleefully, "In another week we will have visitors from every silk manufacturing establishment, and what a price they will pay when we sell them a few of our cards! Yes!"

Even Ikanu giggled at that. He said, "Yes, what a price!" and everyone in the chamber roared with Japanese laughter.

But was *that* enough, Davies wondered. Certainly Suzuki-mura's concern was in a position to charge tremendous prices for the egg-cards which other manufacturers would take to their own silkworm chambers to hatch... but was that enough for the glee here? Suzuki-mura could have made use of the JCCA to get himself going; Suzuki-mura was willing to take pariahs as employees, as Davies had seen, to get in with the JCCA and raise the valuable moths for silk and to sell... but, *It's not enough,* thought Lew, *and I haven't been able to find out anything else.*

It was on the thirty-second day that Ikanu, clad only in a cotton kimono and straw sandals, said to Kitabara, on coming to the chamber after the evening meal, "Send Koropok to his sleeping-quarter now."

Why? It was time for the hatch, one of the busiest of all times in silk production, Davies had overheard. Why, then, send away a worker for whom there should be plenty of laborious and dirty jobs?

"Someone must throw the unmated male moths into the baskets," Kitabara suggested. "That is a task which tires fingers. But Koropok could—"

"Send him off," said Ikanu shortly.

Kitabara relayed the order to Koropok... and, because of it, Davies saw the first hint that something might be going to happen, something which would justify the fact that ordinary Japanese silk workers had been kept away from the silkworm chamber, where they might have seen things which, to Davies, looked perfectly all right. But he had not the least notion what this might be.

CHAPTER V

THE MOTH AND THE FLAME

KOROPOK WENT back to his space on the dormitory floor, waited until the Ainus there were asleep, and then slipped out and returned to the outside of the building containing the cocoons. He encountered no one at all, for all his caution. Once there, he figured where the racks were ranged, inside, and finally selected a location from which he should be able to see into the chamber; he quietly pried apart bamboo uprights, where they were joined by a slender cross-piece, and then slipped one of the wall boards sufficiently apart from the next one so that he could peer into the silkworm chamber. He did this below the level of the eyes of the Japanese who were engrossed completely in what had to be done inside....

His eyes widened at what he saw. The birth, mating, and death of silkworms, of moths; the foundation of the silk industry.

Moths were emerging from their cocoons under the sheets of paper and creeping up to the light through the holes. For newly born things they came through the openings with amazing haste and eagerness.

Davies' first glance showed him that the moths, where he was looking, were, in body and wing, as white as flour. The male as well as the female was white, but was instantly distinguishable by the smaller size of body and wing. And the males who had not found partners were executing furious wild dances, with their wings whirring and their bodies whirling until they looked like circles of incandescence. A soft sound, the continuous whirring of thousands on thousands of wings, was broken again and again by huge and violent sneezes, as one after the other of the Japanese was affected by the soft down which flew thickly from the new-born wings of the excited male silkworm moths.

When a female appeared through the holes in the paper a male instantly rushed toward her, like a blur of white light, and at once the two insects were locked in a tight embrace, during which their wings ceased to flutter.

From what Davies had already heard, the major task in the chamber was to remove superfluous male moths; and, already, the floor was so littered with them that the bare feet of the Japanese gave off crunching sounds when the handful of men, Ikanu, Kitabara, and several others of the staff, moved about. At first, Davies supposed that they were performing this task only. Then he saw that Ikanu always went to a rack in a far corner, and that he would pick out moths from a tray there and, with them, go to other breeding-trays, depositing those moths with the others.

In another corner of the chamber, with piles of the tin receptacles stacked on the floor, were trays on which rested the new and ready egg cards, marked with the correct number of circles. On each of the circles a Japanese was placing the small and bottomless tin containers, while another Japanese placed a single moth within each of the little enclosures of metal, in which the female instantly settled down, as docile as a Japanese woman. Before long the entire circle would be covered with eggs. The male was crushed immediately after mating; the female as soon as the eggs would be deposited.

The ecstatic dancing which Davies was watching, a dancing of white-appearing insects, and what followed, was strangely Japanese. White garments were customary for birth, marriage and death… and the moth perfected in the cocoon was similarly arrayed for all three, which came in such swift succession. The wild dance of the silkworm moths was reminiscent of orgies at Number Nineteen, although the maids there had been attired in strong, violent colors.

Davies watched the dance.…

It took time for him first to see and then to verify two things. The first was that Kitabara and another Japanese kept going from tray to tray and selecting male moths, tearing them away from their embrace if necessary, and depositing them on other trays instead of dropping them to the floor; and the second was that, unless he had been staring too long, those moths which Kitabara saved instead of destroying seemed a little different from the other males. A trifle larger? Perhaps. And the least bit more silver than white? Possibly.

A fine breeding-stock, Davies supposed. By careful observation he became reasonably certain that these moths, which were slightly larger and had a silver tinge, came from the single rack over which Ikanu worked… and then, when his eyes ached from staring, he became positive that those moths were never hurled to the floor, always dropped into the basket.

Once, twice, this basket was carefully emptied into a brazier, and the moths' wings and bodies hissed during the destruction.

It took him longer to be sure that Ikanu saw to it that all of the female moths where he was working were also destroyed, and not permitted to mate except by accident, in which case both went into another nearby *hibachi*.

A better breeding stock? Then why destroy it?

The Japanese wasted nothing. Why would they do away with the finest stock? *Is this why regular, experienced silk workers have been kept away?* wondered Davies. *And is this why Ikanu and. Kitabara are doing the work themselves?*

Even he, Koropok the stupid Ainu, had been sent off so that he would be out of the way, and wasn't that because Ikanu was keeping something secret? If this were not an unusual procedure, what could it be?

Davies, from his years in Japan and from this new experience here, knew the extreme care which Japanese gave sericulture. More varieties of mulberries existed than most people knew; five hundred or more, with each texture of leaf for the production of different kinds of silks.

There were the hot chambers in which cocoons were killed, and rooms draped in black like the setting for a beheading, in which silk was tested for luster and color, and there were intricate machines for winding and weaving… all for silk. Nothing was ever wasted. Nothing should be wasted now, and certainly not the precious silkworm moths for breeding stock, after the long intermission in silk culture.

T H E C A R E which the Japanese took was apparent in the checking of temperature here in this chamber, and in the scrawny Japanese who, stooped over a microscope, examined bodies of female moths, after egg-laying, to make sure that the insect was not affected by infectious disease, in which case the eggs she had deposited, all numbered as to the circles in which the females were placed, would be destroyed. Now and again the microscopist would shout a number, first that of card, then that of a particular circle, and this circle would be cut out from the card.

"No official examination will find anything wrong with *our* eggs," shouted Kitabara once. "Oh, they will be perfect!"

Davies saw Ikanu bare his teeth in a grin, but the manager remained silent as he kept on with his task.

The bacteriologist bowed, and, according to custom, acknowledged the compliment to his skill. He looked up from his steady examination, and then he began to laugh, a cackling and pleased sound,

"*Komatta koto desu,*" he said. "It is a nuisance, but the reward is worth it. I have assisted in scientific experiments, but this is as interesting as any I have performed. It is good," said the microscopist, "because it is simple."

He rubbed a claw of a hand over his eyes, sneezed from moth-wing dust, and began to scratch luxuriously at his bare, itching chest. Ikanu also relaxed, and in immediate imitation, so did the other Japanese, because it would be insulting for them to continue working while the manager rested where they could see him; Ikanu would feel that they were chiding him for his moment of respite.

The manager, smiling, bowed to the bacteriologist at the microscope. "It has gone well," he said. "Suzuki-mura-*san* is sure to reward you."

"It was a simple idea," said the bacteriologist, returning Ikanu's bow. "Not nearly so complex as making soap from the residual oil crushed from the pupae which you yourself suggested, Ikanu-*san*. But my idea, now long in operation, for the manufacture of Fuji Delicious Beef Tea, from the same source, was not simple either. We have reached," announced the Japanese, assuming the customary lecturing attitude which all Nipponese loved, "the synthetic age. Yes. We—"

"Please," warned Ikanu, but continuing to smile. "We have pledged ourselves not to mention what we do and what is intended."

The bacteriologist bowed; and being a privileged person, he said daringly, "I suppose you fear that the pariahs will discover what we do?"

Ikanu laughed with the others.

"It was worth the stink of them about us," he said, "in that the work needed to be done was accomplished by stupid persons. In addition, how else could the Association have received so many favors from the equally stupid Americans who think they control us? In the past, we were without competition, all of us. The synthetic age changes that. And soon...."

Ikanu stopped. But Davies, listening and figuring, waited patiently. *There never was a Nip who wouldn't boast,* Lew was sure.

He was right. Ikanu said, after a pause during which he saw only familiar faces and heard only the gradually diminishing whirring of the silkworm moth's wings, "And soon we will undersell American synthetics, as we have undersold all goods of any description in the past, while here, in Japan, the Association will not have a manufacturer who can compete with us for years.... There will not even be the competition of true silk here, either!"

"Let the experts who will come to purchase eggs from us, in order to make their own start, examine them all they will," proclaimed the microscopist, "and not even when they see the cocoons will there be any warning for them. Oh, in a short time there will be no silk industry at all in Japan. It is a reversing of the theory of the master race," giggled the scrawny Japanese. "Instead of building up the excellence of silkworms, we are, by our breeding, destroying it. We—"

"Oh, the lovely silver moths," exulted Kitabara. "Joyfully mating with true silkworm moths. How pretty they are, these silver moths which we have collected in the woods! And when I realize what is to take place because of them, I desire to dance as wildly as do they as they mate."

Ikanu quoted, while the room shook with laughter,

" *'Kaiko....*
Hane wo tottaro
To-garashi!' "

Koropok crouched lower. He knew the verse: "Pluck off the wings of a shining silkworm moth, and you have a burning pepper-pod."

So that's what they're up to, he thought.

Clever. Diabolically clever. If it worked, it would leave Suzuki-mura the wealthiest and most important man in Japan;
and Suzuki-mura was a fellow without scruples, who hated the
United States.

The scheme, as the microscopist had boasted, was extremely simple. Detection of the plan—the wrecking of the Japanese
silk industry in order that the Imperial Nippon and Far Eastern
Silk Association could manufacture synthetic silks without
competition from true silks—would come too late, would come
after the damage, the ruining of the silkworm moths, had been
accomplished. The destruction of the industry, which would
take years of patience and breeding to rebuild, could easily be
explained by Suzuki-mura: the JCCA's demand for the employment of the Ainus was responsible. The pariahs' stupidity had
been responsible for everything which had happened... and all
Japan would feel that the United States was bent on destroying
Japan in peace as well as in war. Suzuki-mura would profit from
such hatred in a hundred ways. Japan's resentment could one
day become war.

A slow grin appeared on Davies' lips. One of his hands slowly
became a fist. *I've got 'em*, he thought, *just like that.*

And at that moment, in the brief silence within the chamber
during which each of the Japanese there dreamed his own
dream, Davies sneezed. Not the *sssszee!* of a Japanese, but a deep
American *aaaaachoooo!*

He was off his knees and running before Ikanu could scream
the first order; he was running hard, and not toward the dormitory. Every pariah would be examined over and over. Davies'
beard would not withstand such an examination. He dared not
return and huddle in his blankets... he knew, without the waste
of a moment of thought, that he had to get away.

THERE WAS a little millet, and salted vegetables for
relish, and sometimes a pot of thin bean soup in the village
below; and, to Davies in the hills above, any of these would
have been a feast. He was hungry. More than that, he knew

that lack of food was making it more and more difficult for him to clamber down to a vantage point, from which he could see the station of Kofugano, and doubly difficult to climb up to where there was no chance of his being seen. Yet whenever a train chugged into the station, he had to see who emerged from the cars.

There had been an immediate and wild search. Two days later there had been a more intensive search of the surrounding country, conducted by Japanese sent from Tokyo for that purpose.

Davies had realized the impossibility of getting out of the mountainous silk district without being picked up. He had flirted with the notion of removing beard and wig, and, as an American, bluntly returning to the factory; but he knew Suzuki-mura and his men too well for that. Major Davies, who had been Koropok, would disappear. The stakes for the Japanese were too high for them not to take a chance in killing a lone American, whose death could never be proved.

What he had to do was to keep under cover, and alive, until the purchasers of silkworm moth eggs came to the factory, as they would, and to hope, as he reasoned, that JCCA men would come with them to see, first-hand, the result of the work done by the Ainus.

There was water in the hills, but no food. As the days passed, it became more and more difficult for Davies to restrain himself from slipping into the village, at night, in search of food. And as the days passed he became more and more like an Ainu in appearance. His face became gaunt. His hands would clench and unclench without purpose; sometimes he would mutter to himself. When he walked, to go to the place from which he could see the station, it was unsteadily; when he rested, he trembled; and when he slept, it was fitfully and miserably.

When finally he did see well-dressed Japanese step from one car of the train, with American civilians along with them, similarly attired, it took the uniforms of several United States officers in the party to make him realize that this was what he had been waiting for. Even so, his return toward the walled factory was a painfully slow one. Not until he was almost at the central entrance, through which the JCCA officials, the officers, and the Japanese had long passed, did he have the sense to know that Koropok, the filthy, starved, ragged pariah, would not have been permitted to walk through that same gate even if Koropok had not been so badly wanted by Suzuki-mura's men. When Davies stopped shambling ahead, and leaned against the smooth trunk of a tree, he saw that not one but three Japanese stood around where he would have gone, and that there were other Japanese along the wall. Koropok was not wanted inside the factory now.

Davies told himself slowly, *Pull up your socks.* He backed away from the tree. If only it were night... but it was not.

I could wait until everyone comes out, was his first hazy decision, *and then make myself known to our people.*

It was a long minute before he decided that if he were Ikanu or any of the men in on the plan, he would promptly shoot a ragged Ainu who approached, no matter what the seeming pariah called out, because killing Koropok was vastly more profitable and simple to explain, than allowing Koropok—the vanished bearded man who sneezed like an American—to do any talking.

Davies took a slow, deep breath.

How much have you got left? he asked himself. Enough for one try at something in order to get over the wall? *It had better be good,* he thought, grimacing involuntarily, *damned good and clever and smart. Because you haven't got the stuff to have two shots at it.*

Where should he try to get over the wall?

He began to move clockwise around the factory's wooden barrier. He stopped when he came to a tiny bridge over a tinier stream; he knelt and wet his face and the back of his neck, which helped a little. From where he was kneeling, he could see the corner of the wall. A Japanese, as a guard, was near the corner; the Japanese closest to the squat fellow at the corner did not stand in one spot, but, obviously a former soldier, paced slowly back and forth as if on sentry duty. When this ex-soldier's back was turned to the corner... how long a time elapsed before he reached the end of his beat? Enough?

It had to be. And so Davies began to creep toward the corner, first on hands and knees, and then on his belly.

The guard at the corner stood with his back against the wall, not moving, but staring ahead solemnly and dumbly. It became apparent to Davies that this guard's instructions had been to watch where the little indented stream came into the open, because a man could approach, almost unseen, along the bed. Lew was not doing this. He reached the last tree-protection; he calculated the distance between where he lay and the corner guard, and how long it would take to reach him. To rush to the wall, to attempt to clamber over without being heard, was impossible.

But if the pacing sentry would keep to the time it took him to reach the far end of his slow and decorous march....

OFF your dime, Davies' mouth formed; and then he was on his way toward the corner and the guard there, with his teeth biting down on his lower lip. At what moment he must have come into the Japanese' range of vision, at what moment the fixed eyes of the Nip wavered from the spot on which they were fastened, Davies did not care. His hands now contained almost the last strength in his body, and as Lew's right flashed up and smashed the guard on his narrow and hairless and unprotected chin, Davies' left sunk deep into the guard's belly.

Davies was over the wall almost before the guard fell.

He had to wait a moment. He himself had fallen, inside the wall; was he going to be able to rise? Somehow, he did, on shaking legs; somehow, just before the ex-soldier, having turned and seen his companion on the ground, shouted, Davies was

Davies was over the wall
almost before the guard fell.

fumbling his exhausted way toward the offices where the staff
and the guests, the JCCA officials and the officers ought to be.

The thudding in Davies' ears was the harsh pounding of his
own blood, and not the running feet outside the wall which he
would otherwise have heard. He crossed the empty factory yard;
he swerved instinctively when he saw the pariahs, clothed and
clean, waiting to be shown off to the JCCA by Ikanu, because
where there were Ainus there would be a Jap to watch them...
he stumbled around the deserted, old silk-testing structure and
avoided the rearing-chamber... and, as he weaved toward the
building which contained Ikanu's big office just inside the entrance, he did not think that perhaps a guard might be stationed
outside, who would stop him at the last moment... all he could
do was to keep going.

Davies did not remember, even automatically, that Japanese

did little or no inner post guarding in combat or in Tokyo for war-secrets manufacture, but trusted to perimeter guarding. Nor did he recall that the Japanese here would not want ex-soldiers, gendarmes, or anyone else to be near enough to over-hear what would be talked about inside. He was able to think only one thing: *I've got to tell them!* Then he plunged inside.

If the faces of the men there were blurred to Davies, so was what happened. A Japanese hissed warningly, first of them all to understand; and that was Suzuki-mura, sitting in the man-ager's padded chair. Ikanu had been sitting beside the old schemer, and Ikanu, seeing Koropok, reached into a drawer of the desk. Before the manager's invariable smile froze solid on his face, one of the American officers had his own gun out, and Ikanu's hand remained where it was.

On the desk were samples of the egg cards. On the plump knees of the Japanese in the room were order pads and sheets of agreements for the purchasing of silkworm moth eggs, mil-lions of the eggs which would destroy the silk industry of Japan; on their faces was blank astonishment.

The G-2 officer was the first to speak. He said softly, "I suggest that everyone remain just where he is, without moving."

Suzuki-mura ran a red tongue over parched lips, having received Ikanu's report as to what had happened; Suzuki-mura made his try. He said, "This is the crazed Ainu, Ikanu? I can see that he can hardly stand on his feet. Take him away and see that he is given the best of care."

"He is the only Ainu I have seen who does not look well," said the Chief Commissioner, Brown. "Please," he said to the G-2 officer who had drawn his gun, "just because this poor fellow has come here like this is no reason for—"

The G-2 officer broke in, "What's his name?"

Ikanu shrugged. "I would need to see the lists," he smiled. "One looks like another. Asking him would be useless. He is not only crazed but—"

"*Watakushi wa Koropok to moshimasu,*" said the apparition.

"My name is Koropok." The scrape of metal against leather, as American pistols were drawn, extended the sound of the final word. Then Davies' eyes came up until they met Suzuki-mura's; and it was the Japanese, the favored guest of Number Nineteen, who looked away... who cringed... who did not move....

It was so still in the room that the sound of the labored breathing of guards, who had rushed in to say that someone had climbed the wall, was like thunder, and rats, chewing on pupae under the building, clashed their teeth so that the noise seemed like great rocks tumbling down from the mulberry-planted mountainsides.

"And," said Llewelyn Davies, in English, "I have a story to tell."

EARLY MORNING fog was not thick enough to keep the heat of the sun from Tokyo; what it did was to press down the smells of the city and raise tempers. But Major Llewelyn Davies, on his way to see what Public Relations wanted, whistled contentedly as he walked down the Headquarters corridor, and felt very fine, because he never forgot the difference between masquerading as an Ainu pariah, hungry and unwashed and kicked around, and being as he now was, fresh from a shower and having eaten breakfast, and smoking a States-side cigarette.

Public Relations always wanted something from the man who had been in Japan all through the war. While Davies had argued for flight duty after the occupation, and managed to get up a little, he no longer rebelled at being assigned to Headquarters in Tokyo. Japan in transition was a strange place, with its plots and counterplots, and Davies was aware that he served to more purpose by being available to AMG, G-2, and Public Relations than by flying. He himself wondered at the strength of those cross currents, deep, unseen, and not always internal, which were cutting more and more foundation from the Japan of the past.

A sergeant was busy at a typewriter when Davies entered the PRO's office. Major Harrison's desk was piled with papers, but the major was not there.

"Sir," the sergeant said to Davies, "the major was called away—"

"You go call him back," said Lew. "When I get a castor oil assignment I always like to swear at the fellow who's holding the spoon."

The sergeant kept his face sober. "The major dictated his request, sir," said the noncom, standing up and going to Harrison's desk. "He said that if there were any questions he would be available later."

"I know the answer to that one," grinned Davies. "Later will be after I've done what he wants. I suppose it's got to be done immediately?"

"Yes, sir."

"Well, I'll finish my cigarette while you find Major Harrison. Tell him I left my glasses in my room and can't read anything."

The sergeant looked at the alert black eyes under the shaggy brows of the dark, stocky American who had been able to disguise himself so as to fool both Japanese and Ainus, eyes which had to be good to pass the flight physical. He wanted badly to grin; but it would be smarter to play dumb and save whatever face he could for his own officer, Harrison, particularly because the sergeant intended to request a week-end pass where there was supposed to be good food, geisha, and iced Sapporo beer. So he kept his tanned face straight as he said, "Sir, Major Harrison did not say where he—"

"Try the north balcony," suggested Davies solemnly, sitting on the edge of Harrison's desk. "There's usually a morning breeze there. Sometimes it comes down from the north, and sometimes it's being batted around."

"Is that an order, sir?"

Davies nodded; and when he was alone he wondered just what Harrison had on tap this time. It might be something to which Davies would object, or it might be something which the Public Relations officer hated to ask Davies to do, Harrison being a decent fellow with the tough job of trying to please everyone. But, either way, Davies wanted it first hand.

AS LEW had guessed, Harrison was found without difficulty. He said, as he came puffing into the office, "Damn it, Davies, it's sweltering. The whole thing's written out. I'd have gone over it with you except that it's perfectly plain."

"Plain that I won't want to do it?"

Harrison growled, "You've got no more choice than I had. It comes straight down from the C.O." Harrison wiped his face. "I don't see how you keep so cool. I feel like hell. No sleep. Damn mosquito got through the netting."

"You're soft," jeered Lew.

"See how tough you are when you hear this one," Harrison retorted ominously. "I tried to get you out of it. Told the general

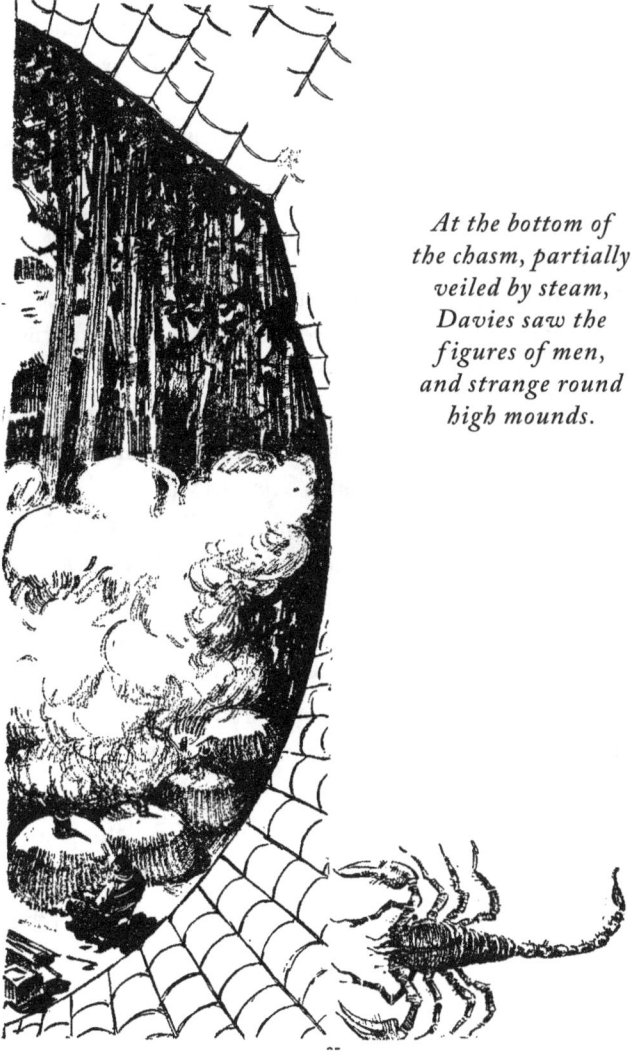

At the bottom of the chasm, partially veiled by steam, Davies saw the figures of men, and strange round high mounds.

that you're checking AMG's information on parties and politics. He brushed that aside. Said he wanted you, and that you've got to be damn careful. Said he was more afraid of having things fouled up by these men than by anything the Jap politicians can do. Said—"

"What's it all about?" demanded Davies.

Harrison said, "Fraternization."

Davies threw back his head and laughed. He said to the sergeant, who appeared deep in paper work, "Which would you prefer, Sergeant, a visit to a tenth century temple or a fat little Nip gal filling your glass of beer?"

"Personnel engaged in work involving military secrecy must not indulge in alcoholic beverages, sir," said the sergeant, thinking of the pass he wanted.

"What the devil have I got to do with fraternization?" asked Lew. "I could give the boys plenty of tips, having been at Number Nineteen. Am I supposed to lecture on the perils of the Yoshiwara? Or—"

"The delegation from the States," Harrison said, "wish to be conducted personally about Tokyo. They know what they want to see. Drinking shops. Tea houses. The sort where girls are sent for. Everything, including the Yoshiwara. They intend to determine for themselves just how far fraternization has gone, and the general's made up his mind that you can show them the fewest seams. I'm damn glad," Harrison grunted, running a finger under his collar, a finger which came out wet, "that now you've taken that damn silly smile off your face."

Davies said, "What's wrong having a geisha pour your beer?"

"Tell it to the delegation."

Davies began to sweat also. "With important things to be done, everything stops while we try to hide what doesn't mean a thing? If a soldier gets a wallop out of having the bones picked out of boiled globefish with chopsticks by the maid who is squatted in front of him, what the hell? And if Joe makes a pass at her, which he does, and she giggles and wonders what it'll be like when he gives her that formerly forbidden and immoral *kisu*, who's hurt? If—"

"Tell it to the delegation," said Harrison. "Convince 'em that Number Nineteen is only a restaurant. The general will decorate you for that. But if the delegation get the proof they're out to find, what you'll get from the C.O. is the Purple Heart." The Public Relations officer ended disgustedly, "He's stuck with the delegation, and so we've got to worry about fraternization when all hell is pulling in fifty directions to get control of Japan."

Davies nodded. He liked no part of what he was to do, but there was one bright spot about conducting the delegation around Tokyo; it seemed to Davies that some of the strange political organizations, learning that Americans from the States, obviously important, were making an investigation, would attempt to reach the ears of the investigators for their own purposes. If this happened, Davies would have a chance to pass along names to AMG and G-2, perhaps those of men who remained well out of sight in the struggle for control.

Much of what was going on politically, seemingly obvious, was below the surface in Davies' opinion. Japan was a rich prize, and there were many players in the grim game. The United States played in it also, but without marked cards, depending on a few men, of whom Davies was one, to keep the game straight.

"When does all this start?" asked Lew.

Major Harrison said, "The delegation is in the general's office."

"And the general," remarked Davies, "has important business elsewhere, just as his PRO did." He got off the desk. "And a staff officer has the job of keeping the visitors in good humor." Davies laughed; he said to the sergeant, "The way to get yourself in strong with a halfway pretty waitress, when there's competition, is to say, '*Moshi kanete orimasu.*' That's the polite way of making a request. She'll put a bigger piece of ice in your *birru*, Sergeant."

"Thank you, sir," the sergeant said. He picked up a pencil. "Would the major please repeat that slowly?"

"Officers are supposed to discourage fraternization," grumbled Harrison. "Now he'll want a pass to see if it works."

The sergeant said, "Yes, sir."

"You're a big help, Davies," the PRO sighed. "Why beat on me? I'm not the one who wished this on you. Lord, but it's hot!"

Davies said, "It may not be as bad as you think," although he was not speaking of the heat.

The fog seemed to be turning into steam. The light was a blend of lavender and gray, like fuming incense, and as hot as glowing incense in a brass container. But the odor was not that of highland Japanese pine nor Indian sandalwood nor Formosan jasmine. It was that of a bombed Japanese city in which many inhabitants lived in the open; it was an odor composed of low-tide mud, fish, condiments, cooking, and sweating garments.

"You wouldn't have the nerve," said Harrison, wiping his forehead, "to suggest to these men that they ought to go to the seacoast! I had a couple of days there. I slept like a rock." He sighed. "But I'd just as soon sweat here as sweat trying to satisfy those men anywhere."

"No seacoast," Lew said. "One of the advantages of being an Ainu is that your clothes don't amount to much. Nice in heat. If those investigators stick with me, they may blow a fuse before long."

Harrison warned, "If they get out of sorts, they may blow up the wrong way. I don't envy you." Quietly, the PRO said, "I needn't tell you how some people have been anxious to oust the C.O. because of his policies." Harrison picked up a paper and handed it to Davies. "I wouldn't say that this delegation is a hundred percent friendly to the Old Man."

Lew examined the list of names. "I wouldn't say so, either," he commented. Then he said, "I hope you get your pass, Sergeant," and, lighting another cigarette and nodding to Harrison, he started for the general's office.

SEVEN MEN in civilian attire were waiting for him. One of the general's staff officers introduced them to Davies, and Lew acknowledged each introduction and did his best to associate names with faces and appearances. The elderly and pipe-smoking man was Hartshorn, the head of the delegation; the man of about the same age, standing near an open window, was Ashton, a Washington man who disapproved of the manner in which Japanese affairs were being handled by the C.O. and AMG; a younger fellow beside Ashton was the expert who would compile the delegation's report. These, Lew was reasonably certain, were the three to watch.

The youngest of the trio said, "Is it correct that you have been instructed to answer all questions frankly, Major Davies?"

"Yes, sir," agreed Lew.

Captain Martin said, "Major Davies is completely at your service, Mr. Malloy. And as the general explained earlier, Major Davies is thoroughly conversant with—ah—life in Tokyo."

Malloy whipped out a notebook and found a pencil. "What is your opinion of Tokyo life, Major? And what part do our boys take in it?"

"Life here is not yet normal," said Davies. *And make something of that*, thought Lew. *Our boys! Nuts.* "Our men," he continued, not wanting to give the questioner a feeling that there was to be any evasion, "take little part in it, and, it seems to me, react in a normal manner."

"I am specifically referring to night life," Malloy prodded. "To be absolutely exact, to fraternization. How much is there of it?"

"Unless I have misunderstood my orders," said Davies, who had no intention of saying anything which could later become a damning statement, "that's what you are here to examine. My orders are to show you about."

The elderly Ashton remarked, "But how much will you show

us? We want more than a handpicked tourists' tour." He went on smoothly, as if the coming question was to be innocent instead of being loaded, "Just how do you qualify for this assignment? Do you know the licensed district well, for example?"

"Yes," said Davies.

"Been there often?"

"I have, sir."

Ashton smiled with satisfaction. "I see," he said, while Malloy began to write in the notebook. "I see. Hmm. Now tell the delegation, Major, how you justify the military orders, such as were shown us, supposedly issued for the purpose of inducing our boys to keep away from the Yoshiwara, when officers such as yourself, you admit, actually engage in fraternization?"

"I don't believe it necessary for Major Davies to give opinions," said Hartshorn quietly.

The head of the delegation continued, "We are in your hands, Major, and depend on you for an honest insight as to what is going on in Tokyo. From what the general has said, you will give that to us."

"He'll make it possible to apply a coat of whitewash," snapped Ashton. "Suppose we let the major, who has agreed to answer questions with frankness, answer what I asked of him. If he intends to be frank. Well, what about it, Major Davies?"

Davies saw the misery on the staff officer's face. Few secrets had been guarded more closely than that of Llewelyn Davies' life as Koropok the Ainu, during which time he had served in the licensed district as an *hakoya,* the most degraded of all servants, at the famous Number Nineteen.

This was no time to fence, nor to come up with anything which might continue the questioning. The thing to do, Lew decided, was to go strictly GI and so he said levelly, "I carry out orders, sir. I do not justify them."

"That's what Hitler's generals said," remarked Malloy.

Lew's lips tightened; but as he controlled himself, and remained silent, he was thinking, *We're going to get along just fine.*

"Mr. Malloy," Hartshorn said wearily, as if similar bickering had worn him down, "you owe Major Davies an apology."

Malloy mumbled something. Ashton, before the unwilling apology was concluded, cut in to say, "I'll have no part of the investigation until I am satisfied we can depend on Major Davies conducting us to the proper places, and before I step foot in Tokyo I want him to state his qualifications. The general hedged about Davies' experience, stating that the major knows Tokyo. I want details. Speak up, Major." He added nastily, "Or are you under orders to keep silent?"

"Suppose we put it this way," said Davies; "you tell me exactly what you want to investigate, and I'll take you to the proper places."

Ashton demanded, "How'll we know you will do that? Why, there has been time to arrange things so that it will all look perfectly innocent when we arrive. For all I know, you've been in touch with the Japs at the places you'll take us, and when we get there all we'll see is one soldier drinking tea, instead of being corrupted by women, alcohol, and drugs."

"If I were Major Davies," said Captain Martin, opening and closing a hand, "I would resent what you have just said."

"The implication," Lew said quietly, "is that I would work with Japs against the good of my own country—"

Malloy broke in, "Isn't that what happens when our authorities attempt to interfere with what the mass of the people really want?"

"Food is what the mass of the people want," said Davies. "They'll vote on the side of the most rice." Staring squarely at Malloy, he went on, "Hidden forces are tugging at Japan, but I am a soldier and these are none of my business." *And let's hope you believe it, too!* After a pause, Lew said bluntly, "I have no interest in politics. I do know Tokyo. Do you wish me to take you around, or don't you?"

ASHTON LEANED over and whispered a moment with Malloy, and, while Hartshorn was saying that the delega-

*A wrinkled vendor
of shaved ice
attempted to sidle
up to the visitng
Amerika-jin.*

tion as a whole surely were satisfied with the general's selection,
Davies thought that he heard Ashton say something about a
dumb soldier. A corner of Lew's mouth twitched; that was what
the Japanese had thought regarding his intelligence when they
had supposed him to be a stupid Ainu. He almost felt as if he
were Koropok again.

What a portion of the delegation wanted was an honest

check on fraternization; what another portion wanted was something to play the devil with the present form of occupational control. Ashton and Malloy were the leaders of the latter group. A belligerent pair who came close to dominating the others.

Davies was sick of it already. No wonder Harrison, the PRO, hadn't wanted to accept any responsibility for what Davies was to do; and that went for the general also. On the other hand, *The C.O. trusts me,* thought Lew, *and if I cheat every GI out of a bottle of beer, that makes me something, too.* Yes, this castor oil assignment was his, and he had to see to it that the delegation accepted him instead of some other officer who might well mess it up.

And it seemed reasonable to suppose, now that he saw another group of men near Hartshorn speaking together, that if Ashton were satisfied with him, thinking him to be only a dumb soldier, the others might not want him.

"Fraternization," said Davies, "is a funny word for what goes on, isn't it? The word refers to brothers; but we use it when a soldier and a girl become friendly." He grinned. "Sometimes I think that what is back of Japanese politics is the desire of unscrupulous men to make fortunes"—Ashton, Malloy, and another man nodded and agreed—"and of the people to simply get enough to eat"—and Hartshorn and everyone else nodded also—"and yet it looks terribly involved to us, who are trying to find something deep and Oriental."

Both sides agreed with the stocky officer, Hartshorn honestly, Ashton because he was now convinced that while Davies might attempt a whitewash of conditions, the major was really a fool and could be managed.

"Let's have an understanding," said Ashton, smiling. "You, Major Davies, are to take us where soldiers are entertained, on which we are to report at home. If an effort is being made by the Japanese to influence our boys toward Japan, or against any of our allies, we want this shown by permitting us to examine soldiers we will find where you take us. If our soldiers, and more particularly officers, indicate any bias toward any of our allies, which they pass on to the Japanese in order that elections are influenced, we intend to investigate that also. If—"

Hartshorn said, "Must we go over that again, Mr. Ashton? The purpose of the investigation is only to examine fraternizing. We—"

This time Lew broke in with, "Gentlemen, it is going to be hotter as the morning becomes later. There are some places to which we can go right now." He turned to the staff officer. "Do we rate cars, Captain? O.K. That's something. I—"

"Major," said Ashton, "you haven't answered me."

Davies said, "What you were saying is too complicated for a soldier, sir. It's hot enough without having to think how to reply."

"Just one thing before we go," Malloy remarked. "Are these unscrupulous men you mention, who are making fortunes at the people's expense, men who sit in with AMG and the occupational authorities?"

He can't think I'm that dumb, Davies was sure. And so he said, "Even if I knew the answer, you wouldn't expect me to say anything, would you?"

"Do you know the answer?" asked Malloy.

"Quite frankly," Davies said placidly, "I don't." He continued in fluent Japanese, "*Todai moto kurashi.*"

"What's that mean?"

"Just below the candlestick is the darkest place of all. It's a proverb which means that a man must be at a distance in order to see what really goes on. As far as what is happening in Tokyo, I expect I'm too close to everything. You gentlemen will doubtless have a better perspective. I—"

Ashton said thoughtfully, "You are very good at evading simple questions, Major Davies. The question was, 'Do wealthy Japanese influence our conduct in supervising the government of Japan?'"

"The answer," said Lew, "is no. But there is another proverb which may operate in Japan as it does elsewhere. *Jigoku no sata mo kane shidai.* Even hell's judgments may be swayed by money."

Malloy said, "Where did you learn to speak Japanese?"

"That is a purely personal question," said Captain Martin.

Ashton, frowning, insisted, "When we go to wherever you take us, Major, I want you to speak in English whenever possible. And when we question any of our boys in teahouses, you are to stand back and remain silent. We do not want their replies to be influenced by your presence."

Lew guessed he had better start polishing his brass, to have it ready when the pair questioned GI's who might be full of beer.

Some fun, thought Davies. And in the meantime his own work would stand still, unless Ashton and Malloy were approached by men who thought as they did, or by Japanese who, for purposes of their own, put on such a cloak. Yes, Japan reeked with plot and counterplot, and scoundrels plotted for gain along with the ideologists. Yes, in Tokyo had collected the scum and scour of the Asiatic gutters, while ranged against them stood a handful of men, including Llewelyn Davies.

"Ready, gentlemen?" he asked.

CHAPTER II

THE FALSE HAKOYA

THE RIDE toward the licensed quarter was not an agreeable one. Davies, seated with Hartshorn and Ashton, in the staff car's rear seat, tried to explain a little about Tokyo, not as a guide but to underline the strangeness of Oriental thinking and habits, and to prepare the men for the differences between America and Asia. Hartshorn was keenly interested, but Ashton cut off Lew's telling of how Japanese, bombed out of their homes, continued to go in the evenings to the city's

outskirts for *mushi-kiki,* the-listening-to-sing-insects, and for *tsuki-mi,* summer-moonlight-viewing. Ashton said that such foolishness had better be beaten out of the Japs. Learning something about their rights would be better for them, and the occupational authorities were remiss in not showing the people that adherence to old customs was an easy way to keep men and women in subjugation. That was what Hirohito had done. But this certainly was going to be changed.

After that, Davies remained silent.

But when the Yoshiwara was in sight, he said, "The tree which you see, outside the entrance gate, is called *mikaeri yanagi.* The

*Inside of the showrooms were
girls, seated in rows as they
displayed their charms to
prospective customers.*

lookback willow. Formerly, when a girl, because of her debts to whoever owned her, could not leave the district, she would go as far as the gate with her lover, and when he left her he would walk to the tree and then turn and look back to see her once more. The Japanese," said Lew, "look at... fraternization... differently than do we. I mention this because, often, Japanese men come here for ordinary entertainment, dancing, singing, maybe drinking, and not for—"

"I intend to examine certain phases of prostitution also," announced Ashton in a sharp voice. "For example, did the girls here have the opportunity to vote? Were they given the chance to hear all sides? Or were they herded to the polls to help uphold the present system? It is not my intention," he orated, as the driver of the staff car began to slow down at the Great Gate, and then stopped, "to permit these unfortunate women to be further exploited—"

"I thought it was our soldiers in whom you were interested," said Hartshorn in an amused voice. He went on with sudden crispness, "Please do not make a speech. I am certain there are none of your constituents here. I am not one, and, unless my feeling is incorrect, I doubt whether Major Davies would vote for you."

"Naturally not," retorted Ashton, "He's an officer."

Hartshorn sighed. "I early came to the conclusion," he said, "that the major has seen through you, Mr. Ashton, and that he is well aware that your interest is not so much in the avowed purpose of this delegation, which is the examination of fraternization, as it is in the political situation."

"I am not interested in the opinions of majors," said Ashton. "I am interested solely in what our boys think. If—"

"This is where we get out," said Davies quickly, returning the salutes of the pair of M.P.'s and the Japanese police near the gate. He glanced around and, when he did, and saw that the machine containing the remainder of the delegation turned the corner, he stepped out of the car.

If the interior had been hot and stuffy, the air outside seemed to writhe with heat vibrations, on which were carried the minor jangle of stringed instruments as geisha plucked at them, and the tap of drums. The latter were like pulsing heartbeats, eager and compelling and throbbing. Real or imaginary, perfume seemed to be in the quivering air and to have replaced the city odors.

A wrinkled vendor of shaved ice flavored with vanilla attempted to sidle up to these visiting *Amerika-jin* who would have money and thirst; one of the solemn-faced Japanese policemen stopped him.

"Let him come," ordered Ashton. "He has a right to make a living,"

The M.P. glanced at Davies, who nodded assent.

"*Yoroshii,*" the M.P. gave permission.

The Japanese shuffled up to the group. Ashton spoke to him, forced to shout because of the din set up by rival stallkeepers in praise of their wares. Holding out his hand, Ashton said, "Me you friendee."

The vendor blinked.

"You talkee to me. Me not letee soldier hurtee you. Me bossee man. You sabbee?" With this explanation, of which the vendor understood no word, Ashton went on, "Me thinkee you hatee emperor who makee you workee too hardee."

When the old vendor merely continued to hold forth his tray, Malloy said, "Perhaps he doesn't know any English at all, Chief."

"Everybody in the Orient understands that sort of talk," grumbled Ashton. "He is afraid to tell me what he thinks, with the military around."

The vendor, deciding that the crazy *Amerika-jin* had no intention of making any purchase, began to back away toward the willow's shade, where he kept the covered pail containing the chunks of ice which he shaved when he saw likely customers arriving at the gate. As he backed off, not neglecting to bow courteously to the M.P.'s and the Japanese policemen, he muttered something.

Ignoring Davies, Ashton asked an M.P., "What'd he say?"

The soldier said to Davies, "Does the major wish me to repeat it?"

"The major has nothing to say about it," said Ashton; and the soldier, in the moment before Davies nodded, with his own face absolutely blank, guessed that Brass had plenty of troubles of their own these days. "Speak up," ordered Ashton, "What did the poor old fellow say?"

"He said," the M.P. began, while his companion on guard

duty looked away in a hurry, "that you say *'ee, ee, ee,'* as if you were a… as if you were howling because a man was throwing rocks at you."

"Nonsense," stated Ashton. When he saw the smiles on his fellow delegates' faces, he fumed to Davies, "Look here, Major, aren't you going to correct the attitude of this soldier? Such a remark calls for disciplining, and—"

"The omitted word," said Lew placidly, "was female dog."

One of the delegation laughed; another said, "You asked for it, Ashton. You'd better take lessons in Japanese, or rely on an interpreter."

Malloy sprang to Ashton's defense. "How do we know that either the soldier or the officer translated correctly?"

"I didn't," said Lew solemnly, "and I'm sorry." *And I've got this coming, too,* he told himself, not solemnly at all, as he decided what to say next. "I erred in translation. Female dog wasn't the word. It was—"

"That'll do," shouted Ashton; and from the glance which he shot at Davies, as almost all of the others were laughing, Lew knew that now he had made a personal enemy in place of the previous impersonal one. But he was satisfied to have it so, because Ashton's importance to the other men in the delegation had been cut down. "How long do we stand here waiting?" Ashton asked shrilly, his face more red and flushed than even Tokyo heat warranted.

DAVIES FELT much better as he led the way through the gate and into Nakanocho, the broad middle street, on which could be seen no signs of visitors, either Americans or Japanese. He did not intend to take his party to a guide-house, the usual custom, where arrangements should be made to visit Number Nineteen or any of the other houses of entertainment; Americans, including an Army officer, were not expected to follow polite routine, which began with tea and cakes and the engaging of dancing girls, with the final geisha not seen unless *naji-mi-kin,* the payment of intimacy money, allowed her to sip tea or sake and also watch the maids whose single task was to dance and serve.

And Davies was keenly amused at the idea of returning to Number Nineteen as an honored, at least outwardly, guest. At Nineteen he had been the *hakoya* always given the dirtiest of jobs. But at Nineteen, frequented by high officials who came for entertainment and Scotch brought in from Singapore, he had picked up those sometimes fragile threads which later he had been able to weave into an understandable dangerous pattern, and then do something to thwart what the Japanese intended.

He thought briefly, as he walked and explained the district automatically, of Suriga, the manager of Nineteen, and of the weight of Suriga's foot and the expertness with which the fat little Nip had planted it where it hurt the most. The Jap had not been sadistic. He never kicked Koropok unless there was an audience, and he did it then because the audience enjoyed seeing the degradation of an Ainu pariah. He did it because it brought profit to Nineteen.

The round-faced manager had been spoken to, but not in such a way as to cause him to believe that he was singled out from the other house managers. Davies, knowing the type of Japanese who had visited Number Nineteen, had seen to it that Nineteen was kept under surveillance, although not obviously. He had doubted from the start whether anything would come of it; Suriga was a clever little devil interested in only one thing, profit, whether it be in yen or dollars.

He was half smiling to himself, recalling his kennel in Nineteen, where he had slept only when there were no duties, which was seldom, and comparing it to orange juice and coffee after his morning shower....

"I see some of our boys down that street," said Malloy. "Are you trying to prevent us from seeing what is going on there?"

Davies knew what it was before he turned his head. He knew exactly what was of interest to the GI's, and, without speaking, led the delegation off the Middle Street, Nakanocho. There had been a flurry when places such as the soldiers were examining had been closed; it had something to do with soldier-officer discrimination because of price differences, Davies remembered vaguely, although this wasn't anything even distantly related to his work in Tokyo. Probably a complaint to the States, and the resultant moans, had changed the original order.

The structures on the side street within the Yoshiwara were European in design and were two-storied. The first series of buildings which the delegation passed or paused before were fenced with bamboo, with photographs of the girls displayed behind the fence, each moon face framed in gold and marked with the geisha name of the particular girl. All had the proper geisha prefixes of "young" or "little" by means of which geisha could always be identified. There was Wakayuki, Young Lucky, and Wakakoma, Young Filly, and Ko-tei, Little Docile, and Ko-hiro, Little Wide Spreading. There was even Wakakiyo, which honored the geisha with the name of Young Pure, in case anyone could believe that.

At the end of each fenced building was the booking office, with a Japanese behind the open window, and Davies noted that where the prices had formerly been one, two, or five yen, there was certainly inflation now.

Beyond these picture houses were the showrooms, and it was in front of the lattice fronted places that the soldiers were gathered, orderly and grinning. Inside of the showrooms were girls, dressed in red and purple, and seated in rows as they displayed their charms to prospective customers. Some smoked long thin pipes, others the cigarettes which had been passed in to them. Their black and shining hair, the color of licorice, was arranged in fantastic fashion, and ornamented with silver bell-like pendants and paper flowers. Heavy perfume swayed out from the showrooms. Some of the girls piped the words they had learned, "How you do?" and "You want *kisu?*" and "You rike me?" while their thickly powdered faces remained blank, dull, and expressionless. Where sweat had trickled down, there were streaks on the brown lustreless skin beneath.

Ashton said savagely, "I have never seen anything more disgusting. Major Davies, order those men back to their barracks."

"I think we'd better not interfere," said Hartshorn.

"If the major refuses to do it," Ashton snapped, when Davies lit a cigarette and had not spoken, "and you have no interest in protecting our boys, I'll talk to them myself. I would be remiss in my duty to their mothers if I did not."

Davies said, "They all look as if they could take care of themselves, Mr. Ashton. They are behaving. They are getting a kick out of staring at the girls, but you haven't seen any of 'em go in, have you? If—"

Ashton had already walked over to the first group of GI's. "Fellows," he began, "this isn't why you came to Japan. This isn't why—"

"Who says so?" broke in a soldier. He was about to continue when a companion nudged him, and the soldier's eyes shifted so that he saw a major. He shrugged; he turned away as he said something.

"What did you say?" demanded Ashton, near enough to have caught something of the words. "Repeat that, young man!"

Davies said wearily, "You needn't repeat anything, soldier." He strode over to Ashton, "I must ask you not to go beyond your purpose here, Mr. Ashton. You are to investigate and to question, but orders"—Lew's voice sharpened, and he guessed he was being bothered by heat too—"are out."

"This is the second time you have interfered with us," said Malloy.

And the third time, thought Davies, *you rate a punch on the nose.*

He remained silent again, however; and by now he gave over the idea that perhaps something more than acting as guide might result from conducting the party around the city. He was too disgusted to care, either.

"We have seen this phase," said Hartshorn. "Let us go on, Major."

Lew turned abruptly and led the way back to Middle Street. What damned foolishness, in Nineteen, would come next?

WHERE NUMBER Nineteen, in Japanese style, was located, it was hot as elsewhere, a harsh Tokyo heat; but it was cleaner than on the side street of picture houses and showrooms, and more quiet. The way was familiar to Davies, although it was strange to be walking to Nineteen, where the red lanterns hung, as a free man instead of shambling up toward it as a tattered and filthy Ainu pariah. And it was even more strange, on entering Number Nineteen, to be welcomed by bowing, smiling maids, and to be directed to the principal guest room into which the manager, fat Suriga, came breathlessly.

He smiled all over his face, and bowed, and said, "Oh! Ssso prenty geisha! Oh! Scotchu whisuky! Oh! Prease down sssit!"

Every time Suriga bowed, which was with every sentence, Davies wanted to kick him. And when the manager hissed, "*Oshii koto ni wa*... it is a pity that we are to be subjected to the illiteracies of these pigs," to the woman in charge of the geisha of the house, "and we will offer them the least attractive girls," he managed to keep his face straight.

"Do you speak English?" asked Malloy.

"Oh! Yesss!"

"We are supposed to sit down," Davies suggested.

Ashton said, "I have no intention of sitting down. I am here as an investigator, not as a profligate."

"Suit yourself," said Lew. He sat, at once, on a soft *futon* in the bare room, and all of the delegation, smiling at their clumsiness, followed his example; all save Ashton and Malloy. "If you want to learn anything," Davies added, "it will come only if you at least put up a pretense that you are not antagonistic. But, as I said, that is up to you."

Hartshorn remarked, "There is a good deal we want to learn, Major Davies, and I, for one, am listening to you."

Plucked *samisen* told Davies that girls were practicing or entertaining. He heard singing—

"Iya no o-kata no
Shinetsu yori ka
Suita o-kata no
Mura ga yoi."

—and guessed that the singer, certainly, had been engaged, because the words of the song assured the listener that better than the kindness of the disliked was the violence of the beloved.

New pale green mats were on the floor, flowers had been carefully arranged in a low bowl, and a valuable painting, one Davies had not seen when he had been at Nineteen, hung against the alcove wall; Nineteen must be prosperous. And the thirteen-year-old serving maids who padded into the room, one with a tea set and the other with sake and sake cups, were both finely attired.

The maids paused on entering the room, and, trays in hand, docilely glanced at Suriga. He blinked momentarily, and then called, *"Kore via do iu imi de gozaimasho? Hakoya! Mo yoroshii ka!"* but without any of the venom in his voice such as Davies, as Koropok, had heard if he had formerly been only half as slow as was the present *hakoya* in placing the stands about for the guests' bowls and cups.

Maybe there's a union now, thought Davies. *Maybe managers don't kick hakoyas around.* He thought briefly of telling this to the delegation, but again didn't care what interpretation they put on anything, although he wanted to give Hartshorn and the other honest delegates whatever break he could.

He began to explain the procedure in Nineteen as Malloy shot a first question at the manager, concerning the number of soldiers and officers who came to Nineteen; he kept on talking until the *hakoya* arrived and went to the corner where the little lacquered stands were nested; and then he talked automatically, unhearing of an expressed wish from Ashton that he be still.

This is the damndest thing I've seen yet, thought Davies. *Who says Suriga is dumb? He's one smart Nip.*

The *hakoya* at Number Nineteen, whose arrival had brought Davies up short, was a stocky, broad-shouldered, bearded man of about Davies' height, and as swarthy as Lew. And the *hakoya,* although in no such rags as had hung about Koropok during his service at Nineteen, was certainly not a Japanese.

Suriga's hired himself another Ainu, Davies could see. *Somebody who's cheap, and easy to kick around.*

He paid no attention to the questioning; it was just what he expected it would be. But it was fascinating to observe the *hakoya,* whose clumsiness was so different in every way from Japanese deftness, and to think, *That's how I must have acted and looked when I was Koropok here.*

Unable to keep silent, Davies said, "Have you gentlemen ever seen an Ainu? The man putting the stands down for you is one. A pariah. He—"

"There is no such thing as caste in Japan now," interrupted Ashton. He stared at the *hakoya.* "Why, he's a white man!"

"An Ainu," corrected Lew. "One of the original inhabitants of Japan, his ancestors were." Davies, of all the men in the reception room, sensed Suriga's interest in what Ashton had said, and wondered whether he himself had imagined that a hasty glance had gone from master to servant. His own eyes began to appraise the *hakoya;* he bit down a greeting in Ainu, or in the clipped Japanese which the pariahs spoke, because while an American officer could explain being able to speak in Japanese, it was doubtful if anyone in Japan believed that any American officer was conversant with the language or dialect of the pariahs.

IT TOOK Davies a long moment before he truly realized so simple a fact that as far as Suriga was concerned, who had been Koropok's master, whatever an officer of Davies' rank might do would only result in bows.

*Hokuyak stumbled over a
stand, upsetting a short-
necked bottle of sake—but
Suriga's reprimand was mild.*

He said, speaking for the first time in Japanese, "*Sono inu wa
nan' to iu?* Has the dog a name?" and addressing the fat manager.

"*Nihon wo go-zanji desu ka?* You speak Japanese?"

Davies said, "Of course I speak Japanese. How else could I
serve as guide for this honorable and important delegation?"

"Oh, then perhaps you will inform me why they are here?
Do they desire whisky? Girls? What is the purpose of the
honorable visit?"

Davies didn't blame Suriga for being confused. He said, "They desire certain information. This they will obtain through your answers to me. As for myself," Lew went on, "I am curious as to why a pariah serves you,"

Suriga giggled. "During the war," he replied, "I engaged as *hakoya*, and cheaply, an Ainu who was called Koropok, and he was a very good servant if you kicked a little speed into him. This one," said the manager, "has the name of Hokuyak, and by hiring him I show my desire to accede to the recommendation from the authorities that pariahs be afforded an opportunity to earn a living."

He bowed after making the statement.

Hokuyak stumbled over a stand which he had already placed down, upsetting the short-necked bottle of sake which a maid had set on it; Davies waited for the torrent of invective which should have followed, but Suriga's reprimand was mild. As Davies wondered about that, he also began to wonder whether the bearded *hakoya* had stumbled because he had been engaged in listening.

"He is very clumsy," said Davies.

"He has been ill," Suriga said, "and, as you know, honorable Major, it is now forbidden to beat the pariahs."

Davies smiled; he knew this, and he knew a good deal more concerning the Ainus and their customs. So he asked, half turning away as if uninterested in what Suriga might reply, "Was he very sick?"

"I feared he would die," admitted Suriga. "Had he died, what a horrible cost I would have been burdened with! But last week, when other medicines failed, I caused him to be treated with expensive *moxa*"—the wily manager was doing his best to curry favor with fool Americans who were interested in pariahs—"just as if he were a profitable maid. As you can see, he is now well again."

One way or another, decided Lew, although he nodded, *you're a liar. If the man is an Ainu, he would refuse to work, after being sick, until he had seen two full moons cross the sky. If he isn't an Ainu, what's going on?*

Now alert, Davies appeared utterly uninterested. He squatted on the nearest *futon* and took the bowl of sake which was handed him. Then, as he heard Suriga order the *hakoya* back to his other duties, something which Hokuyak should have learned in his first day at Nineteen, he said, *"Nesan! Biiru ippon motte kite o kure,"* because cold beer was preferable to tepid rice wine.

Ashton said, "What'd you just say? I hope you've told the Jap that the Ainu is a man just as we are."

Maybe he is, agreed Davies to himself; and there came to him the notion that as this bearded servant reached the doorway to the long corridor that the fellow half paused, as if he might be listening.

Davies had already made up his mind that he wanted a check on a pariah who was named Hokuyak; he changed his mind about a delay, and, leaning forward so the maid could light his cigarette, said, "I wish to speak to the *hakoya*."

"He is very stupid," stuttered Suriga. A pucker of worry appeared between the manager's eyes as he was undoubtedly trying to figure out a better refusal, all of which was being complicated, to Davies' secret amusement, by the fact that the *hakoya* had not hurried away.

"These gentlemen," smiled Lew disarmingly, "desire to hear from a former pariah something regarding his treatment by a Japanese, yourself."

The pucker disappeared and Suriga's face became bland again. Davies was pretty sure that Suriga almost sighed with relief as the manager told his servant Hokuyak to reply truthfully to whatever the honorable officer-*san* asked of him.

"*Hakoya,*" said the man who had been Koropok, "were you very sick?"

"What're you asking him?" demanded Malloy.

Davies explained patiently, "About his health," and waited, while the maid who had returned with his bottle of beer uncapped it and poured it into his glass, for the swarthy, bearded man's reply.

It came gutturally and slowly. "*Wak'r'mas'.*" The black-visaged hakoya spoke in clipped Ainu-fashion when saying that he did not understand.

Hmm, thought Davies. *Maybe he is an Ainu, and ducked the question because it's unlucky, according to the Ainus, to mention illness.* There was another way to get at what had aroused Lew's doubts. He said, "*Moxa itande iru?* Was the application of *moxa* painful to you? Did you cry with pain?"

MALLOY ASKED, "Now what's being said?" and that, Davies guessed, was asked because Malloy wanted to record it all in the notebook. Treatment of pariahs did not come within the scope of the investigation of fraternization, but Lew had found out that Ashton and Malloy had other interests, and how the Ainus were being treated in Japan, particularly if the treatment were such that they could beat on the C.O. about it, was something they wouldn't pass up.

"I asked him how he was treated when he was sick," said Lew.

Ashton wanted to know, "And how was he treated?"

Davies saw that the word, now, referred to the manner in which the *hakoya* had been cared for, and not to actual medical treatment; but he chose to misunderstand. He took a swallow of beer, glanced at the unlabeled bottle, decided that it tasted like fine Dutch beer, took another provokingly deliberate draught, and then began, "When other remedies failed"— Davies did not intend to voice his doubts—"*moxa* was applied as a remedy, and—"

"What's *moxa?*"

"A cautery," said Davies. "The word has become an English one. Properly, in original Japanese, it was *mogusa,* contracted to *moxa. Mogusa* translates into 'fiery herb' or 'burning herb.' Bits of the herb are rolled together to form a crude cone, which is applied to the back or the backs of the legs, and then lit. *Moxa* is said, by the Japanese, to be a cure for all human ailments. The manager of Nineteen," Lew said, just in case Suriga understood enough English to know what was being said, or if there should be anything to Davies' doubts about the bearded *hakoya*, "paid for this costly form of treatment."

Ashton frowned. "Why this sudden interest in something far from what you have been ordered to do for us?" and Davies believed that Ashton's ire had risen after his question concerning the Ainu's treatment had drawn a blank, instead of another opportunity to needle the occupation authorities. "What makes you so curious about a servant, anyhow?"

Davies saw, or thought he saw, a flicker in the *hakoya's* deepest dark eyes, a corresponding one in Suriga's, as if the manager understood the simple English of the question. Lew's irritation rose to anger. He half wished that he hadn't started to check on the *hakoya;* on the other hand, he dared not stop now, if there were really anything fraudulent about the pariah.

He said the obvious thing, ignoring the interruption, and spoke sharply. "Let me see the scar, *hakoya!*"

And if there isn't one, Davies said to himself, *the M.P.'s can come and get a pair of liars, right here and now.*

But, almost to Lew's surprise, there was a scar, the mark left by the burning of *moxa.* And it was a fresh one, too, although on the servant's chest instead of on the back. As a matter of fact there were several scars, all burned on the skin at the same time, and, as Davies stared at the fresh and angry cicatrices, they seemed to writhe into the shape of an insect instead of being separate and distinct scars. But this could have been caused by burning herb-fragments dropping from the smolder of the cones of *moxa.* Even so, Lew believed that his eyes were tracing out the long slender body and the mandibles of an insect....

"Such barbarous treatment must be ended," stated Ashton. "Make a note, Malloy, to remind me to ask the general why it hasn't been done already. Or," he continued, "has the major fooled us? Was the poor fellow actually tortured?"

Davies forced himself to stop wondering about master and servant. He wanted to save the C.O. from more nonsense; he asked, "For what?"

Malloy suggested, "Possibly to make him vote as his master wanted him to vote at the elections."

"Now I've heard everything," said Lew.

Davies was so utterly disgusted that as he picked up his glass he thought, *To hell with the whole business.* Lord, but it was hot! Why get worked up? The general could take care of himself. If a pair of idiots wanted to turn an investigation of fraternization into heaven knew what, was it Davies' affair? If Suriga hired a pariah, as Koropok had been hired, that was Suriga's business. And if the man named Hokuyak worked so cheaply that Suriga was willing to spend good money on *moxa*, why should Llewelyn Davies give a damn? And if the doctor who had applied the burning herb had been so careless that the scar looked like a bug, that wasn't anything to get excited over, either.

The payoff was that Ashton and Malloy believed Suriga had the slightest interest in politics. Suriga thought of one thing, and one only. Money. Gold. Silver. Yen. Dollars. And the shrewd Jap got them, too.

Davies told himself, *Stop looking for trouble,* but that demand couldn't explain away his suspicions about the manager of Nineteen and his *hakoya*.

HARTSHORN TRIED to start the investigation. "Major Davies," he said, "find out how many soldiers come here, on the average, during a week, and how much money is spent, and particularly whether soldiers meet these girls elsewhere on—ah—companionable grounds...."

As the delegation's head continued explaining what he wanted to know regarding fraternization, Davies saw that the scarred *hakoya* turned as if to go. *As if he knows he won't be asked another question,* decided Lew. *And if that's true, he understands English.*

Davies, in spite of his having had enough of the affair,

stopped the departure of the squat, bearded servant with, "*Dochira ye irasshaimasu?* Where are you going? Were you given permission to leave?"

He does a pretty fair job of acting like an Ainu, thought Lew, as the *hakoya* stood with hanging head. *But I did a better job. I wouldn't have stopped until my master, Suriga, gave me the order. He's a phony!*

Taking a refreshing swallow of beer, which was cool and good, Davies remarked, "This is fine beer, Suriga. Where was it stolen from? Java? Sumatra?"

Davies knew that he had two fish on his line; he was trying to play them both at the same time, and yet not let either think the hooks had been swallowed; and he had to handle the delegation at the same time also.

"I bought it from a man," said Suriga. "It is my desire to serve the guests of this house with the finest of everything." He bowed. "May the *hakoya* go about his duties now, officer-*san?*"

"In a moment," Davies agreed. *Anxious to get him away?* wondered Lew. *Afraid he is showing too much interest?* He faced the stocky servant. "*Hakoya*" he asked without a change in his voice, "do you live in a pariah village here in Tokyo?"

Hokuyak said, "No."

Smiling, Davies drained the last of the beer, and waited for the maid to pour the liquid remaining in the bottle into his glass.

"You desire the records of this house?" suggested Suriga. "I will furnish them gladly, officer-*san,* in order that your gentlemen can see who comes here."

Davies gave no sign that the manager of Nineteen had not only revealed that he certainly had learned enough English, since the occupation of Japan, to understand Hartshorn's request for information, but also that the fat, shrewd Suriga wanted to put an end to the questioning of his servant. Why?

"Thank you," Lew nodded. He went on placidly, "This is indeed splendid beer." He was lifting the refilled glass, as if about to drink, when he shot at the scarred Hokuyak, "Quickly! Where is your home?" and, before the *hakoya,* if he were an Ainu, could have done more than pull his wits together, the American had jumped up and grabbed the man by his short kimono. "Speak!"

The bearded lips had tightened, instead of going lax with fear; one of the servant's hands had involuntarily moved to tear the American's hand away.

Suriga said hastily, "He comes from Ikadebetsu," and Davies was reasonably certain that the manager, to avert trouble, had blurted what might be the truth. "Oh, he is a very stupid servant, and illy trained," apologized Suriga. "Do not punish him, officer-*san!* Hokuyak! Dog! Apologize to the *danna-san* for your stupidity. Oh, you have disgraced this house! Apologize!"

The *hakoya* muttered something which Davies accepted; and then Lew was aware of what Ashton was saying, "I intend to report your action, Major Davies, and I intend to ask your commanding officer to have you replaced. Don't attempt to dissuade me, Hartshorn! I've seen enough to know that the major is entirely unsympathetic with unfortunate people. After seeing how he has acted with an Ainu, I can well imagine how he must be with soldiers under his command. I am," said Ashton, "a fair man. I am giving you a chance, here and now, Major Davies, to explain, if you can, your amazing conduct. What have you to say?"

Ikadebetsu, Lew was thinking. *That's in Hokkaido, probably, because "betsu" is the Ainu word for "river". Did this battling Ainu, who isn't one, come to Tokyo by way of Ikadebetsu? And what's he doing at Nineteen?*

Whatever it was, so far as it concerned Suriga, money would be involved, and not politics. Were the pair working together, each for his own purpose? That was a possibility. Or was the imitation pariah one of the vultures who had swooped down here to do some profitable scavenging, as others were doing, gamblers, procurers, pimps, swindlers, gathering from the

corners of Asia, from Macao, Hong-Kong, Manila, from Vlad-
ivostok and Nanking and Calcutta? And what about the mark
of the *moxa*... the scar burned, and not completely healed, on
the *hakoya's* chest which looked like an insect. What insect? A
scorpion?

"Did you hear what I said?" insisted Ashton.

"Why, yes," said Lew mildly; and he had heard it, too. "I'm
sorry, sir. I was thinking about something else."

MALLOY, HAVING done some savage writing in
the notebook, looked up to where Davies was standing. "You
have given us no cooperation," he remarked. "I now realize the
difficulties of investigation, and what is wrong with our occupation where the military refuse to relinquish control. And yet I
venture to say, gentlemen, that an officer of a People's Army
would have accorded us better treatment, although we continue to refuse to allow our allies a hand in governing Japan—"

"We'll stick to fraternization," Hartshorn broke in; but when
he glanced at the major it was not happily, but as if the officer
had let him down.

Major Davies' thoughts had been far from GI's drinking beer
with Nip geishas; he asked Suriga, "Have other servants been
sick here? Was it necessary to apply the *moxa* to anyone else?"

"Not to anyone," said the manager, smiling broadly and
showing every tooth in his head. "Oh, no! Ask them, officer-
san!"

Why are you so pleased? wondered Lew. *Because it didn't cost
you money? Or because I'd get excited if I saw more Nips with scars
on their chests?*

Then he asked, "And yourself, honorable manager?"

He saw the infinitesimal veiling of Suriga's eyes, and the
shifting of feet as the manager sought to stop the tensing of
his pudgy body. What the *hakoya* Hokuyak might have done
in revealing himself, if the man did anything, was beyond
Davies' vision; but now Lew believed that the unscrupulous

manager of Number Nineteen, beneath his fine silks, was branded with the scars of *moxa*.

If I say, "Let me see," he will say that he has been sick, Lew thought, *but he will say nothing, Jap-fashion, unless I press for an answer.*

This Davies did not do. The pair were suspicious, but could argue themselves out of their suspicions if the American seemed too stupid to follow up what had happened. Nor did Davies want to bring matters to a head, not until he knew, for example, what the mark meant; what he did want was to start checking, although certainly not here. And he wanted to get away, and do it without exciting the pair again.

He knew how to do this.

"Gentlemen," said Davies, "I regret that I have lost your confidence—"

"If you ever had it," Malloy said.

"And another officer will take my place," continued Lew. He stopped, picked up the glass of warming beer, and finished it. Headquarters wasn't going to like this. Not any part of it. Even so, and while Hartshorn was saying that after all it was not entirely the major's fault and that he himself disliked trouble, Davies smiled and said, "Good morning, gentlemen."

He returned Suriga's bow politely. Hokuyak, just inside the doorway, stepped aside to let the American pass. Davies did not glance at the other. He was completely satisfied, because the *hakoyo* had moved without an order from the manager, that the squat, bearded man was not an Ainu.

In the corridor, a soldier was being pulled back into one of the rooms by another G.I. When the soldier saw Davies, he shouted, "Ye damn dirty yella devil! What ye doin' in uniform? Get out'f it!"

"Sir," said his companion, "he's seein' things."

"Look't his face," the soldier yelled. "Look't his hair. Yella!"

The black-haired Davies said, "Stick to beer, soldier."

The loud words brought not only Suriga but several of the delegation into the corridor.

"Yes, sir," promised the excited soldier's companion. "From now on, it'll be nothin' but beer, sir."

"Too much sake socks you," Davies said.

"It wasn't sake, sir. We was tryin'—"

Suriga had sidled between soldiers and officer. "Nice eatsomesing," he said to the soldiers. "Nice tea. *Sssss!* Nice sreep on bed? Oh, yesss!"

Davies turned and was gone before any of the delegation could start questioning him about anything. He had a question of his own to ask of the proper person. More, he had his first real inkling of what might be going on.

If he were correct about it, the presence of the imitation pariah made sense; and if the fellow who called himself Hokuyak was convinced that the American knew what was going on, Davies, who knew the vultures of the Orient, had every reason to believe that he himself would get a knife in the back.

CHAPTER III

A BREAK IN THE WEB

IT WAS a strange city, Sapporo in Hokkaido, more like an American city than Japanese, for there were wide avenues, tree lined, and granite and solid brick buildings, and well kept parks. And while there were the customary things found in small Japanese cities, the Shinto shrines and Buddhist temples and inevitable eating shops, and the filthy huddle of squalid Ainu hovels on the outskirts, on this north island where the majority of the pariahs now lived, Sapporo was dominated by an enormous brewery. Major Davies, in his comfortable breezy room in the Occidental-style hotel, could see the brewery buildings, and the tall chimneys there, of brick, cut across his vision of the hills in which the Ainus also lived, those not needed by the Japanese to bury their dead, mend footwear, and slaughter animals for Japanese consumption.

Behind the first hills were the grim forested mountain fastnesses where a few of the sturdiest Ainus remained, partially free unless their conquerors centuries ago had use for them. The town of Ikadebetsu was somewhere in those peaks, in what amounted to a tiny pocket, a sort of trading place, but without sufficient land on which even a Japanese could tear out a living.

In front of the hills was a rich and magnificent plain, where Lew could see, a little beyond Sapporo, the poles of hop-fields.

Even after Japan's surrender, Sapporo was a busy place. Sawmills were engaged in turning out lumber for flattened Tokyo; the brewery was taxed to capacity in an effort to keep up with GI thirsts in the hot season. After the stagnation of Tokyo, Davies enjoyed watching activity, just as he was enjoying the glass of beer which he had ordered on reaching his room.

He was in uniform. The room had been reserved for an AMG officer—which Davies was not, although papers and charts from the bag he opened seemed to indicate that he was. The second bag, unopened, contained clothes, although an offer from a housemaid to open it and arrange his clothes in the closet had been refused politely.

The hotel management knew that Major Davies had come to confer with Americans in Sapporo, and a good thing this was, because strange matters appeared to occur in the city, although it was not to be expected that any *Amerika-jin* would learn about them or do anything if he did. The major had explained in halting Japanese to Matsugamo, the head clerk, that he would leave the city from time to time. The Japanese supposed that a little unofficial hunting and fishing would be involved in the absences, and, wanting to be helpful, mentioned places where salmon teemed, or where woodcock, wild duck, and pheasant could be shot. But from the American's difficulty in understanding what Matsugamo said, it was obvious that the officer only knew such common phrases as "I will go on a journey" and "Bring me a bottle of beer" and "Where is the *benjo?*"

The major was satisfied with what the management thought they knew about him, but much less satisfied with what he himself knew regarding his being in Sapporo on his way to an Ainu settlement, Ikadebetsu.

And I'd better make good, he told himself, legs on the window sill, *or the C.O. will fry me in oil when I get back.*

The general, and everyone at H.Q., were probably pretty unhappy right now, Lew guessed, and were being well needled by the fraternization boys, particularly Ashton and Malloy. Davies was not at all sure but that the C.O. felt that Major Davies, with a bellyful and having messed things up, hadn't run out. The general couldn't sneak off. He had to stay in Tokyo and take it, take the heat and yowls about fraternization and elections and politics and everything else. But the Old Man had been decent about it. He had said, "You may have stumbled on something, Davies. Go have a look. But if you get a chance to do some shooting, or hook on to a big salmon, don't let me hear about it."

Before going to the C.O., Davies had talked at length with the chief medical officer. Davies had based his belief on the fact that anyone associated with Suriga would be concerned, as was the manager of Nineteen, with profit and not with politics, and therefore the imitation Ainu and Suriga were tangled in a deal from which they expected to make money. At Nineteen, money was made from entertainment by geisha, from serving food, and from alcohol; Davies knew the details because of his servitude there. The liquors, when admirals and generals had come to the house during the war, first to celebrate and then to submerge their misery, included everything from a to z, from absinthe to what Suriga insisted was a zombi; there were vintage wines and Culmbacher beer as well as sake and purple local brandy.

The medical officer had agreed that although when the

soldier had shouted the word yellow he might have been using it as an epithet, it was equally possible at Nineteen that the soldier saw Davies as truly yellow in appearance. This opinion was strengthened when Davies told the medical officer that the manager of Number Nineteen had prevented the GI's companion from saying what, exactly, had been served the soldier— which hadn't been beer.

Vision could be colored by drugs, the medical officer had explained; and H.Q. wanted such things kept far from the occupation forces. Too much alcohol, in some cases, caused blue vision. If a person saw things as if tinged with green, an overdose of quinine could be held responsible. Brown vision was often caused by caffeine, and seeing red, the M.O. said, was brought about by an alkoloid called duboisin. Yellow vision came from wormwood, and from wormwood when combined with alcohol, anise, marjoram, and angelica, to make the liqueur known as absinthe.

The M.O. had doubted the presence of absinthe in Tokyo. Perhaps a bottle or two had been brought in from French Indo-China, although it was scarce there. A supply of the liqueur sufficient so that it could be served soldiers was extremely doubtful, although, "The boys would go for it," admitted the medical officer, "because one fellow would tell another what it does."

This included the drinker being carried away in ecstasy, in being a part of imaginary unrestrained revelry. The fascination of the absinthe was intense, said the M.O. Opium, against which H.Q. fought, was no worse.

NUMBER NINETEEN had about everything in liquors, Davies had said, and, during the war, Suriga had strange sources of supplies, even including a naval officer enamored of one of Nineteen's girls. Was the imitation pariah one who supplied Number Nineteen now? Couldn't a supposed Ainu get around, as Koropok had done, safely and without being suspected nor detected?

"But where'd he get quantities of absinthe?" the M.O. had argued. "Manufacture was stopped long ago, Major."

"I don't know. And yet you say that yellow vision is caused by absinthe, a word Suriga prevented the soldier from saying."

The doctor had shrugged; Davies, then, decided that the place to begin checking on Hokuyak had to be Ikadebetsu, even if for no better reason than the fact that Suriga had blurted out the name when cornered.

"Thanks for the information," Lew had said. "I can end a racket, maybe, if my figuring is right, and a racket handled by the dirtiest people in the world, white scum in the Orient." His preoccupation over, he grinned. "Maybe I can square your helping me out by giving you a report on *moxa* as it is used here, if you are interested. I... What's so damn funny about that?" asked Davies, puzzled.

"Absinthe, Major," chuckled the M.O., "is made from artemesia maritima. *Moxa,* the cautery, is rolled or pulverized leaves of artemesia vulgaris. Same family. The sage family, to be exact. The various species are found almost everywhere. In America, Europe, Asia. You—" the doctor stopped; it was he, this time, who looked puzzled—"you seem a trifle excited, Major?" he said, instead of whatever expression he had intended to add.

Davies nodded then; here on his chair in Sapporo, he recalled how excited he had been. Because couldn't there be a connection between the plant from which absinthe was made, one sage, and the plant used as *moxa,* another sage? Couldn't the *moxa* mark be the easily-explained symbol of a gang, the means by which men could identify themselves? And now, in Sapporo, he had two things to work on. The past of Hokuyak, for one thing, and the cicatrices on the false *hakoya's* chest, for another, the marks of *moxa* applications which, accidentally or by intention, had formed the resultant scars in the shape of a scorpion.

The "*Gomen nasai!*" of a houseboy outside the door prepared Davies for the visitors whom he was expecting. Three men entered, two lieutenants, English and American, and a Russian captain. Davies' brass was sufficient so that it was the others who saluted; Davies began playing his part immediately by failing to rise when he returned them. The American lieutenant blinked, the English lieutenant stiffened, and the Russian captain's face flushed with annoyance.

Lieutenant Case, with infantry rifles on his lapels, trusted that Major Davies would not object because the lieutenant had informed his allied colleagues of the major's expected arrival. The major did not object. Lieutenant Abernathy, clearing his throat, hoped that the major had a decent journey north. The major said that he had. The Russian, Captain Ogrodowski, wanted to know if the major brought with him the authority to change the management of the brewery, which was increasingly more profitable, and give the brewery over to the workers. The major didn't have confiscating authority, Davies said, and went on to add, coldly, that personally he'd just as soon not be bothered by opinions on management, and that the one thing he was interested in was facts and figures.

I did that good, Davies told himself, seeing the disgust on the Russian's face. *He's had enough of me already.*

Lew didn't intend to be handicapped by men who would want to stick with him. If he accomplished anything, it would be on his own.

Captain Ogrodowski said in excellent English, "I see that my information was correct, Major Davies. You have no interest in the common people, have you?"

Now who in hell told you that? wondered Lew. And he was aware that if the captain knew about him, or thought that he did, the captain would report back to the Japanese capital concerning what Davies did in Sapporo. *Somebody,* realized Davies, beginning to believe some of the things which G-2 officers had worried about, *must keep a damned good check on what we do.*

"I am interested in carrying out my orders," said Davies.

The English Abernathy said, "We are at your service, sir."

Davies shrugged. "I will call on you later. As regards the brewery, Sapporo's chief industry, has there been trouble there, as the captain hinted?"

"Yes, sir," the American lieutenant said promptly, "but not labor troubles. I don't agree with Captain Ogrodowski. No, sir. The directors and the superintendent have been scared out of their boots. They're afraid to go near the brewery unless they have a police guard. The captain says that the workers they've exploited are getting ready to take their revenge, but that isn't the way it looks to me, Major Davies. But I don't know what's got 'em frightened, sir."

"They fear the wrath of the masses," snapped the Russian. "There can be no other reason. None. I have already told you that, haven't I?"

You and Ashton would make a good pair, thought Lew. *A couple of statement-makers.* He himself had not the slightest desire to get mixed up in the disagreement; he was sorry for the out-ranked lieutenants nevertheless… and, when he stopped to think, beer was sold to the same places where other liquors, including absinthe, were bought, and the whole thing was interesting.

Davies put out a feeler.

"Couldn't be a racket, could it?" he asked.

"Sir," said Case, "if you saw some of the characters who've gathered in Sapporo, you'd say it could be. They—"

"To Lieutenant Case," broke in the Russian, "a man with an accent is always a racketeer. It is my considered opinion, Major, that—"

Davies took a leaf from the stodgiest colonel he had ever encountered. "Put it in writing," he said curtly. "Now, if you will excuse me—"

The Russian captain's hand jerked up in an angry salute; Davies himself was not amused by the fact that an American officer, in Tokyo, had been spied upon and his actions reported.

Undoubtedly he would be watched here, also, which would certainly add to the difficulties normally expected.

But, *Some fun they'll have,* Davies thought, picking up his cap when the three officers had gone, and preparing to follow them, *when they try to figure out, from what I do that they see, what I'm up to.*

HE BEGAN what he had planned right at the hotel desk, asking the head clerk about entertainment to be found in Sapporo, because he, the major, wanted a little relaxation before much dull work… and the entertainment started not far from the hotel, where, according to the clerk and the newly painted sign, COKTALES and LICKERS could be enjoyed within. There was a beer sign on the outer wall, with the Japanese characters painted out and replaced by the information that "Our Biiru is so Sweet and Simpul that no Injury come from Too Much Drink."

Like the signs, the interior of the almost empty place was hybrid. The lanterns and bowls of carefully arranged flowers remained, but the mats and cushions and low stands were gone. The big room was electrically lighted; there were long tables, bare, along which a few Japanese were seated uncomfortably in chairs, with beer, dull in color, before them; at the end of the room was something set up to look like a bar, behind which were two bartenders.

Both hurried forward to welcome an *Amerika-jin* with bows and to lead him over to a table; but the uniformed guest preferred to stand at the bar, which was an American habit. He ordered whisky without *tansan,* another American custom; straight whisky, Lew had planned, was more easily disposed of than beer or highballs, and, of course, would be supposed to act more speedily.

It was at his fourth drink—with the other three in the square Japanese spitting box at his feet, poured there when the bartenders scurried out to serve customers, any of the recently entered ones who might have been checking on Davies as he had been

The rotund Japanese bowed several times. "Oh, prease, can make buy drink for officer-san?"

similarly observed in Tokyo—that he asked, in a blurring voice, "O Yoshiwara mitai mono?" and accepted a card from one of the bartenders. Promise of excellent entertainment was printed on the card, and the address where it could be obtained.

When he turned the card over, because all Japanese advertisements were thriftily printed on the reverse, he began to laugh, and his laughter, spontaneous and not feigned, made the Japanese in the place sure that the American was drunk. All Americans became happy when they drank too much.

On the reverse of the card advertising a geisha house, was printed, TRY BEST ANTI-FLEA PERFUME WATER; *and when you put two and two together,* Lew thought as he laughed, *you certainly have got something.*

His behavior did for him what he hoped it would do; it brought him company in the form of a smiling rotund Japanese, who, after bowing several times to attract Davies' attention, said, "Oh, prease, can make buy drink for officer-*san?*"

And when he does, Lew knew, *I've got to down it, too, because he'll be right beside me.* "O.K.," said Davies. "The same."

When Davies' whisky, and the Japanese' beer, were served, Lew stood sidewise at the bar. He listened to the Japanese prattle about Sapporo and Hokkaido and the fishing and hunting; he saw that two white men were seated at one of the tables, a pair who had him under observation. Davies was feeling better and better, not because of the alcohol but because he was sure that now he was getting ready for a game of wits. Nor did he underestimate his opponents.

He said, to see what would happen, and loudly, "How 'bout showing me 'round in Sapporo. I want to see what's here."

The rotund Japanese was bowing in agreement, but had not yet made it verbal, when the men left their places at the table and came to the makeshift bar. One of them shouldered the Japanese aside and stood between him and Davies; the other introduced himself as a fellow American: "I'm Bill Simpson, Major, and this is Ralph Gentry. If you want to take in the sights, we'll be glad to show you around. You don't want to go with a Nip, do you?"

And while you're doing it, thought Lew, *you'll find out why I'm here, although maybe you think you know already.*

Were these two mixed up with a gang engaged in carrying on traffic in liquors and drugs, common enough in the past, but frowned on in Japan? Or were they connected with a political crew critical of the American administration in Tokyo? If they were either of the two things, wasn't it probable that the rotund Jap, shoved aside but sticking around, would be the other?

"Davies," said Lew, swaying as if under control of the whis-kies. "Sure. Like to see the sights. But I've got work to do—"

"It'll wait," coaxed Gentry. The lack of ribbons on Davies caused the man to add, "Just come from the States, Major?"

Or do you know better? wondered Lew. Swiftly, he went into an act, appearing to be enraged. "Maybe I didn't get into the fighting," he snarled, "but I don't like Japs." With an erratic motion he reached around Simpson, grabbed the rotund Japa-nese by the top of his summer kimono, and pulled it down, but as if it happened accidentally while jerking the pudgy Nip-ponese toward him.

There was no *moxa* mark on the Japanese' chest.

The rotund Nipponese' suavity vanished. He hissed, "*Samu-rai-buta!*" as if involuntarily, very low, with the "sssss!" sound almost obliterating what followed; but Davies' having heard, believed that when the Japanese had called him a pig of a lord, it was pretty clear on which side of the political fence the Nip could be placed. Did this leave the white men mixed up in the liquor traffic; and, if so, could they be identified by the mark of the *moxa?*

This couldn't be determined here, certainly. But if the pair escorted the major to a place of entertainment, where the first thing to happen would be the changing of hot clothes to a thin, cool *yukata,* and nothing else, Davies saw no reason why he wouldn't have a chance for a look-see. It was sufficient reason for him to accept the invitation, which he did.

H E   WA S   about to leave with the pair when two well-dressed Japanese hurried into the shop. Both were elderly; both had worried faces. Up to the bar they hastened, side by side, until they bowed in unison to the apparently intoxicated Amer-ican officer. Their faces were deadly serious; they avoided looking at anyone except the man in uniform.

Keenly alert, Davies saw that while the rotund Japanese jostled rudely against one of the elderly, wrinkled Japanese, as the white man, earlier, had done to him, both white men,

Simpson and Gentry alike, moved slightly aside for the Japanese as they bowed. Davies found the expressions on their faces interesting.

Those are two bad boys, decided Lew. *I'll bet they not only know their way around Sapporo, but Hong-Kong and Macao as well.*

He had the men who called themselves Americans, and the oily, fat Japanese, identified; but what, exactly, was the game being played, which centered around an American officer newly arrived in Sapporo?

One of the old Japanese said earnestly, "*Irasshaimashi;* may I offer my home to you, please? I am Hagawari Shijo, president of the brewery company. I—"

"Pig Shijo," exploded the rotund Japanese, "Dog Shijo. Crusher-of-poor-men Shijo. You wish to get this fool of an American under your control—"

The man who had introduced himself as Simpson began to speak in Japanese, ripping out what he said to the old man so swiftly and slurringly that no American who had learned his Japanese out of a book could have possibly followed what he was insisting; it brought fear to Hagawari Shijo's face, and a slowly growing smile to the round face of the younger Japanese. Davies' own expression remained perfectly blank, stupidly blank. Not until Simpson said finally, to him and in English, "I got you out of that one, Major! The last officer sent here to report was taken to this damned yellow-belly's house, and the old swine filled him so full of lies and false figures that when the officer returned to Tokyo he faced a court martial. It was all kept secret. Did you know about it?"

Davies shook his head.

He knew what Simpson had done; threatened the head of the brewery company with loss of the business by the simple and workable scheme of throwing his, Simpson's, word, as an American businessman, on the side of the movement to take over Sapporo Beer in the name of the people.

That the old Japanese, and his companion, did not protest

seemed to Davies to be proof that while the old men might suspect what Simpson and Gentry were engaged in, they could not prove that the pair were other than businessmen. Davies had no trouble in guessing what interest the scamps had in the brewery workers. *They must be after it themselves,* seemed logical to Lew, *and my arrival has brought it to a head.* It occurred to him also that if the gang could operate under the name of Sapporo Beer, they could get around beautifully, all aside from the tremendous profit to be made from the sale of beer itself to GI's."

It's a tangled web, thought Lew; but he was beginning to see through some of the intricacies. The time had come, he decided, to know if all this was separate from what had started him on the venture, or was part of it.

Ignoring the pleading faces of the two old men, Davies said, "Sick of argument. Too much argument. Don' und'stand. Want to get away. Want to go fishin'. Like fishin'. Don' like girls. Don' want go Yosh'wara. Sleepy."

"Best fishing in the world here," promised Gentry. "You're fortunate, Major. I was planning to go after salmon. Glad to have you along."

And away from here, thought Davies, but what he said, mumblingly, was, "Got t' think. Don' rush me."

It was like being Koropok again and, undetected, watching the wheels go round, except that instead of being the stupid pariah Ainu among Japanese, he was now the dumb occupational officer among scoundrels. The white men, whether marked with *moxa* or not, were bad boys. The rotund Nip, who was in opposition to the manner in which the American authorities were permitting the people of Japan to vote without outside influences, in which view he was encouraged by Captain Ogrodowski as well as by Ashton and Malloy, had the look, to Davies, of a banzai-killer. The way the Jap flared up and boiled over was proof of the latter. A fanatic.

Davies was tired of plot and counterplot. He wanted action,

now that he had an understanding of the forces which were at work. If the two officers on duty here, the American and English lieutenants, sharp young fellows, were bogged down in an effort to keep things straight, he himself, Lew Davies, had no intention of getting involved in a political performance. He wanted to bring matters to a head; and, in a maudlin voice he said, watching closely out of eyes which seemed almost to close with drunken sleep, "Fishin'. Go fishin'. Fish at Ikadebetsu."

He saw the narrowing of Simpson's eyes, heard the quick breath. The rotund Nip began to laugh. Hagawari Shijo said sadly, as if he could expect nothing from an American who knew so little of the north country, "*Dare ni kitta.* There is no fishing there, sir. Only mountains."

There's something there, thought Lew. *Plenty, I'll bet. And I want whatever is there, or whoever is there, to be waiting for me. It'll save time.* He himself took a deep breath, but as if he were attempting to pull himself together. He laughed again; and then, dropping all pretense of drunkenness, said clearly, "If I go on a fishing expedition to Ikadebetsu, I wonder what I'll find?"

He was racing out of the drinking shop before Simpson could do more than start the motion which told of the gun he carried, before Gentry could try to first grab him and then prevent his own companion from revealing the weapon. He was racing at full speed up the street before the pair reached the entrance; but he was, they knew, a marked man. A white man in Sapporo. An officer. So there was nothing to it, whether he skulked in the hotel or sought to reach Ikadebetsu. The damned fool, as Simpson said to Gentry, had to sound off, just like an American.

Soon, Simpson lounged in the shade across the street from the hotel, watchful for the appearance of uniforms which would have probably meant that the major had contacted other officers; Gentry was at the hotel's rear. Simpson had already sent off a message, scrawled on paper and in sufficiently cryptic English, by the first passerby, and in minutes the pair were joined by others, so that Major Llewelyn Davies was going to find it difficult to leave.

Word to the handful of occupational personnel would get him out safely, but to reach Ikadebetsu, with or without an escort, would prove difficult. And if he got there, things would be ready for him.

Davies, able to see from his room what was going on, realized that the stakes were high. He grinned as he continued his preparations; he smoked a cigarette, and thought, sadly, how damned good it tasted.

It was a half hour later, with guests or visitors coming in and out in front, and servants or tradespeople entering and leaving in the rear, that Matsugamo, the head clerk, personally booted out the idiot of an Ainu who must have wandered into the honorable hotel without being seen. The stocky, bearded pariah, clad in filthy blue rags, picked himself up and, head low, shambled away. He passed within a few feet of Gentry, who gave him another kick for good measure; and as he continued on his dejected way, and reached the drinking shop, the rotund Japanese emerged, and stood squarely before him.

"Name, Ainu?" demanded the Japanese.

"Koropok, lord."

The Japanese kicked him also.

CHAPTER IV

KOROPOK THE AINU

IKADEBETSU, FROM Sapporo and the south, could be reached only by a narrow road; the railway, with its bridges and tunnels, avoided the straight line to the north, and even main roads would have no part of the mountains, streams, forests, and impenetrable depths which grew more forbidding as Llewelyn Davies, turned again into Koropok the Ainu, sweated upward in the heat of the short sweltering summer.

There was shade, dense, under the wild magnolias, seventy feet high, and an intense perfume; but the very shade quivered with heat, and the scent of the magnolia blossoms was overpowering. Worse, a giant horsefly, *abu*, abounded in the forests, and made the most of a man whose face, arms, and legs were unclad.

Now and again Davies came in sight of a crude Ainu village, always smelled before seen. He gave all a wide berth, because

"Name, Ainu?" demanded the Japanese... "Koropok, lord." The Japanese kicked him also.

while it had been easy to get out of Sapporo, he did not intend to have anyone from the city, or anyone with whom Simpson might have somehow contacted on the trail ahead, question anyone on the narrow road which led north to Ikadebetsu.

He slept in the open; he ate sparingly of the food which, along with his Ainu tatters, had been in his bag, supplementing it with edible lily bulbs found along the waterways, and with berries. Since he had lived with the Ainus, not only in Tokyo but in the mountains, he knew what to do; one thing he had neglected was a means to catch fish. Enviously, one night, he watched a bearded Ainu standing on a rock in a brawling stream, torch in one hand and spear in another... and while Davies could have taken the salmon from the Ainu after it was caught, for which the fisher would probably have blamed the dreaded earth-spider-spirit, he was afraid that if the account got about, as stories were told and retold in the Orient, someone other than an Ainu might not think that the thief was super-natural. No gentle and peaceful Ainu would rob another Ainu, or anyone else. But a thick slice of salmon, broiled over coals, would have tasted damned good....

Because Davies had been Koropok, where he was under observation every minute, he acted as he had before. His last cigarette had been smoked in the hotel, while he had changed and done some note-writing for the American lieutenant in Sapporo; he had eaten his last decent meal, and even the food which had been in his bag and now was in his pack had been such as a pariah might have. Had he been apprehended, there would have been nothing to show that he was other than a pariah.

To the west, unseen because of mountains, was where the Sea of Japan and the Gulf of Tartary met; to the east, again behind mountains, a railway threaded, and long snow-sheds alternated with tunnels and jungles. Eastward of the railway, however, were rich fields in the valleys, lush with grains, and magnificent orchards where apples, pears, and peaches fruited. The Ainus had long been driven from such land. Left to them were the jagged peaks of the mountains. Those who remained, animated bundles of rags, did the dirtiest work for the Japanese, which included standing in the fields, arms waving, as human scarecrows.

Ikadebetsu came into vision suddenly, all at once, as Davies came out of forest; it was far down, a compact huddle of huts, and, like many places in Hokkaido and Honshu, steam rose from it, the steam of volcanic origin.

Must be the Ainu idea of heaven, thought the weary Davies, because according to pariahs, who spent their lives shivering, life after death was always warm. He saw, from his vantage point, no sign of anything unusual. Thatched huts, one jammed against the next, the roofs black with smoke. The open space dedicated to the feared bear-god, with its peeled pole and wood-shavings at the top. And yet Ikadebetsu was the point from which trouble came. But from the path, which zigzagged down, there was only the squalor of an Ainu settlement to be seen.

If I've come just for the walk, Lew told himself, *I'm ass number one.*

He could see Ainu men in the village, and this surprised him. Every man able to walk should have been out in the forest, hunting the deer and bear which were the mainstay, together with dried fish, of the villagers' diet. He was rather pleased about that, however; it would make Koropok less conspicuous, and, to anyone except another Ainu, all of the bearded pariahs looked alike. The one reason he could figure as to why the men were about was that there must have been a death in the forest—an Ainu killed by a bear—and the others had returned, according to custom, to satisfy the spirit of the dead man.

Davies, adjusting his empty pack, started down the path, his story ready; without hesitation, he entered the first hut, as was proper for a stranger, and, speaking in the clipped Japanese which meant that he had lived in one of the settlements outside a Nipponese city, asked the way to the house of the chief.

A dull word or two from the Ainu inside the hut, uttered

without interest and without an upward glance, gave Davies the direction and location.

The Nips must've been beating on him, decided Lew. *Forest Ainus ought to have more pep.* He did not say anything, but, in true Ainu fashion, shambled away, toward the chief's larger hut, and between rows of hovels which gave a man scarcely room enough to pass. He saw the familiar sights, heard the familiar sounds of women who pounded wild grains to be mixed with bear fat; only when he reached the space of earth where the peeled pole stood, with the chief's hut beyond, did he see anything different; and even this merely aroused his curiosity, and was unimportant. There were three tassels of shavings tied to the top of the pole. Davies had never seen more than one. *Gives me something to ask about, and start conversation,* decided the American as he stepped inside.

REED MATTING was under his feet. The room was so dark, being windowless, that it took him time to determine what or who was in it; whoever was, squatted beside the low sleeping platform, seemed to have moved, to have made some sort of gesture with his or her hands... and this, again, surprised Davies, because when a person entered an Ainu dwelling, those within should remain stockstill, lest the man who entered might think that the hut's owner was reaching for a weapon. Davies saw, shortly, that two men were crouched on the floor, on the matting; at the fireplace, where smoke hovered, a woman stirred at the cooking-pot; but whether she was young or old, a first wife or one acquired in the bearded chief's more recent years, the newcomer could not determine.

He said, "*Kom' wa,*" as was proper; neither of the two men replied. Then Koropok, typically an Ainu, pleaded, "*Membo' g' no'*... I hunger."

The older of the pair, the chief, jerked his head toward the fireplace, which was the invitation.

I've never seen an Ainu act like this, thought Davies. He began again, "*Mako' n' sh'barak.* I have been gone long."

The chief should have asked him where he had been, and about his own village; again the old pariah remained silent. Nor was the stranger invited to set his pack down, nor to accept the house as his own.

"I have killed a Japanese," said Koropok, proudly. "I have run away. Can I be hidden here?"

This was his trump card; but he had not expected to play it like this, not to a silent, seemingly hostile chief.

"*Nan' sh' kit'?*" the chief said slowly, whispering. "Why have you come?"

"To hide," said Koropok.

The man beside the chief muttered, "Nothing is hidden from them."

*There were three tassels of shavings at the
top of the pole before the chief's hut.*

From whom? *What goes on?* wondered Lew. *Was I on the beam, coming here?* The sudden glance which the chief gave toward the woman at the pot began to give Davies an inkling, because the woman was young, rounded, and, while far from pretty, not repulsive. Was someone, not an Ainu, after her? Someone woman-starved? Maybe a fellow accustomed to women, as a fellow from Macao or Hong-Kong would be?

Davies did not say, "Hidden from whom?" but, instead, like a young Ainu before a chief, waited. The old men muttered until they reached a decision. "*War' ko,*" the chief said. "He is an evil man. You must kill him. If you do not, I will tell him you went where no man may go, and then he will kill you."

"When I killed the Japanese," said Koropok, "I was brave."

The chief called to the girl, who ladled greasy bear meat out of the pot and into an earthenware bowl which she brought to Koropok. While he ate, thus putting himself in debt to the Ainu, the chief said, "You will kill him tonight."

Not me, thought Lew, gobbling away. *Not until I see what goes on, and have a shot at identifying whoever's here.*

Ikadebetsu was certainly an ideal hideaway for racketeers; but why Ikadebetsu? Why not any one of a dozen other places? Davies was still bothered about that, and intended to find the answer, even if it were only by chance that Simpson and Gentry and the imitation Ainu, Hokuyak, knew too much about the isolated village.

Davies, when the chief's companion plucked at his sleeve, to lead him out of the hut, became truly Koropok. He whimpered. "I am afraid...."

The chief's eyes began to burn brightly. "You need not be afraid," he whispered. "I will make a man of you."

What the Ainu took out from his ragged jacket could have been what caused the moving of his hands in concealing it when his hut was entered. To Davies' amazement it was a small paper flag of one of the allied nations. "Touch it," promised the Ainu, "and you are a man and not a slave."

"I do not feel any different," said Koropok, after obeying. "What is this? A powerful charm of the bear-god?"

"The Great Bear himself sent it to us."

In a timid voice, Koropok asked, "Did it drop out of the sky?"

"A sacred messenger brought it," replied the old chief. "A bear-brother with a thick black beard. He came from Sakhalin. When I was young, I lived there, among bearded men. *Orosha-jin*, they were called. But the Japanese lied about us. We were sent here, because the Japanese said we belong to them. Soon we will belong to no one." His harangue, amazing for an Ainu, gave him the courage to add, "It will be easier to kill a *danna-san* than a *nippon-san*, Koropok."

Koropok said, "A *danna-san?* Here?"

"A wizard. A magician. But you have touched the sacred charm of the bear, and you will be protected. Go with Pi-shak. He will show you."

This, thought Davies, as he shambled after the chief's companion, *is a twisted course I'm following.* On one hand, unscrupulous scoundrels, well versed in a grim trade, were gathering themselves a traffic which would pile up their wealth and allow them to expand into other ventures until they would have a hand in whatever went on in Japan. On the other hand were men engaged in a political venture which meant trouble for the American authorities and disaster for the Old Man; and what the result of the struggle for Japan's control would be, Davies refused to guess as he shuffled along behind Pi-shak, through the village and up a hill path.

He believed that the chief's desire to kill someone, a white man, stemmed from advances made to the chief's young wife. The Ainu had selected Koropok, felt Lew, because Koropok had already killed a man, something which the Ainus never did, and also because if someone must be given up as the killer, Koropok was not a member of the village nor the clan. Thus if Koropok, detected, were himself slaughtered, his spirit would not return to this village, but to his own, wherever it was.

THE WAY out of Ikadebetsu, to the north, was as steep as the way down had been. The old pariah, Pi-shak, made slow going of it; and when, after a dozen pauses, he picked a spot where it was possible to leave the path, and climb upward deeper into the forest, he went even more slowly. What the Ainu was doing, it seemed to the American, was circling the path. After a bitter scrambling over rock of volcanic formation, but out of which trees, festooned with creepers, grew, the old Ainu was so exhausted that he dropped to the ground.

Koropok asked, "What is the *danna-san's* magic?"

"You will see," panted Pi-shak.

Davies' early knowledge of Ainu folklore and legend stood him in good stead as he prodded for information. "Does the magic require women?"

Pi-shak nodded. "My young wife. Oikik's daughter. Madak's two wives."

"So many women will make much magic for one man," said Koropok.

"There are more men than one."

"They all make magic?"

The Ainu, getting to his feet, said, "You will see." He reached over and patted the *geta*-mending knife in Koropok's belt. "Kill them slowly," he urged, and, getting out his bearskin charm bag, carefully drew out the toe of a bear. As he gave this to his stocky young companion, he whispered, "I give you this. Kill a *danna-san* who has hair the color of a persimmon. Kill him for me. He stole my wife."

Taking the charm, Koropok asked, "Cannot the Great Bear help you? What did his messenger say about all this?"

"The messenger came a year ago. When there was fighting. Before the *nippon-san* were defeated. He said, 'Wait. Your day will come.' And so we wait."

"What else did he say?"

Pi-shak replied, "He said we must say nothing to anyone of his visit. He said that no matter what took place, to remember that one day we would be free men, like he was, and to remain silent. The *orosha-san* remained with us. Oh, such fine tales he told us of his native land, *Orosha!* But when he departed, these magicians came. Evil men who perform magic."

"The *Orosha-jin* is called Hokuyak?"

"You saw him, too? He said that he would talk with our people everywhere, even in Tokyo, to prepare them for the day they would be free."

And so there's a Russian scoundrel mixed up in the business, realized Davies, *a smart boy working out under cover of an ideology.* It didn't matter to Lew whether this was positively the case, or whether it might be the other way around, and the imitation Ainu, Hokuyak, engaged in liquor and drug traffic to conceal his actual purpose of being in Japan. His job was tracking things down.

Pi-shak's caution increased when he started off again. Soon a sort of mist, a fog, sifted down through the trees, and from the smell of it the eruptive springs could not be far off, since there was no wind. Mingled with the metallic odor was one more pleasant, and new, biting and pungent, and it came, Davies determined at last, from the scrubby growth through which he was advancing. He picked one of the purple-stemmed branches, on which the leaves stuck out, green above the white and cottony underneath. The smell was that of sage. Which sage? That which was employed as cautery in *moxa,* or that from which absinthe was produced? From what the H.Q. medical officer had said, it must be the former.

Getting hot, thought Lew; and that was true, also. Heat shimmered where any sun penetrated into the forest. Then, without warning, Pi-shak stopped and pointed. A chasm was at the feet of the old Ainu. At the chasm's bottom, partially veiled by steam, Davies saw the figures of men, and strange round high mounds, from the tops of which light was reflected almost as if from glass, and from the sides of which, near the bottom, steam emerged. Davies had never seen anything like these mounds, nor had he heard anything about them, although, except for the glittering squares atop them, they seemed to be of rock and very old.

Some of the mounds, on the far side of the ravine, sent out no puffs of steam; in front of one of these mounds a man was seated, smoking. His hair, Davies saw as Pi-shak began to mumble in futile rage, was violently red; the fellow was a white man, and, equally obviously, the canvas chair on which he sprawled in comfort had never been made in Ikadebetsu.

WHILE THE Ainu continued to curse, Davies kept on with his examination of an unbelievable scene, here in the isolation of Hokkaido. He saw evidence that more than a chair had been brought here. The steam which puffed out of many of the big mounds came from pipes. There was a stack of small boxes, unlike Japanese containers, near one of the mounds. Whoever was operating the place had come mighty well prepared. *And I don't see how they got the stuff in here without either the Japanese police or G-2 being wise to it,* decided Lew.

It came to him then, that moment, that whatever equipment had been brought to Ikadebetsu could well have come down from the north into northern Hokkaido. Hadn't Hokuyak come from the north?

He was glad that Pi-shak was still dribbling out his venom; it gave the stocky man known as Koropok time to investigate, time to figure out that the tops of the mounds where rock and earth had been replaced by a shiny substance, as if in thin sheets, could actually be split hides, which would let in light. Glass would be a difficult thing to bring, from anywhere, to Ikadebetsu.

What were the mounds?

Koropok asked Pi-shak, "Why does the ground rise like the beads of a necklace? I have never seen such a thing."

Pi-shak mouthed a final curse. "If you kill the one with red hair," he slobbered, "I will tell you."

"If you do not tell me," said Koropok, "I will kill only the

man I have been ordered to kill by the chief." He let that sink
in, and then said, "Which is the man who intends to violate
the wife of the chief?"

The old Ainu placed a trembling hand on Koropok's arm.
"The one with the fire-hair came to my house," he said. "I was
ashamed. I had no sake to give him. But he was anxious to do
me honor. So I thought, because he brought a bottle. When it

*The two men, the live
and the dying, the
American and the old
Ainu, fell together over
the chasm's edge.*

was opened, the smell of the hills came out, like magic. I drank. It was sweet and good. It tasted like flowers on the hills. And when I drank several times, my youth returned to me in sleep. When I awoke, my wife was gone."

Absinthe? *I'll bet it was,* thought Lew.

"Our sacred place"—the Ainu pointed to the chasm with its mounds—"was also taken from us. These men make their magic under the roofs of rock where we came in fear to worship the stone axes of our ancestors. When the magic is made, it is put into bottles. The bottles are taken away."

At the chasm's bottom, Davies realized, must be the remains of pit-dwellings, once occupied by a primitive people. It took someone who knew of the isolated ravine to have selected it for the damnable business; in one way or another, some chemist and archaeologist must have spoken together. How this had happened, Lew felt, was not important, nor was he interested in exactly what was being done in the mounds, nor how the distillation apparatus' might be set up. He would have liked a first hand look-see. The risk was too great. His job, right now, was to get out of Ikadebetsu and back to Sapporo and arrange to have the chasm surrounded and the men caught. The last thing Davies intended to do was to go after the scum who had taken the Ainu girls. That would come later.

He wanted to get rid of Pi-shak.

"When I kill the evil ones, including the one with fire-hair," said Koropok, "I may not live. Some of the evil ones will wonder who brought me here, where it is forbidden to come. I do not wish you to be caught and killed, Pi-shak. Return to the chief. Tell him that the evil ones will die."

And if they put up a battle later, thought Lew, *that's no lie.*

"I wish to see the death of the red one," muttered Pi-shak.

"Slip down, Koropok. He will not hear your hunter's footsteps. Get behind him. Drive the knife into him. Do not be afraid. Look! Now he is drinking. Not from a magic bottle. From a small black, fat bottle of sake. See?"

Davies glanced where the red-headed man sat; and, as he did, the fellow yelled, and what the Ainu thought was a stubby bottle of sake came away from in front of the white man's face. It was no bottle at all, but the binoculars which the man with red hair must have raised from time to time to sweep the approaches leading to the ravine.

Men scrambled out of the mounds. Davies hesitated for the briefest of moments. The chase would be on when these men forced the chief to admit that a strange Ainu had come to the village; and all the blame for having gone to the pit-dwellings would be placed on Koropok. Things would be rough on old Pi-shak for having taken Koropok to see the chasm... but Davies didn't see how that could be helped. He himself, a young man, with a start, ought to get back to Sapporo. The ancient Ainu could never make it.

"Pi-shak," said Davies, "their magic tells them we are here. I will hide in the forest. When they come to find me, I will kill them. You must return to the chief. Go. Go quickly. Say I forced you to come with me. Say—"

A rifle shot cracked; Pi-shak's scream and the echo hammered back and forth in the chasm. But as the Ainu jerked and constricted, his thin old arms snapped once like wires in the wind, and reached Davies enough to circle one of Lew's arms with the sting and force of wire being reeled. The two men, the live and the dying, the American and the old Ainu, fell together over the chasm's edge.

CHAPTER V

MARKED MEN

HALFWAY DOWN, a jagged boulder pulled them apart; fifty feet from the bottom, Davies tried to get his hands on the clump of shrub growing on the least of rocky shelves. And failed. But the impact against the ledge, bruising as it was, hurled him away from the ravine's side, so that he was thrown to the top of a mound. His body tore through the pale-colored square at the top as if it were paper, which it actually was, thick, heavy translucent paper, easily transported. Davies fell into a pungent softness which broke his fall.

The interior of the mound was hot with steaming jungle heat piped into it; the biting pungency from the crushed leaves of artemesia absinthia forced into swift, lush growth in the clever makeshift hothouse. But Davies, partially dazed, thought of one thing only: if he had to die here, he must die as an Ainu and not give the men operating the absinthe production, and heaven knew what else, cause to become suspicious. If they were not positive that he was merely a disobedient and curious Ainu, there would be no one here when G-2 came to see why he did not return to Sapporo. While this whirled in his head, he resisted the instinctive desire to get to his feet. An Ainu would remain, cowering, where he had fallen.

His best hope was that the men here would kill him quickly instead of questioning him, an inquisition in which some of the worst minds in Asia could suggest tortures to produce talking. If they didn't finish him at once, *I've got to take it,* Davies told himself; but it would be a hell of a way to die, now that the fighting was over. A hell of a way, and a hell of a place.

The red-headed man was first inside; Davies managed to roll just enough to miss the wild blow from the rifle butt, and to whimper, "*Kurak' t' m'sen'...* I am only a poor Ainu, lord—"

The second man who had stormed into the mound was cursing in French; he aimed a kick at the tattered figure sprawled on the sage plants while grabbing at the red-headed man's rifle. A third man, behind the first two, stormed at Red Hair thickly in what sounded like German-accented English; first, the gutturally-speaking fellow roared, they must question the interloper....

There was a superstition, the last speaker said, while he and the other two examined the cowering Koropok with their eyes, and the men outside crowded the door to the mound-green-house similar to those around it, among the Hokkaido Ainu that if a man's beard was removed with metal, shaved off, he would be forced to tell the truth. It was a trial among the outcasts; and he himself, who had studied the Ainu people and their pit-dwellings, would like to see how it worked.

At least it would be amusing, in this isolated place where the only amusement was found in the Ainu women.

And when it happens, thought Lew, turned to ice despite the terrific steaming heat, *I'll be a gone goose, because the beard is a phony.* Worse, the gang was sure to leave Ikadebetsu, only to set up shop elsewhere, and continue to raise hell. If a GI couldn't find whisky, he'd have a try at absinthe. Nothing was more habit-provoking. *I'm a gone goose anyhow,* Lew told himself, *so I might as well go out in doing something.*

Grab a rifle? He had to rise to get at one; he'd be smashed unconscious before he could get his hands on a gun. Use his hands, his fists? Again he'd only be knocked out. Being killed had to be O.K., but not merely becoming insensible. If he were killed, the beard business would be forgotten.

The red-headed man reached inside his half-open shirt, scratching the red pelt on his chest, heat-irritated. Davies saw the marks made by *moxa,* the scar shaped like a scorpion. Yes, it must be this which identified members of the gang to one another, to men unknown to one another save for the mark of identification. Knowing this did Davies no good now, as, head down, he tried to formulate something, anything, which would result in instant death.

Beside him, close enough so that he could feel the heat of it, sufficiently intense so that his arm was almost being seared, was one of the pipes which heated the mound, a pipe through which flowed the steam jetting out at the far end of the mounds, along with a number of similar pipes. Carefully, Davies managed to get a look at it; but as a weapon it would never serve, even if he could wrench off one of the lengths. He would be beaten down, he was positive, before he could rise to his feet and swing a length of the pipe. But....

Would it work? thought Davies. *Will it?*

He didn't want to die!

Davies did not so much as run the tip of his tongue over his lips. He was going to try what he had in mind; but to the three men in the mound which smelled of the pungency of absinthe he continued to look like a terrified Ainu.

It's got to be done all in one motion, decided Lew. He knew the cost of failure; that didn't matter. Not the way things stacked up.

One hand, the nearest, was already on the pipe; he had his other hand on it, to sear it also, before Red Head had his rifle up, or the others made their first move toward him. He didn't feel the heat of the pipe as he wrenched at it, getting into the movement all the strength of his shoulders and stocky body. He gave one fierce, furious jerk; he rolled away from the blow of the rifle, and was actually on his knees when steam from the pipe, wrenched apart at a joint, hissed into the mound like scalding mist, like the falling of sulphurous fog, like what it was, a steam from the volcanic formations of the Ikadebetsu chasm.

H E   F E L T   no pain from his seared fist as he drove it into the face of whoever was in front of him; but when he had done this, he dropped to his knees again, unable to see, but with the advantage of knowing that whatever body came in contact with his own was that of an enemy. He crawled across fragrant leaves again; at the wall of the mound, with the hiss of the steam no more deadly than the shouts of the scorpion-marked men, he worked his way toward the more brilliant whiteness of sun slanted on the emerging steam at the entrance.

Steam billowed up through the spot where Davies had fallen through the mound's artificial top; steam clouded out at the entrance, sulphurous and heavy enough so that while some of it rose, more of it crawled along the ground, like poison gas in warfare. And Davies crawled along with it, first avoiding the legs of the gang who sought to get inside, next following the outside of the wall of the mound... and lastly, when the steam began to thin, running and never turning.

Not until he was above the chasm, taking the way he had seen when on the brink with Pi-shak, did he stop, prone and protected from vision from below by a rough, spined bush, and look back. The steam still billowed out of the mound; but by this time armed men were tearing about the strange pit-dwell-ings, and some already were preparing to search elsewhere....

For an Ainu, thought Davies soberly. He hoped grimly that the scum of all Asia would argue themselves out of any doubts they might have, although, *What doubts?* Lew asked himself. *They'll suppose I grabbed the pipe to use it as a weapon, being the one Ainu in a thousand who'd try to save his own life. What they'll concentrate on,* Davies was sure, *is in getting me, whether I'm an Ainu or anything else.*

And so the chase began.

Davies swung out of the forest, at last, running, and avoiding the village of Ikadebetsu; and at first he stuck to the trail. He had the advantage of a start, a trail he had already used, and a hard, trained body accustomed to fatigue and hardship. He had the advantage of knowing his destination. This latter the men marked with *moxa*—and because it was a Japanese medicinal mark, Davies believed that Japs were also in the gang—did not have; they couldn't know whether he would go north or south, nor where he might leave the trail, if southward bound, instead of continuing on to Sapporo.

But they had one advantage. Some of the men, perhaps in good condition, could take food with them, or take it from the pariah settlements on the way; Davies, on the other hand, knew that he was going to be desperately hungry before he ever reached Sapporo. But that was O.K. For it was fine to keep going, to have a goal, to be alive, even if certain that his pursu-ers would be close behind him and were armed, or perhaps might get to Sapporo before him, because they might pass him at night, when he would sleep off the trail. When he thought of that possibility, he began to grin, for the first time since he had turned himself into Koropok. It was a broad grin; but what he was thinking amused him.

The return began to sap Davies' ability to keep going swiftly. When he drank, at a stream, hunger gnawed more bitingly; and when he slept, no matter how exhausted, food entered into his dreams. Even such scraps as had been flung at him when he had been the *hakoya* at Number Nineteen, instead of the equally false Hokuyak, a man marked with the scorpion scar of the gang, would have been wolfed down. A bowl of slippery macaroni-like *oden* would have tasted wonderful; so would a few shreds of fish mixed with millet. And when he thought of American food....

By the time he could see the brewery chimneys above Sapporo, he looked utterly an Ainu, a field scarecrow. Hair and beard were matted with dust, sweat caked his dark face; what had been a tattered blue jacket was brown from dust and sweat... and the first Japanese who stared at him when he reached the outskirts giggled until the filthy pariah was out of sight.

If any of the Ikadebetsu gang got here ahead of me, thought Lew, as he had so many times before, *I'll damn soon know it.*

He didn't want a quick, silencing shot to be the way he'd find out; he seemed to shuffle along like a dispirited Ainu, but was keenly alert. His exhaustion had vanished, and was replaced with an exhilaration which tingled through him strongly, setting his seared palms to aching as a reminder of where he had been and of what had happened there.

Davies believed that if any of the scorpion-marked men had reached Sapporo, to be ready for him, there were two possibilities as to what preparations had been arranged for his welcome. One would be that any pariah entering the city would given a quick examination and, if there were the least notion that the pariah had been at Ikadebetsu, there would be a dead Ainu. The other possibility was that if the Ainu who had escaped from the chasm was not an Ainu at all, the masquerader would head for wherever the Allied H.Q. of Sapporo might be... and be killed before getting inside to tell what he had discovered.

But Davies was headed for the hotel.

THERE HAD been time for the note which he had sent to the American lieutenant, before disguising himself, to have been relayed to Tokyo. Time for action to have been taken. However, before starting out, Davies had not known that it would be necessary for the men on duty at Sapporo to watch for a perilous return... although he was now aware that a figure had detached itself from shadow, not a Jap figure from the size, and was following him.

But not one of the gang, reasoned Lew, *or he'd do more than follow me, if he had any kind of look-see at me.* Obviously, word had come to Sapporo; one of the Ikadebetsu gang must have passed Koropok on the trail. *He'll wait until there's no Nip in sight,* thought Lew, sticking to his first figuring, *and then drag me off to question me, and then, if I know anything about Asiatic scum, kill me.*

Davies quickened his pace. So did the man behind him. Japanese blinked at the sight of a rapidly-shambling Ainu.

When the next intersection was reached, from which the hotel could be seen on Sapporo's principal street, the man whistled twice. Davies did not wait to see who was being warned by the signal. He ran. Like a terrified Ainu. He kept his stride a jerky one, and not smooth, as an American would run. He waved his arms. And when the man behind him yelled, a warning in a foreign language unfamiliar to Davies, Koropok ran faster. No shot yet....

He isn't sure, thought Davies; and then the doubts of his pursuer must have become complicated by the appearance of a Japanese policeman, who shrilled to the *inu* from the hills to stop running in an improper manner dangerous to pedestrians. But the policeman, about to knock the Ainu down with a club, stepped aside politely on seeing that a white man was chasing the pariah.

People of Sapporo goggled at the sight of a foul pariah running away from the foreigner. This was better than a *no* play, any day of the seven. Oh, how the bearded dog ran, and how the beardless one ran after him! What an amazing spectacle! *Ai!* And now another crazy *Amerika-jin*, or *Orosha-jin*, or perhaps even a *Doitsu-jin*, one of those yellow-hairs who were formerly allies, was attempting to cut off the equally crazy Ainu! Oh, the Ainu was so terrified that he leaped over the little wooden fence which protected the hotel's grass and flowers, as if the sign there were not there at all! But of course no Ainu could read, neither the Japanese characters in black, nor the strange words which had been added, for visitors, which warned, *DO NOT TROMPLE GRASS OR BRAKE FLOUR....*

Why, the crazed pariah was running up the steps! Oh, how the honorable clerk would catch him, and throw him out!

The honorable clerk, inside, was busier than usual; the hotel had more guests than for a long time, including important men from Tokyo, who had come from the United States. He gasped when he looked up; but before he could shout at the wild figure which had burst in, the bearded apparition had bounded through the filled lobby and was making the turn into the corridor. A white man, and a second, and, in another moment, two more, hurried into the hotel, breathless; the pariah, said one, had grabbed his pocket watch and chain... which way had he gone?

The policeman had come in also, bowing to the clerk, but making no effort to go after those who were following the clerk's pointing finger.

Davies raced up the flight of stairs. His jacket was already off; and when he reached the door of his room he grabbed tentatively at the knob. Locked. He backed off slightly, wrapping the jacket around his right hand; he mounted to the transom with his left foot on the knob and his body flung against the upper portion of the door, and, as he went high, smashed the glass. As his fist wound about with cloth went through, Davies hooked his elbow on the transom frame. He steadied himself a moment, and then pulled himself through and dropped to the floor.

His bag was there. So was the bathroom. Koropok grabbed the bag, hurried into the bathroom, and, grinning, locked the door.

It was minutes, as the searchers examined room after room while an intent audience, sprinkled with uniforms, watched, before the broken glass of the transom was discovered. Matsugamo's master key unlocked the door; an instant later a fist pounded on the locked bathroom door. "Come out," squealed the irate Japanese head clerk, "or it will be worse for you. Oh, you will be beaten!"

Davies, buttoning his shirt, whistled to himself.

A deeper voice said, "*Machi wa Orosha shimanesu…* do not make me wait. I am a Russian officer, your friend, and you will not be hurt."

That would be Ogrodowski, decided Lew, as he picked up his tie. He thought, *I don't see why I didn't put cigarettes in the bag.*

"If you don't break down the door," snapped another voice, "the damned fool'll stay there until he rots. I've lived in the Orient most of my life," continued the speaker, "and this is the first time a pariah has ever stolen anything."

"When a man is downtrodden and hungry," another man retorted, "and we do nothing to assist him, what do you expect?"

What do you know? Lew told himself. The first speaker was Simpson or Gentry, one of the Asia-style racketeers; but the second voice was Ashton's. *Right along to see what happens,* decided Davies, *and I wouldn't be a damned bit surprised if Ogrodowski tipped him of that I was here. Not that it matters now.*

Davies turned to the mirror over the washbowl and went to work on his tie. He grinned at the face he saw. No beard. No matted hair. He was looking at Llewelyn Davies again, a little darker from sun, a little more gaunt, and very tired. But feeling pretty damned good.

THE WAIT, he could guess, was while an axe was being brought so that the door could be smashed down. He finished putting on his uniform, belted himself but not with the old hole, because he was thinner, patted his holster, and picked up his cap.

A word from outside brought him up short. He had been inattentive to whatever had been previously said, because he knew now that the principal people involved in what had started in Tokyo must all be outside waiting to see the pariah.

"Not the slightest cooperation," the Russian captain was saying. "Interference. Stubborn interference. And when we prepare to do something, without American assistance, he slips away, this Major Davies gone off fishing."

I caught something, thought Lew.

"Our own Professor Kajenski is expected in Sapporo," continued the Russian. "A famous and learned man. A great chemist. He can help the poor pariahs. But will he be able to combat the—the—"

"The stupidity of this Davies?" said Ashton. "You needn't tell me about him, Captain. I've seen an example of his stupidity. Only he won't be able to prevent making Japan a nation of the people, Captain Ogrodowski. I think that I can guarantee that! We, as members of the people ourselves, no longer need Davies or his like to tell us what to do!"

Davies opened the door and stepped out.

A fly buzzing on the windowpane was the one sound for immeasurable time. Then Davies was saying softly, "Simpson, Gentry, you two next to them, don't move," and everyone could see that the American had a gun in his hand. "Search them," ordered Major Davies; men in American uniforms did so.

The buzzing of the fly seemed to grow and grow, only it was

not a buzzing at all, but the hiss of indrawn breaths. The bath-room door was open; there was not a sign of an Ainu within.

"Oh, where can be?" whispered the head clerk, beginning to tremble. "Ainu go in …*Amerika-jin* come out! Oh, where are gone? Elsewhere?"

Davies said, "Why not go look?"

He strode over to the four men, nodding to a G-2 officer up from Tokyo who had helped disarm the four. Swiftly, roughly, Davies ripped buttons from Simpson's shirt in order to expose the man's chest. The scorpion mark was there; and it'd be on the other men's chests, too, Davies knew. The gang mark.

"What in hell're you doin'?" snarled Simpson.

Davies said, "Explain the scar."

"That? Why, you ass, that's *moxa*. Had a Jap physician. Anybody who's been in Japan for more than five minutes knows what *moxa's* for." It was at that moment the renegade must have recalled exactly what Major Davies had said at the saloon, concerning fishing and Ikadebetsu, because fear replaced the rage which had burned in Simpson's eyes. He said, "Ah," and that was all.

"Does Professor Kajenski know?" asked Lew.

"What do you say of him?" demanded the Russian captain.

Ashton bustled forward. "I am well acquainted with the professor," he insisted, "and I don't propose to have his work interfered with because of the stupidity of a man like yourself, Major. So let's have it clear now—"

"It will be clear to you shortly," said Lew grimly. He turned to Ogrodowski. "And to you as well, Captain. It will surprise you."

"Coming from an officer of your type," interrupted Ashton, "it will probably be as clear as what happened to the Ainu."

Davies suggested, "If he came in through the transom, maybe that's the way that he left. All I know is that I didn't see him in this room."

But I saw him in the bathroom mirror, thought Lew, *and he looked like hell.* He had orders to give, concerning Ikadebetsu, and wires to get off to Tokyo so there would be action at Nineteen. But right this moment something was pretty important.

"Who's got a cigarette?" asked Major Davies.

As a G-2 officer snapped flame to a lighter, and Davies took the first deep inhalation, the Intelligence officer winked briefly.

"Remember this," said Ashton, "when Professor Kajenski arrives, I intend to see to it that although his opinions regarding Japanese occupation do not conform with your general's, he is to be afforded every courtesy."

"I'll see to it," promised Davies. "There will even be a reception committee, sir. I wish," added Lew, "that I could do for you what I'll do for the professor." *What a tangled web,* thought Davies. *Renegades of all nations. And these boys have so managed to mix a damnable racket with political ideologies that it was hard to tell where one began and the other left off. And they had damned jackasses such as this one to help them.* "I'll take care of the professor," repeated Lew.

Ashton did not soften. He pressed what looked like an advantage by saying, "I suggest that you give him a dinner, Major Davies."

"Dinner?" said Lew. "Dinner?" He sighed deeply. "Dinner," said the man who had been Koropok, "would be wonderful… right now!"

THE YEAR OF THE DOG

THE TRACKS of the railway on which the troop train loaded with Marines moved cautiously inland from the China coast followed what had been the sluggish course of the river a few days earlier. Now, flood water swirled so high that it lapped against the roadbed; the channel could be told only by the rusting smokestack of a former floating go-down which the Japanese had bombed at the start of the war, and bombed gleefully, because the ship had flown the American flag.

The highway between tracks and river was buried deep under mud and water, with sampans, on which families lived, made fast to the telegraph poles. Turbulent and mucky as was the flood, Chinese were fishing in it, with scant hope for any catch in such water. But China was starving. One small, bony fish, boiled with weeds or bark, could mean another day of life for a fisherman's family.

On the far side of the sullen flood, the plain stretched to the stormy cloud-piled sky, and the clouds were settling lower and lower.

A gray Marine officer remarked that there would be more weather, and there was immediate agreement. Almost all of the officers in the rear car had seen long-time service in the Orient, as had the non-coms up ahead with the rest of the outfit. Old China hands. Asiatics. Men who, before the fighting had started, had missed too many boats. This was no group of replacements, but hard-boiled Marines who knew the difference between boondocks and boondockers.

Except for a handful of junior officers, they had already had their fun with the lone Army officer in the car, who was younger than any of them. Had he started out as a general, after O. C. S., and by now worked his way down to being a major? Or did Air Forces promote a man every time he got back safely?

Major Llewelyn Davies, who had spent almost all of the war in Japan, disguised as an Ainu, had only grinned at the deviling. He liked these men; he liked the way they shrugged at what was going to be a difficult duty for them, stationed as they would be between Chiang's forces and the Communist Army of the North. Davies didn't envy the iron control they must maintain over themselves, no matter what happened, no matter what they would want to do, no matter how they were goaded.

Behind the deviling, Davies knew, was understandable resentment. Here he was, assigned to a duty which Marines felt belonged to the Marine Corps. And it was the sort of duty they would have enjoyed carrying out, from the shrewd Old Man down to the worst knuckle-head in the outfit, although the accomplishment would have been with rifles and mortars, and not as Davies intended.

LEW'S ORDERS were to attempt to find out what had happened to Marines reported missing from patrols and convoys. The Corps' way of learning this, and recovering the men if alive, would have been simple; they would have gone for them, and gone fighting. But nervous Washington wanted no new situations, unless the Marines were attacked. More, officials in the capital were desperately worried about the intentions of the Northern Army; something was in the wind, but what it was, and when it would be tried, and what it could mean for the United States, nobody knew. To Davies, under cover of a more obvious duty, had been given the job of finding out what was going on.

None of the officers had asked him how he proposed going

after the missing men; but once the colonel remarked soberly
that if Davies expected a pilot's uniform was any protection
against a slit throat, he was apt to learn that he was mistaken.
A bandit, the colonel said, was a bandit, even if he joined an
army.

Now, as the train's wheels clicked along, the colonel said, for

THE YEAR OF THE DOG

With the two Red
Army officers almost
in line now, Davies
had both covered.

the benefit of juniors in China for the first time, but with a
glance to where the stocky Davies was looking out at the flood,
"Have a look-see at a Chinese cemetery on the other side,
gentlemen. Cemeteries are to be out of bounds. Remember
that."

"Are they held sacred, sir?" asked the lieutenant.

Colonel Mathews said, "That's part of it. The other and more important reason is that some jackass will spread the yarn that the Chinese sometimes bury pieces of number one jade with bodies, and tell what fine jades are worth, and then some other jackasses will start out chop-chop on a treasure hunt. And," the colonel reminded grimly, "enough incidents'll develop from causes beyond our control."

"Yes, sir," the lieutenant acknowledged, because the colonel was staring at him as if the C.O. intended to hold him responsible.

"A grave," continued the colonel, while the cemetery went out of sight behind a low, bare hill, "should face a river, have a cliff to the rear, and elevations to the right and left. If the aspect is to the south, so much the better, because the Chinese believe that devils come down with the cold from the north. And if the dead are made unhappy by demons, they take it out on the living." He ended, "Our own troubles come out of the north. Eh, Davies?"

Lew smiled.

When the talk veered to the place where the battalion was to be stationed, and what a fellow could do there, the dark, stocky major sighed involuntarily. Out of the frying pan of Japan and into the fire of China, Davies was thinking; and he began to wonder how long it would be before he sat around with Americans again, once he really got going on the strange assignment.

He would be entirely on his own. But, unlike when in Japan, he would be on unfamiliar ground, with greater chances for making mistakes. Yet he realized why he had been selected for the duty, after the failure of men who knew China and the Chinese far better than did he, and who spoke the Mandarin of the north as well as the dialects. Handicapped as he would himself be, there was a possibility of success, and it was worth the attempt.

Davies could understand some Mandarin, the language of

China's officialdom as well as of the north, and something of the dialects and Cantonese, and he had been carefully trained to speak what common words had been taught him with a Japanese accent. The written language, for a man who could read Japanese with ease, wouldn't cause him much trouble.

He turned when the colonel sat beside him. *The old boy doesn't care much about my doing what's a job for Marines, thought Lew, but that's not why he wants to talk with me. Nor is he just going to pass the time of day.*

"I have an interest in what you want to do," said Colonel Mathews, without any finesse whatsoever. "Let's put it this way, Davies. I'd hate like hell to have you go fouling things up so we never get our men back. Tell me, what damn good'll come from your asking General Li Chou a lot of questions? Eh? He'll deny everything. I know him. Bandit from the ground up."

"I won't ask him any, sir," said Davies.

Mathews snapped, "Whoever you ask'll go running to him. Spread the word. Don't argue. I know China. That's how it's done."

"I'm sure it is," agreed Lew. "Just the same, my orders are to make the attempt to find the missing men, and that's what I'm going to do."

"Mind telling me how?"

Davies said slowly, not liking what he had to say but recognizing the need for saying it, "Sir, my orders are that I am not to discuss what I am to do with anyone. I am sorry, sir."

The colonel snorted. "First time I ever heard of anybody in Air Forces worrying about obeying orders," he said. He had a word of caution. "If you do happen to learn anything, keep it to yourself, or old Li Chou will cut your throat and throw you into the river. I know what I'm talking about."

"I don't think General Li Chou will know what I'm up to," said Davies quietly. He paused while a Chinese train boy came into the car from ahead, and said nothing until the boy went to the rear platform to smoke an American cigarette. "Unless he is smarter than the Japs," said Lew, "I don't think that Li Chou will know."

"Well," growled the colonel, "he's smarter." He blinked. "If you think," said Mathews soberly, "that disguising yourself as a Relief Commissioner, or an oil company man, or any other damn thing, will fool old Li Chou, think again. That damned devil can smell out a disguise. You couldn't fool him," snapped the Marine Colonel, staring at Davies' stocky figure and curly hair, "any more than you could fool me. I tell you that for your own good."

Davies smiled slightly.

Colonel Mathews was not looking. Staring straight in front of him, he muttered, "Those men are our men. If I had my way...."

He left it unsaid.

"If I had my way, sir," said Davies, "I'd like to be with you when you went to get your men. Anyhow, wish me luck, sir."

The grizzled Marine said, "When I was younger, I didn't count costs, either," as he shook hands. "All I've been trying to say, son, is that you're starting out on a fool's venture, all because some jackass in Washington is playing diplomatic games when this is the time to get tough. 'Mustn't hurt anybody's feelings!' What the hell is being done to us all the time?"

Having raised his voice, the colonel jumped up. "Gentlemen," he snapped, "my personal observations have nothing to do with orders already issued you. First officer who starts or encourages an incident will have the pleasure of office hours with me." He added to Davies, lowering his voice but not altering his tone, "Keep away from disguises. D'ye hear?"

"Yes, sir," said Major Davies.

He had heard; that was what he was admitting. He had heard every word, although the only thing of importance which he heard concerned General Li Chou, leader of a division of the Army of the North; and this information was verification of what had already been drummed into him. It was important.

Mathews wasn't the man to be fooled by reputations. Mathews knew what he was talking about when he expressed an opinion about General Li Chou. It wasn't scuttlebutt.

Look out for Li Chou! Davies thought about this as the rain began to fall, the expected rain, first softly, and then with the turbulence of China, swelling a river already beyond its banks. Look out for Li Chou! Yes, look out for a man who had lived profitably all over the world, in England, the United States, Russia, Japan. Look out for him! One day he led ragged bandits and kidnaped missionaries for ransom, the next he popped up in Europe, buying ammunition with hard dollars, a third and he was playing the tables at Havana, a fourth and he was in North China. Some boy, Li Chou. It took quite a fellow to drink Tojo's tea, smoke Stalin's tobacco, be entertained in Hong Kong… and get away with it.

Rain slanted against the window of the car.

Five minutes before the train was scheduled to arrive at Kunhwei-kwan, with a three minute stop, Davies stood up and rubbed his cheek; and no Marine officer in the colonel's battalion, or any other, would have had even the trace of a shadow on his face. Good-natured banter followed the Army major to the washroom… and at Kunhwei-kwan the officers in the car hurried out for a breath of air under the roof of the newly repaired station. It was still raining; if anything, it was raining harder than before, a dull, numbing cold rain.

COLONEL MATHEWS was standing with several of his senior officers when a pariah shambled up to him; the pariah's hand was extended in the universal gesture of begging, a shaking, fearful hand.

"That's what China's done for the Ainus," grunted Colonel Mathews, giving the pariah a coin. "Taught 'em to beg. They wouldn't dare, in Japan. The Nips," went on the colonel, "shipped Ainus around during the fighting. Formosa. China. Anywhere a dirty job was beneath Jap dignity. Why the hell," demanded

Mathews, "haven't Ainus been returned to Japan where they belong? What's holding it up? Eh?"

His officers knew that he expected no answer.

"Well, I know why not, even if you don't," announced the colonel. "Nobody has done the paper work on it yet. Paper work! And the poor devil looks like he hasn't had a meal for a week." Colonel Mathews grabbed the arm of the stocky, bearded man below the tatters of a sleeve which was already thoroughly soaked with rain. "Boy! *Ni'i ying wa?* Eh? What li'l piecee talk you catch?"

The thinly clad and sodden figure groveled until its head and the matted, wet hair on it touched the colonel's shining belt.

At first the pariah's words must have been Ainu, because the colonel could make nothing out of, "*Yairapp, yairapp,*" nor any of the other mumbling. But when the man in tatters whimpered, monotonously and uninflected as a Japanese would have spoken in Chinese, and with the Ainu whine in the speech, "*Ng'-u-kon si'-si',*" the Marine C.O. managed to understand him.

For the benefit of junior officers who had come up and were waiting for Mathews to board the train ahead of them, the colonel said, "He says he can speak a word or two in Chinese." Another coin passed. "*Chang chang,*" Colonel Mathews said, turning the trembling pariah loose with the goodbye.

When the train pulled slowly out from the Kunhwei-kwan station, officers were looking out of the window. One of them said, "Colonel, I'm afraid that the object of your charity is losing what you gave him," and Mathews crossed the car's aisle to have a look for himself.

The pariah had already been tumbled to the mud and water beyond the station; as the colonel watched, the men who had followed the shambling Ainu were jumping up from where they had held him down, and were running off. A couple of M.P.'s yelled, but did nothing which might be protested by the local authorities as unwarranted interference with civil rights; and the Marine colonel, before the train puffed ahead on the mild up-grade toward the next town, saw the broad-shouldered pariah-beggar rise slowly and dejectedly to his feet, wipe filth and muck from his beard and eyes, and, head low, shuffle off and disappear behind the slanting curtain of China's rain.

"What can you expect of people like that?" Mathews wondered. "No fight in 'em. No guts. Been kicked around too long."

When the Marines settled down for a continuation of the journey, a junior officer asked, "Sir, just who are the Ainus?"

Colonel Mathews was about to say, "Major Davies is the man to tell you. He was some years in Japan, I believe." He was about to say that; but when he looked down the aisle and didn't see Davies, he almost said, "Did he mention Kunhwei-kwan as his destination? Or did he miss the train, which would be just like the Army?"

He said neither. He blinked. Wrinkles appeared on his leathery face, although he had no intention of grinning.

When he finally spoke, all he said was, "I'll be damned."

Nobody asked the C.O. what he meant.

CHAPTER II

THE FEAST OF DEATH

WHEN DAVIES was out of the town, after twice missing the way, he hesitated before going on. What he saw must be the road leading to where he wanted to go; the Bitter Water shop was on one side, where the road began at the town's edge, and an abandoned bellows-maker's shop on the other.

This was how G-2 had indicated the start of the road. But it was lower than the fields around it, and farmers had turned it into a drainage ditch, There was no choice, even so; the fields were a grayish ooze. And so Davies splashed along, on the road north, often through water up to his knees.

Davies could have walked with longer strides, shortening

the time he spent in the rain. Not that he had much hope as
to what shelter there would be, later. But he was acting, when
alone, as he would act under observation; and so he walked as
a pariah would have walked, not hurrying despite the slashing
rain. He looked exactly as he had looked not only to the Marine
colonel but also to the beggar-ruffians who had grabbed away
the coins he himself had begged for, and also as he hoped he
must have looked to anyone around the station when he had
sneaked, on the far side, off the train. An Ainu. A pariah named
Koropok.

No savage dogs raced out of the fields ahead of him, nor
slunk up behind for a mouthful of leg-meat. There were no dogs
in starving China.

As Davies slogged ahead, he wondered what luck he would
have in putting together the pieces which G-2 had given him,
and making them work. In itself, the affair appeared simple
enough, if he managed to pick up any real leads. It was in the
ramifications that there was no way of knowing what might
happen.

Somewhere to the north was Yeungwi, a *chen-tien*, a formerly prosperous market town. Located as it was, north of the
Nationalist lines and south of the Communist lines, and with
roads radiating from it into the country around, Yeungwi had
been selected as an excellent spot from which to distribute
Relief.

When starving men had slipped up to the moving trucks,
and slipped away with whatever food they could find, Central
Government guards began to accompany every convoy. Soon
after, a convoy was openly attacked, and not by desperate villagers or farmers; the Nationalist soldiers escorting the trucks
were killed or driven off. Not only was the rice stolen, but the
trucks disappeared as well. Marines replaced the Nationalist
guards; the Marines were never driven from the convoy, but
had been forced to fight against fifty to one odds. Marines had
been killed; some, undoubtedly wounded, had been reported
missing.

*A pariah shambled up
to Colonel Mathews,
begging for coins.*

Air recon showed nothing in the way of any Northern Army
forces near Yeungwi. However, Intelligence added up the reports
made by the detachments which had been under attack, and
was reasonably certain that the attacks had not been made
bandit-fashion, nor with bandit weapons. More, the uniforms
of the convoy raiders killed by the Marines were those of the
Northern Army, although the replies to continued protests by
the United States announced that the dead raiders had stolen
the uniforms and really were Chiang's men trying to make
trouble for the Communists... or perhaps the United States
military officials lied about the uniforms. And, if the United

States didn't like it, why not recall the Marines, who liked trouble and were much too fond of fighting, anyhow.

Whoever the raiders were, they were skillfully and aggressively commanded. G-2 had cause to believe that their commander was General Li Chou. With his flair for international intrigue, which would profit him one way or another, and his bandit background, making things difficult for the United States and at the same time being able to feed his own troops with American rice... nothing would please the suave, cold-blooded Li Chou more.

"If you are anywhere near him," G-2 had warned Davies, "don't underestimate a scholarly-appearing Chinese who seems the most gentle fellow in China. He changes his coat every time it profits him. Be afraid of him, even if he's merely in the same town, Major! He is not only bad; he's smart. But if you can find out what he is up to, after his visit to Moscow...."

This was Davies' real job. He was well aware that putting complicated numbers together wasn't as easy as adding two and two. He had no feeling that simply because Li Chou had spent a month in Moscow there would be trouble. The old so-and-so, according to G-2, had been in London, and Washington.

What was annoying to Davies, as he plodded ahead, was that he had passed up a chance to have added a couple of chops to the breakfast he had packed away; it was going to be a long time before he did any important eating again. And from now on eating would be a problem, because he had to remain alive in order to do anything about the problem assigned to him. And smoking would be something to dream about, probably when his belly was empty. In Japan, when Koropok had been a despised and kicked brothel servant, he had been fed enough to keep him active. What would it be like here, in China?

IT WAS hours before Davies finally saw the walls of Yeungwi and the square of black which was the gate. With the rain pelting down on him, he stopped. Because no convoy had reached Yeungwi for weeks now, G-2 had no way of knowing what went on in the market town, nor who might be in it; but, anxious as was Davies to have a look at the once prosperous village, he dared not do it. Not yet. First things came first. He had plenty of time. Or did he? Washington was worried; Davies' orders were that he was to work as swiftly as he could.

Circling the walls of Yeungwi, far enough away to remain unobserved should anyone be watching, was a slow performance. Where Davies' legs had been wet, mud of the empty fields seemed to plaster them with layer after layer until walking was difficult. He kept a wary eye on the low, small farmers' houses; he crossed first one road, leading southwest, and then another, more west by south; Yeungwi was a true market town. A damned good place from which to start operations, Davies was aware; a finger pointing into the China controlled by the Central Government. At this season, however, the roads were practically impassable for large bodies of men, whether on foot or in vehicles.

Davies kept too far from the walls, and the gate at each radiating road, to be able to observe whether the Japanese had left any marks of their occupation. Rain obscured his vision anyhow; and the continuing torrent so obscured it that he was actually where he wanted to be before he saw the ruined huddle which had formerly been the extensive walled dwelling bought by the town money-lender, according to G-2, after he had worked with the Japanese during the occupation. When the Japanese surrendered, the place had been torn apart by angry villagers, although more of it was left than of the money-lender.

The posts of the place still stood, and here and there, against what remained of the walls of thin slab-bricks, crude shelters had been fashioned and roofed with reeds and sorghum stalks. Davies saw an opening in the brickwork of the nearest of the shelters, and, after glancing automatically behind him, making certain that only the rain was following him, shuffled stolidly past the peeled twigs thrust in the ground to keep out devils, and into the black, unlit interior.

The inside of the shelter was damp and nauseous as it was dark. Davies could make out figures, in rags, sitting on other rags and on reeds; but if any of the men on the floor saw the entrance of the newcomer, they gave no sign. Nor did any of them move. There was no sound except the rain on the stalks above, a sound as if rats were scurrying across.

Davies extended his hands and waved them inward, the customary Ainu gesture of salutation. He made the gesture toward the *k'ang*, the elevated north-China heating apparatus around which the shelter had been formed, because he saw a man's shape lying on it, and whichever person was on the *k'ang* would be the oldest and most important. But the figure on the brick heating-and-sleeping stove did not acknowledge the salutation, nor whisper the *kiaki-ni-guru* words of welcome.

It was then that Davies was able to see, in the gloom, that the old and bearded pariah on the *k'ang* was as cold as were the bricks under his dead body. No fire burned in man nor stove.

Nor was there much life left in the Ainus who sat around the *k'ang*, according the dead man the three days of worship. Bearded lips were gray, cheeks sunken, eyes dull. Here, Davies saw, were starving men. Here were pariahs who had been shipped into China by the Japanese, and who had been forgotten. G-2 had been correct; the ruined dwelling of the money-lender housed men who had been pariahs in Japan, and were pariahs in China, where the Chinese themselves lacked food. The Ainus were a problem on paper, too, Intelligence had told Davies. Nobody knew exactly what to do with them… and here they starved and died.

Davies, who had not only lived in Ainu settlements in Japan during the war, but who as a boy had been with his missionary-doctor father in Ainu villages in northern Japan, said humbly, *"Apt' shan."*

A sad-faced Ainu looked up, and said, *"Tschup' rai.* The sun is dead."

The sun, Davies knew, was believed to be gone because a

man had died, and, being a good man in life, was protected in his journey to the Forest-World of Death by clouds, which prevented devils from devouring his spirit.

Davies had seen a good many pariahs die. His response was proper: *"Uku Ainu buri-kuru.* The sun will shine for us again soon."

A PARIAH whose stringy beard could mean that he was part Japanese stared up at the newcomer. "Name?" he asked; and the question, indicating to the others that a stranger, and not someone from another shelter, had come inside, brought up a few heads in dull curiosity.

"Koropok," said Davies.

"Yani! Go away!"

The sad-faced Ainu mumbled, "No. That is bad. He is one of us. Sit, Koropok." Then he whispered, "Did you bring food?"

Koropok hung his head.

"Another mouth," muttered the half-caste, "where there is nothing." Rising to his feet, and approaching Davies, he asked, "Where did you come from?"

Davies was ready with the answer; where he had been, he said, everyone starved. The Old Men had heard that here there was a little food, and had sent him, Koropok, to find out whether this were true. "You hunger also," ended Davies.

The half-caste said, *"Oship' ishu kanna,"* and jabbed Davies with a stubby finger. "You do not look hungry to me."

The same to you, thought Lew, aware of the strength behind the poke at his belly. Then, *Just because the guy looks part Nip is no reason for me to dislike him. I don't want anyone to question my being an Ainu. Not anyone. This has got to be my base of operations. I've got to be accepted.*

More, if the half-caste were shrewder than the other pariahs, the dumber that the fellow considered Koropok the better it would be.

So Davies fumbled under the tatters of his jacket until he

The Ainus were a problem. Nobody knew exactly what to do with them... and here they starved and died.

pulled out the bearskin charm bag. He opened it carefully, lest other eyes than his observe the charm which protected him; but instead of taking out what the Ainus expected, a pinch of powdered seaweed which he would swallow to purify himself in the presence of a dead man, he took a long time before producing two coins which as they came to sight, gave out a little clink. Davies' slight movement, eluding the grasping hand of the half-caste Noma-us, was so subtly executed that not even the pariah who was part Japanese saw anything in it save concealment from those evil spirits certain to be hovering around the dead, and who would be attracted by the sound of metal.

"The Old Men, the *onné,* told me to buy food," said Davies; *and,* he was thinking, *from the way the half-caste is trying not to grin, he now considers me more stupid than anyone he's ever known. For who but a fool would expose money to men who starve for what the money will buy?* If the statement were not sufficiently one to convince Noma-us, Koropok added, "But I do not know this village. Perhaps someone will help me in the buying?"

Noma-us said, "Assuredly. I myself will do it. But how, Koropok, will you take food back to your own people? You will be robbed of it."

Koropok lowered his head. "Will I be robbed?" he whimpered. "I have not even a bear knife with which to defend myself."

Smiling in his scraggly beard, the half-caste bent and whispered in the ear of one of the seated Ainus, the one who would become chief, because of his age, when the burial was over. The ancient pariah, drooling and slobbering into his luxuriant white beard, listened. He had to clear his saliva-clogged throat before he quavered out the words which Noma-us had put into his head.

"Koropok, when you return to your Old Men, bring them my words. These are the words I send: 'The chief died. There was no food for the death-feast. No *sake.* So the god ordered me to make a feast.' Say that."

KOROPOK DROPPED to his bare knees and put his head against the edge of the cold *k'ang.* Rain rattled on the reeds and stalks. Along with it, Llewelyn Davies heard the breaths of the Ainus coming in anticipatory shudders, sounding like wind from the north.

What a spot this is going to be, thought Lew, while the Ainus believed that he was making his prayers. But he was thinking of more than hunger, cold, and food; he was realizing that if he were permitted to remain for the funeral feast, bought if possible with the coins, he would eat what otherwise would have been eaten by the pariahs. If none of the numbed older men figured this out, it was a foregone conclusion that it would occur to the half-caste. Davies had no intention of having Koropok sent out of the shelters. Here was where he had to stay.

Hell, decided Davies, *I might just as well get accustomed to no chow right off. The funeral food wouldn't be any good anyhow, although in a week,* Lew was ready to bet, *it'd be the finest stuff I ever ate.*

Lifting his head, decision arrived at, he thought, *Here's where I pull one out of the hat.* He said, "*Onné,* it is the law in my *kotan* that no man may eat of a funeral feast except men of the same *kotan.* Oh, I would like to eat with you, but if I eat it will anger the god of my *kotan.* Yes, you must have a funeral feast." Koropok pleaded, "But if you eat the food bought with the money I have, and I do not return with food, my Old Men will say that I ate it myself."

"Tell them you were robbed," said Noma-us.

Koropok whimpered, "Will they believe?"

"Then," said the half-caste, reaching out imperiously for the two coins, "if you fear to return, perhaps the new chief will allow you to stay here."

"Will I be fed?" Koropok added whiningly, "I do not mean at the feast. I mean will I receive my share of other food?"

Noma-us scratched the chin under his thin hairs. "That depends on what we can find to buy with your two little and almost worthless coins. But even so you will be better off here. If you return, foodless, your Old Men will curse you and your spirit. Give me the money! There is too much talk."

Koropok kept it in his fist.

"*Shirri kun'!*" said the half-caste. "Night is coming, which is a good time for me to make purchases of what is unsold in the shops and would spoil before morning. If there is anything to be bought. Come! Open your hand, Koropok, and give the money to me. If… *ho!*… where did you get this money?"

Davies had allowed Noma-us to open his fist and seize the coins, which, first seen in the gloom of the shelter, might have been copper instead of silver. Sharp eyes had caught the difference.

Soberly, the American disguised as an Ainu, and accepted as one, played a card in the job ahead of him.

"The Old Men," said Koropok, speaking furtively, "gave it to me."

"Where did they get it? Tell us!" Noma-us, despised by the Japanese, seemed to have inherited a good trace of the inquisitor as he thrust his face close to Koropok's. "If you do not tell, I will report it!"

Nuts, thought Davies. But, as Koropok, he moaned, *"Kora Amerika-jin tag'r att' tscharu'...* captured sea soldiers of the Americans gave the money to someone of us to tell someone else something about which I know nothing."

Davies let that sink in.

He believed that he could see cupidity grow in the half-caste's eyes as Noma-us reckoned what this information might be worth. *You'll pass it on,* decided Lew, *and since the information is worth nothing to the Central Government, whoever you contact'll be one of Li Chou's men.*

What Koropok's explanation implied was simple; a Marine, captured after an attack by General Li Chou's men on a convoy, had attempted to bribe a pariah so that the Ainu would get word to either the Nationalist Army or to Americans. Davies was entirely prepared for any future questioning, since sooner or later he had known he would be questioned. His story would hold up.

The man-to-be-chief muttered, "When will you obtain food, Noma-us?"

"Soon," said the half-caste. "Very soon. I go for it now."

He glanced at the newcomer, the brother Ainu, as if expecting that Koropok was going to insist on going along during the spending of the money; but when the newly arrived pariah said nothing, and did not move, Noma-us' opinion of him became even lower than previously. Koropok was a fool.

This suited Davies perfectly. He would have liked seeing where the half-caste went, but he would learn that soon enough, and without volition on his part. Yes, Koropok the Ainu would soon be sent for, and questioned.

So far, so good, thought Lew. Then, as Noma-us hurried away, Koropok added his mumble to the prayers of the Old Men as they promised the spirit of the dead chief that shortly they would feast to do him honor.

"To the sea which nourishes us," chanted the starving pariahs, "and to the forest which protects us, we present our thanks."

Koropok prayed with them.

CHAPTER III

DEVILS FROM THE NORTH

NOT EVEN a mockery of sleep came to Davies when he huddled into the remains of cotton quilts in a corner of the black, unlit shelter. The old pariahs, half alive, half dead of hunger, continued to sit around the fireless *k'ang* and the cold occupant lying on it, as they waited for the return of the half-caste Ainu. It seemed to Davies that what the old men must be thinking was whether Noma-us would return with food, or, instead, fill his own belly.

But the gentle, beaten-down Ainus gave no thought to this. The few words which were spoken showed trust in the half-caste. Perhaps the food-shops were empty. Yes, there was little food. Or perhaps they were closed for the night. Robbers came at night. Or perhaps the *Shina-jin* merchants refused to sell to an Ainu, who had no right to eat when Chinese men were without food. Or perhaps an evil spirit, that of the unfeasted dead man perhaps, had caught Noma-us in the night and devoured not only the food Noma-us was bringing, but their brother's soul as well.

The soft, sad voices, hopeless voices, and the rain above, should have brought sleep to Davies; but it was cold, and damp, and more than strange, and he was very wakeful. The half-caste was up to more than the pariahs had the sense to realize, if Davies' reasoning were correct: Noma-us was bargaining for whatever he believed the information about having a pariah act as messenger for captive Marines ought to be worth. If this were what the scraggly-bearded fellow attempted, Noma-us was entirely willing to sell out brother Ainus somewhere else in China....

"Perhaps Noma-us is captured," mumbled an old man.

The man-to-be-chief said, "He has done nothing."

"He will go to someone who has said we will be brothers," said a third. "Noma-us is a wise man."

"Such men are not shopkeepers."

"They who are shopkeepers and rob the poor do so only because an evil spirit named Chiang protects them," said the man-to-be-chief, mouthing, Davies knew, what Noma-us must have said previously.

A different voice mourned, in the blackness, "We starve because the *Amerika-jin* refuse to bring food to us any more."

A good deal of venom was being distilled in China, as the man disguised as Koropok could hear, if drops of it dripped clear to where pariahs starved. Well, he was hearing about what he had expected to hear, and this included what the Old Men continued to mumble about—how the *Peri-kamoi*, the pariahs' own Bear God, must be related to the *Peri-okkai*, the Bear Men from the North. Even more, the sacred color of the Ainus, kuré, was the color of their brothers, red.

On and on went the talk, endlessly, coming from mouths hungry for food. Always verification. But useless to Davies, whose twin problems were, firstly, discovering what had happened to the missing Marines, and, secondly, finding out what General Li Chou and the Communist Army might be planning. He had high hopes that there was a good chance to work out the first portion of the problem, although what he might learn about the second seemed worse than a remote possibility.

Why the devil don't I sleep? Davies beat on himself.

He was finally willing to admit to himself why not; he hoped that Noma-us, accompanied by North Army soldiers, probably in disguise, would come to the shattered dwelling and take Koropok off for questioning. And when that came, he didn't want to be awakened; he wanted to be awake and alert. After all, this was China, not Japan, and not familiar to him. And Li Chou's reputation was enough to worry Davies. The man was without scruples, and he was disarmingly smart… and G-2, as well as the Marine colonel, had warned Davies that disguises had been penetrated before. All of which kept the stocky American awake.

But when footsteps, of shod feet, broke the interminable talk and the rattle of the rain, Koropok appeared deep in sleep. His final precaution was to bury his shaggy head in his arms, as Ainus often slept in the presence of devils… and the manner in which he was awakened proved the wisdom of this, because a flash was snapped down to where his face would have been.

Davies allowed whoever stood above him to jerk Koropok's arms from his face to expose black beard and black, staring— and seemingly frightened—eyes. Then the stocky newcomer to the shelter began to whimper a plea that he not be beaten, talking disjointedly in clipped Ainu-fashion Japanese.

He was pulled to his feet when Noma-us said that this was the stranger who had come this night, and he was able to see, when the light which blinded him was lowered to take in his bare, muddy legs, that there were four or five Chinese with the half-caste pariah. Two of these men grabbed him, without saying anything, and shoved him toward the entrance to the shelter. The last thing Davies saw, while all of the Old Men sat wordlessly, fearing even to ask what had happened to the food Noma-us was to bring, was the dead Ainu chief on the *k'ang*.

THE WALK to the market town of Yeungwi was made in absolute silence. Koropok shambled along with head low, but even so, and in the night, he was reasonably positive that

his captors were being kept dry in GI slickers and were marching in GI shoes. Army. Not Marine equipment.

Several men slouched at the gate through which Koropok
was taken into the dark and silent town, and past the Red
Temple, which G-2 had said had been taken over by the Army
of the North, which didn't believe in temples. Davies marked
the place because of location and style, although the red plaster
which had given the temple a common name had fallen off
long ago. But G-2, as regards the temple, was wet as the rain
which was drenching Major Davies… his captors, with never

*His captors took him
down one crooked shop-
street into another.*

a glance at it, took him past it, and down one crooked shop-street into another, and then along a zigzag way partly open, partly closed in by the side walls of houses. And through another, smaller gate, inside of which were other armed men, and across the paved courtyard with its single tree, and into the house. Another guard, who brought his rifle to attention, was posted in the hallway.

If this corridor was dim, the room to which Koropok the Ainu was taken hissed with gasoline lamps and was bright with light. There was a desk in the room, with papers on one end, a number of small bottles on the other, and, seated so that he was between the two, a smiling, wrinkled old Chinese.

In spite of what Davies had been told to expect of General Li Chou—and the general physical description made it obvious that this was the dreaded strategist of the Army of the North—his first impression was that of astonishment at the contrast between his outward appearance and the reputation he bore. He looked like a benevolent old grandfather in his black, padded robe, out of which the tips of his old fingers peeped. He did not shake his own hands, in Chinese fashion, when he spoke to the pariah standing before his desk; but he did speak gently and kindly when he said that after all when a stranger came to a town, in these days of conflict, it was necessary to ask his name and see him. Did not Koropok—that was the name?—agree with him?

Davies did not reply to the softly spoken query. He was Koropok the Ainu now, and so what he said was, in terrible mixture of Japanese, Ainu, and northern dialect, " 'S'an' l'o hakkir' wak'r'mas' tanni…. Headman, I do not understand. I am stupid. I am only an Ainu. I—"

"Here," smiled General Li Chou, "there are no headmen, Koropok. We are brothers. So do not be afraid."

Koropok merely blinked.

"Are you hungry?" asked Li Chou.

"Yes, lord."

"Nor are there any lords," the general informed him. "You say that you are a hungry person, Koropok?"

"Yes, lord."

General Li Chou snuggled his thin frame deeper into the warm quilted robe which he wore, examining and appraising the stocky, bedraggled figure standing in front of his desk. The general's eyes, Davies was pretty sure, were the coldest and most unwavering he had ever seen, and were unfathomable pools of narrow blackness. Was the general satisfied with what he saw, satisfied that Koropok was a pariah? As yet no real questioning had come up; did Li Chou trust to observation only? Davies doubted this; he was uneasy under the icy scrutiny, and unable to so much as glance around a room which he would have liked to examine. There was never any way of knowing exactly what a man might see... but he did not dare.

This is a smart boy, Lew was sure. *Smart and bad. No jumping into things. Not Li Chou. Nor will he ever do any boasting, the way Nips did, and give me a hint as to what cooks.*

The general said in fluent Japanese, *"Ryoko menjo wo o mochi...* have you papers to travel from one town to another?"

Koropok hung his head.

"If you had been captured by the men of Chiang," smiled Li Chou, "instead of being brought to me, your head would have been cut off."

One of the men who had brought Koropok to the general said, when the tattered, sodden pariah merely blinked, "Sir, this one was too stupid a pariah to be afraid of evil spirts hovering around a dead man. He slept when we came for him."

"Did he?" said Li Chou gently; and Davies was aware of new interest momentarily shown by the general, although quickly concealed.

What he's thinking, Lew believed, *is that no matter how dumb a pariah is, no Ainu would dare sleep near a dead man.* Davies could have said, "Lord, I had walked far, and was hungry, and therefore I could not help sleeping," but did not. Instead, he swayed, almost imperceptibly, on his feet, acting out what he believed would not be wise to mention, not to such a shrewd antagonist.

LI CHOU'S delicate fingertips, slipping in and out of the sleeves of the black, quilted robe, fascinated Davies. The general's hands, after the fashion of Chinese of importance, were beautifully kept; but what caught Davies was the fact that the nails were red. At first Lew supposed that this must be some strange affectation. Then he recalled, from stories he had heard from patrons of Number Nineteen in Tokyo, that male Chinese attendants on Flower Boats, or in Chinese brothels on land, painted their nails as did the women themselves.

Take a leaf from Li Chou's book and don't go jumping to conclusions, Lew told himself; and finally he was able to see that only the forefinger and middle finger of Li Chou's right hand had been stained red.

Davies had all he could do to keep from looking immediately at the small vials on the desk. Even when he was able to do this, by wagging his head numbly back and forth while Li Chou studied him, he learned nothing, since each bottle was wrapped with paper clear to the stopper. If anything was written on the papers, those sides facing Davies were blank.

And you don't pick up things with forefinger and middle finger anyhow, reasoned Lew. *Maybe it's a sign so all good fellows know each other when they get together. Sign of top dogs,* thought Lew, because he hadn't noticed the red color on the nails of the general's men. *So what?*

General Li Chou reached his right hand deep into his left sleeve, and drew out a silver cigarette case, opening it slowly and gracefully. *Is he going to pull that old one?* wondered Lew, when, with the cigarette lighted, Li Chou paused before replacing the case. *Is he going to say, in English, "Will you have a cigarette?"* But the general said nothing, although his eyes bored away into Koropok's.

Davies had no way of knowing whether the general had

thought of doing just that, and finally discarded the old way of unmasking a masquerader. But what Davies did know, now, was that Li Chou had started to lift out the cigarette between thumb and forefinger, in the usual manner of men, and, instead, had picked up the paper tube with his fingers instead. As the general of the Communist Army smoked away placidly, Lew saw the reason. The thumb's end was scarred and roughened.

Li Chou remarked, showing that his thoughts had never deviated from that which had made him suspicious, "Did you not fear to sleep beside the dead?"

"I was praying, lord," ventured Koropok meekly, "and I slept. I did not know I slept. Do not beat me for sleeping, lord."

"We are not going to beat you for anything," Li Chou said gravely. He said, in an amused aside to the man who had been in charge of the party, and in Mandarin so swift that Davies only caught a few words, "These Ainus believe that evil spirits descend to earth whenever a man dies. We, at least, confine that superstition to the New Year, eh, Wang Fong?"

"We are not going to beat you for anything," Li Chou said gravely.

Since the general winked solemnly, Wang Fong chuckled, and the other men standing in the room all grinned.

Davies had managed to pick out a few of the rapid words. *"Shan sao"* and these were devils from the north, and *"Yuan Tan,"* the New Year. Combined with these were Ainus and death. Although Davies did not guess exactly what Li Chou had remarked, he was able to come close enough. He saw no importance in what was said. It was a natural enough remark for the general to have made, especially because the celebrating of the New Year was not far off.

"Koropok," said Li Chou idly, "how did you get to Yeungwi?"

"I walked, lord."

The general nodded. "How many li?"

Now he's getting to work on me, realized Davies. So Koropok said, *"Wamb' li,"* apologetically, and continued, *"Hots li, ito hots li.* A long distance, lord. I was tired, lord. I was hungry. It was a long way." *And make something of that,* thought the American calmly.

Not until Li Chou had rubbed out the cigarette, again holding it between forefinger and middle finger instead of more naturally, did he say, "And why did you come so far to Yeungwi,. Koropok?"

"Yeungwi was the great town to which I was sent by the Old Men," said Koropok. "I swore to come here. I was sent," he said, in what sounded like a confidence, "because the Old Men decided, after prayers, that it would be lucky to send me. And I was less starved than the others."

"Ah," said Li Chou. "I see. Yes. Very good. But tell me, Koropok, what is the name of the town from which you were sent?"

"Town?"

Li Chou lost none of his patience. "Yes. Its name."

Koropok said sadly, "I lived in no town, lord. The Japanese lords gave us one field in which to live, lord, while we worked."

"Ah," the general said, and again, "I see." Then he asked, "And how did you acquire coins, Koropok?"

Davies repeated the tale he had told Noma-us; *Amerika-jin* soldiers, he did not know how, had given the coins to his Old Men, in order that a message be delivered. He Koropok, knew nothing of whatever decision the Old Men had reached, nor why the message was not delivered. Nor did he know why he was sent to Yeungwi to buy food, although the Old Men said that it was a safe place for an Ainu to go.

At this last, Li Chou nodded briefly. *He thinks,* decided Davies, *that word-of-mouth stuff has been circulated by his men, which is why Ainus got the name Yeungwi hammered through their thick skulls.*

THE GENERAL stood up and went to a hanging map. Davies could easily guess that Li Chou was tracing the course taken by the captors of the Marines reported missing, in an effort to locate the particular group of pariahs from which Koropok had come. He watched the general, but with extreme care, lest he himself be under observation of the general's men in the room. He saw the long, red-nailed forefinger following a heavy black line on the map, probably from Yeungwi north; and once, where the finger hesitated, Li Chou's face darkened.

The general turned from the map, started to speak, and then shifted to what Lew knew was a different dialect as Li Chou spoke.

"Heung ni pin hai... they escaped in that direction," the general said icily. But only from the hesitation of the tracing finger, where Davies had seen no crossroad on the map, and from the swift expression of rage, instantly concealed... and, lest even a pariah understand much of the northern dialects or Mandarin, the shift to what was probably Cantonese, did Davies guess what the general was convinced had happened. Li Chou now believed that the money had been paid the pariahs by Marines who had somehow escaped.

When inventing the story, Davies had supposed that Li Chou

would think that a Marine, somehow, had managed to slip the coins to an Ainu, en route. This was a complication. The general was apt to want the escaped Marines—who actually existed—captured; and for that purpose he might send Koropok, under guard, back to the field from which Koropok had said he had come... which Davies would never be able to find, because it didn't exist.

When I don't find it, thought Lew, *I can play dumb, of course, and have lost my way, which is a lousy yarn. Wasn't I supposed to have come here for food which was to have been taken back? And when I lead 'em nowhere, I end in a field and have my head chopped off. Some fun.*

General Li Chou returned to his desk, and seated himself, and lit another cigarette. He did not resume his study of the sodden, tattered figure standing before him; he had accepted Koropok to be what Davies said Koropok was, but, *What good is that going to do me?* wondered Lew. *Damn it, I've outsmarted myself.*

He had mentioned a field instead of some town in which Ainus lived for an excellent reason; checking would prove difficult and would be done only in case Koropok failed to convince Li Chou that Koropok was a pariah. Now, Li Chou was entirely convinced, and believed the manufactured story.

Wryly, Davies thought, *Why couldn't those confounded Marines have remained prisoners?* He came close to grinning as he guessed what the colonel would have said to that. Not that the situation, right now, was funny.

General Li Chou said, "Keep him here."

"In this house, General?"

Li Chou reached into a desk drawer and took out a tiny snuff bottle, amethyst glass with a coral stopper. Unscrewing the top, and holding the bottle again with fingers instead of thumb, he allowed a drop of perfume to fall on a paper spread in front of him, and sniffed the fragrance delicately.

"No," he said. "He stinks."

Same to you, thought Lew.

A non-com grabbed Koropok's arm, swinging him roughly around. Davies had time for one direct look at the map, and tried to relocate where the general's finger had paused; then the map, as he was swung, was replaced before his sight by books on a shelf, by a long white silk placard on which black characters were painted, and finally by the oblong of the door.

"Where will you keep him?" asked Li Chou.

Wang Fong, apparently in charge of the men, said, "The walls of the great Red Temple are thick, General Li Chou."

"They are thick enough," agreed the general, "but I do not want him there. No. I do not even want a stupid Ainu there."

Captain Wang Fong smiled as he saluted. General Li Chou returned the smile; in that smile, if Davies could have seen it, was utter satisfaction.

"Kung hai fat choi," said Li Chou, and both men laughed.

Again, Davies knew that the words were not in any north-China dialect nor in Mandarin, and were not intended to be understood by an Ainu, a man who had been in the north long enough to have picked up a few common words. Certainly Davies didn't understand what had been said, and, as before, he guessed the talk to be in swift Cantonese of the south. But he did know, from the outburst of cackling laughter, how satisfied these Communist Army men were with themselves.

CHAPTER IV

THE WALLS OF YEUNGWI

EVEN BEFORE Koropok was marched, after a brief discussion between Wang Fong and his men, into the night and rain and to a nearby requisitioned house, he was trying to add up what had happened. When he was shoved into a bare room, and two quilts, and their fleas, were flung in after him, he was so deep in the puzzle that he had to force himself to remove his ragged jacket, dry himself with one quilt, and roll up in the other. His teeth chattered as he thought, *What have I got that makes any sense?* but what did make sense was that if someone came in during the night, and saw that an Ainu pariah had dried himself off and was sleeping without garments, it would instantly arouse suspicions.

All body-warmth was gone from the Ainu jacket when Davies, on the floor, picked it up. He had to get into it, and he did, shivering; he moved the worn fabric in such a manner that little of it touched him except across the shoulders: then he bundled himself in the dry quilt, and pulled the damp one across him. Because it did no good above him, he shoved it off, and rolled himself over and on it. Then he settled down for his first night in Yeungwi.

As regards the missing Marines, one or more, or possibly all, he had nothing on which to go except a red-nailed finger which had hesitated on a map. Without examination of that exact map, he could get nowhere. And even if he had a look-see at it, little could be accomplished, because the Marines certainly had too much sense to stick around where they could be easily captured.

Those boys beat it, chop-chop, Davies was sure. *They headed south, keeping away from town, and particularly from Yeungwi, where they probably were questioned by Li Chou or somebody. Maybe they'll manage to make the Nationalist lines, unless a starving man turns 'em in for the reward.*

Doubtless a reward had been posted. For several minutes Davies pondered on what might be done about that fact, turning it this way and that to figure whether use might be made of it. Right off, he didn't see how.

As regards Davies' greater duty, which was to find out what the Communist Army might be planning, he knew this much: Li Chou had something in mind, something he was happy about.

There was no sense in wasting time wishing that he himself

could be free to get around as an unsuspected Ainu, although this should have made everything far simpler. Perhaps he would be sent back to the pariahs; but, in the meantime, he had to keep going, although he had to wait to see what could be done.

Davies grinned to himself as he thought of the sort of thing on which he had to work, and which added up to zero. Old Li Chou had red fingernails. Something about the Red Temple was important to the general.

I'm seeing red, thought Lew, amused. *Probably the temple's being used to store arms, ammunition, and supplies, meaning Yeungwi is to be an advance base, which G-2 has already realized.*

What else was there? Well, Li Chou had concealed words he had said, first with lightning-fast Mandarin and next with a different dialect. Davies had not been able to understand anything of the latter, but had recognized a word or two of Mandarin; what Li Chou had said then referred to the dead and to devils.

"Shan sao," the general had said, which meant Northern Devils, and, *"Yuan Tan,"* which meant the New Year.

Davies tried to form the four words into a sentence which included "Ainu," also used by Li Chou, although the general had given it the Japanese pronunciation, *ano.* Dog. Hmm. Had the number-one strategist said, "The Ainus believe that Northern Devils come to earth when a man dies, but we know that demons come only at the New Year?" Was that it? No. Nothing about that to have made Li Chou wink, to have made everyone in the general's room laugh. So that wasn't it.

Was it the obvious, when a man stopped and thought about it?

Rolling over on his back, eyes wide in the darkness, Davies slowly became willing to admit that it might be. He was afraid of obvious interpretations. Usually they resulted from lazy reasoning, from an unwillingness to dig deeply. This was especially true in the Orient. How did the Japanese put it? He remembered: "In the glare of the obvious we are blind to the truth." Perhaps this was the other way about. Perhaps the obvious was the truth.

Had Li Chou said, "The Northern Devils will descend at the time of the New Year, and attack"? By Northern Devils, did the general mean the Communist forces? Why not? But... *Where do the pariahs, who were mentioned, come into that picture?* puzzled Davies. He didn't know. But he was certain of this much: his first figuring was entirely wrong, because the leaders of the Northern Army didn't believe in demons any more than in gods. And yet suppose Li Chou had mentioned Ainus and their superstitions, and Chinese New Year beliefs, ironically?

Wouldn't this have caused winks and laughter?

Now I'm getting nowhere faster than ever, Lew told himself disgustedly. And so he settled himself for sleep. Not until then, having been deep in the problem, did Davies fully realize how Yeungwi's fleas had been dining.

He did not have a good night; he had to simulate sleep in the gray morning when the door was unlocked and he was ordered to his feet.

IT WAS a shame to waste good American rice on the useless Ainu, one of the non-coms gathered about the cooking-pot remarked; but the taunting was given over when bowls were filled with rice topped off with shredded pickled cabbage, and the chopsticks began to click. Koropok, unwashed and stiff and flea-bitten, held his bowl as close to his mouth as did any of the Chinese, and, his own chop-sticks flying, gobbled down his full share without a grain remaining in the earthenware bowl, although when he held it out, empty and polished, it was not refilled.

What was to be done with this rice-destroyer during the day? The sergeant said that Captain Wang had merely given instructions that the fellow was not to be permitted to escape, if, indeed, the unintelligent bearded one had the courage to try; therefore should not the Ainu work for the rice which he had eaten? And work the pariah did, in the driving rain, following the rolling of the *cha t'in kau* dice and their good fortune in the hands of the sergeant, who sold Koropok's service to the highest bidder, whose burdens Koropok carried all day long.

There was nothing to be gathered from what he carried; and if some of the bales contained food which had been taken from American convoys, and if others, smaller, might have been packed with ammunition which had been shipped down from the north to Yeungwi, both facts were known to G-2. So all that Koropok the burden-bearer was able to add to his scant store of knowledge concerned a Chinese crossroads town, a place on which advance units of the Red Army had descended, cleaning out the shops and breaking down the stone walls of the square, high pawnshops, and taking the best of the walled residence as quarters, along with whatever women remained in Yeungwi. Li Chou's men had as yet done no fighting, but they had brought war to Yeungwi, although the general called it brotherhood.

Yeungwi, in peace, would have been dreary enough during the rainy season; now, it was a place of desolation. There was not even the solace of a visit to the Red Temple, where men would have liked to utter the prayers which General Li Chou had announced could no longer be pasted on doorposts as the New Year approached. No, "May Heaven send down upon our

It was a shame to waste good American rice on the useless Ainu.

home peace and happiness." No, "Honor and wealth as well as
poverty and lowly station are in the hands of Heaven." Nor
could men take strength from the presence of the stone temple
tiger, with its massive jaws, which was the protector of Yeungwi.

Nor was it possible for women to bow before the temple's
Kwan-Yin, goddess of mercy, not even to ask her sympathy for
those things which happened when an army came to a town.
It was rumored that the Kwan-Yin had been broken, although
no one in Yeungwi knew of this positively, because since the
arrival of General Li Chou only his men were permitted to pass
through the temple gate.

There were guards at this gate, as Davies soon discovered,
and there were additional guards posted around the walls.

Davies gave little thought to this, as the days passed and Li
Chou appeared to have forgotten about a pariah who, with
Marine money, had come to buy food. None of his burden
bearing had taken him inside the walls, although a good many
times he, along with the labor detachment, carried boxes and
bales as far as the gate. There, guards sent for soldiers stationed
inside the temple, who carried the loads inside after an officer
checked the contents.

What did amaze Davies was the fact that as the New Year
came nearer, people of Yeungwi found little subtle ways in which
to circumvent the posted orders that the old superstitions regarding the New Year must be forgotten. Of course there was
the *Shun Hsing,* the Homage to the Stars, curtained as they
were by rain-clouds; and who could say that when men walked
out at night and, when unobserved by soldiers, dropped bits of
paper fashioned like star-lanterns, they were following tradition
old as China? Or that some families ate less of little, in order
to save enough pounded rice to make boiled New Year dump-
lings?

True, this would be a New Year without firecrackers which,
exploding, would exorcise the demons of darkness and the
north; but it had been years since the custom had been permit-

ted by the Japanese, who saw to it that no powder was wasted. As Davies overheard, it would have been splendid to celebrate China's victory at the New Year by letting off strings of firecrackers; but, to the people of Yeungwi, again under domination, this was too much to hope for. But, in whatever ways were going to be possible, men wanted to greet the New Year, with incense burned to meet good spirits even if there could be no firecrackers to drive off the bad.

Because Koropok worked without protest, relieving whatever Communist soldier won his services, he continued to be fed; but rice, plus shreds of vegetable, was not enough to keep off hunger. While this was an annoyance, because it made some of the burdens a weight which buckled his legs, what bothered him more was that he was wasting his time. He could, he was sure, escape from his night-quarters; but why do so? To climb the wall of the temple and look inside? What for? He knew just about what he would see, guns, ammunition, G-2 knew that already.

I T W A S when Koropok was carrying a heavy, square, three-foot package, different from those being handled by the Chinese of the detachment, that he saw General Li Chou standing with members of his staff at the temple gate.

If I call myself to his attention, decided Lew, *that moment, he'll either send me packing back to the Ainus, or stop this damned coolie business.*

Deliberately, Koropok stumbled, and as he did so gave the big, square package a shrewd pitch, so that it landed in front of the strategist in command of the advance force. It fell with a thump, sending water splashing up.

I didn't figure on that, Davies thought uneasily; mud had splashed high. Even so, he was unprepared for Li Chou's icy fury, directed not at him but at the trembling non-com in charge of the detachment. The general whipped words at the cringing Chinese which were as damaging as blows from an iron, jointed bone-crusher in the hands of an executioner. More, the general gave the order which was sending the soldier off to be shot.

Not until the non-com was marched away did Li Chou look directly at the stupidly-standing Koropok. The latter looked only at his own feet.

Li Chou snapped a command to a major; all of the labor detachment turned and moved away when the major relayed the order. Major Hing Ma's next order brought a half dozen soldiers from inside the wall, men well-uniformed, well-trained. "Sir," said Major Hing to General Li Chou, "is the Ainu to be shot?"

At least I'll be finished by men who can shoot, thought Davies, *and all because I was tired of packing their damned supplies.*

It was, of course, more than that; Davies had wanted desperately to be able to shamble around Yeungwi, instead of always being with the soldiers.

He kept his eyes on the mud. While he waited for the order which he feared was about to be issued, he waggled his shaggy head a little, in a gesture of complete stupidity; and as he waggled it, and saw for the first time what must have caused Li Chou's rage, he wanted to live long enough to learn what there must be about the contents of the package, where he saw something red where the wrapping had broken a little, to have sent one man to death already.

Red paper. Or cloth? *No. It's paper,* decided Davies. *Cloth wouldn't have been that heavy.* What paper? Placards, in the thin red rice-paper which the Chinese always used; placards marked with orders, either obvious or for Fifth Columnists to carry out, perhaps previous to attacks on the Nationalists?

Red paper. Into Davies' head popped remembrance of Li Chou's red fingernails; had the old boy been going over some of the placards? Again, no. This would have stained the balls of the fingers, and not the nails.

Not only was the paper red as blood, but as Davies forced himself to act like a man who had no realization that death confronted him, he believed, as his head moved from side to side, that there was a metallic shine to the paper, silver perhaps, or a pale gold. And while this might have been illusion, there was no sun to be brightening the bloody redness. The paper was flecked with a different color, a metallic color. And what could that mean?

General Li Chou wiped mud from the trousers of his uniform. He shrugged, then he smiled. "Koropok," he said, speaking fluently in the Japanese which a pariah was bound to understand, *"chitto wa hanashi no tane ni narimasho...* another general would cut off your head for what you have done. Go back to your people, and talk about the kindness of the Northern Army."

Good old propaganda, thought Davies, fighting down the relief he didn't want to show in his face. *And it's more than that. Li Chou wants his own men, who get doses of this brotherhood stuff, to know that while the general is severe, he is just. He punishes a non-com of his own forces, but he is kind to dumb animals. All of which, the American knew, has nothing to do with red paper.*

"*W' s'kosh',*" promised Koropok meekly.

General Li Chou glanced around; none of the labor battalion men remained, but only soldiers from inside the wall, and the staff officers.

"Koropok," said the general softly, *"ketchaku ch'i huo? Chin pan? Erh t'i chao? Fei t'ien shih hsiang?"*

If the first word were Japanese, and meant, "do you know" the words following were in Mandarin. Here and there Davies caught a little of the meaning, but only a little. He took the moment during which Li Chou paused, and in which he himself only blinked, to get those words indelibly in mind.

"*Pa'o ta hsiang yang chen?*" continued Li Chou. "*Wu hwei nao p'an? Yen huo kan tzu? Ho tzu? Huo tzu?* How many do you know, Koropok?"

"I am only an Ainu," said Koropok. "Do not beat me, lord. I do not understand. I am a stupid person. I—"

"Send him back to his fellows," said General Li Chou.

Koropok waited, even after the words were repeated to him, until he was given a push. Then, without a word of thanks, he shambled away.

What Davies was thinking was, *What I think I know doesn't make sense. Not any.* But if the general's words, plus the testimony of the gold-or-silver-flecked paper, made no sense, it was damned good to be alive.

CHAPTER V

A BALL OF MUD

KOROPOK RECEIVED no welcome from the Ainu elders, and expected none. Noma-us, the sly half-caste, was gone; no, it was not known where. He had returned, days and days ago, with a little food, but not much; now, he had gone to get food again, and had not come back. In response to Koropok's prodding, the Old Men insisted they had not the slightest idea where Noma-us might be.

Davies, since the obvious had been the truth once before, was willing to gamble that the half-caste was trying to pick up the trail of the escaped Marines; this might easily be the case. Northern Army officers might have financed the journey; Noma-us might have started out on his own.

But if Lew hoped that the scraggly-bearded and slippery Noma-us failed to pick up the trail, his hopes were higher about what he now knew about one thing—one anyhow—which went on inside the walled Red Temple, even if it made no sense. He did not remember all of the Mandarin words which Li Chou had used; he did remember some, and these were words which a man being sent behind the Communist lines would have been taught to recognize.

While he squatted down in another shelter in the ruined dwelling, being of too young an age to stay with the Old Men, he repeated these words to himself. Yes, he could tell to what they referred, even when knowing only a word or so of each of Li Chou's phrases. "Fire. Bombs. Smoke. Explosions." Although an entire phrase, such as *"Fei t'ien shih hsiang"* meant, exactly, "Ten explosions flying to heaven," and the general's *"Yen huo kan tzu"* when properly translated, meant "Smoke and fiery bombs," yet the single words, which Davies recognized, when considered along with the thin, red rice-paper, which was flecked with typically glittering splotches of metallic color, added to only one thing.

Firecrackers.

And that, decided Davies, *is what doesn't make one damned bit of sense, not as I see it.* Observance of the New Year, with or without the customary firecrackers, was forbidden to all Chinese within the zone controlled by the Red Army. *Then why are they being made?* worried Lew.

Well, suppose the firecrackers, after manufacture, were smuggled through the Nationalist lines, to serve as the signals for attack, to get Fifth Columnists to work? Might that be their purpose? On the other hand, there certainly must be any number of easier ways, involving less work, which would serve that purpose. Dozens of ways. Messages. Or shrewdly worded placards, seemingly innocent.

Although Davies told himself that he ought to attempt to get over the wall of the Red Temple, into which the sheets had gone, and where there was certain to be powder for the making of firecrackers, he did so half-heartedly. What good would verification be? None. But what puzzled him was the reason for secrecy. Perhaps because Yeungwi Chinese would demand some of the red-paper tubes? No. Any request to General Li Chou would be brushed off.

Something was in the wind in which firecrackers were involved, those powder-packed red tubes with the strange Chinese names mentioned by Li Chou to find out whether Koropok the Ainu knew to what the names referred. Davies had connected a portion of the names with the thin, typical red paper;

the entire names would have been immediately recognized by
any Chinese anywhere in China. Bombs for frightening devils.
Silver flowers blooming at night. Double-kicking feet—tubes
which exploded once on the ground, and, flung up by the force
of the explosion, burst a second time in the air. A thousand
devils splitting apart.

All I'd see is how the things are made, Davies told himself
finally; but when days became a week, and he shambled aim-
lessly and uselessly about in Yeungwi, he began to realize fully
how magnificently guarded were the temple walls, and the
impossibility of scaling them, unseen.

*Koropok was booted
out of every drinking
shop in Yeungwi.*

All because firecrackers are being made there? the American disguised as Koropok asked himself. Nuts.

TOWN GOSSIP, what he managed to overhear, did him no good. It was difficult to pick up anything, actually. He could not hang around the food stalls, because the merchants ordered him off, because he was penniless. The drinking shops were even worse; soldiers there shouted that when they drank they desired to see objects of beauty, and not a bearded apparition who looked like a mountain devil. Koropok was booted out of every drinking shop in Yeungwi; and Davies was beginning to give up hope that he would learn anything.

He had to be careful when anywhere near the walls of the Red Temple, although he continued studying them. Whatever went on inside was kept secret… and there was nothing Davies could do about it. He went so far as to follow some of the soldiers on duty there, following them into drinking shops; but

they were picked and silent men, grim dark Buriats, Mongols, Tartars, and—during the short time Koropok would be in the shop, before being ordered away—they drank without much talk save about women.

And yet the Red Temple drew Davies like a magnet. He never stood still when he was anywhere within sight of the walls, but, he hoped, out of sight of the guards; he would shuffle along one crooked street, along another alley... and he was doing this on the morning that he heard, from within, a long, terrible scream, into the echo of which came a second scream, of stark, terrible agony.

Was someone being tortured? Only a man beyond breaking-point would have cried out like an animal; and it came to Davies that perhaps someone had penetrated the secret, and was now paying for the knowledge.

But the sound he heard next indicated that his guess was wrong. He heard the roar of a motor; he crouched down, against the blank side of a house, on seeing how a jeep came careening through the gate, to go roaring down the street. Pressed as he was in shadow, he dared look squarely at the vehicle.

Davies saw that one soldier was holding another in the rear of the jeep, holding him by force, not as a captive, but because the second man's anguish made him twist and writhe. The second man was not screaming. A gag, white on dark face, was across his mouth. He fought the soldier who held him, vio-lently, terribly; and as the soldier sought to restrain him, and to keep him under the cloth, blanket, whatever it was, which enveloped him, the man's head jerked horribly. His eye-balls, Davies saw, all in the flash as the jeep passed, seemed to have been rolled back into his head.

Then the car was out of sight.

For the first instant Davies wanted to follow the jeep. Where was the man being taken? The hospital, which once had been American? To Headquarters? Following at once, when there were guards who, at the gate, stared along the street, was out of the question. But a jeep wouldn't vanish in Yeungwi, and Davies' immediate supposition was that it would not return at once, not if he knew soldiers.

Even so, it was difficult to remain where he was until the commotion at the gate was ended, and it was safe to shamble, as Koropok, down the street.

What had happened inside the Red Temple?

If ever I saw agony on a man's face, thought Davies, as he shuffled along next to the wall, *I saw it a moment ago.*

A fight between men? No. Torture? No. If it were that, the fellow would never have been rushed off. Well, what? Some accident. What accident? Powder burns? To Davies, this latter seemed logical. Possibly the dark man's clothing had caught on fire; the cloth or blanket over him might have been used to envelop him, to have smothered flame. Fire could have caused the screams....

Then, as Koropok shambled down the street, back to the gate, his eyes were attracted to an irregular two-inch piece of something which lay flat on the mud between the tread-marks of the jeep's wheels. Something red. A bit of the rice-paper used in the manufacture of firecrackers?

Must be, figured Davies. *The fellow was probably working on firecrackers.* How the paper had clung to the dark man was unimportant; but as Davies was about to walk past the red bit, his eyes told him that the little scrap appeared criss-crossed, as if it were fabric, and not paper. The rice-paper had been perfectly smooth and shining; this was neither.

One lifting of Davies' eyes was enough to see that a couple of soldiers were a hundred feet away, and coming toward the temple gate, while several Chinese men had come out of a nearby house. And so Koropok slipped in the slickness made by the jeep's tires; and when he rose, to the laughter of everyone who watched, the red object plus mud, was in his hand. As he rubbed mud from himself, he slipped the hand which had scooped up the red bit inside his jacket, and, balling the mud so as to hold the thing which he wanted above his hairless bearskin belt, he continued on his way. The Ainu.

Davies could hardly wait to turn the first corner. He had the ball of mud out swiftly. But when he examined it, while crouched again against a wall and acting as if he searched for fleas, in case anyone could see him, he found no trace at all of either red paper or red cloth. Not as material. All that he could see was that the mud had become brown, instead of the black mud of the streets. Whatever Davies had picked up had disintegrated.

His first thought was, *Of course. Damned stuff was charred.* Then he realized, *Charring means it'd have been black, and it wasn't. It was red. Like firecracker paper, but it wasn't paper. Fabric. Red as blood.*

Red as General Li Chou's fingernails on his forefinger and middle finger. And it was that moment in which Davies recalled the scarred thumb of the general who was the strategist of the Red Army.

H E H A D no time for more than the flash of the thought. Davies had been so intent on examining the ball of mud that he was unaware that Northern Army soldiers had come out of a house, and curiously, were watching him.

"What are you doing?" asked one.

Koropok looked up stupidly.

"He is going to eat it," another grinned.

The first soldier said, "Do you eat mud?"

The pariah shook his head.

"You are going to eat it now," he was told. "If your belly is filled with mud, you will not eat food intended for us. Do you think our great general steals food from Americans merely to feed you?"

Koropok crouched lower.

The soldier ordered, "Eat!"

And the man disguised as an Ainu had no choice. But when

he choked, none of the soldiers knew why, and gave credit to the mud; and when he seemed to swallow, painfully, the mud was again believed the reason.

They went off pleased with themselves. What a story this was, how the bearded fool gobbled down mud as if it were a lump of roasted pork, and how he made noises when it stuck in his throat!

But Davies, slowly rising, was just as pleased as they. Part of his choking, true, had been because of the nauseous mud; the major reason was because of the way it tingled hotly on his tongue and was sharp-tasting in his mouth, both proof that what he had been forced to swallow was neither alkaline nor neutral. It had been acid. The sensation had been caused by the skeletonized, acid-eaten fabric, cloth fallen away from the Red Army guard's uniform when the soldier, spattered in the temple, had struggled in the jeep.

Acid caused the soldier's agony. Acid, the self-same red acid, had gnawed and roughened the ball of General Li Chou's thumb. Red acid, the same red acid employed in the Red Temple, had stained the more resistant and impervious nails of the general's forefinger and middle finger.

There could be no doubt.

The fact that it was red made Davies smile in Koropok's beard, although the color, red, was actually incidental.

I may be a dumb Air Forces guy, he thought elatedly, as he moved slowly away, holding his hands over his middle, the sight of which made the soldiers laugh, *and the Marines got a wallop out of kidding me, but who else in the service would know about the stuff, and what it's used for?*

Men outside the service, those men who had studied and worked on liquid oxidizers, would know, of course. They would know how a mixture of nitric acid and nitrogen dioxide had been developed for use in rockets and rocket-propelled planes, after rigorous eliminations. Red fuming nitric acid, it was called. It oxidized a new fuel.… Major Davies, while in Tokyo and

assigned to Headquarters, had done a lot of reading and studying himself, trying to catch up on what had happened to planes
while he had been disguised as Koropok in Japan....

The Red Army was not using the red acid in rocket manufacture; whatever they were doing with it involved small, confined chambers. Firecrackers. China, for a good many centuries,
had made hundreds of varieties of firecrackers, and it was Davies'
belief that they were again fashioning them, differently, as a
weapon, a deadly and diabolical weapon. As he ambled along,
he was already figuring out many ways trouble could be caused
by firecrackers such as must be being made within the temple,
and he was weighing what ought to be done about it. He could
get away from Yeungwi and inform G-2, who would do everything possible to prevent the discharge of any firecrackers anywhere behind the Nationalist lines or anywhere near where the
Marines were stationed.

That was one choice. The other was that he himself could
have a go at destroying the explosives where they were made
and must be stored.

Me and my big ideas, Davies thought wryly, knowing how
well the Red Temple was guarded. *But what a damned swell fire
it would make!*

As Koropok passed a drinking-shop, and heard the soldiers
within singing about women—

> *"Shen hou t'ui chin*
> *Chu p'ei tou*
> *Pu ju sh eng ch'ien...."*

—one thing kept recurring to him; if he attempted to get
over the wall, and were detected, or if he got over it and were
caught inside, no warning would ever go to anyone, and General
Li Chou would be able to carry out his intentions—in which
furiously explosive firecrackers were involved—exactly according to the Red Army plan. Davies knew that the right thing
for him to do was to leave Yeungwi as soon as darkness came,

turn in his report, and have the affair cared for by those men who would know how to handle it.

O.K., he told himself. *That's it.*

He would pass along what little he had overheard, and guessed from the map on Li Chou's wall, to Headquarters. There was nothing else he could do about that, if indeed he had accomplished anything. All that he could say was that the Marines, or some of them, had escaped. Here, he could do nothing, although he had not altered his guess that Noma-us, the half-caste, had set out to secure the reward which would be paid for information about the Marines.

He almost continued on past the drinking-shop entirely before pausing; no Ainu would do such a thing, but would enter and beg for any dregs which remained in a drained bowl. To have gone by, if anyone happened to be watching, would have invited suspicion. So, fumbling at his beard, Koropok slowly shuffled along at an angle until he walked beneath the hanging Pilgrim's Bottle, the red gourd which, above the door, promised thrice-fired wine inside.

CHAPTER VI

INSIDE THE RED TEMPLE

A N ARGUMENT was going on within the drinking-shop, between several soldiers of the Red Army, punctuated only when the shopkeeper refilled the bowls. Davies could see down to the skeleton of the argument, and at any other time would have been amused by it: one soldier, in debt to another, was insisting that the ancient habit of paying debts before the arrival of the New Year was a barbarous, uncivilized, and capitalistic custom. Since celebration of the New Year was forbidden by order of General Li Chou, the lean, dark Manchu insisted vehemently, it was no longer necessary to meet a debt previous to the coming of the New Year. And if the debt were not paid as in the past, no face would be lost, either.

The shopkeeper, who ladled out pale *samshu* from his fat jars only when he saw money on the crude counter, could afford to smile.

It was easier for Davies to translate Chinese characters than it was to keep up with the crackling sing-song of the argument. Sometimes the thin Manchu soldier and the sullen-faced Szchuan creditor both spoke at once, and during the babel of sound Davies slowly translated the worn, old placard fastened to the railing which separated customers from the jars.

"Tsui li ch'ien k'un to, hu chung jih yueh chang," read the placard. "From the depths of intoxication the heavens appear to expand; from the bottom of the cup the days seem to lengthen."

Nice little thought to get drunk by, Lew agreed. Having been

in the shop long enough to have been refused a drink, he began to sidle away.

"But how can I pay you before the New Year?" he heard the dunned Manchu state in a voice which rose higher and higher. "How? It is not until after the New Year that we will be robbing the fat merchants to the south. Then I—"

"You talk too much," someone growled.

One soldier was
holding another in
the rear of the jeep.

The debtor shrilled, "I say what everyone knows."

"If the Great General wishes nothing to be said, your mouth should be sealed," retorted the creditor. "Besides," argued the Sz-chuan soldier, "when the fun has started, I will have plenty of money, as our general has promised, but now I have little. Therefore it is now that I wish to be paid what you owe me."

His voice, also, had risen high. Davies, almost at the door, wondered if argument would become physical violence.

The shopkeeper must have thought the same thing. He said genially, "Let there be less talk of owing and owed. As for you," to the Sz-chuan creditor, "I intend to change my custom. Here, you may drink and pay later. Let there be no quarrel. Why, if you fight, there will be questioning by General Li Chou, and something will be done to us all. Come! Think of the good American rice which has been cleaned, softened, and sprouted, and which is fermenting in the tubs, so that when you return in triumph there will be warm white *samshu* and burning yellow *samshu* waiting. What more can you ask?"

The storekeeper had been refilling the bowls while the words flowed out of him in a stream; but into the words, as Koropok was leaving, after having heard verification of what actually needed no verifying—that the New Year was to be the time of an attack by the Red Army—came a new sound. At first it seemed no more than a rumble under the words, and then it grew and grew, to become what it really was. A roar of voices, becoming louder and louder. Wild, triumphant, jeering voices. Into the bellow was blended, and almost smothered, the blare of a horn.

Koropok, who had been at the door, stepped back into the drinking-shop as the din increased. The tremendous noise made by hundreds of throats must have penetrated the wine-fogs in the soldier-customers' heads, and they bumped against door and pariah as they rushed drunkenly out. The shopkeeper followed them, but only as far as the door, where he stood with his hands in his sleeves.

The crooked, narrow street was filling up magically with men, with soldiers of the Red Army who were quartered everywhere in Yeungwi. Davies, soberly, could see that whatever was causing the wild excitement had brought out only a few of Yeungwi's inhabitants; and because he knew the curiosity of Chinese, and their love of excitement, it was this fact which gave him his first inkling as to what the soldiers were waiting so jubilantly to watch… and which the Chinese townspeople apparently did not care to see at all.

The screams of the soldiers grew and grew. Davies' heart began to pound angrily against the wall of his chest. What he thought, just as the first jeep in the procession of three followed a horde of gesticulating soldiers into the street of the drinking-shop, was, *It's a damned good thing Colonel Mathews can't see this.* A slow, cold smile moved Davies' lips when he thought this, a smile which seemed to be frozen on his face until it was replaced by the laxness of expression which was a part of Koropok's make-up.

General Li Chou sat in the first jeep. The Red Army strategist sat immobile, as woodenly and ominously as if he were the devil Mara, the arch-fiend, about to pronounce sentence. The second jeep, driven by a Tartar or a Buriat, was filled with Marines, bound together and to the jeep also, and so was the third. Marines. Unshaven. Haggard. Stiff-lipped. And somehow, in spite of their bonds, they were as erect as was the strategist of the Red Army.

DAVIES' EYES, as he watched the slowly-moving procession, which he knew was adding hugely to the general's prestige in the minds of his soldiers, were black and hard as obsidian, and not the mild, sorrowful eyes of an Ainu pariah. He had all he could do, as he stared at the gaunt, grim faces of the Marines, to remember to keep his own face stupid and blank, and to keep his hands hanging lankly against the tatters of his filthy Ainu jacket.

He was torn by a long instant of impotent, icy rage, as the

horde gathered from North China and the north beyond yelled, and the horn of General Li Chou's stolen jeep blared away triumphantly... and then, as more and more soldiers of the Red Army, coming from all directions, slowed the procession until it was moving hardly at all, and seemed stalled, he blinked.

Could I? he asked himself.

It came to him that he dared not violate his assigned duty, which was to find out whatever he could and return to report. But as he kept watching the faces of the Marines, he thought, *I was given a double duty.*

The first thing he had to do, if he could do anything, was to get away from a street now packed solidly. Nor was there time to be lost. His guess, and a reasonable one, was that Li Chou had left Yeungwi quietly, on receiving the word about the recapture of the Marines, in order to make this triumphal return; obviously, the procession would end at the general's headquarters, and when the Marines were taken inside, the crowd would disperse. Whether he could slip through the mass of soldiers he didn't know. But he intended to try.

He intended to get to the Red Temple, where he had reason to hope that every guard off duty had gone tearing away to see the excitement... and where every guard on duty would be looking, from wall or temple roof, in one direction. It was worth having a look-see at; and if he actually succeeded in getting over the wall and into the temple, and doing what he wanted to do there to thwart the basic purpose designed by Li Chou, mightn't he, after, actually go to the general's HQ and again take advantage of a new excitement?

Davies was already on the street while he had been figuring; with his back to the front of the drinking-shop, he began to work his way along, sometimes unable to move forward, sometimes advancing the width of his stocky body, sometimes being pressed back and cursed by Red Army soldiers in languages which he did not know at all. Once a dark soldier shoved a greasy hand in his face.

Now and again he would turn his head. The procession was not yet beyond where the street turned off and into one which, Davies' aimless ramblings told him, led toward General Li Chou's headquarters.

When Davies was near the first gap in house walls, where a narrow passageway ran off the street itself, and for which he had been aiming, he turned for a final look. The procession appeared stalled; General Li Chou was accepting the plaudits of his men. Li the Conqueror. Li the Captor of Marines. And General Li Chou, in satisfied but grim response, had stood up, and, as the horde roared, had saluted gravely with the salute of the Red Army.

Somewhere in the crowd a man shouted, as Li Chou's officer had said earlier when Koropok was being questioned, *"Kung hai fat choi!"* and the entire horde took up the shout, so that it battered back and forth from wall to wall. But if some of the soldiers and officers bellowed the Cantonese words, others howled, *"Yuan tan! Yuan tan!"* and Davies guessed that both meant the same thing.

He thought grimly, *Happy New Year to you, too!* and then a hand was on his arm, with fingers gripping him like cat-claws.

Noma-us, the half-caste, was jammed up against him; but whether the part-Ainu, part-Japanese, had been standing still, or whether the scraggly-bearded pariah had moved toward him, Davies did not know.

He knew this—the half-caste's eyes were spitting out hate.

Davies could smell *samshu* on the breath which came from a mouth only inches away from his own. *He found the Marines,* thought Lew, and *he's been drinking up the portion of the reward which has been paid him.* The remainder of the blood-money, after the fashion of the Orient, would be paid over only when the prisoners were actually in jail. *The damned little swine is afraid that I'll claim part of the cash,* realized Davies.

Hoarsely, inflamed by avarice and *samshu,* Noma-us whispered, *"Ra' k'ra kayer' n'satt'...* go away or I will kill you."

"Pi'rik'," begged Koropok in agreement. But the half-caste's arm was already moving, and Davies was certain that Noma-us, uninterested in the acquiescence, was trying to get out his short bear-knife. Lew could feel how Noma-us was struggling to get the blade out of its skin-sheath, difficult to accomplish because of the press of bodies. *"Pi'rik',"* promised Koropok again.

There was no space in which to grab at the half-caste's knife arm, nor any way of knowing that Noma-us wasn't going to be able to draw the knife. The very last thing which Davies wanted was any commotion which would call attention to himself, something which might prevent his getting away.

The soldiers, on tiptoe and with eyes only for the Marines, paid no attention to what was going on, and saw none of it.

To wait, Davies knew, might mean a knife dug into his belly, and what he hoped to do at the Red Temple needed, he knew, guts in more ways than one. Noma-us' red and slitted eyes had narrowed even more from the fellow's efforts to get out his knife; Davies' arms were as they had been, elbows to his sides, hands up because he had been using them slyly to help him slip through the crowd. He could not lower them. But he could raise them, and he did.

He had his hands, unseen by the shouting horde, around the neck of the renegade pariah. The muscles of Davies' forearms, where the tattered sleeves fell away, in stiff and muddy folds, rippled once, and then were rigid.

One pariah, so close were they, might have been embracing the other; and when a soldier, without lowering his eyes, protested because someone was kicking at him, Davies knew that this must have been the half-caste. Davies hastily pulled the renegade's head down so that the face was flat against Koropok's chest.

And Koropok faltered, *"Samshu* sickens him, lords."

The soldiers, thinking of their uniforms, inched back as much as was possible. Koropok was able to carry the body of the half-caste the few feet to the passageway between walls. He did not put down his burden until he was out of sight of the soldiers, behind him, and until the way ahead was empty. Then he ran.

I T W A S an old town, Yeungwi, and the streets, the walls, the houses, had been laid out in accordance with *Feng-shui*, that magical art which the Marine colonel had mentioned when speaking of cemeteries. Consequently, the racing Davies was able to anticipate every turn, just as he knew that within the walls of the Red Temple he could find his way. A path would always curve left from a clump of bamboo; if a low structure stood before him, inside the wall, there would be a higher one, called the green dragon, just beyond it The temple itself, with its central chamber and principal deity seven paces from the door, and its Hall of the Old Men for the priests, and the opening with its ladder to the bell tower, would be just exactly as he expected it to be, and what was being done inside he had already learned and drawn the basic conclusion for.

The emptiness of every street of soldiers was proof of two things; one, the excitement caused by the parading of the Marines, and two, the tremendous curiosity of the Chinese. And Davies, as he ran, was grinning. Because, should he be able to accomplish what he had decided to do—destroy what Li Chou intended to use in making the attack on the Nationalists—he could, during the destruction, make the soldiers run in the opposite direction. And then, given luck, he could give General Li Chou something else to howl about.

The wall surrounding the temple was, like almost all Chinese walls, of brick, rough, octagonal old brick, and not glazed porcelain brick. When Davies neared the wall, that which faced the scene of General Li Chou's triumph and the disgrace of men who did not support him, he saw soldiers along the wall's thick top. But when Koropok ambled past the gate, on the far side of the street, only a single officer and one non-com stood guard there, and the wall on either side of the gate had no guards at all.

Davies, shambling along, picked his spot carefully. He passed by spots where the brick had crumbled. The right-angled corner suited him; he could climb up on the protruding bricks, and, with a hand around the wall's corner, get a good purchase and grip... and, without pause, he was up, and dropping inside the Red Temple grounds. He had no eyes for ancient cypresses nor the little rocky mound a little beyond, called the Peak of Extreme Joyfulness, nor for the pool from which the carp had long been taken and eaten. He slipped from one clump of bamboo to another; he crouched behind the open-mouthed Stone-head Fish, and, flat on his belly, began to creep toward the side of the temple, aiming for the small door once used by the priests in entering their dormitory.

When he came to the twin stone tablets with their carved and worn phrases of good omen, placed so as to protect the temple priests from any evil spirits lurking in the grounds, he took one swift look around, from their protection, and saw nothing. No one. No pacing guard. But he did see the door.

Davies came to his feet, and crossed the stone flags of the open space. Even as he reached out for the door's lion-head which operated the bolt within he was wondering whether he would dare try to enter by the Great Door to the central chamber if this one were bolted... and then the bolt, unsecured inside, clicked as he pulled. The sound, the clack of metal, almost stopped Davies' heart. Then he was inside, with the door closed behind him.

The ancient sleeping quarter of former priests was not so dark but that Davies saw how it was again serving the same purpose. Blankets were on the floor, gear and uniforms scattered about, and guns stacked in a corner. The American major's roving eyes, as he stood a moment and made sure that no soldiers were rolled and asleep in the blankets, were caught by a familiarly shaped oblong package, and he grinned as he picked it up, together with the matches beside the cigarettes.

A fool for luck, he told himself. It was because of the matches, however, that he thought, *Now I don't waste time being a Boy Scout.*

Davies slowly opened the door which, he knew, would show the corridor beyond. Crooked and narrow, it would end at the great chamber. Every creak of the unoiled old hinges sent shrill sound down the corridor.

Could it be heard in the great chamber? Or had everyone there, once the place for worship, gone to witness the humiliation of the Marines? Davies didn't believe so. Some men were sure to be in the big room... and he was positive that what was being done in the temple was being done there, because nowhere else could men work in complete secrecy and have enough space for operations.

The corridor was black as the pit, at first. When Davies passed around a right-angled turn, which would stop passage of evil spirits, the corridor was gray. Beyond the next turn, it was a shade lighter. Two more sharp turns... and then he could see into the Red Temple's great chamber.

CHAPTER VII

HAPPY NEW YEAR TO

THE GENERAL

NO BUDDHA was seated on his brass lotus where the altar once had been, nor any lesser divinities at his feet, their hands clasped in supplication. Only a single deity remained, and it, partially effaced with red paint, was painted on a far wall. Davies, at the corridor's end, first saw the strange, savage male figure seated on its peacock, a bird with a wattled cock's head, dimly, in the dim chamber. No other evidence remained to show that this had been a place for worship.

There were men in the place, and women, shadowy figures whose own shadows were grayish yellow and not black in this lamplit chamber where, for secrecy, all trace of daylight had been shut out. Like ghosts, the Chinese worked in utter silence at long, makeshift tables, boards laid across trestles, on which were stacks of straw-colored paper and of red paper splotched with telltale gold and silver. With the rougher uncolored paper as foundation, and the brilliant paper as outer wrapping, tubes were being fashioned on iron rods by thin fingers which flew like machinery. Red tubes. Firecrackers. Firecrackers by the thousands. Machines were also involved, crude swinging arms with blocks of black wood, convex beneath, which, on being swung down, tightened the paper.

The only sound was the constant thump-thump-thump as the blocks were brought dexterously down on the tubes. Thump. Thump. Marching feet.

China-fashion production line, thought Davies, seeing how the formed red tubes were bunched and shoved along the table, where other workers spread something like a heavy paste or clay over one end of the bunch, plugging each tube. When this was done, a Chinese spat on the plugged ends, and tamped them tight.

The next operation, logically, should have been filling the tubes with powder, inserting fuses, plugging the upper ends, and turning the edges of the red paper over the ends, with the fuses protruding.

This was not being done. Instead, the bunched, empty firecrackers were taken far down the great, dim chamber. There, Davies saw what he had believed he was going to see. On the stone pedestal which had once upheld the sculptured image of a god, was a stoppered glass container, which reflected, but in red, the lamps burning in the chamber.

That's it, Davies' bearded lips formed. *Red fuming nitric.*

The tremendous care taken by the short, squat, swarthy Asiatic who was decanting a little of the liquid was additional proof.

Davies was unable to see exactly what operations went on at the table beyond the flame-colored acid container. As nearly

*He took one swift look
around, and saw nothing.*

as he could make out, each firecracker in the bunches was being
individually worked on; but if at first he thought this was a
filling with powder, or whatever they were intended to contain,
he saw that the actual filling was done only after some preliminary operation. Were the tubes being lined? With clay,
undoubtedly impervious to acid or an acid compound? While
possibilities were racing through his head, the Chinese were
working with backs to him, and he could see little.

According to jet propulsion and rocket practices, red fuming
nitric had become the amazing oxidizer for new propellants....

Each firecracker, Lew thought soberly, *can be a miniature pro-
jectile. Whatever is being done here must be producing firecrackers*

with contents which are inflammable as hell. What would happen if they went off was easy to guess.

Strings of firecrackers for the New Year. The man disguised as a pariah could see, to the right of the container about which only men worked, the smaller table where women were twisting the fuses of completed firecrackers around a long thick fuse, forming the strings of miniature explosives which, when hung from balconies, and lighted, would explode one after another.

Davies wanted one of those firecrackers. Could he find where the strings were stored? Suppose he did discover the place; the storage room, if not actually under guard now during the excitement in Yeungwi, would be securely locked.

G-2 can find men to figure it out, Davies decided, while words like turbojet and thermojet and ramjet popped out at him, along with combustion chambers, blowout plugs, ignition squibs, aniline fuels. What I've got to do, he continued to think, staring at the silent figures until his eyes burned, *is to make sure that those strings aren't set off… not behind the Nationalist lines at the start of the New Year, when Li Chou's forces here, and Red Army units everywhere, can be ready to move against burning key cities, where Chiang's men, celebrating the New Year, would be demoralized by fire and destruction.*

It was the type of intricate plan which General Li Chou, the strategist, could have designed, according to everything G-2 had told Davies about the man. And General Li Chou, a martinet, would have worked out all details, not being one to leave anything to chance. Certainly, Davies realized, the Red Army general must have had a hand in checking on the firecracker manufacture… or a couple of fingernails, anyhow, plus the thumb which had been seared by acid.

While Lew started, in his attempt to ascertain how the firecrackers were being handled and filled, he thought, ironically, how it was from China, centuries ago, that gunpowder had come. And crude bombs, bamboo tubes filled with gunpowder. And rockets. And flame as a weapon of attack.

Firecrackers. Couldn't these firecrackers here have two chambers, one containing red fuming nitric, perhaps plus something, and the other an incendiary powder or compound? Mightn't there be a clay plug between, with a fuse running through? A plug, figured Davies, somewhat similar to the copper disc blowout plug where new propellants were used in jet-assisted jobs about which he had read in Tokyo, but which he had never flown? Why not? The Chinese themselves were clever in fashioning a hundred varieties of firecrackers and fireworks; suppose, added to this, was information which Li Chou had picked up, or been furnished, and which originated in the eastern portion of occupied Germany?

How near the truth Davies was, or how far from it, he had no way of knowing, as he risked detection in his effort to see what was being done. Nor did he know, before, that Li Chou, when naming firecrackers, had shrewdly mentioned those called ehr t'i chiao, double-kicking feet, which, exploding once on the ground or, if on a string, in the air, exploded a second time, from a second charge, far from where they had first burst. The force of the initial explosion sent the remainder of the red tubes flying high and far.

No wonder those in the real know about what I think has been planned keep saying, "Happy New Year!" and laughing when they say it, thought Lew. Then, under his breath, and with a final futile look at the strange scene in the Red Temple's prayer chamber, where now only the defaced Fire God rode on his rooster-headed peacock, the Fire Bird, he said, "Happy New Year. What's sauce for the goose...."

S O F T L Y, O N bare feet, he backed away, turned, and followed the passageway back to the priests' room. The first thing he did was to pick up not one but several of the rifles, and the ammunition belts looped about them. Two were Garands. He wrapped these in a blanket along with two additional blankets, making a pack, oblong, which did not give away the contents. Around the outer blanket he put a piece of the straw-cloth which had been under a sleeping place. He fastened the pack with an unraveled strip of the roughly meshed cloth, made certain that there was no rattle, and then placed the pack beside the outer door.

The wood of the ancient Red Temple was dry as the straw cloth. Davies moved about the room swiftly now, grinning to himself once when he crumpled up newspapers which soldiers had been reading, grinning because of the fiery headlines. Outside, he could hear the patter of the rain; inside, he struck one match, lit a cigarette and drew deeply on it even as he stooped and touched the match to the first pile of papers and straw cloth he had prepared... and to the second... the third. Flames licked up. Wood began to crackle. Davies flung his cigarette into one of his fires, stepped to the outer door, and picked up the pack. When he opened the door, the flames leaped not only to the wooden ceiling, but into the dark passageway to the great chamber.

Davies was over the wall before the outcry went up... and while the shouts rose high as the flames which were following smoke up to the pinnacles, Koropok the Ainu, under such a pack as Chinese, soldiers and townspeople alike, had often seen him carrying, shuffled away from the Red Temple.

Not once did Koropok turn and look back. He could see the brightening overhead; that satisfied him.

Davies heard no roaring of flames. The ancient wood must be burning as swiftly and silently as the red tubes had been manufactured... until there was the hoped-for crackle of explosions which meant that a string of firecrackers had been found by fire. Instantly, after that, there was sound unequalled by the celebrating of a New Year anywhere, a pandemonium of continuous discharges growing to one great and wild and fierce din, a deafening roaring boom.

And that, guessed Lew, increasing his pace as much as he dared, *ought to take care of any evil spirits around here.*

Then he said, "Ah!"

Across his vision, first one and then another flash of yellow light appeared, tiny meteors... and ahead of him, to the right and left, sizzling silver-white glitters lit up roofs, and began to hiss there, and next to change color, as the roofs caught fire.

Outside the closed door, he cradled the rifle on his arm.

And the streets filled, not only with the Red Army soldiers whom Davies had expected would go rushing for the temple when it was seen to be burning, but with all Yeungwi, because Yeungwi was catching fire.

The pariah was knocked this way and that, but no one paid heed to him. And he, even while wondering why he had not followed his reasoning to its logical conclusion, which should have been that what could happen in cities behind the lines of the Nationalist forces could happen here, plodded rapidly toward the headquarters of General Li Chou.

And Yeungwi continued burning.

Why didn't I figure on this? Davies accused himself; but, even if he had known that this could happen, what could he have done about it? He was very sure of one important fact: General Li Chou would not be in position to make a deadly assault on the New Year. Not now. Not with incendiary firecrackers. And if one town, Yeungwi, was afire, cities elsewhere would be saved.

The strategist of the Red Army was going to be unhappy. *He could take his rage out on the Marines,* worried Davies; and it came to him that Li Chou, who sniffed at perfume and who shuddered at a pariah's lack of elegance, was hardly the man who'd risk his life in the streets nor where a temple blazed. Li Chou was a strategist, a man of plots and counterplots, and not one to be where bullets whined. Such a person, Davies had learned from his years in the Far East, would take satisfaction in avenging himself on whoever was available. The Marines.

And so Koropok struggled to work his way through the throng as he prepared to attempt the second part of his original plan. What he had decided to try had seemed reasonable; its failure, if it came after the destruction of the firecrackers, principally involved Koropok's life. Would it be possible now, with Yeungwi burning instead of merely the Red Temple? Davies was hopeful and fearful.

Soldiers banged him out of the way as they pounded along the narrow, crooked street. Once a maddened villager sought to tear the pack away from him, screaming that the bearded one had stolen it from his house. Everywhere people were dragging out whatever could be pulled, adding to the confusion outside. One old grandfather was wailing every prayer he could remember, addressing every deity from Po-lo-t'o-she to the bearded Carpenter God worshipped by white men. Nor did the old Chinese forget to address the devils in the sky and under the ground....

In Davies' ears was the old man's stark terror—*"Ku mu lei wei t'ien! Sung po ts'yi wei hsin!"*—as the flames leaped higher and higher, until the slanting rain seemed turned to steaming red fog. Nowhere was it so bright as above where the Red Temple blazed.

KOROPOK THE pariah, pack Ainu-fashion on his back, slunk along until he could slide between the walls which brought him near General Li Chou's headquarters. No townspeople were milling about, where houses had been commandeered; a few keepers of shops seemed torn between desire to carry out goods, and fear that if they did the shops' finest wares, probably kept out of sight, would be seized, although no soldiers were visible save a single guard standing at the headquarters door. He was watching the merchants.

The three jeeps which had brought the Marines into Yeungwi in the procession ending here were up the street past the entrance, empty not only of captured men but of drivers. All three.

Li Chou's inside, the presence of the vehicles assured Davies. He'd never go on foot. How many will be with him?

For a moment, as Davies approached the entrance, he saw no way of employing any of the subtleties which he had used in Japan; and then, as he saw how the one guard kept narrowed eyes on the merchants, he remembered that what men wanted in one country would be the same in another. Perhaps he himself needn't take the long chance he had intended, which was to pass the guard, whirl, and smash him down. A better way might be possible.

"*T'ai to lok*... so much gold for one man," mumbled Koropok, but so loudly that the guard heard him. "*T'ai to lok*...."

"You speak like a monkey from the south," growled the soldier. "What gold?" A turn of the guard's head toward the merchants indicated his belief. "Speak quickly, or I will cut off your beard, and your head with it."

Davies had already pieced together the words for his reply. "Gold," he muttered. "Gold. In a bag. Those men—"

The guard's appraising glance back into the house was followed by one look up and down the street; then he was running toward the merchants. Davies was inside before the soldier could accost the shopkeepers, inside, and at the first angle of the corridor, on his knees, unfastening his pack. One of the M-1's suited him; he shoved the other weapons against the wall first, grabbed them up next, carrying them down the corridor, to put them down just outside the door of the room where he had been questioned by Li Chou.

He cradled the rifle on his arm; he heard, through the closed door, "You have no choice. Sign the statement, Lieutenant. It merely states that you took orders from Chiang's officers. If you do not sign," Davies heard Li Chou continue coldly, in the best of English, "you and your men will be burned to death in Yeungwi, and your government will be perfectly satisfied it was accidental."

The next voice was curt. "Go to hell," said the Marine.

Li Chou's laugh was silky.

"If I thought," he said unhurriedly, "that it had been you who fired the Red Temple, instead of having something gone wrong there, I assure you that you would already be praying for hell. Come, Lieutenant! It is necessary for me to leave a burning town. I intend to take something with me which will temper the anger of my own superior. Sign!"

Davies pushed against the door, and as it opened he raised his rifle.

He saw what he expected to see. The bound Marines, their backs to him Captain Wang Fong. No soldiers at all. And, behind his desk, delicately fondling his snuff-bottle in his long, beautifully-kept fingers, General Li Chou.

Davies wanted no questions, nor did he have any wish to savor the change from the strategist's opening mouth, to curse a pariah, to a mouth which drooped and began to drip saliva down the front of Li Chou's uniform when he saw what the pariah was pointing at him. No questions. This had to go fast.

Captain Wang Fong was reaching for his holstered, stolen Army .45 when a shift in the rifle's direction stiffened the captain's arm, holding it rigidly at right angles to his body. Li Chou's imperceptible movement also froze when Davies swung the rifle at him again, at the same time taking three swift steps to the desk, to snatch up, with his left hand, the long, thin paper-knife there. With the two Red Army officers almost in line now, he had both covered.

THE MARINE lieutenant was nearest the desk; Davies slashed apart the ropes behind the American's back, and immediately handed the lieutenant the silver-hilted blade. He himself, while the lieutenant was releasing his men, gave

General Li Chou a shove which pushed man and chair away from a desk which must hold a weapon, and then took Wang Fong's gun away from him.

The guard outside, who had left his post for a bag of gold, would suppose that the pariah had gone shambling up the street... but even if he left his post again, and came inside, he would find no reward. Danger lay in returning officers, making reports; danger lay in men who would accompany Li Chou away from the burning city. And Davies, all in the same fraction of time, heard a crackling; and if it might be the sound of rats gnawing somewhere, it could be fire, also. No time to lose. No time to reply to the sudden outburst of questions from the lieutenant.

He said, "Let's go!" and the widening of General Li Chou's eyes made Llewelyn Davies aware that he had spoken in English.

"So that's what you are," the strategist croaked.

Hell, thought Lew. He had, he realized, given himself away. But when he saw the grins on the gaunt Marines' faces, he said, "Happy New Year, General."

"Dog," said Li Chou.

Davies was grinning. He said to the lieutenant, "Bind 'em. Loosely. Enough to give us a couple of minutes." Then he told Li Chou, "That's me. Dog." He patted a grimy hand where his tattered jacket was stuck with mud to his chest "Last year, General, was the Year of the Monkey. The Jap. This is the Year of the Red Cock. I remind you that next year will be the Year of the Dog. Happy New Year, General Li Chou. Maybe I'll see you around."

The two Red Army officers were tied enough to hold them for a little time when Davies added, "Rifles just outside. One guard at the entrance. The jeeps are still there. If I know any-thing about the Orient, the keys'll be in 'em."

The jeeps were slammed into high gear before the Marine lieutenant said, as he stared at the brilliance of the sky. "What happened? The general damned near went crazy." Then he asked, "You're a Marine?"

"Mac," said Major Davies contentedly, knowing that even if there were guards at the outer gates these men would shoot their way through, "it took the Army to get you boys out of your mess." The jeep gave a violent lurch as it careened around a corner, headed, after Davies' directions, out of the town. "Go easy," Lew yelled. "The war's over!"

The lieutenant was laughing. "The Army never could take it," he said; and in the laugh, and the words, Davies knew that there was sheer relief. "Sir," said the Marine, voice steady, "I don't know what you did, or how you did it, but… for all of us… thanks."

Davies nodded. The gate out of Yeungwi was ahead; a guard had jumped into the middle of the road. Davies saw Marine rifles rising. He himself, however, turned, and as he looked back there was a sudden spatter of furious flame, and then a huge column of black smoke as the tower of the Red Temple crashed down. The shots of the Marines seemed only a far echo to the sound.

ABOUT THE AUTHOR

MY PEOPLE came across the plains just behind the ill-fated Donner party, which makes me a Native Son, although I've never practiced the profession. Born in San Francisco, in 1893. As a youngster the family business was in the Orient; two years there, a year in the States. The Philippines in the days when garters were worn without stockings, and shoes carried in the hand by the natives; when the pariahs in Japan did not show their faces along respectable streets; when the Chinese believed foreigners originated from the hairs of curly white dogs.

University of Wisconsin, ex-1914; ex-salesman, ex-advertising manager, ex-reporter. For the first, saw no reason for waiting a few months merely to get a degree; the second, promised everything the sales-manager told me was true about his wares; the third, didn't and don't play golf; the fourth, quit after seeing 42 executions and refused to cover any more.

In fact, I seem to be ex-everything except husband; have the same wife I started out with thirteen years ago, plus two potential Badger halfbacks.

Started writing in 1923; and consequently have to my credit many short stories and five novels. Once won a tennis cup. Voted for LaFollette for President. Have seen Clara Bow at close range and wasn't even singed. Like trout fishing immensely, especially in the high Sierras.

For the rest, we live on the top of a hill in a small sleepy

California town just north of San Francisco; there are iris and columbine and poppies and mission-bells not a hundred feet from the house. And the birds come within a yard of the house to get bread in the rainy season (I'm Native Son enough not to say Winter) and right how we're trying to get a gray squirrel to eat almonds out of our hands; he'll come a foot away, but that's his limit.

Sidney Herschel Small

That's about all, except that I insist it was the fire and not the earthquake that did the damage; maybe I'm a worse and more rabid Native Son than I thought I was.